Instructions for Heartbreak

Instructions for Heartbreak

Sarah Handyside

MACMILLAN

First published 2025 by Macmillan
an imprint of Pan Macmillan
The Smithson, 6 Briset Street, London EC1M 5NR
EU representative: Macmillan Publishers Ireland Ltd, 1st Floor,
The Liffey Trust Centre, 117–126 Sheriff Street Upper,
Dublin 1, D01 YC43
Associated companies throughout the world
www.panmacmillan.com

ISBN 978-1-0350-3275-4

1 3 5 7 9 8 6 4 2

A CIP catalogue record for this book is available from the British Library.

Illustrations © Shutterstock and Sinead Hayward

Typeset by Palimpsest Book Production Ltd, Falkirk, Stirlingshire
Printed and bound by CPI Group (UK) Ltd, Croydon, CR0 4YY

Visit **www.panmacmillan.com** to read more about all our books
and to buy them. You will also find features, author interviews and
news of any author events, and you can sign up for e-newsletters
so that you're always first to hear about our new releases.

For the girls – women – who healed mine.

GIRLS / WOMEN

Rosa walked with a bounce and a small, secret smile. He was a *nice* man, wasn't he? A *good* man? They had stayed for five drinks; they had made each other laugh. He had shivered his hand across her knee; he had brushed his mouth over her cheek on saying goodbye. Flickers of electricity down her back.

How magical, these moments that everything can spring from. How extraordinary, that she couldn't yet know who and what and how he was going to be. How *they* were going to be.

Her red hair curled around her shoulders and she made herself think *mane* not *mask*. A mantra for the formerly shy, a determination to be open to the world. Her hands twitched in her pockets and she imagined his skin beneath them.

The world is full of wonder. Frissons and fireworks; roses and riptides.

This is what it means, to be The Last Romantic. It means to live in hope.

*

1

Back in the flat, Liv lay under her shabby duvet, crumpled and warmer than she would have liked. She had washed perfunctorily, muffled by alcohol, and could still taste vodka on her breath.

A TV show she had seen before was playing on her laptop; shutting her eyes was making her head swim too unpleasantly for sleep. The paradox of drinking so as to stop yourself from thinking: drink too much and you were unable to do anything but.

She stared at the crack that cobwebbed out from her light fitting. It bisected the room; on one side the plaster and paint were pale and, if not pristine, intact. On the other, a lightning storm of smaller cracks made the paint look darker, yet also shimmery.

Nikita had said how lovely it was, that the flaking, splintered side looked shinier. Like that Japanese art of fixing broken things with gold. What's it called?

Kintsugi, Liv had replied. The flaws in something make it stronger.

Right, Nikita had said. You know everything, don't you? I love you so much.

Her breath was hot on Liv's neck, and whispers of adulation flittered like moths around her ears. But over her beautiful, earnest, anxiously adoring girlfriend's shoulder, Liv's gaze was distant. She stared at those cracks and wondered whether she could scrape filler through them, paint over them, or whether in trying to disguise them she would only make them uglier.

Nikita had whispered then, Are you okay? Where are you?

Too many places at once, Liv had wanted to say, but never would.

*

In the toilets of a bar, a mile or two away, Dee stood in front of the mirror, turned left and right, appraised herself. She realized that her hands were balled into fists, her fingernails gouging into her palms. His name flitted momentarily into her head. She swatted it like a mosquito. Seven words that waited in every mirror; seven words that echoed on every run.

She pursed her lips and applied another layer of red. When she returned to the table, he would look at her mouth and think of the shiny skins of apples, Valentines, blood, bed. She would hear her own laughter as if from a distance; she would drink another glass of wine; she would go home.

Ten-miler tomorrow, if the weather was okay and the hangover was the sweat-it-out kind. It always was.

*

Katie listened to the click of the lock, felt the deep exhale that always followed the jittery walk down the road, keys bunched firmly in hand, smudgy relief in the knowledge that the maybe-shadows had stayed maybes for another night. The comforting, cake-like presence of Chris in the flat. She wondered, not for the first time, what it was that meant she *knew* he was there, even though the place was silent. Was it a pheromone thing? Was her body attuned to some wavelength that her consciousness couldn't access? Like twins who knew when the other was hurt?

He would be playing a video game, she thought, or perhaps already in bed, getting in his eight hours before Sunday football.

Her stomach lurched as she saw him sitting on the sofa, pale and sweaty. He had been crying, she said afterwards.

Soon, she was crying too.

Chapter One

GUTS

Rosa heard her first. A sort of mewling noise. A cat? As she passed the last three houses before her own it became both louder and more human; shatteringly human. Katie was at the front door, knocking in a frantic fervour. Hearing Rosa's footsteps, she turned. Her face was streaked with makeup and tears and incomprehensible pain.

As Rosa ran to embrace her, the door opened and Liv squinted into the night. It was beginning to rain; of course it was beginning to rain.

'Pretty tragic,' she said five minutes later, having deposited Katie on the sofa with a cup of tea, 'that it's only eleven on a Saturday night and I was tucked up in bed.'

Rosa eyed Katie's shivering form, and looked back at Liv. 'I'm not sure that's the *real* tragedy here.'

'Point taken,' Liv said, sitting cautiously next to Katie. 'So. What's happened?'

What was it he said? This isn't working? Did he say that? Did I dream that? It sounds like a line. It is working, isn't it? What does working mean? How does a relationship work? I have to go to work on Monday. Every Monday, every week, every month, and now Chris isn't in any of them.

She clasped her hands around the mug, a buoy in a stormy sea. Interlaced her fingers until the skin turned white. *Hold on. Keep on holding on.*

She didn't know if she'd spoken or not.

'What does he mean, not working?' Rosa asked.

'I don't know. He's been – work has been – it's been stressful – you know that he wants to move up – get promoted – and all that saving for a deposit – feel like we're getting nowhere – there's all that pressure, but—'

She broke up and off, and was crying again, trying to relay the conversation, the look on his face when she came in late, just out for a few drinks with my friend Suzy, I'd been shopping earlier, looking for clothes for the holiday, the fucking holiday, we're going to France at Easter, just booked, how is this happening now, how long has he been thinking this, we've been arguing but everybody argues, don't they? Why didn't he talk to me, he can't just *decide* something like this. All in the wrong order, soaked in tears, ringing in her head, like staying out for too long, on a comedown, feeling sick, teeth grinding, tongue swollen, all wrong.

Rosa and Liv wrapped around her and caught each other's eyes above her soggy hair, running a wordless gamut. *Did you have any idea? Is it a blip? Is it for ever? Do we tell her he'll be asking for forgiveness tomorrow, or that she should never see him again?*

'And he's at the flat?' Rosa asked.

'Yeah. He said he'd sleep on the sofa, but . . .' She shook

her head and cried again. 'I couldn't stay. And we couldn't talk any more. He was – it was like he was . . .' She steadied herself on the precipice, preparing, for a second, to vocalize for the first time what she had heard just hours earlier.

'I really think it's over. He said he'd tried, and he said he knows.'

'You don't know that yet,' Rosa said. '*He* can't know that yet. It's an argument. It's one night. You've been together nine years, that can't be undone in an evening.'

Liv opened her mouth in protest, and thought better of it. 'You don't need to decide anything yet. You don't need to do anything. You're here. You're with us.'

A series of clicks at the front door.

'Good, you're up,' yelled Dee, voice wine-lubricated and bad-date-sharpened. 'We'd better have some bloody gin in.'

She appeared majestically in the doorway, resplendent in knee-high boots, black leather skirt, red polo neck and a slick of matching lipstick. Her coat slid damply off one shoulder.

'Another one for the posh-boy chronicles,' she announced, stumbling elegantly to the kitchen for a glass, apparently without taking in Katie's crumpled form. 'Talked for twenty minutes about catching his first salmon.'

Katie giggled gently.

'Fuck. What are you doing here?'

Katie trembled into tears and breath.

'Chris,' Rosa said. 'He's. They've.' She shrugged helplessly.

Dee's eyes travelled languidly across each of the three. 'And you're drinking *tea*?'

One of the flat's many idiosyncrasies – the landlord called them 'design quirks' but 'conversion fuck-ups' was closer to the mark – was that the living room had been carved from the centre of the property and was therefore windowless. In an effort to encourage some light into this dreary cave, the kitchen was attached via a set of sliding glass doors which in other settings would have led on to a patio or decking. Glasses of chilled white wine and civilized barbecues. Dee lassoed her bag into the wall as she made her way through them, and there was an otherworldly sound of breaking glass.

'It's okay.' Rosa scrambled over and picked the photo out of its shattered frame. 'We're all still here.'

The picture had been taken in Manchester, where the four had met, at a fancy-dress party celebrating the birthday of someone whom none of them had seen since. The theme was 'circus'. Liv and Rosa were a pair of acrobats in lurid leotards and leggings and glitter face paint; Katie had bought reams of cheap scratchy fur and fashioned herself into a lion; Dee, in a top hat and cracking a whip, was the ringmaster.

'Fuck, we look young.'

The strangeness of seeing your own face, simultaneously harder and softer.

'That's the night I met Chris,' said Katie suddenly.

'It's not, is it?'

'Yes. Remember, he stayed over, and we were all laughing when he had to get the bus home in his costume the next day.'

There was a simplicity to that, wasn't there? Catch someone's eye, dance and turn your head again. The unspoken parameters of university parties – you're studying here too, right? Arts or science? Right, like my housemate, do you know them? You'll be the same age, give or take. You'll live in the same part of the city, and your house will look the same as theirs. A *Trainspotting* poster, photos from home or travelling, empty wine bottles on the windowsill, damp. You'll knock together, press together, grow together.

By the end of their first year in Manchester, Liv and Dee and Rosa and Katie had formed an impermeable unit. Liv and Rosa met first, both studying for the same literature degree and attempting to mould appropriately bohemian identities out of the countryside and London suburbs respectively. Each had felt a brittle affinity to the other across their first seminar room, Rosa admiring Liv's 10 a.m. black eyeliner, Liv Rosa's Botticellian red hair, and both suspecting, secretly, that their liking for each other would always be inflected with envy. Or perhaps, that their jealousy of each other would always be saturated in adoration. Rosa talked romance where Liv talked passion, and so Rosa was forgiving where Liv was demanding. But after a session on *Little Women* in which Liv gave an impassioned defence of Amy as the true heroine of the piece, they went to the nearest bar and shared a bottle of vinegary wine. They talked about books and music and cities and escaping. They talked about the newspapers and websites they wanted to write for, and sneeringly dismissed what passed for journalism in the student paper. They didn't talk about money.

The bottoms of their overdrafts loomed quickly. Rosa made a plaintive phone call to her parents, which Liv noted with a mixture of scorn and resentment. She got a job in a bar where the toilets were wallpapered in supposedly ironic cut-outs from nineties men's magazines. Dee was already bartending around her graphic design course and used a black Sharpie to add speech bubbles to the women on the walls, announcing that they were nuclear physicists and Nobel Prize winners and prime ministers. She had been brought up in Brighton by her mother alone – a mother who, Liv and Rosa learned with thinly disguised admiration, maintained shelves of second-wave feminist literature, a purple stripe through her hair and the kind of spiky attitude they had always assumed washed away by the time you reached your forties. Dee's blood was as hot as her mother's; she had, on more than one occasion, thrown drinks into the faces of punters who, in her words, 'crossed the lewd line'. Liv loved her immediately, and when Rosa joined them after closing to drink whisky while cashing up, so did she.

Katie met Rosa and Liv in a research skills seminar, diligently studying history and looking off-puttingly angelic with her cloud of blonde hair and pastel scarves and dangly earrings. But she had a liberated, head-thrown-back laugh, and drank Guinness and Tia Maria, and danced to techno with her eyes closed, and after three post-seminar drinks which turned into clubbing which turned into chips on the bus home the four of them felt aligned, like trees that the wind had bent the same way.

They shared a house in second and third year, one of the crumbling red-brick Victorians which characterized most of

Manchester's student suburbs. It was ramshackle and glorious and obnoxiously impermeable to outsiders. *No – I'm going out with the girls. No – I'm staying in with the girls.* So they rejected offers they considered lesser; so they laughed at themselves, ironically imitating the language of lightweight TV shows and magazines. Because *girls* was a term to simultaneously scorn and revere. It was infantilizing and condescending; it spoke of walking with arms linked out of fear of standing alone, of keeping voices artificially light and giggling amenably at people's jokes, however unfunny. Yet it spoke, too, of joy and freedom. Of dancing on tables and sharing secrets and linking arms in the luxurious scaffolding of steely friendship.

They knew that girls were young, and prized for being young above all else, and they found this both unnerving and delicious as they entered their twenties. They held a power that they knew to be problematic but also knew – or thought – they would miss one day. So they said *girls* to bathe in their youth, and *women* to hope at their wisdom, and throughout it all, other parties – other bodies – came and went from the house.

Chris, though, had lasted longer than any of them.

Dee reappeared with four martinis – accurate in their composition if not the glasses they were served in – which she had shaken, as ever, in an old, well-washed pickle jar. Rosa draped Katie in her Hangover Blanket, its faded florals a comforting echo of all the mornings after that had come before. Each took up their established position; Dee sprawled on the floor, Liv on the armchair, Rosa on the sofa next to Katie. And Katie's voice began to skitter over fragments of description: the way her back slid down the wall like something from a film; the way she sobbed; the horror when Chris did too; the circling of their words around *future* and *love* and *I think* and *I feel* and *no*. And each of her friends shivered in silence as her descriptions ricocheted them back in time, as her broken heart recalled the scars on theirs.

Katie was wrapped only in herself, her world that was smashed, the fire, the flood.

Eventually, her shoulders shuddering, she said, 'Tell us about this salmon man.' Dee arched an eyebrow. 'I mean it. I can't talk about it any more. I can't think about it.'

Storyteller incarnate, Dee obligingly turned onto her side.

'I was thinking about it all the way home. What is it, what is that *look*, that means you know how rich someone is? I was thinking – is it the clothes? He dressed *expensive*, right? But I swear, even if he was bollock-naked, there's still something I'd have put my finger on.'

'Floppy-haired?'

'Floppy-haired. And floppy-*faced*. But good bones at the same time. Like – chiselled but also doughy. And there's something in the shape of the mouth. Silver spoons, right? Anyway. So we meet at this wine bar – his pick – and I get there ten minutes early, so I get a seat, buy a drink.'

'Sure.'

'Sure. I'm not waiting around in the cold like some teenager on their first date in a coffee shop. I'm a big girl – *woman* – I can get a glass of wine by myself. And I message him, say what I'm wearing, so he can recognize me when he walks in.' Dee expertly swallowed a substantial mouthful of gin.

'And when he turns up, I think he's a bit . . . *pissed* that I've got there first. Not doing the fashionably late thing, maybe. Or that I haven't waited outside like some damsel in distress. Like, it's fucked with his plan for how he's going to be on a date, opening the door, picking up the tab.'

'Ohh,' Rosa murmured peaceably. 'That can be nice, though. Can't it?'

'Subtext though, isn't it?' Liv said tartly. 'You can repay me later?'

'Exactly. It's not even the money. It's the *power*, right? It's who's chosen. Who's *choosing*.'

Liv nodded vigorously, while Rosa looked hesitant and Katie sat, lost.

'So anyway,' Dee continued, 'we get a bottle, do the chat, where do you live, what do you do, and then – drumroll – *where did you go to school, then?*'

'Hah,' Liv tutted, while Katie was mystified.

'I don't get it?'

'Only,' Liv explained, '*only* people who went to an expensive school – and who *care* about expensive schools – ask that question on a date. It's the phrasing, right? Not "where did you grow up?" They want a name. Then they can start asking if you had maths with Lady Whoever.'

Katie's head twitched. 'Wow. Okay.' She bit her lip against the flow of something she couldn't quite touch, whirling waters that boiled green and purple like a bruise. *Is this it? Is this how it is, outside of Katie-and-Chris?*

'But this is not an attack on the privately educated men of London!' Dee continued, splashing her drink onto the carpet. 'This is an attack on the *self-obsessed, judgemental* men of London.'

'There's an overlap,' Liv muttered.

Dee nodded wisely. 'True. Believe me, I've met a few of them in the years since – in the past few years. So. It was downhill from there. The salmon was the high point. Fourteen pounds, apparently. Why are salmons in imperial?'

'Substitute babies for the rich?' Liv suggested.

Dee laughed. 'Yes! Right there. Right there. That's why I love you.' She lay back on the floor, gazing upwards and away. 'But I wasn't going to love Salmon Man. Or pretend to. Even for the sake of getting laid.'

'Must have been bad,' Rosa said.

Dee cackled. 'Touché! But you know, if a man's asking whether your parents have money in the first half-hour, you can bet he's going to make you feel cheap the morning after. No matter how much it takes two to tango. How was your drink, anyway?'

'Nice,' Rosa said. 'It was nice.'

'Uh oh.'

'What?! Nice is – nice isn't always a wet blanket word, you know. It can just be – it was nice. Warm, and safe, and sort of *anticipatory*.'

'Aha. So, second date, third date, shacked up with two point four kids and a golden retriever?'

Rosa laughed and shook her head gently. 'Well, who

knows. That's the joy, right?' She looked quickly across at Katie. 'I'm not sure we should be talking about this.'

Now Katie shook her head. 'No. We should. How'd you leave it?'

Rosa tried to keep her smile small. 'We said we should do it again soon.'

'Good. And you?' Katie turned to Dee.

'Awkward hug. He'll feel the same way and we'll just pretend it never happened.'

'No!' Rosa squealed. 'No more of this ignoring each other! We start off pretending first dates never happened and then we're into pretending weeks of relationship never happened. When did people forget how to *say* things to each other?'

'About the time we got smartphones,' said Liv, darkly.

'I'm pretty sure it's mutual,' Dee said. 'He'll be going out with a Kate Middleton lookalike by next week.'

She rolled over elaborately, like a panther, and fixed her eyes on Katie. 'So, not a great night. But I think you win.'

Katie, drained and sunken, looked at the floor for miles. 'I don't know how to do this,' she whispered. 'I can't.'

'You can,' her friends said back.

'No.' She leaned forward and wrapped her arms around her torso. 'It genuinely feels like I've been punched. I'm not just saying that. When I walked in, he was sitting on the sofa. He looked at me. There was this silence. And you know what? For a second, I thought something so different. Had this – this *vision* for what he was about to say.'

She broke off, appalling herself. A proposal? Seriously, with the myriad tiny problems that were now so amplified, with the creeping realizations that *he might be right* and *but I want him to be wrong* and *Katie-and-Chris no longer exists*, all that and there had been part of her that was expecting to be sitting, right now, with a ring and a glass of champagne?

'And then he said *we need to talk*,' she stuttered. 'We need to *fucking* talk. He said that to me. And it's like, everything dropped. This hardness, here, and it's still there.' She pressed on her stomach and screwed her eyes shut.

Dee stroked Katie's feet. She took a huge breath, and said, 'I remember the same thing.'

Katie looked at her, somewhere between incredulity and gratitude. 'Really?'

'Yes. Four years, and I remember it like yesterday. It's crazy, isn't it? How physical it is? That pain in your stomach? This *weight*. Like something's been physically swung at you.'

'I think I didn't eat for a few days, when I – when I found out about Joe,' Rosa said carefully. 'I mean, when he told me. That he'd met someone else. Can you imagine? Me, no interest in food? It was bizarre.'

'Yes!' Liv cried. 'It hurts you in your stomach more than anywhere else. They say it's all about your heart, your chest, but it isn't. It's your guts.'

Katie shook her head. 'I don't know how to do this,' she repeated.

'It takes a few days,' Liv said. 'I promise. I remember. You sleep on it, and tomorrow it'll feel a bit lighter. And then you sleep on it again, and the day after it'll feel lighter again. Those feelings of for ever – they're not real.' *They're not permanent, no. But other things are, aren't they? Liv, you*

16

broke up with Nikita. You stood while Nikita cried. You broke it, and you broke her. And where are you now? A job you've fallen into, a man you're fixated on even though you know nothing about him, a life that feels as fragmented as you do. Shame, and guilt, and lingering wondering. Is this really what you wanted? And if it isn't, what now?

Katie turned her bleary face upwards and managed a watery smile. 'That's nice,' she said. 'I mean it. It helps.'

And then she dissolved again. 'But I don't know how to do *anything*. Where am I going to live? Who am I going to live *with*? How do you *do* this? I can't – I can't figure – my life has just been *Chris* – nine years – how pathetic is that – how do I *do* anything?'

'Doesn't come with a handbook, sadly,' Dee said, thoughtfully. Sympathy with the slightest edge.

'Yeah, well, it should,' Katie mumble-sobbed, smudging her sleeve across her face. 'That bit about my stomach. Telling me that. It helps. I'm glad it's not just me.'

And that, *that* was the moment. A flicker of recognition, an eye-catch between the four.

'Well, we'll make you one,' Rosa said. 'We've all done this. We know what it feels like. We can write it down. Your stomach feels like there's a rock in it, but it won't soon. You need soup and hot-water bottles and things.'

Dee stumbled upwards and out of the room. Some vague rumbling, crashing sounds. She reappeared triumphant, holding a book aloft.

'Perils of being a graphic designer,' she explained. 'Sketchbooks are fallback Christmas presents for *everyone*. I never use them, obviously. What fucker's got time to sketch?'

It was hardbound in a pleasing tactile black material, and the pages were thick and creamy coloured. Dee placed it on the floor between them. Liv opened it, folding down the cover and running her hands down the first empty page. Rosa shuffled clumsily through the stacks of magazines, flyers and general detritus under the coffee table, eventually sourcing a thick blue marker pen.

'So we'll all write in it,' she said. 'Everything you need to get through your heartbreak. And this is the first bit. You're going to feel like you've been punched in the guts. It's physical. But we can make it better.'

Guts

The first lesson of heartbreak is that heartbreak is the wrong word. Because the pain isn't in your heart – or even the heart-inside-your-head. The physical pain of heartbreak is in your stomach. You feel like you've been punched, and then like a football has been dropped inside you.

Or a rugby ball. A tennis ball. A briefcase or a backpack. A pint of beer or a dirty martini. A specific pair of shoes. A particular brand of cigarettes. That pretentious guitar. Whatever it is that makes you think of them, them above all else. This weight, this appalling weight has crawled inside your guts and taken up home like a spider under a rock.

Heartbreak is physical, more physical than you ever imagined when you saw it through the filter of other people's lives. It takes your breath, your hunger, your strength, your control. Your life has been split open, and so your body feels like it has been too.

So protect your stomach. Hug hot-water bottles, hug pillows, hug people. Make cauldrons of soup and sip it like an invalid. Stretch and curl up and stretch again. Undo the top button. Breathe deeply, in the air beyond your bedroom. Breathe deeply, and know that this pain will pass.

That's your stomach covered. Your mind is a different matter.

Chapter Two

TEARS

How long was it, that gap between waking and remembering? That moment in which her life was not shattered; that bliss of feeling that Katie-and-Chris were solid and whole; that eternity crushed into a singularity?

Next to her, Liv was still and silent.

In Manchester they had folded themselves into each other's beds constantly. Because it was the morning after, because it was cold, because they were sad, because they were happy. Had she been in a neutral box, blindfolded, she would still have known it was Liv next to her. The way she curled her body around her pillow; the jigsaw curve of her spine; the coconutty smell of her hair; the precise cadence of her breathing. Her presence was at once comforting and appalling; an old yet brand-new bedmate after all these years.

Katie was shaking then, and Liv turned and rubbed her back, and whispered, not Are you okay? because that was ludicrous, but, I'm here.

'How's your stomach?'

'Better, actually,' Katie said with light incredulity.

'D'you want a coffee?'

'Yes, please.'

Liv boiled the kettle, swallowed the slight hangover nausea rising in her throat and stared distantly at the cafetière. It was made of copper and self-conscious styling, a birthday present from a year or two previously. Liv had asked for it specially, following a series of complicated internal calculations as to what her parents could afford, what they were likely to choose in a small-town branch of John Lewis, and how much guilt she felt about judging them accordingly. Judging them! For living the life *she* had lived for eighteen years: Radio 4 and a Ford Focus and cottage pie for tea; weekends in the garden or walks across farmland; a gin and tonic at seven and a whisky with the ten o'clock news. News which always spoke of places a very long way away.

Nikita had asked repeatedly to visit her family home. At first the requests were easy to bat away; having grown up in a large but nondescript town, Nikita found the idea of fields romantic, but was easily persuaded into imagining pursed lips and disapproving shakes of the head behind net curtains. But after a couple of Liv's parents' occasional visits to London, when it became apparent that they were not only perfectly accepting of but actively interested in her girlfriend, it was harder to explain. It'll make me closer to you to see your childhood home, Nikita would say. The place where you caught the bus to school, the river where you went for those moody walks. They were moody because I was sixteen, Liv would say, wanting to scream, and isn't it strange they've kept my bedroom exactly as it always was? They love you, Nikita would reply. And so do I.

21

They call me Olivia, she'd say back. So? That's your name. That's what they named you. And she couldn't articulate, then, how its intricate four syllables and rolling rhythm felt too prim and proper, like an Amelia or an Elizabeth, when she had tried so hard, so very hard, to turn herself into something sharper and harder – something that belonged in the city, where people queued on concrete and sent cigarette smoke dancing under the lights. What do you mean, you tried, Nikita would have said. What is it you're longing for? You're perfect just the way you are. And Liv's shoulders would have stiffened, and something would have caught in her throat.

The cafetière fitted with an idea of herself that hadn't quite worked yet, the way she had imagined herself forward.

What do you do?

I work in PR.

Wow, in London? That must be so glamorous.

It's a riot.

Back in her bed, Katie was crying, and scrolling through her phone. Liv handed her the mug and sat watching her.

'I'm sorry,' Katie said.

'Don't say that,' Liv said. 'You've nothing to be sorry for.'

'I just want to be able to switch it off, just for a minute.'

'It'll come. It takes time.'

Katie shook her head. 'It feels like *I will never stop thinking about it*. Like, it's colouring everything. *Everything.* I was looking at the ceiling before, that crack up there, and suddenly I'm remembering when I got on his shoulders to change the lightbulb and he fell over and broke his collarbone.

Remember? That godawful evening sitting in A&E, and it was a Saturday night and everyone was pissed and fighty and shouting and it was horrendous, but I was looking at him thinking, *I love you so much, even this is right where I want to be.* And then I'm thinking *him* and *us* and it doesn't make sense that we don't exist any more.'

'It's shit,' Liv said hollowly.

There was an uncomfortable echo inside her head as she spoke. The expression on Nikita's face as she rolled the words around in her mouth, expelling them in a shorter, uglier way than she had practised. She had drunk beforehand to steel herself, and felt guilty about doing so. It was as though she were placing a film of something between them, failing to do Nikita the service of being soberly authentic. Authentically sober?

Katie looked at her. 'Can I ask you something?'

'Mm.'

'Nikita. You and Nikita. You don't talk about it much.'

'Mm. It's been three months, I guess. Move on, move up, you know?'

Katie hesitated. 'How long had you known?'

'That it wasn't right?'

'Yes.'

Liv processed this. Katie needed to be protected, and she deserved honesty, and honesty was sometimes painful. 'I don't know,' she answered, truthfully. 'More than days. A month or two?' She looked hard at Katie. 'Did Chris talk about that?'

Katie gave a weak shrug. 'I feel like – I've been trying to

work it out. All these little things . . .' She trailed off, trying to set a path among her meandering thoughts, a compass in the storm. She took a deep and crackly breath.

'When we moved into the flat. Last summer. So what – eight months ago? I told you we were arguing.'

The word unfurled in her head like a weed. *Arguing*.

They hadn't moved far. Same borough, different Tube stop. There were no duplicate kitchen utensils or concerns that they might uncover wildly different attitudes towards cleaning the bathroom. Their joint belongings were neatly boxed and they hired a by-the-hour van. The new flat was let unfurnished. It had a balcony. Both of these things were delightful novelties.

Katie had cultivated a private vision of the evening ahead, stitched together from the internet and other people. They would do the essential unpacking only, make up their mattress on the floor (they had bought their own bed for the first time, and it would arrive a week later) and dig through the boxes for a couple of glasses and the portable speaker. They would order a takeaway, and buy a bottle of something cheap but fizzy, and sit on their balcony in the fading sunshine listening to old blues and eating pad thai, wrapped in the cuddly contentment of another piece of the puzzle slowly coming together. There would be a photograph and a caption – a conscientious display. People would be jealous, and she would pretend that she didn't know that.

Only it hadn't worked out that way. The van was difficult to park, igniting a tense discussion about the deposit. The flat was dirty, and they disagreed as to whether to clean first or unpack first. And a box of Chris's clothes initially appeared to be missing, which was sourly blamed on Katie's packing abilities. Each conversation rapidly became far more complicated than the problem it was addressing. Katie wanted to hang pictures; Chris wanted to double-check the list of faults from the estate agent. Everything took longer and felt heavier than it had in her head, and Chris had a meeting on the Monday morning and started talking about going into the office the next day, just to get ahead of some things, a plan which always came with a simmering subtext throughout those six weeks of her school summer holiday. By the evening, the idea of clinking glasses in celebration, no matter how cheap the bottle, seemed like a party dress at a funeral. They went to the pub around the corner and had a beer and burger deal and ate mostly in silence.

'It isn't one thing, is it?' Katie said. 'So much has changed since we met. You're at university, you're writing your essays, you're going to happy hour, you're doing fancy dress, everyone's lives are basically the same. And then you graduate and it's like – whoosh.' She gesticulated with her hands and coffee slopped onto the duvet cover. 'Shit, I'm sorry.'

'Don't worry about it,' Liv said. 'Carry on.'

'He's so focused on the future. Doing that job, working that hard, and for what, so we can buy a bit of a flat an hour and a half from the office and say we're making progress?' She shook her head. 'It's like it doesn't add up, what you get at the end doesn't justify it. And he's furious, but he doesn't want to acknowledge it. And I'm *not* furious, but is that because I'm naive? Or just resigned? I think I always imagined we'd end up back in the South West, you know? A bit more travelling, I hoped, but then – yeah. Somewhere to live, a bit of grass. And that would be enough.'

'Of course it's enough,' Liv said, wondering whether she meant it.

'I mean yeah, sure, maybe a few years ago I imagined something different. I thought I'd be like my brother maybe, teach abroad. The funny thing is, Chris is the one who wouldn't have been able to – or wouldn't want to – move overseas, I mean. But isn't that growing up? Recognizing how unrealistic some of the stuff we used to think was? Or is that just really depressing? Isn't Chris being – I don't know – ambitious, and exciting, and *romantic* even, wanting to keep on pushing? Or is he just being greedy?'

Liv half laughed on her outward breath. 'There's probably more overlap between all that than we like to think.'

Katie shook her head. 'But we were meant to be doing it together! We were meant to be in it together! The past few months it's been like – like I should feel *guilty* if I'm enjoying my job. Or ordering a bottle of wine that's a step up from the house. Buying a pair of expensive jeans. You know – I said we could go and see my brother in Argentina this summer. Stay at his flat, he could take us around, show us where he teaches – it'd be the cheapest, easiest way we ever have of visiting South America, right? But even my *suggesting* that – it's like there's all this weight behind it.'

And what exactly was that weight, she wondered, trying to migrate herself into Chris's head. Wanting life to be a certain way, and trying to calculate what was worth sacrificing to get there? An involuntary image of him as a teenager flashed into her mind – was it from a photo she had seen, or entirely imaginary? Scruffy blond hair and a too-big blazer, clammy-handed and trying to check his accent among boys who possessed a lazy ease of everything. Boys who would grow up to tell women about fishing for salmon while trying to surreptitiously calculate their date's parents' wealth.

'He's got a chip on his shoulder,' she said slowly.

'That's not your fault,' Liv said gently.

Katie let out an exasperated something, and then suddenly, unthinkingly, she was crying again. 'Then why can't I help him?' she choked. 'Why can't we talk about it, when we talk about everything else? He's meant to be my best friend, right? That's what they say, isn't it? We *love* each other. How can we love each other, and suddenly find this barrier between us? I have to talk about it. When I go back to the flat. We have to talk more. This can't be it, I can't . . .'

She had dissolved into tears and sounds of anguish. 'And this,' she managed. 'Crying, like this. This can't be right, can it? You know, yesterday, it was the first time I'd ever seen him cry. Even when I went with him to his grandmother's funeral, no tears. Stiff upper lip, I don't know. But you know what? I was *glad*. It was horrendous seeing him cry, but it was good too. It's like – it's like the evidence that it was real. That *we* were real.'

'Of course you were real.' Liv kissed Katie on the forehead. Then she floated to the bathroom, locked the door and sat on the toilet. She stared at the scorpion tattoo on her ankle, the suggestion of sinister movement across her skin. She thought of fear, and the strength to resist it.

*

The secondary school where Katie taught was Victorian, red brick. It had been added to over the years, morphing from clear architectural idea to mutant conglomerate. The roofline was haphazard, concealing a multitude of patches of flat roof and hidden space. Doors to these were, of course, kept locked to prevent rogue smoking and sex, but Katie had worked out long ago how to access one of them.

She clambered into a pocket between two sloping roofs, imagining herself held, as if by a parent. Or Chris, the way he scooped his arms around her. The sky was grey and light and unbearably huge.

What happens next? How can anything happen next?

Her life, she now saw, stretched out behind her as a linear thread. Go to school, do your exams, go to university, make friends, sew a costume, meet someone in another, you've done a better job than me, dance and drink and screw (and listen to Pulp), fall in love, join graduate schemes, rent a flat, open a savings account, lay out the map. She could join the dots so neatly, explain how *this* led to *that*, so that Chris had been waiting at that party in that bar in that ratty homemade elephant outfit (he was right, she had done a better job at sewing than him), until that exact evening she walked in to be beside him.

To stay beside him.

And now the thread was cut. Where was the next piece to grasp onto, knot to herself?

She was tucked back from the edge, hiding from the swarms of children below – yes, she thought spitefully, jealously, they were all still children, even as they hitched up their skirts and down their trousers and patched together mosaics of countless photos. As if capturing fragments of their lives through lenses and filters would grant them certainty, some permanence. Children who thought they were heartbroken.

No. You have no idea, none of you. This is heartbreak. This is broken.

She was hugging herself around the knees, and was embarrassed when she realized it. There was an echo of her body on Saturday, the wall against her spine. Her flat. *Their* flat. She was going there on Friday to – to what? How could these shattered pieces possibly be put back together? Before she could detangle it she was crying again.

She could barely see as she tapped at her phone, but Dee answered instantaneously.

'Katie?'

She hiccupped and choked out that she couldn't stop crying. 'And it's fucking ri-ridiculous. I'm twenty-nine years old, and I've got a great job and great friends and a great family, and I feel like *I cannot see what comes next*. It's like it's empty. The rest of my life, without Chris in it. It's too big. And I ha-hate myself for thinking it's too big.'

Dee closed her eyes as she tipped backwards into the moment. Four years ago. Leo's face before hers, seven words

29

unlocking a chasmic future. Day after day, week after week of refilling that space, piece by piece.

'Babe,' she said. 'It's normal to feel this way. Your life is wonderful, I promise. There's so much you're going to be and do. You feel this way now, but it's only now. Really.'

Katie gulped and bubbled. 'I hate that I'm crying. I can't help it. I can't stop. Every time I think I've got it, it's gone again. It's like it's not my body.'

'I know,' Dee soothed. 'It's a bitch. Where are you?'

'I'm hiding on the roof. How the fuck can I go and teach looking like I've been crying? I'm all pu-puffy and grotesque. They're ruthless. They'll be savage. They can't know.'

'Okay,' Dee said firmly. 'Stand up.'

Katie found herself obeying without thinking.

'Is it windy?'

'A bit.'

'Face into it. It'll dry your face and cool you down.'

Katie lifted up her chin and almost laughed.

'Now deep breaths. Literally in for five, out for five. Yoga, right? Until you're not doing that shaking thing any more.' Dee counted along. 'Is there a bathroom near?'

'Yes.'

'Go there. You work in a school. You know the power of the wet paper towel.'

Katie did laugh this time. 'Thank you.'

'Always. See you later.'

Dee put her phone down and suddenly became aware of Simon's face, two feet from her own, plastered with a knowing grin. 'Jesus, you made me jump.'

'Quite the little therapist, aren't we?' He raised an eyebrow coquettishly. Simon had been seated next to Dee since he joined the agency two years previously, and after a bumpy start in which each directed their spikiness, standoffishness and superiority at the other, they had slipped into easy companionship. It was companionship with a guard and a filter – all Simon knew of Leo, for example, was inferred from jokes and caricature, his beard and his bike and his craft beer, rather than his heart, his humour and his eventual cruelty – but it was companionship, nevertheless, which delivered welcome entertainment to Dee's work life.

'I wish. I don't think I'm helping much.'

'Well, quite. When did you last cry, 1999?'

Dee rolled her eyes to cover biting her lip. Leo's name in her head again, a flick on the synapses like a finger on a guitar string. Guitars. A strain of old music. Seven words.

'No need to look quite so pensive,' Simon drawled. 'What's happened, anyway?'

Dee relayed an abridged version. Simon soaked up the intricacies of other people's relationships with relish. 'And what do we think? Good thing, bad thing?'

'Oh god, I don't know. Chris – he's very – straight.'

'Heaven forbid,' Simon said tartly. Dee snorted.

'You know what I mean. Very – organized. Spreadsheets of his savings. I think Katie said he got a scholarship to some posh school? He does this corporate, techy job, very focused on the future. Two point four kids and all that.'

'Aha. And she's not?'

'Well. Parts of her are. I guess you'd call Katie romantic.'

Dee said this with more than a little loadedness. 'But she's got a sense of adventure too, you know? Travelling, new places, all that kind of thing. And she's tougher than you expect. You know, a few years ago, when she first moved to London, some man tried to snatch her bag when she was walking home. It was late at night, dark. Anyway, as he goes to pull the bag off her shoulder she screams, pulls it back, punches him on the side of the face and runs home – bag in hand. She swore afterwards it had just been a reflex. We couldn't believe it; she looks like a baby angel and she manages to deck some mugger. Chris was furious, thought she'd been reckless.'

'Maybe she'll cope with heartbreak better than you think, then.'

'Maybe.' Dee stared at her computer screen, where an email of precisely ten words had just arrived. *Looks fantastic. I'd like you to lead on the presentation.* She couldn't prevent a tight smile of satisfaction.

'Let's see,' Simon demanded, reading over her shoulder. '*Fantastic.* Still with your head up Margot's arse, then?'

His eyes flickered to the glass-walled office which usually housed their frighteningly youthful managing director. It was dark and empty.

'It's not sticking my head up her arse to do my job.'

'Whatever you say, protégée.'

'Don't be jealous, it doesn't suit you.'

'Oh darling, everything suits me. But anyway. Back to Katie-and-Chris. So he's a boring sod, she's a flighty free spirit, that's what we're saying?'

Dee laughed despite herself. 'Didn't anyone tell you not to slag off your friends' exes? At least, not 'til you're sure they're not getting back together.'

'Aha!' Simon said triumphantly. 'So a break, not a break-up?'

Dee considered.

'She's devastated. You remember my housemate Rosa, a year or so ago?'

Simon whistled. 'He hasn't cheated on her?'

'No. At least, we don't think so.' Dee stabbed her pen violently onto the table. 'Joe's still with her, you know. The woman he left Rosa for.'

'The heinous anti-sisterhood bitch?'

Dee shook her head. 'Don't call her that.' Simon raised an eyebrow.

'I mean it.'

'So, let me get this right. This woman's broken up your best friend's relationship, shattered her dreams of a white taffeta dress and cubic zirconia earrings and dry chicken, ruined her life and you don't want to have even a *little* dig?'

Dee shook her head again. 'It's not like that. Christ knows I don't want to see her, don't want to speak to her, don't want anything to do with her. But – *he's* the one who cheated, right? I'm sick of the woman getting the most shit when this happens. My mum always said the same. Don't shit on the woman he left me for, shit on *him* for leaving me with a two-year-old.'

Her mother's face was in front of her, then. Eyes like diamonds, hair like flowers. Wrapping Dee's first boxes of drawing pencils in paper scattered with pink and purple stars. Holding her hand and telling her to look up; guiding her through the meanings of windows and rooflines and the sky.

'Anyway,' she continued. 'Rosa – Rosa's amazing about it. Ridiculous, even. I've never met anyone who – she believes in *love*, right? Big, grand, old-fashioned, black-and-white-movie, ballgown love.'

'How sickening,' Simon said.

Dee snorted. 'I know. But she means it. That Last Romantic column she writes – she actually *lives* it, you know? Even after all that – even after what that *arsehole* did to her – she cried for a bit, and then she stopped crying, and then out she skipped, ready for the next great romance. It's insane. She's – she's the only person I know who's actually gone for a drink with someone she met on the Tube. Someone she caught eyes with in the park. She went out with someone the other night from speed dating – *speed dating*?!'

'Christ, what's wrong with a nice friendly hook-up app?'

'Just that, apparently. *Casual sex does not equal love*, yada yada.'

'No, casual sex just equals a good time.'

'Exactly.'

'Anyway. Time for a drink before you head home tonight? Commiserate and bitch about the general shitness of men?'

'Right. Ice cream straight from the tub. But nope, I'm hitting the gym.'

'Christ. It's *Monday*.'

'Exactly. Leg day.'

'I swear to god . . .'

'You should give it a go, you know,' Dee said, standing. 'Few squats. Some lunges. Perk you up a bit.'

'No, thank you. My body is a temple. Coffee, cigarettes, vodka. The gym bunny thing is atrociously Gen Z.'

'Suit yourself. I'm going to the loo.'

And there, in a small square space with no windows, Dee leaned into the glass and stared at herself. Seven words to close her ears against; seven words to swallow down. Her eyes – dark brown, white flecks. No tears. There was a philosophical rabbit hole there, somewhere, in that you never saw your own eyes except through the mediation of a mirror, a lens, a portrait. And you could never make yourself cry on cue. Actors, sure, who trade in masks and imitations of feeling. But the rest of us, who have to live close to our own surfaces. Why was it that Katie's spilled over, and hers did not?

*

One day later? Two days? Katie blinked, still disoriented on waking. Now, the body next to her was Rosa's; they had decided on a rotating system. She gazed for a moment at Rosa's hair – auburn waves; they called her Ariel sometimes. Her hair was *there* because Katie was *here* and Chris was *elsewhere* – and the prickling heat ran across her eyelids again. Again.

What an additional layer of cruelty this was, the unpredictable white water of tears! The way each cry felt like the last one, and yet never was. She swallowed the sound, shook,

tried to slow the carousel of *Chris-and-I-have-broken-up,
Chris-and-I-have-broken-up*.

And how pathetic, how preposterous that she was crying
in this way, with this frequency and intensity, over this? Hadn't
only last term, a girl – Charlotte Archer – come to school pale
and blotchy and bleary-eyed, hung back accidentally-on-
purpose after registration, garbled to her that *My mum's really
sick* as she shook and broke? Hadn't the school, too, run a
fundraising drive for children seeking asylum, children who
arrived at the very edges of the country like ghosts, layer upon
layer of horror etched on their faces? These were the things
that deserved tears. Somewhere nearby, not even a mile away,
Chris was lying in bed (the bed they had shared) in the flat
(the flat they had shared) and he would go to work (the work
they had talked about, over and over, in the life they had
shared). He was alive, he was well. He would go on being so.
Her tears were selfish, ludicrous.

She brought her hands to her face, stretched out her skin
from ear to ear, rolled onto her back, tasted salt. And as her
body shifted, a new pain foregrounded itself – pain beyond
the gut-punch they had written into the sketchbook – nausea
mixed with iron. Twisting between her back and her
abdomen; ricochets down her thighs. She gasped; she felt
wetness between her legs.

And now she was crying again, crying in and at the way
her body overflowed from itself. Crying at how *pain* was just
one word but so many millions of everything. There was being
told about pain in the diminishing abstract: that you *may feel
some discomfort*; that you *may find a hot-water bottle or a*

paracetamol helpful. There was questioning pain in the bewildering present: *Is this 'mild'? Seriously? Am I weak? Am I breaking?*

There was the pain of embarrassment, of sitting in front of a dismissive GP at fifteen, and then another at sixteen, and another at seventeen. Stuttering words that were so wholly inadequate at capturing the claws, the flashing lights, the blinding. Later – and how appalling just how much later it was – there was the pain of learning a new word, of one's tongue tripping over six syllables of clinical grimness, of searches through webpages which admitted *no cure* but blithely suggested *an operation to remove part or all of the organs affected.*

There was the pain of sharing, of wincing in front of the people you cared about – for how could you achieve intimacy if you were unable to peel open this most terrifying part of yourself? The rushing relief of acceptance, of three girls – women – who cossetted you each month and lit candles in the bathroom. And later, a boyfriend who stumbled, yes, at this bloody, frightening femaleness – but then found his own way to be a stalwart too. Holding her through the parts where she thought she was going to pass out, the parts where she was sobbing over what might be to come. And now he would never hold her again.

She sat up, grimacing as the shards shifted, and more tears shivered down her face, and she saw the sheets. *Shit.* Rosa stirred, and made to roll over.

'Rosa! Don't move. Oh no, I'm so sorry, this is horrible, I forgot I was due, oh it's all over the sheet.' Katie used her sleeve to scrub uselessly at the blood, simultaneously startling and banal. She gripped her stomach.

Rosa squinted as she sat up. 'Oh darling, don't worry about it. We've all been there.' She stripped the sheet in a single practised movement, and gazed at Katie with familiar concern. 'Do you want to go lie on the sofa?'

Katie shook her head firmly. 'Bathroom first.'

They stood at the sink, and poured cold water, and scrubbed side by side. Rosa wordlessly took painkillers from the cupboard, and Katie nodded as she swallowed them.

'How is it, these days? The endometriosis?' Rosa asked.

'The same,' Katie said carefully. 'Give or take.' She exhaled raggedly. 'The last time I was at the doctor – they said – they said things about not putting off trying to conceive, you know – I mean hey, at least that's not something to think about any more . . .'

And as her voice broke, so did the matter-of-fact shrug, the fatalistic trill in her tone, and her shoulders were shaking as Rosa stroked her.

'Crying's a good thing,' she recited.

Katie sniffed. 'Tell me it ends?'

Rosa smiled. 'Of course it ends. Remember how much Liv cried, after breaking up with Nikita? I'm sure you said something about rehydration salts, you lunatic.'

'I'm a teacher! The first-aid training kicks in.'

'Yeah, yeah. The point is, she cried like that. Then. And look at her now. It was a phase. It *is* a phase.'

What seemed solid dissolves; a permanent partnership becomes, in the end, temporary. But what seems transient can grow roots, too, Rosa knew. The world was full of possibility but Katie couldn't see it, not yet.

Katie stopped rubbing the sheet against itself, and rubbed her eye instead. 'It's exhausting.'

Rosa reached across and touched her cheek in quiet intimacy. 'I know.'

They looked back down at the sheet, the red fading to a hint, a flush of some feeling, a trace of old knowledge. The water in the sink running paler and paler pink.

'D'you remember being new to all this?' Katie said. 'Thirteen, fourteen? I remember waking up, it used to look like someone had died.'

'Yes! I used to have everything – tampon, those massive pads like bloody *nappies* – and I'd still wake up and it had got everywhere. It felt so messy and dirty and out of control. I couldn't believe that women did this for years and years. Crazy, right?'

'Crazy,' Katie repeated. She placed her finger on the damp centre of the sheet. The contrasting shades of her skin and her blood; the metallic, maternal smell. 'I used to be so embarrassed. I'd get up really early, lock myself in the bathroom, desperately doing this, except badly, because I didn't know how. I was just – *mortified*. And then my mum found out and *she* was mortified that I felt that way. She'd always been so – you know – matter-of-fact and upfront about periods. Like she could stop me from feeling all that shame *she'd* felt, with her mum.'

A chain of women flashed into her head. Her mother, amber drop earrings and turquoise eyes. *Her* mother, long skirts with elasticated waistbands and arthritic fingers.

Forever in her seventies, forever washing plates and bowls.

'Yes!' Rosa exclaimed. 'I know we go on about how hard and complicated it is being a grown-up, but I'm so, so glad to be over that bit. It all felt so unmanageable, so alien.'

'That's what crying feels like, too.' Katie met her own face in the mirror above the sink. Her eyes, simultaneously swollen and sunken. Her skin, blotchy and slick with tears. 'It's a sick joke, right? You feel like shit and then crying makes you look like shit too. Or, you've just talked yourself, *thought* yourself into feeling better for this tiny moment, and then you start crying again whether you like it or not.'

'But it's normal. It's all normal.'

'I don't want him to see me cry,' Katie said.

'What?'

'On Friday. When I go over. Talking.'

Rosa nodded slowly. 'I get that.'

'I want to seem – I want to seem like I've got it under control. I don't know why.'

'Self-preservation.' Rosa paused. 'What do you want him to say?'

Do I want him to say it's a mistake? Do I want him to say let's not do this? Do I want him to cry to me? And if he does, what do I want to do then?

'I don't know.'

*

Friday. Katie's finger was suspended over the buzzer. The keys rattled in her other hand. What a schism this had become, a stranger outside her own building.

'I'm outside,' she said into the intercom. It felt pointless, and bizarre.

'Come on up,' he said back. It was artificially bright, she thought. Or was it artificial? His voice was clear like a bell.

Her heart was skipping frantically, and her stomach felt gripped as if in a vice. Dulled by days of writhing and pain-killers and hot-water bottles and blood, so much blood. Sharpened by being here.

There were so many more ways of entangling your body with a partner's than sex; there was sharing blood, and tears, and anxiety for the future. She had been so very terrified of talking to Chris about it; it had taken months, and when she finally found her way through the layers of angry shame, of course he hadn't even heard of it. *Endo – endo – what?* he stuttered. But he had surprised her then, not only by his tender care each month but also by his throwing himself into reading and research, until he knew almost as much about it all as she did. He was angry for her, and with her, and he pushed their conversations into places she would have been embarrassed to take them on her own, and yes, perhaps it was part of that oh-so-Chris desire to map out the future, make it solid and predictable – but perhaps it was also his love for her laid bare, the desire to stop the one you adore from hurting.

His footsteps were heavy and deep as she waited at the door to the flat. She could picture precisely where he was at each moment, measured out on a mental floorplan.

But what was written on his face? What was he planning to say? A million lifetimes flashed before her, and each began with Chris undoing the horror of the past week with a word, a hug, a sob. How easy, how easy it would be.

And then the door opened, and he was there, his flesh that had been *her* flesh. The slight roundedness of his shoulders, which he was constantly trying to reshape in the gym, but which always hinted at the nervous schoolboy he had been. The hair she had buried her fingers and face in, which she knew would smell faintly of peppermint and eucalyptus. The dusting of stubble, the deep green eyes. A million lifetimes of love.

But immediately Chris's stiff stance, his wary expression told her that this was the million-and-first lifetime, the walk across the bed of nails. How could a body that she had known so well now, already, be so separate? How could a greeting that had once been embraces, kisses, warmth, joy, now be this shaky awkwardness, this empty air? It was like she was looking at him from the bottom of a pool of water.

'Shall we . . .' he said awkwardly, and she realized she had been standing absolutely still. 'Living room?'

'Sure,' she said, and her voice sounded like dead leaves.

She walked first, folded herself onto the sofa. It transported her instantly to the evening of its purchase, the irritable feet-dragging around a too-big furniture store. And then somewhere else again, hot nights lying on it, knotted bodies, falling to the floor. She picked helplessly at the fabric, and Chris nodded in recognition.

'You can have it, if you want?' he said.

'What?'

'The sofa. I mean, we should talk about all the joint stuff, I guess. But I'm – I'm moving in with someone from work, actually. Nat. And she's already got a sofa, so . . .'

Chris sat down meticulously on the armchair opposite, and the stomach-weight that had been gradually fading since *then* rotated and shifted inside her. The armchair opposite, a hundred miles away. The armchair opposite, built for one. She blinked, feeling the slightly tacky mascara that she had applied through breath after rattly breath. Big eyes, he used to call her. If she could only make her eyes look beautiful enough, she could take this encounter down a different path. If she could only make him remember all the time before, he would kneel at her feet and cry onto her. If she could only be the Katie she had *been*, she could keep the thing she wasn't sure she should.

'You're moving in with a girl – a woman from work?'

'Yeah. Nat. I mentioned at work, what's happened, and it turns out her flatmate's moving to Berlin. Some start-up thing, so . . .'

She felt a fizz of anger, and swallowed it.

'Serendipity.'

'Yeah. Her place is close to the office, actually, so . . .'

She flinched at the repeated trailing off. This was how it was, now? She was no longer deserving of the second halves of his sentences, his complete thoughts? She focused on his face instead. On Saturday it had morphed and crumpled, choking out thoughts that she had pushed firmly away whenever they surfaced, these past months. *I don't think we're happy. I think we've grown apart.* She had felt them but

Chris had made them real, and she hated that he had done it first.

Now, though, Chris watched her with a mixture of anxiety and impassiveness.

'And is Nat single, then?' she said, spilling it out quickly so that she couldn't stop herself.

'Katie.'

'Is she?'

'It isn't like that.'

'Isn't like what?'

Chris stared at her. She felt horribly aware of her own face.

'This isn't like – a me and Nat thing. There *isn't* a me and Nat thing. We both need new housemates, and she's in a two-bed. That's it.'

That's it. This is it. How can this be it? If I keep talking, something will shift. If I keep talking, you'll remember how much more than a housemate *I was, I am, I can be.*

'I've been crying all the time,' she said. '*All the time*. It's like a reflex or something. Like I'm allergic to the air. I have to keep hiding at work, locking myself in the toilets and things, and—'

'Katie.'

She pressed her hands to her stomach, and she wondered if he knew what she meant. His eyes flickered with something like sympathy, and something like relief.

'This isn't right,' she whispered.

And it wasn't, was it? That she was sitting on their sofa in their home, crying now, of course she was bloody crying now. A week ago, if she had cried, this man would have comforted her. A week ago, if she had cried, they would already be skin to skin. He didn't move.

'I know it's hard,' he said. 'But we talked about it all on Saturday. You know it's what we need to do. It doesn't mean that it hasn't been amazing. But we've grown apart. We want different things. We're – pulling on each other instead of, y'know, pulling together.'

'But I do know what I want. I want you,' she said simply, and unexpectedly. His lips made a pursing movement.

'You don't mean that.'

'I do!' she said ferociously. 'Don't – you *can't* tell me what I want! You can't tell me what's right for me. You can't . . .'

She was shaking.

'I mean,' he said, and his voice was unbearably precise, 'you only want parts of me. We only want parts of each other. Staying together, now – it would be the easy thing. Not the right thing.'

And what's wrong with easy, anyway, she thought? Who wouldn't want their life to be easy, a calm skate across smooth surfaces? If they were characters in a game, a script, a play, she could push them together, wrap their arms around their trembling bodies, press them to taste each other's sweat. They would lock together again and all those words wouldn't matter, because they were two bodies and nine years of love and intimacy, and that couldn't, *couldn't* be undone.

Her eyes were closed, and his voice was gentle. 'It'll get easier.'

'I don't know what to do,' she said. Drifting, like a plant at the bottom of the sea.

'You're such a strong person, Katie. You'll be fine, you'll see.'

Strength. *Strength.* Bitter strength. She was gritting her teeth in silent fury now. How dare he call her strong? The strength that had held him night after night, the strength that had talked him through the anxiety and the ambition and the imposter syndrome. *You're clever and brilliant, my darling, and all the more brilliant because you've worked so hard, you want it so much.* The strength that she had poured out of herself and into him.

And him saying her name. It sounded different to how it had before.

'We should sell the bed,' she said.

'What?'

'The bed. eBay or whatever.'

He nodded. 'Okay. I can sort that out.'

'It'll help with a deposit. On a new place, I mean.'

He nodded again and she hated him.

'Do you know where you're going to go?' he said.

'I'll start looking this week.'

She wanted him to feel guilty. She wanted him to feel jealous. She wanted him to love her. She wanted to tell him she was leaving. She didn't want to leave.

'So Nat's place is free in two weeks. If you'd like the flat to yourself 'til then, I can stay with friends. Either way, I'm happy to deal with the estate agent, serve notice, all that. Good job we're on a rolling tenancy now, right?'

Good job.

'Right. And no. That's okay. I'd rather stay with the girls. The women.'

'Sure.'

There was more after that, about furniture and boxes and dates and deposits, and when she left she tried reflexively to hug him, and his body felt a different size and shape to how it had before.

In the park around the corner she sat on a bench. In other parts of the city there were benches with views for miles. Yet the horizon from this one, surrounded by trees and sunken and damp, was the furthest of all. The world felt too large, far too large, and horrifying because of it.

She sobbed. Somewhere nearby, a child was screaming and the world was split open. An ice cream dropped on the ground? A grazed knee? The pedal boats packed away for the winter; a pigeon too close?

She clutched her bag to her chest. Inside, the sketchbook was nestled between her work folders and her purse. Her friends' words, their own heartbreaks transformed into messages of resilience and hope. *Hug hot-water bottles, hug pillows, hug people.* She hugged the bag, and she willed her stomach to lighten, but it curled and clenched beneath her skin.

'Are you okay, sweetheart?'

Katie recoiled before realizing that the speaker was a grey-haired woman. She was wearing a navy duffel coat, and her face was etched with gentle concern. Katie wiped her sleeve over her face, feeling simultaneously childish and uncaring.

'Yes, thanks. Just having a moment.'

The woman rummaged in her bag, and pulled out a miniature packet of tissues.

'Never be without,' she said as she handed them over. 'Believe me. My dog died last month. It catches you short.'

'I'm sorry,' Katie said, wondering if she meant it.

'Thanks. It's getting better. Pear drop?'

Katie hesitated. The tangle in her stomach had so many different layers. The rigid refusal of food, the sensation that anything she ate would turn to concrete, sink her. The woman said go on, you'll be surprised. Katie rolled the sweet around her mouth. The smell of nail varnish remover and sugar. Somehow, it shifted the focus of her head away from her stinging eyes and swollen mouth. Sweet-sour. The woman nodded with satisfaction.

'Told you. Don't ask me how, but it works. You can keep the tissues.'

'Thanks,' Katie said. 'What kind of dog did you have?'

'Oh, a mongrel. Bit of everything. Bloody nightmare, but he was the best.'

'We always had dogs growing up. I miss them.'

'Ah, they're a lot of work though. You're young, you want to be able to stay out all night, jet off at a moment's notice.'

Katie half smiled. 'Something like that.'

Tears

When you're young, it's easy to explain why you're crying. I fell over. He pulled my hair. She took my toy.

When you're older, it's harder. There's crying out of frustration, because you've pushed yourself to the precipice and it still isn't enough. There's crying out of desolation, because the view from that precipice is unbearably vast and unknowable. There's crying out of imagination, because you are dreaming through a thousand different ways things could have been but aren't, but won't, but can't.

There's crying that takes you by surprise, crying which ambushes you like a tiger in public, at work, on the bus. There's crying alone, in the dark, which feels bigger now than it ever did before.

Crying is multi-layered. When you cry your heartbreak – when you really, really cry it – then not only will you be appalled at the visceral nature of it, as though your body is a piece of fruit being peeled apart to bleed in the sunlight, but you will also hate yourself for crying in the very moment you sob. You will know, with each wail and wash of tears, that you are crying, not over war or terror or devastation or destruction, but over your own very private catastrophe. You will cry while telling yourself not to cry. You will cry while telling yourself this is not worth crying over.

But it is. Oh darling, it is.

Crying is ferociously human. Crying is chemical, biological, physical. Crying is connection. And crying will help you. Crying is a mining operation, an excavation of pain from the deep and a shuddering, juddering, shifting of it to the surface, where it can dissipate and cool. Let that slick of tears, that raw wail, that prickly heat happen. It is all inside you. Let it fury over and over again. In time, the storm will subside.

Until then, here's what you need:

* *Tissues – in your bag, your pockets, in your desk drawer, next to the bed.*
* *Wear makeup? Switch to the waterproof kind, as though every day is a wedding and a funeral. Carry wipes for when the tears beat your mascara.*
* *Teaspoons in the fridge – the old magazine stories about them soothing your eyes are true. Who knew?!*
* *Eye drops and concealer – for temporary removal of the red. Fake it 'til you make it.*
* *Sweets, gum, cigarettes, whisky. Distraction for your mouth, for your eyes, for your stuffy head and your aching insides.*

And if you don't cry your heartbreak? If they don't cry theirs?

Play the forest game. If a person cries alone in the woods and no one sees their tears, did they actually fall? If a person's face is dry and their eyes are clear, it might be by accident or design – it might just be for now.

Be neither too demanding of yourself, nor too quick to

assume their detachment. Crying happens alone and inside too. Crying is not a marker or measure of distress, and it is not a competition. Your heart can howl while your eyes are dry.

Chapter Three

SMALL STEPS

'I can't decide,' Rosa said, plucking at the sofa, 'whether it would be better if Chris falls to his knees and tells her it was all a mistake, or if the next man she meets becomes an even better love story.'

Dee and Liv caught each other's eyes. Rosa didn't need to.

'Don't say it.'

'What?'

'Call me hopeless, or deluded, or tell me romance was never actually alive, or whatever else it is you're thinking.'

They laughed the familiarity of old teasing.

'Fine,' Dee said. 'What a beautiful little optimist you are. Speaking of, what happened to that man from the other night? When Katie turned up on the doorstep.'

'Oh.' Rosa's earnest expression faded a fraction. 'I haven't heard from him yet. I'm sure I will, though.'

And she would, she knew she would, because people wanted to fall, and feel.

Liv clamped the next bottle between her thighs as she attacked it with the corkscrew. The good one was lost, and the bad one had rusted stiff. 'Gah. You know they call these things a *waiter's friend*? Ten years of bar work and I still feel like I'm going to break my wrist off.'

'Ten years?' Rosa said, and wished she hadn't. Liv looked at her sharply.

'Okay, seven. Six. Started in the local pub at sixteen, finished in the magazine bar after graduation. Maths. Whatever. I wonder if it's still going? The bar, I mean.' She directed this last at Dee, who immediately scoffed.

'Course it will be. Immortal, that place. Or rather, stuck in the past.'

'I think they secretly liked the – *additions* – you made. Didn't bother papering over them, did they?'

'You know, they had *some* good ideas, the magazine bar,' Rosa added, trying hard. 'That Korean kitchen they did? That was a step up from your regular bar food. Their bibimbap was nearly as good as the stuff the teacher made on that cooking course last year.'

'God, I could go for one of those chicken wings right now,' Liv said, to the air as much as to Rosa. Rosa bit her lip. Finally, the cork was extricated. Liv poured generously, and said, 'It's never easy, is it? The first contact thing, I mean.'

Now Dee took a heavy swig. 'I don't know. Never did it.'

'What, really?' Rosa rounded on her. 'The last time you saw Leo was the day you broke up?'

'Yep.' Dee smacked her red-stained lips, and pushed the seven words away without voicing them. 'Why would I?'

'Picking up your stuff? Trying to get back together? Closure, right?' Rosa giggled awkwardly. '*Closure*. That's what they say. As if it's ever *closed*.'

Dee snorted. 'A – nothing to pick up; I took it all with me. B – are you joking? C – how are you going to get closure by *seeing* them?'

'Bish bash bosh.'

'Exactly.'

'You're crazy.'

'Oh really?' Dee turned to Liv. 'Go on then, what was it like, seeing Nikita after you ended it?'

Liv tipped her blurry head backwards, knocking it on the radiator harder than she had intended. 'Ow. Horrible,' she said, wincing. 'I just felt guilty. *So* guilty. It was like kicking a puppy. Twice.'

She said this to make them laugh, and they did, but her brain was pulsating, as though Nikita's face were in front of her. *I don't understand. I thought we were good. I – I love you, Livvy.*

I love you too. I just – I can't—

The unspeakable cruelty of unspeakable feelings towards the person to whom everything is meant to be spoken! Like the moment of breaking up itself, she had wound it round her skull so many times that there seemed to be a clear logic to it ahead of the meeting. But there, in the moment, it all collapsed.

Because how could you tell someone, really, that *I just don't feel the same way any more* or *I just don't think we have a future together* when their own thoughts seemed so neatly stacked in the opposite direction? There had been no great event, after all – no moment of betrayal or broken-ness. Step by tiny step, each merely a question, or a moment of doubt. A wince, or a wish for something else. So she had fizzed with uncertainty and ambivalence, an Alka-Seltzer in a glass of water; so she had moved incrementally to the point of no return. It was ludicrous, surely, that Nikita could feel so calm and comfortable, the other half of that same relationship?

And why did she keep saying *just*? Why did she keep trying to package it up into something smaller than it was? It was enormous, and devastating, and she knew it.

Her phone sat on the coffee table, with that series of messages that she couldn't bear to delete, didn't know how to explain to her friends. There was a comfort, wasn't there, in keeping Nikita's words close to her, scrolling through them in the dark? And not just her words, but her image too – pictures Nikita took together, and apart, pictures which spoke of an intimacy long shattered.

It was an uncomfortable comfort, a hook and a line to something she ought, probably, to let go.

'Well, *I* think it's a good idea, anyway,' Rosa said. 'You have to – you have to make *sure*, don't you?'

Dee made kind noises, and Liv did too, generosity and sympathy and love flooding any residual irritation. After all, they had made the same noises through the deliberations all those months ago, Rosa turning right and left in front of the mirror, trying to breathe clarity into her body. The sustenance of hope in the face of the bleakest task, going back to her betrayer for the final bag of belongings.

Rosa laughed gently at herself. 'I thought about it *so much*. That dress I knew he liked. I even bought a new lipstick that day! As if—' She broke off, and steadied herself. *As if that would make him change his mind. As if Joe would look at me in the green dress with the white flowers and want to tear it off me again, push me against the wall again, bite my neck again, under my ear, the way he did. The way he did before he met her.*

'But it was still the right thing,' she said resolutely. 'To make sure. To know that – okay, there's a line there. Time for a new story. Not –' and she directed this to Dee – 'that I think you needed to draw a line. With Leo, I mean.' Dee smiled companionably and didn't say what she was thinking, which was, *If I'd gone back to see Leo, I would have collapsed on the floor.*

A scratching noise broke the moment. Dee took an enormous glass of wine to the front door with her, and, clutching it, Katie swept into the living room like a gust of wind. She threw her bag and scarf into the corner, gulped wine, gulped air.

'He's moving in with Nat.'

'Nat? Who's Nat?'

'This girl – this woman – from his work.'

Rosa gripped her glass so tight her knuckles went pale. 'He's not . . . ?'

Katie shrugged ferociously. 'Maybe. Maybe not. Maybe now. Who the fuck knows?' She drank and drank, and some of it dribbled down her chin like a line of blood.

'As if, as *if* I went there thinking we'd make up. As *if* I thought he was going to be in pieces. No, no, Chris has got it all worked out, all lined up perfectly. Her flat's *close to the office*, you know? So he'll get up and make his coffee and she's probably got one of those stupid shiny pod machines just like him and then they'll walk to work together and he'll tell her all about how I just didn't understand what work is like for people like them and how I never wanted to go the gym and was only a teacher, *only a teacher*, so obviously *we'd* never have been able to look at flats like that, and then they'll go out for a drink after work or just get a bottle of wine to have on the sofa, and then they're going – they're going to *fuck* and they're going to get together and Chris is going to have everything sorted before I've even found a place to *live.*'

She was crying and shouting at the same time and pulled a sleeve across her face. Mascara, makeup, wine all streaked miserably. 'This *isn't fair*. How come I'm like this and he's like that? I mean, seriously? Does he just not care? Has he been planning this for months?'

'No,' they chorused.

'It's a front. He's just being that way with you to get through it.'

'Bloody stiff upper lip thing, right?'

'He's probably in a huge mess.'

'Fell apart as soon as you left.'

'He's just putting on a face.'

Katie hugged a cushion to her stomach and leaned against the back of the sofa, shaking her head.

'I can't,' she said, and she didn't know how much she meant. 'I called my parents on the way here.'

'How were they?' Rosa asked. She had a sharp recollection of her own parents' faces as she stumbled up the crazy paving. How they crumpled into fury and pity, and her bloody frustration at the cliché of it all. The cheating boyfriend, the angry father, the devastated mother. How they missed Joe, and she was glad they did because that made it real, and also hated them for stealing some of her grief. She gave herself an imperceptible shake. Her grief was then. Now was new.

'Okay. Sad, I think. But trying not to be sad, you know? They wanted to come up, but I can't. They're asking questions. I just – I can't.'

Oh, Katie darling. Oh, what a shame. Oh, what's happened?

What's happened! It was violently impossible. She cradled her face in her hands.

'Right,' Dee announced, clapping her hands together deliberately. A plastered-on smile and a conscious rationalization of what lay ahead was needed, she knew. She remembered. When all was too enormous, you made it smaller. You stuffed your toothbrush and underwear and book and phone charger into your bag, and you wiped from your memory anything else you might have left behind, and you lied to your friends about this later. You looked in the mirror, and you gritted your teeth, and you pulled on your trainers. You sweated and stretched and breathed and, slowly, you changed. 'We need lists. The break things down into manageable chunks thing. Where's the sketchbook – the handbook thing?'

Katie obediently fished it out of her bag, and Dee passed it on to Rosa. 'You can write. I think I'm seeing double.'

Rosa giggled gently as she took the lid off the pen, and spilled a Rorschach pool of wine across the empty page. 'Whoops. Okay. No promises. Go on then, Dee?'

Dee leaned back against the foot of the armchair in which

Liv was curled, spilling a streak of her own wine down her front. 'Shit. Oh well.' She held up a hand, conducting.

'Step one – somewhere to live. That's the big fucker, right?'

'Right,' Katie said.

'It's so annoying we've got six months left on the tenancy here,' Rosa said, and Katie was grateful she had mentioned it.

'I know.' She exhaled brutally.

'But,' Rosa continued. 'That means you need a place for six months only. Because after that – it's obvious, right?' Katie threw herself across the sofa and enveloped her in a clumsy hug. 'Thank you.'

'Don't be stupid,' Dee said. 'Think we're all ready for a living-room window.'

'About time we recreated the Manchester glory days.'

'Let's try to find somewhere without rats this time.'

'Anyone you know at work?' Liv asked. Katie shook her head.

Nobody asked if there was any way she could rent on her own. Katie hung her head.

'Internet, then,' Dee said. 'We'll all help. Operation find-Katie-a-houseshare. Preferably with a six-foot-four Adonis in situ, right?'

Katie smiled weakly.

'We'll each do one site,' Rosa said as she wrote. 'List tonight. Viewings asap.'

'You'll stay around here, yeah?' Liv said, and Katie's eyes widened helplessly at the scale of it all.

'Um. Yes, I guess? Yes. It's good for work. And I don't want to be far from you. And it's – you know, I can afford it, right?'

She was saying words to will it into truth. The contrast against flat-hunting with Chris! The companionable scrolling on his iPad, the gentle safety net of life admin that was built for people in pairs. And that moving-in day. How could she have allowed that argument to happen? How had she not realized the extraordinary fortune of a place to live with the person she loved? She should have been cracking jokes, smiling, being light. She should have been wearing denim dungarees over a bra with no T-shirt, her hair forming gentle waves, dust on her face in a way that was cutesy, not deranged. She should have been making him think, *You are wonderful*. She should not have had hard edges.

'We'll find you somewhere by this time next week,' Liv interjected, and Dee threw her head back in agreement.

'Next week. Yes! That is a Manageable Chunk. Then, step two.'

Katie looked at her in anxious expectation.

'Step two,' Dee said. 'Is pack up the flat. When you know where you're going. We'll all help, right?'

There was a rush of agreement, and Rosa squeezed Katie's foot as she wrote. 'We can ask at the corner shop for some boxes. Get a van.'

Katie visualized it as she spoke, and felt a complex flood of different kinds of love. The way these women scaffolded her; the knowledge that without them there, placing a single book in a single box would break her. The flat was going to be packed up. All those layers of life. The photos she had meticulously framed for the kitchen wall – the adult symbolism of migrating from Blu Tack to picture hooks – where would they go now? Would she dismantle them, replace them with photos of someone else? Would Chris take them? Would he show them to Nat, *I've got some frames, shall we get some pictures on the wall?* Would Nat laugh delicately?

'Step three,' Liv said, 'is keep busy,' and Rosa jabbed the pen in the air in wild agreement.

'Yes! Keeping busy. Busy is the key.'

'Every day we need a plan,' Dee said. 'Things. Stuff. What day is it?'

'Friday.'

'Friday. So, tomorrow. What'll we do tomorrow?'

'I need some space,' Katie said.

'I can sleep with Liv or Dee,' Rosa said immediately. 'Have my room.'

'No. I mean – outside. Can we go for a walk?'

'Yes! Great idea.'

'Train out to the countryside.'

'Pub for lunch.'

'Blow the cobwebs away.'

'Definitely.'

'And what about Sunday?'

'Sunday roast, obviously,' Rosa said. 'I'll cook.'

Katie's stomach lurched emptily against the pear drop and nothing else. She smiled an unsure agreement.

'Come to the gym with me on Monday?' Dee said, and laughed at Katie's mock-horrified expression. 'Seriously. I'll be easy on you. And lifting something heavy will make you feel better. Promise.'

'Okay.'

Later, they sat surrounded by further bottles and Friday-night fug. The sketchbook lay open on the coffee table, a to-do list on one page and a more abstract list on the other. Small steps; increments of reconstruction. Katie counted her breaths. Each of them was scrolling through places where she might be able to live, strangers with whom she might be able to share something.

'*Imagine living with four well-educated professionals who actually follow the cleaning rota and keep the communal areas in a fit state for all to enjoy,*' Rosa recited. 'Well. I mean, I'm doing a lot of imagining right now.'

'Jeez. I've got a "cosy single" over here. "Cosy" meaning – ooh, what do you reckon, two metres by one and a half?'

Seeing Katie's expression, Dee tossed her phone onto the floor. 'But that doesn't matter. We've got – what – twenty? Got to be something decent in there, right?'

Liv and Rosa hurried to agree, and Katie smiled a weak acknowledgement. 'I'm going to need another massive wine, please. Wine. Whine. Haha. Both.' She tipped her head against the back of the sofa and her vision swooped like a shoal of fish. She righted it, and blearily stretched her mouth into something like appreciation. 'Thank you, though. This would be – impossible.'

Later still, she lay back to back with Dee, a line of air between their spines. So much love there, but so different from the kind with Chris. And it was Chris that she was looking at, her phone screen casting a cold glow into the space between her arms, her head and the duvet. The way you could move through someone's digital life, and from there into others. Was it Natalie, or Natasha?

Natalya. A prettier name than Katie. A name with more possibility, further horizons.

Her job title is Analyst, which can be interpreted both as boring (what, she analyses stuff for a living? Who dreams of doing that? Just how *anal* is she?) and as intimidating (she clearly earns a lot of money). She studied Economics at a good university and she went to a school which sounds like it was paid for. This is both to be scorned (she won't know anything about real life, will she? She got where she is because of someone else's efforts. How can she possibly know the depths of her privilege?) and envied (privilege is what we are all working to, after all. The ease of lifting the curtain, the champagne of ordinary things).

She has long dark hair and large sharp eyes and very white teeth. She's not intimidatingly beautiful but she looks polished, put together. Her body looks tight and clipped and predictable; no ragged terms like *scar tissue* and *adhesions*. She looks like babies will come precisely when she wants them, neat balls of unappreciated good fortune. She looks like she knows what her future will be.

There is a photo of her on the company website with her arms folded so as to look businesslike but her head thrown back in laughter so as to look approachable. She is wearing a silky blouse and a very well-cut blazer which is not black or grey or navy but the intimately adult colour of an oyster.

Small Steps

'The rest of my life without my love' is overwhelming. It will sink you. Split 'the rest of my life' into smaller pieces.

Begin with tomorrow. You need to wake up.

Continue with the day after. You need nice things to do. Not ridiculous, challenging, mad-new-me things, but things you already like. The company of good people. The distraction of mindless television. The stretching of sore limbs. Segment out your time and fill it with easy plans – plans that will distract you, plans that might even make you smile. Walking from one place to another. Cleaning out a neglected cupboard. Buying and reading fifteen magazines, one by one. Making pancakes. Swimming. Drawing a picture. Painting your fingernails. Buying flowers. Write down every idea you have, even if it doesn't appeal today. It might tomorrow.

Continue with what needs to be done to complete the separation. The belongings which need to be boxed up. The migration from our bed to my bed. The place from which you will live the next chapter.

It sounds appalling, right? How have you shifted from one life to two? How can you drag yourself through the processes of searching, packing, moving, rearranging, when you can barely cope with breathing? How can you now be dismantling that which you took for granted until the moment it was no longer yours?

It is appalling. It is painful. It is also the ripping-off of *the plaster, the exposing of the wound and the beginning of the better.*

Sometimes the small steps will take you backwards, not forwards. That's okay. Love yourself for it, not in spite of it.

Know your strength. Know you are strong.

Chapter Four

OUTSIDE

Katie leaned her head against the train window and didn't speak. It was a perfectly clipped, cold day with a blue-white sky against which the trees and buildings seemed to stand out more sharply than usual. She watched the transition from city to suburbs to Sussex countryside, and throughout the same thoughts pounded her. *Chris and I have broken up. Chris and I have broken up.*

How she had taken for granted all the years when she didn't have these words clustered at the front of her brain! Like how having a cold was the only thing that made you appreciate the calm reflex of breathing.

Dee, Liv and Rosa drank coffee and talked softly. The sketchbook was open on the table; Dee doodled hills and trees and a pathway meandering through them.

'My mum's going to come and stay on Friday, if that's okay?' Dee asked, and felt a familiar wave of pleasure at their equally familiar expressions of enthusiasm. 'Some photography exhibition she wants to combine with checking in. She's promised margaritas in exchange for a bed for the night.'

'*Mel's margaritas* . . .' Rosa and Liv echoed in unison.

'Sounds good.' And each quietly thought of their own mothers, who had never visited with tequila in hand or to share their beds, and whom they loved, and whom they compared.

'How are things with Margot?' Liv asked.

Dee smiled. 'Good. Really good. She wants me to present to a big client next week. Rebrand project.'

'What's the client?'

'Ha. You'd call it *feminine hygiene* back in the day. Period pants and things, basically. Good politics – eco-friendly, not scared of actual blood, you know?'

'They sound great.'

'They are. Be even better when we're done with them.'

'Margot wins interesting projects, doesn't she?'

'Yeah.' Dee leaned back in her seat. 'Her career, it's just incredible. All these amazing names, award wins, tick tick tick, even before she set up on her own. And she's grown the place to this level in what, fifteen years? The clients are great. The work's *good*. She's – she's how we want to be.'

An image of Margot glided into her head. The delicate corkscrews of dark hair, the deliberate, chunky silver jewellery. Margot looked how Dee had imagined London when she was a teenager. She was a leapfrogging of the years of long nights and short pay cheques, a fully formed forty-something with money to spend on facials and no wedding ring. She no longer got involved in junior interviews, but she did meet every new recruit. Dee had twitched nervously opposite while Margot looked through her portfolio in cool silence. She commented just once.

These are good. Very striking. Not patronizing.

Thanks. And that was all she had said! How different from the ways Dee thought – or hoped – herself to be, vivacious and bold and articulate. How different from how Margot must have been at twenty-two. Afterwards she had phoned her mother, gabbling excitedly in the way she guarded against with everyone else. She's brilliant, so brilliant, reminds me of you a bit actually, like really smart and no-nonsense but creative too, I mean obviously she's creative, she runs a design agency, but she's the polished kind, not the art student kind, you know? Even her name's a bit like yours – Margot, Mel? Her mother smiled down the line, another brick of women building the world better.

And after *that* she had met Leo, telling him fizzily – yet smoothly – about her first day in the new job, how inspiring the managing director was, how she hoped to be like her someday. He had gently placed his forefinger in the dimple on her right cheek, and told her he loved to see her so excited. That she was beautiful.

And frustratingly, awfully, embarrassingly – that *mattered*.

'You're lucky.'

'Yeah. How are things at the paper, anyway?'

Rosa shrugged. 'Valentine's was a bit depressing. My editor made me do a listicle for the column – "Gifts To Show How Much You Care". I tried to tell him The Last Romantic's meant to be about – well, just that. Old-school romance. *Emotion.* Not, you know, buying your way into someone's bed.'

Dee snorted into her coffee.

'Anyway, he wasn't having it. Told me the city's full of clueless boyfriends who need help choosing – I don't know, sexy underwear and non-clichéd chocolates. Even the romantic ones.'

'Sounds about right.'

'But I made the last one "Go dancing, walk home, say *I love you*", and he let me keep that, at least.' Rosa smiled in honeyed satisfaction. 'Anyway, what about you, Livvy? Any unsatisfying work stories?' She bit her lip as she spoke, and wished she had used different phrasing.

Liv pursed her lips. 'I feel like I should have some big exciting tale for you now. But no. Press releases, bylines, smarmy emails to journalists. You know the drill.' She too bit her lip, and wondered if Rosa had noticed. 'But!' she added. 'I haven't told you about *Felix* yet.'

Even Katie looked up.

'Felix,' Liv continued, inflecting his name with relish, 'might just be the most beautiful man I've ever met. He's head of a division at one of my clients – *not* the water cooler people. A good client. The biotech people. They're doing this really amazing research in respiratory – anyway, that's not import-ant. The point is, he looks like a young Marlon Brando.'

'Retro.'

'I know, right?' Liv said. 'He's like – remember that shift up you do, from the baby-faced one in the boyband who couldn't grow facial hair, to the one with the tattoos and the piercings? *That's* what Felix looks like.'

'God, yes. Quite a few of those on the bedroom wall.'

'Exactly. Anyway, let me tell you, there's something

completely discombobulating about being reminded of your adolescence like that. He even smokes in the same way. Rollie, raised eyebrow. I thought we'd gotten over smoking looking cool, right? But no.'

'Single?' Dee asked.

'No. No no *no*. Not whether he's single or not. The hooking up with a client thing. I mean, it's not forbidden. Not exactly. But frowned upon. And, you know, it's a bit harder to tell someone that no journalist is going to give a shit that they've just repainted the office toilets once they've seen you naked, right?'

'Simon had a thing with a client once,' Dee mused. 'We were out celebrating this big project – branding for a hotel chain – and he ended up going home with the head buyer of towels and napkins or something. They used to do these coy little smiles at each other in meetings. But it never seemed to affect anything. They were completely cool. I could never tell if it was a guy thing or a gay thing. Maybe it was just a Simon thing. *Please, I'm a professional*, he used to say when I asked him about it.'

Katie giggled softly from the window, and Liv rubbed her back.

'How're you doing, K?'

'Okay.'

It was a lie, because she would never feel okay again, but it was the truth too, when they got off the train in the chosen village. The air in London was so *full*, so packed with stories, and there was joy to that but pain as well, as though you had to compete for each gasp of it. But here, as they walked through the sleepiness, over a gate and out into the green, she noticed that the sky had grown and contracted at the same time. There was more blue and more white and more clouds and more sun. There were birds here. Birds didn't have breakups and broken hearts; birds just flew.

She tilted her head upwards and tried to make sense of the horizon as they walked towards it.

'*Keep the wall to your right as you walk through two fields and down to a gate with a cattle grid beyond*,' Rosa was reciting in exaggerated confusion from the route she had downloaded. 'I feel like such a townie. Wanna navigate, Livvy? This was your whole childhood, right?'

Liv rolled her eyes as she took the phone. 'That's right. Sunday walks in our wellies and evenings cuddled round the wireless.'

She felt a mental twinge as she spoke, picturing a hurt expression on her parents' faces. *We wanted to bring you up in the countryside, darling. We thought we were doing what was best for you.*

And it *was* good for her, wasn't it? She gazed across the greens and browns, felt tree bark beneath her hands and river water between her legs. It was all so far away, and that was the point, the pull – and yet also the pain, the push. Her distance from home was deliberate – and yet home was still what she called it.

'This way,' she said.

Katie took a rattling breath and Dee grasped her hand. 'Come on. Race you to the gate.'

Dee was a runner, of course, and was probably going

slower on purpose, but as Katie moved her legs faster, momentum and mud pulling them down the hill and drawing tender knives of breath into her lungs, she was amazed to find herself laughing. The cold was like chewing chillies or plucking hairs one by one out of her skin; it was making her *feel*. Her body could still do more than tears and tragedy.

They crashed into the gate, and the tears were rolling again as she laughed, and shook her head, and tried not to think about Chris, except she was going to think about Chris for ever. She gazed up the field towards Liv and Rosa, who were picking their way down the path with a lot less speed but rather more elegance. They were so much smaller than the world! And the world was full of people who had been through precisely this. Every day, everywhere, relationships ended. Heartbreak was a million movies. Lost love was endless lines of poetry. She wasn't alone. She wasn't alone.

Except she was alone, because she had lost Chris. No one else had lost someone so perfect, so utterly right, so spectacularly better than every other human being that she had been monstrous for ever questioning him. Everyone else could navigate this but her. Even Chris could navigate this, in his new flat and his new future.

Was he thinking of her?

'Is it making sense yet?' Dee asked.

Sense! The turbulence that her mind was rearranging and replaying and reordering, the Rube Goldberg machine of *Why has this happened?*

'I think,' she began. 'I think we've become different.'

There. She had translated the thoughts into words, shifted

the atoms of air in front of her mouth, flapped the butterfly's wings.

'The best thing, when I first met Chris, was how much I knew he adored me,' she said. 'I don't mean that narcissistically. Or maybe I do. But I mean – I could trust it. He put himself out there so completely, and his morals. It feels amazing, having someone look at you that way . . .'

She trailed off, embarrassed, but Dee squeezed her hand encouragingly.

'And that made all those years so *safe*, you know? Applying for jobs, and moving to London together, and sharing with his friend and girlfriend, and then getting a place of our own. I – I know I've had it easy, right? Me and Chris – Chris and I. It was like, we were doing things in exactly the way the world expects you to – the world wants you to. Paired up. Boy, girl. Nine to five, savings account. It was *simple*.

'But somehow, somewhere along the way, it's changed. I didn't even notice it changing, but it has. He doesn't look at me in the same way. Like, when I talk about travelling, have ideas for new things – he used to find it exciting, and now he finds it frivolous, or childish. And I never knew – is that just what happens? Is that just nine years? Or is it something else? How he's doing his thing and I'm doing mine, and I thought they were, you know, parallel, right next to each other but maybe they're actually like this.'

She dropped Dee's hand to gesture into the sky, spreading her arms and her fingers outwards, staring at her bleak outline against the white.

'He's got such clear ideas about how he wants his life to

73

be. And when we were younger and we talked about that, it seemed abstract, you know? But now. I'm even wondering if it's a money thing. Is that fair? You start off the same, don't you? Teacher, corporate graduate – they're not so different. But now they are.'

Dee made a comforting, noncommittal noise.

'And then I think – that's horrendous! We *love* each other, right? How horrific if that doesn't stand up through – through him getting his pay rises and planning out where we should try to buy a flat, and me – and I'm doing great too, you know? Christ, if being a *teacher* isn't enough to make things stack up neatly any more, what is? And what's wrong with us if we can't stay together through that? What's wrong with *me* if I'm thinking about us in this way?'

'He's in your head constantly,' Dee said. It wasn't a question.

'Yes. *Yes.* I have these moments of forgetting, of just focusing on what's around me, there, in the moment, and then it's like my brain goes *Hah! You nearly thought you had it then, but no!* Especially when I'm trying to go to sleep. Or when I've just woken up. Or when I'm on the bus. Or when I'm at work. *Everywhere.*'

Dee nodded. 'Your brain does what it does. You'll be processing, or something.'

'It doesn't seem possible. That I can live the rest of my life with this at the front of my head the whole time.'

Dee opened her mouth, and his name was there again before she could speak. The guitar, and the finger in the dimple on her cheek. The savagery of those seven words.

'It does change,' she managed. 'It just doesn't feel like it yet.'

Katie looked at her, eyes shiny. 'Do you still think about Leo?'

Dee swallowed. 'Sometimes. I try not to. But sometimes.'

'Does it still hurt?'

'Yes.'

Another bird darted across the field like a ghost.

'But,' Dee said, 'in a different way.'

That was the nature of scars, she thought. The way the wound knitted together into something harder, tougher. The way a vulnerability gained strength but lost suppleness. She placed her forefinger softly on Katie's cheek. 'Come on.'

They picked their way gingerly over the cattle grid, the strange acrobatics of the countryside, and walked on. The path was only just visible through the grass like an idea, a memory of other people. Katie noticed the changing textures of the earth through her boots; the way sometimes she slipped, and at other points felt anchored, as though she were tethered to the underground. One field after another undulated and rolled them down the valley.

'Thanks for this,' she said. 'I thought it would be good. Being outside. Fresh air. Somehow.'

'No, definitely. Running's the same.'

'I can't believe how long you've been into it. Years now, right?'

'Four. Since – well, you know.'

'Right,' Katie said again, and she looked sideways at Dee's taut body, her upright stance. Dee always looked *sprung*, as though her muscles were wound more sharply than other people's. 'Maybe I need to take it up.'

'Always happy to go with.'

Katie took a long breath. 'And when you think about – when you think about you and Leo. Do you feel – you know when people say *over*? I don't know. Is that a real thing? I feel like I'm just repeating what I've heard other people say. Because it can't be true, can it? How can I get *over* this? I feel like . . .'

The skeletal call of a crow from somewhere nearby.

'. . . I know this is ridiculous, especially after everything I just said, but I feel like how can I ever meet someone like Chris ever again? I was so, so lucky, I met this wonderful brilliant man and I got to be with him and live with him, and I've never met anyone who's even come close. Never. And I *know* there's all these contradictions. I know things haven't been right. I know I've been feeling these doubts, and wondering whether it was right to carry on, whether I'd end up getting sadder and sadder. I know we've been arguing about things we used to laugh about. But they were just part of something bigger. I loved him – I *love* him – so, so much.'

She was crying now, and Dee took her hand and squeezed it. Katie's was clammy and hot, and Dee's was cool and soft, and as they walked skin to skin their temperatures gradually evened out.

'It's weird, the things your mind does,' Dee said. *It's weird that it's been four years, and I still think about Leo. It's weird that I wake up sometimes and think I've seen his face while I was sleeping. It's weird that I've blocked him out, but still look for traces of him, even though I know it will hurt. It's weird that I think about him every time I look in a mirror.*

'It takes time. I know that's a shitty thing to say, but it's true. You just have to trust that it changes.' *And it has changed. But it's still there.*

'I know that's the theory,' Katie said. 'But I can't understand it. Like, right now, I'm wondering where Chris is. What's he doing? How does he feel? How could I know all that stuff so exactly two weeks ago, and now I don't know any of it? And how can I stop myself thinking about him?'

'Practice? Just like running, actually. Practice and time.'

A few metres behind, Rosa and Liv were talking in a dancing way. Rosa's lifestyle desk – centred on her column, The Last Romantic – and Liv's roster of corporate clients never overlapped, but their foundations – Manchester, books, short stories, sardonic smiles – were wrapped around each other. There had been a time, which both knew and neither voiced, when they imagined their twenty-nine-year-old selves as, if not colleagues, then certainly peers.

'It sounds like you're doing so well,' Rosa said. She meant it, but she also meant more.

'Thanks,' Liv said. She meant it, but she also meant less. 'It's good, mostly. You know. There's always that wondering whether you could be doing something else, right?'

'Yes.' Rosa gazed at Katie and Dee further along the path. They were walking hand in hand. 'I guess they've always been much more sure than us.'

'Dee and Katie?'

'Yeah. Katie talked about teaching from the minute we met her, right? And Dee-the-designer. They're vocations, aren't they?'

'I guess so.' Liv bit back a rush of unwelcome thoughts. *Isn't writing? Didn't we sit together, drinking wine out of mugs and talking about newspapers, poetry, screenplays?* How glorious they had been, those long hazy evenings when she knew with blissful arrogance that their words were going to be printed, somewhere, somehow.

Liv's parents rarely travelled to Manchester – there was so much traffic, and it was expensive to stay in a hotel. On the rare occasions they did, it was like the hard shell the city was gradually layering onto her – that she was layering onto *herself* – was temporarily dissolved. She would walk them excitedly around the gothic buildings she loved best, and tell them how she was putting together ideas, a kind of portfolio, needed for applying for work experience and *further training*, you know? They would smile and blink and agree without knowing what they were agreeing with.

And how quickly it all disintegrated, when the reality of rent and bills and *highly competitive* and – oh god, *internships* – began to circle. How blankly her parents looked at her from all those miles away; how she hated herself for wishing something of them that she didn't even believe was right. For weren't they effusive in their pride, when one of the graduate schemes she applied for as an afterthought came good? Weren't they excited to talk about her working in the *city*, for a company with offices all over the world and which brought in a photographer to take her headshot for the website? Liv's parents loved her, and were proud of her, and that would always matter more than money.

'But I know what you mean,' Rosa said carefully. 'The wondering about other things, I mean. I think that. I've been at the paper what, three years now? And it's great, but it's – it's also making my love life into this narrative, this *story*. I pushed so hard for the column to be about what I actually believe – *feeling*, you know, and connection, and kindness, and then when it actually comes to it, it feels like I'm pouring out so much of myself. I believe in love, Liv. I really do. I believe it's out there. I believe there's something bigger and better than Joe. But I don't want to turn that into – what, light entertainment? And I know I'm lucky. I know there's a queue of people who want my job. But actually, that's what makes it . . .'

Harder. It's hard, Liv. It's hard to question what I'm doing when I know how lucky I am. It's hard to question what I'm doing when I know it's what you want.

Liv paused for a second too long. 'I know. Things are different on the inside, right? And it's not luck, you've worked so hard to get where you are.'

She truly meant it, she thought. Rosa had *grafted*. The postgraduate degree by day, the freelance sub-editing by night. The embarrassing blog detailing London's takeaways and greasy spoons in a pastiche of the most breathless broadsheet restaurant reviews. The months of unpaid interning. It was all extraordinary work. And yet it was all anchored in the ordinary: a north London cul-de-sac; a childhood bed; understanding parents; a travel card. The different things money meant, here and there.

'Thank you,' Rosa smiled weakly. 'Well, cheers to hard work, right? We're doing okay.'

'We're doing okay.'

Dee and Katie were waiting at the next gate. 'Well done, guys. Girls.'

'Women,' Katie added reflexively, but she was wondering at how she felt neither young nor wise.

'The pub's just opposite the church,' Rosa said. She had suggested this particular walk not just for fields and views, but for the promise of a celebrated menu in said pub. Katie's response, stomach still churning, had been lacklustre, but even she could see the appeal of its glowing windows now.

Inside, there was a proper fire and several proper dogs. Liv immediately fell to greeting them while Dee went to the bar, and Rosa and Katie squeezed around an empty table. Rosa grabbed a menu delightedly.

'What do you feel like? Lamb! I haven't had lamb for ages. Oooh – Jerusalem artichokes. Have you ever cooked those? They make *the* most amazing soup.'

A smile of pained amusement. 'We're not all as geeky about food as you are.'

'Hah. Yes.'

'I'm not hungry, actually.' Katie paused fractionally before she spoke, and Rosa looked thoughtfully at her.

'You didn't have breakfast and you've walked five miles.'

'I know. I just.' Katie took a shaky breath. 'I haven't been eating. That sounds dramatic. I mean, I haven't been eating normally. Much.'

Rosa opened her mouth, and said something different to what she intended. 'Stomach?'

'It's a different feeling, now. It's like being nervous each time I try to eat.' Yes, that was how to capture it. She recalled the soup in the staffroom the day before – nothing elaborate – a tin that made her think of being younger, or ill. The domestic ping of the microwave, the steaming bowl, and the lurch inside her. As though her hunger had been ripped from her.

Rosa nodded. 'Okay. I won't do the mum thing.'

'Thanks.'

'Glad we came, though?'

'Yes.'

Katie pulled the sketchbook from her bag, opened it and turned to Dee's picture. She traced her finger along the winding pathway. She thought of Chris.

Outside

We all know the duvet-and-sofa clichés. There's a place in heartbreak for your pyjamas, for shutting out the world.

But fresh air and space and moving through them can be a better medicine than you expect. Walking makes it easier to think and to talk and to unpack what has happened. Moving makes you feel more alive than staying still. The outside can be frightening because it is so open and enormous – but it can be uplifting for the same reasons.

So call a friend and ask them to go for a walk. Embrace that for these delicate days they will rally, will go above and beyond. Find a field or a park or a pavement. Wear your warm coat. Put sweets and hipflasks in your pockets. Look. Listen. Breathe.

The scale of the world will grant you perspective, though not necessarily in the ways you think. It might feel terrifyingly, impossibly huge. It might feel like you're the only one within it. Other people will remind you that you are not alone – and also that you are.

Gaze at the outside, listen to the outside, dance in the outside. Soak up all the little beauties. Let yourself be amazed, arrested, awed.

Scream into the outside. Because anger can feel good, and noise is a release. But send that scream into the air, the ether, *not towards them. Look at how much more there is – time, and space, and possibility. Trust that one day your movement through it all will not be saturated in them.*

Keep moving. Keep towards the horizon.

Chapter Five

HOME SWEET HOME

Mel arrived as she always had: in glorious Technicolor, fizzing with energy. The tequila and triple sec clanked in her bag, and as she embraced Dee she tossed a lime to Liv, Rosa and Katie, who jumped for it like wedding guests, laughing.

'Hello, you gorgeous women,' she said unselfconsciously, and she hugged them too, lingering slightly longer on Katie. 'Dee's caught me up,' she said. 'Hold fast.'

She laughed at the pickle-jar cocktail shaker, variations of which had adorned all of their shared homes to date, and laughed, too, at the practised roles they each took: glasses, ice, salt. Makes me proud, she said, and her hand was on Dee's shoulder. Drinks in hand, she and her daughter curled on the sofa like cats, and talked very quickly.

Rosa coated tofu in cornflour and dropped it into sizzling oil, smiling as it goldened, and delighting in the dextrous flicking of it backwards and forwards. How simple and how magical. Peppercorns popped; spring onions glistened green. She carried portions into the living room, frowned as Katie shook her head, but decided not to protest. In the kitchen, she covered the unwanted bowl with foil and left it on the countertop, hoping and worrying.

Liv sat on the floor, scrolling. Nikita's photo had changed. *Then* it had always been one of the two of them – fireworks over the Thames; slightly tacky, Liv privately thought – and Nikita had waited a full month after their breakup to remove it, reverting to some default shape, white on grey. Now it was a picture of an apple. Nikita's own photo, clearly, not a stock one – Liv recognized the kitchen table. What did it mean? Nikita had rubbed an apple on Liv's jumper, once, laughing. They'd turned it into a joke, which meant that she did it with every apple from then on, and each time Liv had found it slightly more irritating, and each time she had said nothing.

Line after line of messages, which even now she read in Nikita's voice. Kisses and cries, unwrappings and unravellings. She scrolled herself back in time, past *that day*, past the banal exchanges about the pub and milk and meeting times, to the photos and messages that felt like vitamins and bubble baths and cashmere. Images of them arm in arm, lip to lip. Images each had taken of themselves, sent like sweets to each other's beds. *You look beautiful when you're sleeping. I can't stop thinking about you. Love you always.* Which wasn't true, because Nikita couldn't love her now, how could she, after what Liv had done, the things she had said? And that was what she had wanted, the cut she had made, the tearing.

'What're you so engrossed in, Livvy?'

Snap. 'Nothing. News.'

'Aha. What's going on in the world?'

'Um. Client news, I mean. Nothing important. What's going on?'

'Flat chat.' Dee nodded towards Katie, whose knuckles were white on her glass as she tried to inflect her narrative with enough humour to avoid dragging the room into gloom, and enough realism to convey how depressing the viewings had been.

Flat one. New-ish build. Third floor. The housemate who opened the door looked about seventeen, which was a bad start. The second housemate, who didn't look up from his computer even once, was a depressing middle. And the bedroom, with its unmistakable musky, sticky smell and floor littered with crunchy, crumpled-up tissues, was a hideous end.

Flat two. Victorian conversion. Promising, initially. It was actually nicer than this place; the living room had a window, after all. But the two women sat on the very edge of the sofa, as though sinking into a cushion would be an outrageous display of excess, and their handshakes were damp dishcloths. 'We've agreed that we don't get in later than nine thirty on weeknights. Ten thirty on weekends.'

Flat three. Lodger situation. Skye must have bought the place many years previously; the beaded door curtains and incense surely spoke of someone who couldn't have afforded it in the past decade. She sniffed between every other word and wiped her sleeve across her face. 'Sorry. Bugs going around, aren't they? So, this would be your room. Oh – shoo. Sorry. The cat likes it in here. Anyway. It's a vegan house, and that's cleaning products and clothes as well as food, please. And my tarot group meets here on Thursday evenings, so you'd need to keep out of the living room then. Sorry. Oh, and I don't have Wi-Fi – because of the vibrations, you know?'

Flat four. Not actually a flat at all, but a four-storey townhouse (though far more dilapidated than the genteel images that conjured up), a tiny kitchenette and a damp shower cubicle squeezed onto each floor with even less elegance than this windowless room. Which might have been bearable, had the corridors not been strewn with abandoned recycling sacks, and the smell of several different kinds of smoke not permeated the entire building.

Flat five. The flat she hadn't mentioned then, and wouldn't mention now, because it was several hundred pounds a month out of her budget. But it was a twenty-minute walk from Chris's office and the balcony looked exactly like the one on Nat's profile photo, where she stood with a glass of – well, it wouldn't be prosecco, would it?

And it was a beautiful flat – of course it was a beautiful flat – with brilliant white walls and engineered-wood floors and a view of space and promise. The owner – the *live-in landlord* – was a man whose face looked like it was carved out of a piece of granite, who was an inch taller than Chris, who had described himself on the advert as *I'm Finn. I'm thirty-four, I do mobile development and techy stuff (don't worry, I won't bore you about it). I like wine, reading and playing squash. Looking for a flatmate who's happy to cook together and head to the pub together every once in a while.*

Her mind had raced from there, because if Chris was going to live in this block with successful shiny sparkling Natalya then she could do the same, she could sculpt something better out of nothing, she could leapfrog the maze that her mind kept stumbling over and transport herself to somewhere better. She could *win*. And Finn was charming and pleasant and offered her a coffee (there was a pod machine on the countertop) and asked her what she did for a living and said he'd get back to her, and if he did call then she would have to lie and explain that she had found somewhere else, and if he didn't call then something, somehow, was lost.

'The thing is,' Mel said, 'there are two things at play. One – you're trying to find somewhere to live in the insanely expensive city you've all chosen, in the insanely expensive era you all haven't. Two – you're comparing everything you see to what you've just had. Neither makes for especially clear vision.'

This was simple and complicated at the same time.

Katie smiled weakly. 'I could relocate, couldn't I?'

Mel raised her glass. 'You could. And you might have more money left over each month. And you might miss everything you moved here for. And you might find new things you liked even more.'

'Where would you live if you weren't in Brighton?' Liv asked Mel. Mel smiled in pleasure.

'Great question. I travelled in South America before Dee was born. I could live in Buenos Aires, Santiago. Sometimes I think about a little cottage in the countryside, the South West probably. The whole honeysuckle over the door thing, let the cats roam wild. Or maybe I'll buy a van and not live in one place at all.'

They all listened to this and believed it.

'What about you?' Mel continued.

Liv startled and then shrugged. 'I don't know. I wanted to leave the countryside as soon as I could. I love cities. I love the busyness, the anonymity, the buzz. I never understood why my parents left.'

'They wanted the best for you.'

'That's the line.' Liv checked herself. 'I mean, yes. Rosa, what about you?'

'Oh god. France somewhere? I'd go to cooking school, learn the classics.'

'You can say Paris, you old romantic.'

'It's not too clichéd? Paris, then. I'll go there, you can live out your secret New York dream, Dee, and we'll be basic together.'

Dee rolled her eyes, and Mel shook her head in mock confusion. 'You women. You think too much about the outside looking in.'

Katie swallowed more margarita and noticed grimly how, after a mouthful or two, the hard edges of *Chris and I have broken up* had been filed away. Now it was something grey and gloomy at the heart of something bigger – swirling waters, distant horizons.

'Mel?' she said.

'Katie.'

'Do you think money can make you happy?'

Mel threw her head back and laughed. Dee rubbed her

foot and looked at her mother. Liv licked the rim of her glass, and waited.

'Oh, darling,' Mel said. 'No one ever specifies *how much money*, do they?'

'What was it you used to say?' Dee said. 'Enough. Know what's enough.'

'Exactly.' Mel turned back to Katie. 'Trust me, those first few years after Dee's – after *he* left. Moving back into my mum's – and of course there wasn't any help forthcoming from him – yes, that was a tight time. Not having money made for more *un*happiness. It made for stress, and anxiety, and feeling like I'd failed. But later on – as things got better – it wasn't about buying a particular *thing*, you know? It was about knowing we had enough. A roof I could keep on paying for, food in the fridge. Confidence in the next month, and the month after that. That's the basis, that's the *foundation*. And it's a huge bloody privilege. Much more than it should be. Especially for women, let me tell you. If your life goes to shit, money can be a pretty important lifejacket.'

Salt crystals melted on Liv's tongue, and she rocked herself imperceptibly.

Confidence in the next month, and the month after that, Katie thought. She had that, didn't she? A job, and a salary, and a family waiting to scoop her up if she called them. Privilege, *huge bloody privilege*.

'But you know,' Mel continued, 'sure, thousands in the bank would have made the practicalities of those early days easier. They wouldn't have taken away the heartbreak though. That sits somewhere else.'

Somewhere deeper, darker, Katie thought. It was true, wasn't it, that no matter how smooth and gilded the base building blocks of her life, her heart would still be aching? She looked at the message again. *All sorted with the estate agent. We need to give the keys back on the 28th.*

The breathy days after they met. The nervous adding of crosses to texts – one was too few, but two looked like overkill. The anxious skittering around how long to wait before replying; the delicious thrill of seeing he had messaged her even when she had been unable to fashion a question into her own text. The gentle transition into unselfconscious outpourings of affection – and now this, a death rattle.

'You're so wise,' she said to Mel. 'Please write all of this into my heartbreak handbook.'

'Your what?' Mel asked. Katie pulled it from her bag and passed it over.

Mel began reading with an expression of wry amusement, but it shifted, soon, into something more like admiration: Oh my darlings. I remember it so, so well. The stomach ache, the tears, the walking for miles and miles. And you say I'm wise? One foot in front of the other, Katie, one tick of the clock after another.

Dee tore open a bag of crisps and began offering them around. Katie shook her head, and Rosa raised an eyebrow, but said nothing. Liv tapped her phone against her thigh, feeling a rush of gratitude that she and Nikita had never moved in together, and a rush of guilt for thinking so. The webpages Nikita used to pointedly leave open on her laptop.

Saying *Yeah, it's a pain with four of us, to be honest* when her bathroom was busy in the morning.

Katie let out an animal noise of frustration. 'But it's still so *hard*. I'm twenty-nine years old. I'm a *grown-up*, right? But I can't . . . there's all this stuff to do.' More tears, and she pressed three fingers frustratedly to the gap between her eyebrows. 'I promise I'm not being fussy. Those places were not okay. I think – I don't think I can . . .'

Her phone was vibrating then. 'Oh, shit.'

'What?'

'It's Chris's mum.' She held the phone away from her body like a grenade. 'I haven't spoken to either of them.'

Dee, Mel, Liv and Rosa watched her expectantly. 'Fuck. Fuck fuck fuck.'

In a rush of movement she stood, placed one hand over her eyes and answered.

'Fiona, hi.' She was mortified to find her voice cracking like glass.

'Hello, Katie.'

There was an embarrassing pause before Fiona continued. 'I just wanted – we both wanted – we wanted to see how you are, darling.' *Darling.*

'Oh, that's kind of you. Yeah, I'm okay.' *Okay! The lies we bind up in that word.*

There was another excruciating silence. *What has he said to her? Did she expect this? Does she know about Nat? Natalya?*

'We're obviously very sad about it.' *Obviously! Obviously!*

'Me too.' Her voice shattered.

'You've been together such a long time.' *Nine years. Nine years, Fiona. Don't say it in that trite way. That's a lifetime. That's my adulthood. That's not just a 'long time' to say casually, like you're commenting on your husband's trip to the pub, or the drive to Cornwall every July.*

'Yes.'

'But it's for the best, isn't it, if things aren't working?' *Working. That word again. What does it mean, and what do you mean? What has Chris said to you, and what have you conspired about together?*

'Yes. I'm just figuring it out. You know, a place to live and everything. Obviously Chris has his new flat sorted.'

She cast the hook and the line, willing Fiona to bite, to supply her with venomous crumbs of *Yes, we've seen pictures* or *Yes, we've met Nat.* But she was cleverer than that, of course – or perhaps kinder.

'You're a lovely young woman, Katie. Of course we wish it had worked out, for you and Chris, but I'm sure you're going to – to have a wonderful life, and be very happy.' *You're sure? These are just words that people say, Fiona.*

'Thank you. That's kind.' She bit her tongue. 'And how's Chris?'

There was a pregnant pause.

'Yes, he's – he's well. He's working very hard, as you know. Such a driven boy.'

Katie almost laughed. 'Yes.'

'Okay. Okay, I'd better go. You take care of yourself.'

Fiona hung up before Katie did, a clinical beep echoing

down the line. She gasped herself back onto the armchair in frustration.

'Mothers and sons,' Dee said. Mel made a short, knowing sound.

'Tell me about it. It starts young, you know. We see it at parents' evenings. Our world invents all these clichés of daddy's girls and overprotective fathers but the mother–son dynamic is *so* much more consistent. It's worship.'

Dee laughed tightly. 'It's masochistic is what it is. Women building men who'll screw over women.' Mel pulled her daughter's foot onto her lap and smiled gently at her.

'Women building men who'll love them,' Rosa said quietly.

'She doesn't know about where Chris is moving?' Liv asked.

'Not sure.' Katie was shaking her head. 'I'll probably never see her again. I've been to her house hundreds of times, I've literally helped her brine bloody Christmas turkeys, and now I'll never see her again.'

She had been a fluttering kind of nervous when she met Fiona and Pete for the first time. There had been a boyfriend or two before, but in the casual way. Come back after school, watch TV, come for a walk after school, reach under clothes. With Fiona and Pete it was the deep end of a weekend at their house in the home counties, shoes off at the door, air kisses and you have a lovely home. Over nine years, just as she and Chris had softened and deepened, so too had she and Fiona and Pete. Fiona would sit with a glass of wine (rosé), ask her questions about her work, oh it's just so much harder in the state sector isn't it, the resources you have to work with, and the pay not so good? Yes of course, but I feel like I'm making a difference where it's actually needed, and you must have been so pleased when Chris got his scholarship, the fees would just be impossible otherwise, wouldn't they?

Barbs, yes, but there was kindness too, a recognition that she was helping Chris, that she made him more than he would be. On the train back to London Chris would roll his eyes at the beige carpets and pine furniture and she would want to shake him, tell him how golden he was there.

'No more comments on *how casually* you dress for work?' Liv said. It was a gambling statement, she knew, but it hit well. Katie laughed out loud.

'This is true. No more mumbling about the deposit when I put picture hooks in the wall.'

'No more tutting when you leave the glasses to wash up in the morning.'

'Exactly!' Katie turned to Dee. '*Exactly*. People who wash the glasses before they go to bed . . .'

'. . . haven't drunk enough.'

They laughed together, the kind of laughter with a layer of melancholy underneath.

'You never heard from Joe's parents, did you?' Katie asked. Rosa hesitated.

'They tried. I had a couple of missed calls, some texts. I just – I couldn't face it.'

They nodded, and she wished she could tell them the fuller truth, the acknowledgement that speaking to them would have further concretized the unspeakable. Because whether

Joe's parents were apologetic or angry or even ambiguous, contact with them would have been a savage way of bringing into the light what had happened, what Joe had done. And, more than that, it would have been a shadow across any future reconciliation. How could she hope, or think, or *believe* that their relationship was to have another chapter if cast in the middle of it was her wailing to Joe's parents about how he had met someone else? How could she return to their house, continue to smile in their photographs? No, refusing their contact was an insurance policy, a layer of armour, a shard of hope.

'I think Leo's mum was embarrassed,' Dee said suddenly. They concealed their surprise at hearing her say his name aloud. Her face slipped into a moment of something painful, and she got up and went to the bathroom.

Mel's eyes flashed around the three, daring them to tell her something she didn't know.

'I asked her about him, on the walk,' Katie said.

'And?'

'Nothing, really. She said she still thinks about him.' Rosa and Liv nodded their empathy, and Mel whistle-inhaled over her teeth.

'If they could see the trails they leave, these men – these people,' she said, and it was unclear whether she meant the adjustment to her words or not.

In the bathroom, Dee looked at her reflection. She forced her mouth into a smile, and the dimple folded into her cheek. Was this how her face had looked, then? Her hair would have been shorter. She might have been wearing lipstick. But surely her eyes, her expressions, the Dee in this mirror was the same one who listened to those seven words and swore she wouldn't let him see her break.

She breathed, counting. It was as though she could see herself from a distance, performing her steadying. Her eyes didn't prickle, but she splashed cold water on her face anyway, and pressed her forehead hard into the glass.

When she walked back into the living room they didn't comment, and she spoke in a firm clear voice: 'That's what we need. More things Katie has to look forward to. When you move, I mean. Like – playing the music *you* want to play, always.'

Katie had been about to protest, but now she laughed. 'That's right! No more Eagles and Springsteen while he pretends to be a white American road tripper.'

'Exactly. What else?'

Katie picked the lime out of her glass and turned it over and over between her fingers. 'I can have flowers. I can buy fresh flowers without him doing the eyebrow thing and saying they're a waste of money.' She snorted. *'They just die, Katie.'*

Bells of laughter. 'Yes!'

'I can put only the pictures *I* want on the walls. The *V-J Day in Times Square* print, the maps. He said they were contrived.'

'Yes! God, as if I could ever have moved in with Joe, the junk he had on his wall,' Rosa lied.

'I can sleep and wake up exactly when I want. No more getting woken up when he comes in late, or feeling guilty when I lie in and he's putting on his gym kit.'

Mel was laughing too, and telling them this is right, you know. Home sweet home. And you're moving on up, my loves – don't you remember the damp and the mould in Manchester, Liv storing her clothes on a rail on the landing because her box room was so tiny? (Liv laughed along, and remembered her lower rent agreement, and was thankful, and tasted lime juice on the back of her throat.)

'We'll come with you to the next viewings tomorrow,' Liv said. 'Not, like, chaperoning you inside. But we can walk together, right?'

'Thank you.'

*

Rosa undressed with the unsteadiness of drinks and thinking. It was true; Joe's interiors taste was the masculine equivalent of live laugh love and prosecco o'clock; a row of expensive whiskies and a framed Pulp Fiction poster. He would have an exposed brick wall if he could. But it was also true that she didn't care; Joe could have wanted to live in a flat decorated entirely in yellow corduroy or magic eye wallpaper and she would have done it, lain next to him soaked in bliss.

Because I was in love and that's what love is, the translation of irritation into irresistibleness, and I found it then and I will find it again, I will, I will.

*

As Dee and her mother got ready for bed, Dee was meditatively rolling Leo through her head, and if Mel could see something in her eyes, she didn't say so. Katie-and-Chris had pulled Leo into a different place in her thoughts, Dee knew. Like taking a book down from a high shelf, his face had a clarity to it now that she had worked for years to blur.

So the thing to do was to work harder. They would walk Katie around the neighbourhood tomorrow. They would find her six-month home, the pause before a return to living as a foursome again. A loop to how they had been in Manchester. A backwards step, is that how Leo would have described it? She realized that she was gripping her thigh too tightly, and her mother had noticed. *Be strong, my darling star. Be strong.*

*

Liv and Katie undressed together. Both noticed the evolution, the way they had moved forward from the embarrassment of teenage PE lessons and sideways from the glow of long-term relationships. A pyjama top over a head, the glimpse of the curves of a friend's body, wholly unerotic but gloriously intimate. How they no longer tried to hide themselves. Feels like home.

Home Sweet Home

Breakups don't just end a relationship. They end something extended: bedrooms; ways of living; the threads of friends and family; routine. They edit the familiar; whether or not you lived together, they change your home.

This is disorienting, discombobulating. This is a loss too.

Try to remember that homes are never static. That image you have in your head now – the home sweet home of a photograph, of your memory – is a snapshot, frozen. Home keeps on turning, and it always would have done.

Try to remind yourself that you create home wherever you go. That your home is held by so much more than walls; that the people near you, the cadence of your days, the mug you like best for your tea will keep you upright.

Try to search for elements of excitement. The ways in which you can reshape your home without compromise or concession.

The ways in which you can twist and turn and map out a route entirely of your own. The ways you can turn up the music.

Chapter Six

FOOD

'Rise and shine and all that.'

Katie blinked blearily as Liv placed a cup of coffee on the bedside table. It smelled like mornings and a frenetic kind of emptiness. There was a savoury sizzling in the background.

'Rosa's making bacon butties.'

Katie twisted into seating and took the cup gratefully. The coffee was strong and rich with whole milk. Her stomach felt simultaneously glad for it and resistant; it warmed her down to her pelvis and then just seemed to wait, grimly, emphasizing the hollowness of the past days.

The kitchen was a comforting chaos of steam and spitting fat and smoke and music. Dee was bouncing from one foot to the other as she made mugs of tannin-heavy tea, while Rosa, in a tiny camisole, turned the gas higher and flipped bacon with a combination of reckless confidence and dextrous skill.

'The best bacon sandwich,' she announced, 'is smoked streaky – cooked 'til you can snap it – and you need to put the bread in the pan for a minute or two as well. Mustard and red sauce.'

'With you 'til the mustard. Brown sauce all the way,' declared Dee, transferring the mugs and said brown sauce to the – 'dining' seemed grandiose – tiny square table. 'Liv?'

'Red, obviously. And hot sauce.'

'Curveball. K?'

Katie inhaled the headiness of countless lazy mornings with Chris, and shook her head weakly. 'No, thanks. I'm not hungry. Coffee's good.'

The opposite of hunger is not satiation; it is lack of desire. She sat awkwardly on the chair by the wall, suddenly fancying that she could feel a new kind of hardness in the seat. That was ridiculous; it was only a few days of not eating properly – ten? A fortnight? Her heart scurried in her chest, faster than the radio, as she imagined her bones pushing closer to the surface of her skin, shapes through tracing paper.

Desire. She had lost it in so many different ways. Ten minutes' walk away, Chris was in their flat. Saturday morning, ten o'clock. Perhaps he had already gone for a run, or to the gym. Sweating purposefully, that muscles-as-machine approach she liked to scorn in men's magazines, while secretly kneading her thighs between her hands. Wishing she wanted merely to be strong; knowing she wanted also to be thin. But living without food, it turned out, meant living on a frantic, skittering surface, ever threatening to crack and sink her. Fragility might look pretty in a picture, but it felt like exactly what it was.

And yet. And yet. She thought about bacon sandwiches. She thought about bread and milk. She thought about the chocolate she had always used to comfort herself, pillowing earlier, gentler heartbreaks and the monthly agonies through-out her body – and she felt sick.

The other three were clattering around the table, passing and spilling tea, chatting over the music.

'Sure your mum doesn't want one?'

'No, no, she's had a coffee, she's heading off soon.'

'Any more encounters with the famous *Felix* this week?'

'I forgot to tell you, he called me about something yesterday. My stomach did that – *mm* – thing, just hearing his voice.'

'You sure it was your stomach?'

Rosa and Dee threw their heads back in screeching laughter, and Liv tried to stop herself from spitting tea onto the table.

'Yeah, okay, okay. You know exactly what I mean. But Jesus – his *voice*! It's like—' Liv tried unsuccessfully to begin her imitation several times, contorting her posture into a sort of exaggerated suaveness, while Rosa and Dee cackled, and Katie tried hard to join them.

Mel appeared in the living room, smiling and blowing kisses through the doorway. Thank you, gorgeous girls, wonderful women. Look after yourselves. Dee embraced her, breathed in her patchouli and her power. I love you, darling star. Katie found her chin shaking as she smiled, and tried to stammer out a fraction of her thanks.

When breakfast was over they all got dressed. Katie almost cried when she saw them lined up in the living room. Dee: biker boots and miniskirt; coat with fur at the collar and cuffs. Rosa: woolly hat over her red hair; emerald-coloured scarf; floaty dress. Liv: head-to-toe black; leather jacket; kohl-rimmed eyes. They looked like they always had: her beautiful best friends; her memories; her promises. They looked like anchors and like ladders, and Rosa linked arms with her as they walked with purposeful, optimistic bounce.

'I think you found this one, Rosa,' Katie said.

'Aha,' Dee said, 'Liv and I'll wait on the bench down there. Four standing at the door might freak them out a bit.'

'Good thinking.'

The flat was on the ground floor of a Victorian terraced house. The road was wide enough for plane trees; the windows had bays.

'It's a nice street,' Rosa observed, looking left and right, and not adding, *Joe lives along there. I used to cut through here to get to the off-licence.* Instead she said, 'Who're the flatmates again?'

'Um. Laura and Aaron.' Katie shrugged. 'Fingers crossed, hey?'

And she kept that wound-up *maybe, maybe* feeling through the ringing of the doorbell, the footsteps, the door swinging open to reveal a man about their age, quite attractive (why, oh why does that thought *have* to be there, even now?), in Saturday uniform of grey tracksuit bottoms and a baggy navy jumper. She kept it through him extending his hand and smiling with dimples, and through the woman, also about their age, who appeared behind him and wrapped an arm tenderly, performatively around his waist.

'Hi, I'm Laura. Nice to meet you.'

It *was* nice to meet them – they were sweet, and their flat was pleasant, with the homely, lived-in décor of a long-term rental and a garden which had caught the morning sun – but each time Laura placed her hand on Aaron's arm, or smiled at him with more breadth and depth than she had offered to Katie and Rosa, Katie's heart pulled in her chest. The spare bedroom, and the relative positions of the two head-boards, decided it.

'I can't do it,' she said as they hurried down the road towards Dee and Liv. 'I can't pay a hundred quid more than I have been to live with a couple that loved up. It's too much.'

Rosa thought better of protesting. 'She did touch him a *lot.*'

'It's like – a display, right?'

'Exactly. You'd be hearing them have ostentatious screamy sex through the wall, and then they'd have mad fights during the day. Throwing knives.'

Katie found herself laughing. Dee and Liv stood up expectantly, and she shook her head.

'No can do. Onwards!'

It was only half forced, the positivity, because the sun was shining and London was glorious and she was out in the crisp air with her three favourite women in the world. *Chris and I have broken up.* She kept it up through the next viewing, which was a raver household of the sort she hadn't seen since Manchester. Glow sticks and polystyrene trays and empty baggies littered the living room. Only one of the four housemates was up – in dark glasses – and he banged apologetically on the door of the room which was to rent, before giving up and saying well, you get the idea, anyway.

Chris and I have broken up.

By the next, in which the spare bedroom was in the lean-to at the back, with a menacing spread of grey damp up half of one wall, she was swallowing down a lump in the back of her throat.

Dee took the initiative. 'Ten past twelve. Pit stop.'

They sat in the rapidly filling pub with four pints and four packets of crisps, which Katie ignored. The beer scraped at the edges of her empty stomach, but it soothed the edges of her scratchy mind, and her breathing steadied.

'Okay. There's one more. Might be the one. And we can do another round on the websites tonight. It's been a week, there's always new stuff coming up,' Liv said bracingly.

Katie shook her head. 'Do you ever think this can't be worth it? London, I mean?'

A pregnant silence.

Rosa broke it. 'Please don't leave us!' she wailed, half seriously.

This broke something else and Katie was crying again, but angrily.

'For god's sake! I've done everything I'm meant to. I've got my degree, I've got my Proper Job, I've got my savings account and my budgeting app.'

And you've got your parents, Liv nearly said, but didn't.

'I just want to find somewhere to live that isn't falling down, or with people who're going to remind me every day how much sex I'm not having, or who think pills and vodka is a balanced diet.'

The final word reminded her again of how her stomach

felt both empty and unhungry, and she downed the rest of her pint in fierce defiance. Her head spun. The others shared a momentary look.

'How long 'til the next viewing?'

'An hour.'

'Shall we go for a walk through the park? It's Saturday, that farmers' market'll be on.'

'Good plan.'

The market was the gentrified kind, with food arranged artfully in wicker baskets and hessian sacks. Plump tomatoes; bunches of dark spinach and greens; potatoes with chocolatey soil on their skins; peppers which looked like they had been polished. They walked through waves of fragrance: pungent, lactic cheeses; billowy freshly baked bread; cured sausages.

Katie inhaled headily and tried to think of eating. A tarted-up fish and chip van with a calligraphed chalkboard sign was handing out paper parcels and the smells of a hundred holidays hit her, salt and batter and oil and vinegar. But as soon as she imagined chewing, swallowing – something contorted inside her. She absentmindedly felt the bones on her wrist, and wandered on.

Rosa, always the most excited by anything food-related, dawdled at one of the stands, tasted a salty, crumbly cube of cheese, smiled and nodded at the stallholder and got out her purse.

That was when she saw them, wandering down the next row in the kind of blissful bubble she recognized with a ferocious ache. Joe in the brown leather aviator jacket she used to gently tease him about, while loving the way it had sculpted to the shape of his body over the years, the creamy woollen collar against his dark stubble. He was pointing at something, and his other hand was scooped protectively over her shoulder. Her jacket was vintage, floral – the kind of jacket which should have looked like a pair of curtains but instead, across her elegant frame with the sweep of dark hair, looked lifted from the pages of a glossy magazine. He was smiling into her face, and Rosa burned.

Stumbling backwards, away from don't you want the cheese, love – *love* – she found herself caught in the Saturday pace of the crowd, everyone strolling too slowly in their unguarded clouds of coupledom. She couldn't see her friends. She felt herself panning out from the market, seeing streams of people gliding in the opposite direction from where she wanted to go, Joe and *her*, Joe and his partner, his lover, his Rosa replacement moving inexorably towards her, which was ludicrous because they hadn't seen her, though if they had surely they would want to run away, because wasn't it horrible, painful, embarrassing – yes, weren't they *embarrassed*, here, in front of her, showing her what they had done, what they had taken from her?

She was pushing now, barging through people with no pause for permission or apology. One or two muttered, or protested more indignantly, but she was beyond and through and suddenly at Dee's side, white-knuckle clutching onto her arm and saying we need to get out of here, Joe's here, we need to get away.

They went to a different pub and ordered four more

pints and a bowl of chips. Rosa was embarrassed to find herself shaking.

'Sorry.'

They all made noises of encouragement, nothing to be sorry for, don't be ridiculous, he's the one who should be sorry.

'I thought—' she began.

I thought I was okay. I thought I had moved on. I thought I had forgiven.

Because he's moved on, hasn't he? She's there, now, clinking glasses and making photo collages of their holidays. Has she made friends with his housemates, growing through that awkward phase of morning hello-goodbyes and evolving into beers and pizza on the sofa with the football? Have her belongings started to appear in his drawers, on the bathroom shelf? God – what if Joe doesn't even live there any more – what if he's made a home with her already? What if she has changed his taste the way I never did? What if they cook spaghetti together in a tiny kitchen and dance?

'A year,' she said. '*More* than a year. And I see them and it feels like it's all undone, I've just been pretending. I mean what am I playing at, really? The Last Romantic? Bullshit articles about walking hand in hand through cemeteries and renting vintage cars?'

Dee and Liv eyed each other.

'I've tried so hard,' Rosa said, and her voice was cracking.

Katie was rubbing her shoulder as the bartender brought them the hot chips, golden and glistening, with edges caramelized into crackly brown. The fragments of sea salt looked like snowflakes. The smell, Katie knew, was delicious, but it wasn't translating.

Rosa, however, selected the fattest chip and then cried at it.

'I'm sorry,' she said again. 'K. This is meant to be about us helping you, not me in a state.'

'Don't be silly. If I saw Chris with . . .' She trailed off, and sipped some more of her beer.

'They shouldn't be allowed to stay living around here,' Dee said. 'If you do the fucking around, you should be kicked out of the area, right?'

Liv ate two chips hurriedly. 'What's the last viewing, Katie?'

'Um. Two guys, I think. Rafee and Jack. It's on the street off from that off-licence, the blue one.'

'Handy.'

'Yeah. It looks like there's a little garden.'

'What do we know about Rafee and Jack?'

'Um. I think it was Jack whose name was on the advert? He works for the NHS? Sounds nice enough.'

'Fingers crossed.'

Time fluttered and no sooner had Rosa scraped the last chip around the bowl than Katie was checking her phone. 'I'd better head over there now.'

'I'll come with,' Liv said. 'You guys stay here. Rosa – have another big drink, right?'

Rosa smiled weakly. 'Thanks.'

Dee bought two gin and tonics, placed them on the table like soldiers and looked hard at Rosa.

'What a load of shit, hey?'

Rosa again smiled weakly. 'Cheers to that.'

As the bitter liquid slid down her throat and diluted the pounding of her thoughts, she felt simultaneous gratitude and vague alarm at the need for it.

'Do you want to meet someone else?' she asked. 'I mean, for a relationship?'

Dee's turn to take a deep drink. 'Wow.'

'What do you mean, wow?'

'Hah. Just that. An expression of surprise, or something.'

'Well. Do you?'

Dee looked at her pointedly. 'What do you think?'

Rosa looked back. 'I don't know. That's the point.'

They broke the face-off with sharp laughter, and Dee rolled her eyes.

'I don't think a relationship would add anything to my life right now. How's that?'

Rosa nodded slowly and stared into the middle distance. 'God, I wish I felt like you.'

'Well, why not? Our lives are pretty similar, you know. Good friends, good job. We don't hate our parents – or parent, at least. We've got enough money for a decent Saturday night. What else do you need?'

'I know. *I know.*'

Dee sighed. 'But. If a relationship's what you want – well, that's okay too.'

'Is it? I've made it sound good, haven't I? The dates and the drinking and the dancing. The *sex*, right? The kissing, the holding hands. I mean – it *is* good. It's exciting, it's anticipatory, meeting these men and wondering if there could be something there.'

Dee gave half a smile. 'Hard to tell, isn't it? The difference between the exciting new and the something that'll stick? God, it's so much aggravation.'

Rosa nodded passionately. 'Yes! Like the speed-dating man from the other night, when Katie came round. That was a *high*, walking home from that, before I saw K, anyway. I felt buzzy, and fizzy, and – Christ – *alive*. But then – I've heard nothing. I've messaged him, asked him if he'd like to go out again, and nothing. So all that energy, all that effort – where's it gone? Was that just me, putting it out into the ether? Because it *is* an effort, Dee. Seeing the good in people, seeing the potential in people – it's labour, it's *work*. And Joe's made it harder work, and I hate him for that. It's not just feeling sad about the breakup, it's knowing why it happened. It's knowing that he chose her instead of me. It's knowing that he lied to me, for weeks. I feel like – I feel like Joe's stolen something from me. Like he's made things that bit harder for me, now, for ever.'

Dee nodded for longer than she intended to, and swallowed half of her drink in one. 'I guess – I guess I can understand that. I mean . . .' She tapped on the table. 'I remember it so exactly, you know?'

The time she had spent trying to distance herself from that moment; the ease with which she could magic herself back there. A glass shattering into a thousand pieces; a knife somewhere tender and private. Dee was a *strong woman* – she knew this, this was important – but she was trembling now as she trembled then. Leo had at least had the decency to look ashamed, but he hadn't been able to meet her eyes. And then there was a dissolving, and a breaking. She shouted things ferociously; she demanded an apology; she hated herself for showing him this fury; she left; she ran; she kept running.

She breathed deeply, and repeated those words – his words – the breaking. '*I just don't fancy you any more.*'

Rosa took Dee's hand.

'I know it's not what Joe did,' Dee said. *Seven words.* 'But—'

Rosa cut in passionately. 'That doesn't matter! It's awful in a different way! It's another bit of bullshit that stays with you, right?'

Yes, oh yes. The bullshit waiting in the mirror, in the photographs, on the scales. What did it mean, when someone who was once so hungry for you changed their mind? The precise pain of knowing that your worth should lie in your mind and heart – while hating that a blow to your body and face made you shrivel. Dee shook her head against the reverberations of Leo: his curly dark hair; his fingers on the guitar, on her cheek; the expression on his face; his echo. She raised the end of her drink. 'To taking no bullshit.'

'No bullshit.'

*

It was a narrower street than those from earlier, lined with cottages rather than townhouses. There was something comforting about the scale of it, Katie thought. It felt like knitted jumpers and cups of tea.

'Here we are. Twenty-one. Please cross everything you've got.'

The man who answered the door was about their age, with glasses and a Dungeons & Dragons T-shirt. He smiled broadly and extended his hand.

'Katie, right? I'm Jack. Come on in. Oh – is this your friend? Hi, I'm Jack.'

There was an endearing fumble of handshakes and smiles and hi, I'm Liv, here for the walk, and come through, Rafee's in the kitchen. Katie took a deep breath and walked forward.

The front door opened straight on to a combined kitchen, living and eating area which had clearly last been refurbished some years before. Scratches and chips. There was a squashy blue sofa and matching armchair, and a TV with two consoles and a neat pile of video games. A complicated-looking board game was set up on the coffee table.

'Yep. Two self-confessed nerds in this house, I'm afraid!' Jack said cheerfully and without embarrassment.

Katie smiled. 'I like it. It's really cosy.'

Which it was; soft and welcoming. As was Rafee, in the kitchen half of the room, but moving purposefully towards them, holding out his hand, saying hello, grinning. It was all contented and unabashed.

'Welcome to the palace,' he said. 'Bit scruffy, as you can see, but the landlord's pretty good at sorting out anything really desperate. Want to see the garden?'

She did. They walked to the back of the kitchen, where a rickety glass door opened onto a tiny square of grass and dandelions, with a trio of wooden-framed planters backing onto the fence.

'We took one each, us and Phil, who's moved out,' Rafee said. 'If you're into gardening at all – or want to give it a go? We've done well with tomatoes and courgettes, but the strawberries were a disaster.'

Katie laughed. 'I managed to look after a chilli plant for a few months.'

'Oh, brilliant! Are you into spicy food? We like doing a curry night every now and then.'

They were both charmingly earnest. Back in the cottage, Jack showed her the bathroom on the ground floor; a tiny white shower room with a few missing tiles but which was nevertheless clean and warm, with a neat shelving unit divided into three. 'We've found it's easiest, to keep things tidy – one space each,' Jack explained.

And then they went upstairs, and showed her the bedroom. The bed was pushed against the window, overlooking the garden. Above it was a single shelf, next to it was a chest of drawers and opposite a clothes rail. The floor was honey-coloured wooden boards and the walls were white, with a blue roll-down blind at the window and a dark-framed mirror above the drawers. There was little room for anything else. Phil had evidently already left; the rail was empty, and the bed was a bare mattress, brand new and still in its plastic wrapping. It reminded her of being a child.

'It's not big,' Rafee said, 'but it means the rent's a bit less on this room, and you're on your own at the back, so it's quite private.'

It was the epitome of small but perfectly formed, Katie thought.

'I love it,' she said, truthfully.

'Great! Why don't we go back downstairs and you can tell us a bit about yourself?'

They squashed into the living area, Liv and Katie perched on the sofa, Rafee in the armchair and Jack on a cushion on the floor, and talked. Katie found herself explaining not only that she was a teacher, not from London originally but it's where everyone ends up isn't it, always lived roughly in this area, but also that she was looking for somewhere to live because she had just broken up with her boyfriend. It was, she reflected, a detail she hadn't mentioned in the other places.

'Ah!' said Jack. 'Can't say we've been in the same boat, but it must be a right hassle when you've lived together?'

A right hassle, she thought, wryly. It was so much more than that, and yet there was a twisted comfort in hearing it phrased that way. A right hassle. A logistic complication. An unexpected addition to the to-do list. She could protest, try to communicate to them the devastation, the way her stomach had frozen and her body kept overflowing with tears – but at the same time, there was grace in hearing it interpreted from this distance.

'Yes, we're both perpetually single in this house, I'm afraid,' Jack continued, before laughing awkwardly. Rafee joined in, and Katie felt a rush of warmth for them both. She covered the moment graciously, saying, 'Some other things about me: I love reading – history teacher, you know – so I come with quite a few books.'

'Oh, that's no problem. You can see there are lots of shelves in here. We like reading, too! I go to a book group, actually, if you're interested? And we could always do an Ikea trip, get one of those bookcases.'

They carried on chatting for fifteen minutes or so, sharing polite but comfortable opinions on television, food, the local pubs, the park, running, the gym. Jack was a project manager for the NHS and Rafee worked for an environmental charity. Katie felt as though she had known them for a long time.

'Well,' she said eventually. 'We'd better get going. I guess you've got more people to look round?'

'Oh. Yeah. A few more today. But we'll be in touch by – um – Monday, yeah?'

'Yeah, Monday. The landlord wants someone in asap.'

'Really good to meet you, Katie.'

'And you.'

'You like them, right?' Liv asked as they walked back down the road, cuddling onto Katie's arm.

'Yes!' she exclaimed. 'They're so nice. *So* nice. Gah, so now it's that will they won't they pick me thing.'

'Oh, I'm sure they will. They got on with you so well.'

'Maybe they want to live with another man?'

'Nah. You put them at ease. Although! You and two guys. First ever go at that dynamic?'

'I know! I thought it might be weird, living with two boys after – you know, just living with your boy*friend*. But – they're lovely, aren't they? And it might be good. Different, you know? Not like – a competition with what I had before.

117

Or with you and Dee and Rosa. Just – something different. D'you know what I mean?'

'I do.'

*

They reconvened at home. Liv and Katie went via the off-licence; Dee and Rosa, having determined that enough time had passed for Joe and – and *her* – to have left, went via the market for a chicken, a bag of potatoes, vegetables, herbs. Rosa had spun herself onto a different plane; she poured an enormous glass of wine and began her work. Butter smeared on the chicken's skin; half a lemon, rosemary and thyme. Peeled potatoes in a huge pan; water as salty as the sea. Carrots and parsnips cut into chunks; whole cloves of garlic – unpeeled, so that in the heat of the oven they would soften in their skins, forming a creamy paste to squeeze onto the plates.

Cooking was chemistry; food was magic. Rosa screwed up her eyes against the flood. The first time Joe cooked for her: rigatoni and tomato sauce from a jar; the puppy-dog pride that he had chopped his own peppers and bought cheese in a block, not a pre-grated bag. The first time she cooked for him: ribeye steak and béarnaise sauce; the uncomfortable comfort of feeding him, of serving him a plate of slightly clichéd but delicious food that she knew his friends would elbow him about in the pub. Lucky fella, hey, hey?

Then, a flash of looking forward. The black sketchbook was open on their tiny dining table, scribbled with their thoughts on how to make a home. Rosa turned the page; oily fingerprints and the smell of citrus. She wrote about hunger; she wrote about satisfaction. She wrote the food that comforted her stomach and her mind; she wrote sustenance.

Every so often Katie or Dee or Liv called through from the living room, offering help over the soundtrack of Motown and disco – Manchester traditions re-formed in a new city – and she called back saying no, no, everything's perfect. And it was, she thought: the alchemy of it, the way heat and time transformed the chicken's skin and the potatoes into burnished gold, made the vegetables sweeter and richer. She poured juices into a pan, whisked flour and wine. She dunked broccoli into boiling water; melted butter; poured.

And then the four women crowded round their tiny table, served each other food and wine through a fug of good music and good smells and comfort, and Katie found herself with a plate: a shining piece of chicken; a roast potato with perfect shards of cracked brown around its edges; jewel-coloured vegetables; a generous pour of rich red-brown gravy. She smelled sustenance, and she brought a forkful of food to her mouth, *tasted*. It was like something had stopped sleeping. She waited for her stomach to twist and shake, but as she chewed and swallowed the warmth of nourishment slid into her, and she felt the hollowness of the past days gently unknot itself.

Food

Heartbreak can do strange things to your appetite. It can freeze your insides, choke your hunger. It can make the simplest cooking feel impossible, the tastiest food turn into sand. It can compel you to fill yourself, to flood your body with sweetness or beige or bulk or heat – or to empty yourself, make yourself into an outline, a shadow.

Listen to your body, but try to hold a perspective about it. If you don't eat you will eventually feel weaker – and you need to be strong. If you eat unusually you will eventually feel strange – and you need to be yourself. You deserve to be hungry for more – you deserve to feed your hunger. Food is the fuel of your future – move yourself into it.

Here are some things which are easy to eat when all you want to do is lie down on the floor, which taste like comfort when all you feel is pain:

* *Eggs. What is more perfect than an egg? Eggs scrambled gently with butter and a grind of black pepper, a sprinkle of sea salt. Eggs fried in a spoonful of hot oil so that the edges turn frilly. Eggs boiled in their shells to the perfect ooziness for you. Hot buttered toast. Marmite soldiers.*
* *Take one chicken. Half a lemon, herbs, garlic. Oil or butter and salt on its skin. A hot oven. Time. You have a dinner which smells and tastes and feels so much more complicated than it is. You have nostalgia on a*

plate. You have crispy skin and juicy meat and bones to make the best soup in the world.

* *Speaking of . . . soup. Enough said. (The best soups are: chicken made with aforementioned bones. Instant noodles with extra chilli sauce. Tinned cream of tomato – you know the one – with grated cheese. French onion, also with grated cheese.)*

* *Your favourite takeaway.*

* *Vegetables. Their bright colours are cheering, and the knowledge that you are eating something Good For You is bolstering. The trick is to not make them hard work. Coat them in oil or an unctuous sauce or a piquant dressing. Cook or chop the effort out of them. Throw them in the oven. Caramelize; calm.*

* *Risotto. You are standing at a cooker. All you have to do for the next half-hour is ladle stock and stir. This is all that is required of you. At the end there will be butter and cheese.*

* *Yes – cheese. When nothing else is possible, go to the nearest shop that will sell you good bread and good cheese. Have a plate of both. Have a glass of wine. Feel full.*

* *Ice cream.*

* *Chocolate.*

* *Chips. Chips with everything.*

Chapter Seven

FISH IN THE SEA

E veryone looks good in red lipstick; you just need to find the right shade for you. Who had told her that? Nikita had preferred her without, saying she liked to see her mouth just as it was, to think of kissing her. It was a charming thought initially, and then yet another irritation, a confirmation that she wanted Liv to be someone slightly different: bare, plain. Liv blotted her lips and leaned into her reflection.

Felix. Arriving for the meeting in an hour: later enough that she wouldn't look like she'd put on the lipstick specifically for him; soon enough that it wouldn't wear off. The delicate frisson of expectation, and the knowledge that this was all, probably, a bad idea.

But then, why shouldn't she seek out these flashes of something special? It was important not to think too much about the sadistic routine of work; important not to tip over backwards into recognizing that it was all just meetings and phone calls and spreadsheets and sentences, day after week after month after year. You had to punctuate it, surely, with winding imaginations and things which made you smile secretly to yourself?

Somewhere across the city, in an office that she knew was scruffier and more crowded than this one, and yet which seemed so much more glamorous in her head, Rosa was writing words that would have her name next to them. Somewhere much further, her parents were pottering around their village. Errands and parish council meetings.

The door swung open and Carrie entered. The same level as Liv, she worked on the financial communications team – one which Liv privately thought sounded both tedious and intriguing. Every team in the communications agency was the same, after all, running a spectrum of clients and responsibilities from the boring and humdrum to the genuinely novel and exciting – and the latter end of Carrie's work was all mergers and acquisitions and drinks with the *Financial Times*. Liv held an equally contradictory set of opinions on Carrie herself, never quite sure if she wanted to be like her or resented her. They went out for cocktails every few weeks. Carrie always seemed like someone who drank dirty martinis entirely because she liked them, rather than because they made her look a certain way. Liv was annoyed that she had noticed this.

Carrie also managed to maintain an insouciant yet articulate manner throughout the drinking of said martinis. Everything she referenced sounded aspirational, whether shopping with her mother or drinking tinnies in a field, and as a result Liv had imagined some kind of gilded background. There was a grim comfort in assuming that Carrie owed her ease and elegance to parental money, unearned privilege – and, then, more than a little irritation in learning that she in fact came from a nondescript Midlands town, a comprehensive high school and a family which sounded perfectly average.

She was dressed elegantly but interestingly: shirt; cigarette trousers; brogues. As if on cue, Carrie said I love your lipstick, and Liv said thanks, your trousers are great, and they both turned back to the mirror, looking at themselves and each other.

'All set for the meeting?'

'Oh. Yep, all good. We've had a good month. Got a nice profile of the CEO in one of the trades.'

'Great. Yes, we've had some positive conversations with investor journalists this month. Really getting some traction now.'

Traction. Who the fuck says 'traction' outside of a meeting?

'That sounds really good.'

'Really good?' Chrissakes Liv, has your personality gone to sleep?

'Absolutely. And how are things in the team? Still working on Crystal Clear?'

Liv winced. She was happy to relay the farcical irritations of working for a water cooler company to her friends, but the context here seemed abrasive, belittling.

'Well, you know. Keeps the numbers ticking over.'

'Of course.' Carrie produced a plum-coloured lipstick and proceeded to apply an immaculate coat. 'What are you doing after work? Want to come out and toast a renewed contract? Assuming we get it, right?'

'Ah, I can't. Meeting my housemates. But next week some-time?'

'I'd *love* that. Right. See you in an hour!'

*

Dee walked to her desk as if on air. Simon caught her expression and laughed.

'You look like the fucking Cheshire Cat. Period pants went well, then?'

'Very well, thanks,' she said briskly. He snorted.

'Fine, fine, keep the details to yourself. Well done, anyway.'

'Thanks.' She sat down and controlled her smile. 'They loved it. Want us to look at a full-on advertising campaign next. TV, social, the works.'

'Well, Margot's going to be even more all over you than normal. Where is she, anyway?'

'Gone on to a pitch, that makeup thing.'

'Right. Mascara and nail varnish. Sounds riveting.'

'Depends on how daring they are, doesn't it? Bravery is everything.'

Simon snorted. 'Christ, you sound like a motivational teacup.'

'*Teacup?*'

'Well, you know. Suspiciously slogan-like, anyway. Like a picture of an iceberg and some blether about hidden depths.'

Dee laughed tightly.

'Anyway. How's your heartbroken friend getting on?'

'Katie? Better. She got a message – a house she looked at last weekend – they've asked her to move in.'

'Aha. New beginnings, fresh start, all that jazz.'

'Exactly. We're going out after work to celebrate, and doing the boxes and stuff at the weekend. I think it'll help her, being out of the flat.'

'Is she speaking to what's-his-name?'

'Chris? Don't think so. She has a little rant every now and again.'

'Ah, the anger stage. Thing of beauty. Especially good when it lasts for years, am I right?'

Dee pulled a complicated face, and Simon laughed at her. 'Come on. You might not have spilled the beans about exactly what went on with Leo, but it doesn't take a genius to—'

'To what?' she demanded, eyes flashing.

Simon, never a wallflower, stared back.

'To figure out that *something's* sitting underneath it all.'

'I don't know what you mean,' she sniffed, turning back to her computer screen.

Simon snorted again. 'Sure you don't. Remind me, what gym day is it? Abs? Or arms?'

Dee pursed her lips, and opened her emails wordlessly.

'Suit yourself.' Simon swivelled back to his own desk.

*

Rosa bit the edge of her cuticle and pulled. The skin peeled and she tasted the tang of blood. Her finger throbbed.

Her phone buzzed, and she let out a minute groan as she saw the group name – then immediately berated herself. Nina was one of her oldest friends, after all. Her parents still lived next door to Rosa's own. Summer barbecues still switched back and forth between their gardens, the trampolines and plastic toys long cleaned up and given away. In some ways, Nina and Rosa's friendship had never really changed; it remained captured in that pair of semis, those lawns divided by a low fence and an untidily rambling rose. A Christmas glass of fizz and a mince pie; an Easter lunch with lumpy gravy.

And it was sweet, really, that Nina had invited her to the hen weekend – of course it was going to take up an entire weekend. Inviting her was an echo of childhood games with Barbies marched down makeshift aisles; it was an acknow-ledgement of history, and intimacy. But god, there was some-thing acrid in its predictability: the games she knew would be played; the phallic accessories she knew would have been purchased. Where was Nina in it all, where was Nina-and-her-fiancé, Nina-and-Gav? How had something that was surely intended to be the most personal, intimate celebration of all become so formulaic?

A memory lurched into her brain; lifting a pillowcase over her tangled red hair and giggling. She and Nina throwing their sticky hands over each other's shoulders, and grinning into the mirror. They were drunk on being too young to understand cliché.

We'll be friends for ever, won't we?

Yes, for ever.

The innocent projections of the other side of adolescence. And the best way they knew to underscore them was to promise to be each other's bridesmaids. The most exciting way to imagine their future friendship was to picture each other's weddings.

She tried to focus on the computer screen. The Last Romantic. Could she bear to write about weddings being a wonderful way to meet someone? The thought made something acidic rise in her throat. There had been a time, not so long ago, when a wedding would have been a culmination, not a beginning. *And what about Joe, now? Do they laugh at weddings on TV, and poke gentle fun at things they are starting to concretize? Do they have houseplants, and ironically call them their babies? Perhaps they giggle together, knowing that bound up in the irony is something more serious, hints of a future.*

She jammed her forehead onto her hand in exasperation. A year – longer – and here Joe still was, invading her days, polluting her thoughts like an oil spill. Oh yes, she could write affected wisdom into Katie's heartbreak handbook, she could act out distance and perspective, but it was laughable, really. Sure, her stomach was no longer knotted, her appetite no longer suppressed. Yes, she no longer had to run to the toilets several times a day to sob. But as Katie thought of Chris, so Rosa thought of Joe.

'Rosa.' She snapped her head back as if electrocuted. Her editor – Ty, forty-one, firm but fair, exacting but not unkind – was standing in front of her desk.

'Yes?'

'I've been having a think. About The Last Romantic.'

Her stomach churned. 'Mmhmm?'

'I think – look, I know the whole *point* is this old-fashioned, analogue thing, but I think we need to switch it up a bit.'

'Switch it up?'

'Yeah. You know, people also want advice on how to get out there, meet new people, navigate the hurly-burly of modern dating life.'

'The *hurly-burly*?' She tried to suppress a smile, and he grinned too.

'One of those moments where the twelve years between us is actually two hundred?'

'Something like that.'

'Duly noted. But you know what I mean, yes? We need some stuff on – I don't know, apps, and sex parties and things.'

'You're asking me to go to a sex party in order to write a column called The Last Romantic?'

'No! Fuck, I'm not asking you to go to a sex party at all. Unless you want to. And then that's nothing to do with me! God, this is starting to sound like an HR nightmare.' He raked a hand through his hair. 'You're doing this on purpose.'

'A bit.'

'What I'm saying is, a bit less on where to go for candlelit conversations, a bit more on how to get those conversations going in the first place. Please.'

'Okay.'

'And no doom and gloom about modern technology, okay? More – how to make that technology romantic. How to bring romance into the twenty-first century. The Last Romantic goes digital. Or something.'

'Okay.'

'You at your best. Funny. Uplifting. Adventurous.'

'Absolutely. Got it.'

She wondered if he was going to comment on her staccato tone, but if he was, he thought better of it, turned on his heel and marched off to another part of the office. Rosa exhaled sharply. A funny, uplifting, adventurous article on modern romance. Simple.

*

The bell rang and thirty teenagers clattered upwards and out, shouting about each other. Katie sat at her desk and watched them leave.

There was something about the sound of a school. A playground would be even worse, she supposed – higher pitched and inflected with mummies and daddies. Yet even here, even with the broken voices and swearing and heady hormones, the sound was one of children, hundreds of children who departed each night to be cosseted by parents, and this was agonizing both because she wasn't one of them, and because she wasn't welcoming them home.

Katie-and-Chris-*and-a-baby*.

Of course she had studied their faces and imagined how they might be blended into a third. Of course she had watched prams and slings in the park and tried to think herself into the future. And of course she had winced at each doctor's appointment, each prickly scroll through medical websites and confessional journalism pieces, running her hands across her stomach and feeling the great betrayal of her body.

As she and Chris moved through their twenties, so their conversations had nudged closer to those questions, those possibilities, those potentials. Chris had said things about bedrooms and schools, things which were strangely brisk but gorgeous all the same. His consistent focus on making the abstract concrete, on translating *might* into *will* – there was a romance to that that she wished she had appreciated more. And while even Chris's pragmatism could not force a schedule onto her scars, her blood, the insides she imagined clenched and angry – his acceptance of them was like a warm blanket. We'll make it work, he would say, and she knew that if anyone would tear through medical notes and specialist referrals and statistics to do so, Chris would.

How many years it had taken to feel that safe, that secure. She tried to imagine starting such a conversation from the beginning. *I have this condition. It might be difficult for me to have children.* How could she say those things to someone new? Dating – god, there was a word she hadn't imagined using – was meant to be light and fizzy; how could she possibly inflect it with something so heavy?

She opened the message again. *Hey Katie, sorry for the delay in getting back to you. We've had all the viewings now and we'd love it if you wanted to move in! Let me know. Jack (And Rafee!)*

It was clean and simple and straightforward, and it felt like something tense and crumpled had started unfurling from the moment she received it. It felt, too, like a promise. A looking forward. She tried to picture Jack's face, but it was blurry in the way a person is when you've only met once. She remembered dimples and curly brown hair and something endearing. She remembered the Dungeons & Dragons T-shirt and thought of how condescending Chris would be.

Because there Chris was, for ever. She would always think about which meal Chris would order from the menu, where he would stop to take a photograph, the comment he would make about an item on the news. Her shadow, her ghost.

She flicked to his name. *Hi. I've got a place now. I can move in this weekend. I guess that's when you're moving into Nat's? xxx*

Heya. Great news! Yeah, I'm going to do the big move on Sunday. Do you wanna do your packing up on Saturday then?

Sure. Think the girls are going to help. Can we come round about 11? Xx

Absolutely. I'll be out, actually. If you leave your key in the postbox I can drop them both with the estate agent.

Okay. Thanks. Kx

Oh and I put the bed on eBay, like you said. £100. I'll leave your share in the flat.

Ah, brill. Kx

Did you decide whether you wanted the sofa at your new place?

Um, I don't think there'll be space.

No probs. Turns out that Nat's got room for it, so how about I buy it off you? I can leave some money for that too.

Okay, that probably makes sense.

Great! Let me know if anything changes.

She swiped away the stream of messages and bit her lip. *If anything changes.*

*

'To Rafee and Jack,' Dee declared, raising the first of four overpriced cocktails. 'May you have many happy evenings together playing board games.' Katie smiled organically as she sipped vodka and vermouth and lemon.

'Abso-bloody-lutely. How were your days?'

'Well,' Liv said, 'I can tell you that I spent a very product-ive hour staring at Felix's face.'

'Aha!'

She shook back her hair and recounted from the lipstick onwards – Felix and his team arriving, hi there, won't you come through to the meeting room, tea or coffee? She described their handshake and how his skin was Goldilocks perfect; not too hot or cold, nor too clammy or dry. She described the crease between his eyebrows and how frustrating it was that women are expected to fill or freeze them, but on men they look thoughtful, refined. She described him catching her eye over the table as his boss talked through the next campaign – his boss with the droning voice which sounded like a lawnmower – and how she and Felix seemed to be sharing something secret, something which made the edge of his mouth rise up quizzically, and his eyes sparkle wickedly.

And then. The fifteen-minute break in the middle of the meeting, with chrome jugs of coffee and tea and platters of pastries and fruit, where everyone got up and milled around semi-awkwardly. Carrie was immediately pulled into a conversation with her own account director and the client CEO, and Liv was watching this with a slithering sense of envy – until Felix purposefully stood up and walked across to her. He was drinking black coffee too.

'So, Liv. Sounds like you've been busy?'

The way hearing your own name spoken could send shivers around your ribs! And this, even the most banal of statements, he managed to drip with suggestion, his lip curled into something knowing.

'Well, we like to keep you on your toes.'

She knew exactly what she was doing, she decided: a coquettish smile; a twist of hair between two fingers. His smile was sardonic.

'You're not a smoker, are you?'

'Quite the look, that. Smoking while your company researches treatments for lung disease.'

He laughed at that – a scathing, knowing kind of laugh.

'You're right. Very off-brand. I'll just have to catch up with you another time.'

'*Woman*,' Dee said in delight. 'This is you've-got-it-bad territory.'

'I know,' Liv said. 'God, it's a real old-school crush, isn't it?' She gulped her drink. 'And I don't really know anything about him! Just that he's hot. So I get to sit there making up all these things about what he's really like, what *it* would be like . . .' She fanned her face dramatically. They laughed. And she felt the same clenching sensation, her blood heating up and bubbling like sherbet.

'Oh, I say embrace it,' Katie said. 'Believe me, if all you had to lust over at work was geography teachers with – for real – leather elbow patches . . .'

'Hah! This is true. But – oh god – it's risky, isn't it?' She recalled the eyes of her colleagues on her in the meeting.

Carrie's eyes sparkling from behind her laptop. The unspoken, simmering competition between two women of similar age and ambition, still seated below a man, Zachary, the associate director who had won Felix's company's account a year or two previously. The balance *they* had to strike between looking polished but not overdone, effortful and yet effort-less – while *he* wore the same shirt every day and jaunty cufflinks to suggest a semblance of personality. It was under-stood that a female employee who caught the eye of a male client might be a good thing, a sharpener, a lubricant – and yet a female employee who was *catching* said eye was unpre-dictable, a loose seesaw, a rogue grenade.

She was musing on this aloud, and Rosa said that this could be useful, actually. Politics of the office crush. She told them about Ty's request to update The Last Romantic, giving voice to a sticky frustration.

'It's pretty shitty timing, isn't it? Bump into the ex you haven't seen for more than twelve months, feel really fantastic about yourself, and oh, by the way, make the dating apps you hate sound funny, uplifting and adventurous. And that's an *exact* description of what he's after, by the way.'

'Sounds good to me,' Liv said tartly. 'I mean, it's still your column, isn't it? Your byline? He's just telling you how to switch it up. Anyone up for another drink?' She said the last sentence as she rose. Dee nodded, while Rosa and Katie indicated their half-full glasses.

'Switch it up. Those are exactly the words he used,' Rosa said. She sighed. 'But god, he's deluded, isn't he? The whole point of The Last Romantic was to get away from how horrible all that app stuff is. The hundreds – no, *thousands* – of men whose opening gambit is *Want to sit on my face* or a description of how massive their cock is.'

Dee snorted, and Katie looked aghast.

'But why do you have to write about this stuff at all?' Dee asked. 'Isn't it a bit predictable, getting the young female lifestyle reporter to write about dating? I mean – look, I love you, but The Last Romantic, really? Never mind switching it up, can't they get you to write about – careers, or finance, or something like that? Actual pertinent modern lifestyle stuff?'

'Everyone wants to be in love,' Katie said quietly.

I'm falling in love with you, Katie. Oh, wow. I'm falling in love with you too, Chris.

Dee snorted again, and tried to cover it. 'Sorry. I know it's – uh – not your best time for reflecting on romance. But, come on. We can do better than that, can't we?'

'I'm not saying love's the be all and end all,' Katie said, swirling her drink nervously. 'But it is a nice thing, right? It makes people happy?'

'It makes them *un*happy too,' Dee said.

'Well, why do you bother ever going out with anyone, then?' Katie said. 'Salmon Man? You must have been hoping for something better than that?'

Dee shook her hair back. 'There's a difference,' she said loftily, 'between wanting to be in love and wanting to have sex.'

'And if you can combine the two? Isn't that even better?'

Not necessarily. Plus, you risk a hell of a lot of aggravation.

Dee, recognizing the anguish sitting behind Katie's firm expression, pulled herself back from this harsher edge and instead smiled sanguinely.

'Well, like I said, he's asked for funny, uplifting and adventurous,' Rosa cut in quickly. 'So you're going to have to help me make something up, looks like.'

Katie laughed shortly. 'Well, I'm hardly the person to ask, am I? I don't have a clue how dating works. No one *dated* at uni, did they? You just danced with people and went home with them. It was simple.'

Dee and Rosa made noises of agreement, and Katie shook her head in exasperation.

'When we went on the walk,' she said, 'I told you – Dee – that feeling that I won't meet anyone like Chris ever again.'

Dee bit her tongue, and nodded.

'God! I know that can't really be true, right? Or that it's emotion over reality, or something. Like, it can't be measured. There's not some score that Chris has next to his name, that no one else can live up to? But when I remember what our relationship felt like earlier on – or when I think about all the *good* things – it just feels impossible. All that intimacy. You know, like the dancing in the kitchen stuff. The in-jokes. The nicknames. The – the *bodily* stuff, the mess and the blood and the shit. *That* feels impossible, anywhere else.'

'It's too soon,' Dee said.

'Well, what is too soon, anyway? Chris is all ready to move in with *Nat* this weekend. She's – I mean, I bet she's *beautiful*.'

They eyed each other.

137

'What I mean is,' Dee said smoothly, 'you can't make judgements about this stuff now. Not when you're in the thick of it. Like you say, it's emotion over reality. You need time to adjust.'

Rosa nodded vigorously. Katie downed the rest of her drink, and was embarrassed to find her hands shaking. 'Then when *will* I?'

'Um,' Dee broke off. 'Katie. There's not a formula for this stuff.'

'Well, why not? Rosa, how long after Joe did you feel ready to meet someone else? One month? Two?'

'Katie.'

'I'm not – I just want to know.'

'Okay. I think about three months. I remember, actually, because I did that pastry-making class. And there was a man there – just a nice man. Red hair. I remember, he made a joke about ginger . . .'

She trailed off in gentle astonishment at her own optimism.

'You went out with someone you met at a pastry-making class?' Katie said incredulously.

'No, no! Nothing happened. That would be, like, a film script, right?'

'Right.'

I wrote about it, though. I wrote six hundred words on how signing up to classes is a beautiful old-fashioned way of meeting someone, and I never saw that man again.

Rosa laughed wryly. 'Maybe that's where I've been going wrong. Insisting on meet-cutes, and catching people's eyes in bars. I'm not sure I should be your model for this.'

'No. That sounds good. This Saturday – moving day – that will be three weeks. So in nine more weeks I'll be ready to meet someone new.' Katie nodded firmly. 'I'm going to the bar. Ready for another one, Rosa?'

'Sure.'

Dee made a noise of exasperation as Katie departed. 'You know what I meant, right?'

'Of course. But – I get Katie, too.' Rosa bit her thumbnail awkwardly. 'Can I tell you something embarrassing?'

'Always.'

'I have this feeling – this theory – that once I've met someone else – once I'm *with* someone else – that's the one thing that'll make all the bad feelings with Joe go away.'

Dee breathed in half the world.

'I know. I know how dodgy that is. I know that's anti-feminist and ridiculous, and I know that I need to love myself before I can be with anyone else, and I know I'm the only person in control of my own happiness and I know it I know it I know it but I can't *help* it. A year, Dee. A whole year, and I see him and her and it's like I just *collapse*.'

'Joe and The Woman?' Liv asked, reappearing, a vision with two drinks.

'Exactly.'

Liv nodded and sipped. 'It's a headfuck.'

Rosa looked at her with a slick of incredulity. 'Yeah. It is.'

Liv immediately felt a rush of something like guilt. 'Sorry. Don't mean to be trite. It's *all* a headfuck, I mean. Or something.'

And she meant it, she thought, as she imagined Nikita swimming into her field of vision, a pained expression on her face. And somewhere else, Felix. Everything Nikita was not: the suave confidence; the knowing smile; the tension.

They gave smiles softened by alcohol and Dee explained that Katie wanted to meet someone new. 'Like, now. Or soon. Asking about timings and things.'

'Timings? That sounds a bit – artificial.'

'Exactly.'

'It'd be nice though, wouldn't it?' Liv said. 'Like – a calculation? Wait exactly four weeks and three days and then you'll meet the next love of your life? *Certainty*, right?'

Yes, certainty. That, *that* was what she had been trying to grasp. That was what had gone wrong. Nikita was a good person, wasn't she? And had loved her so very much? But when you didn't feel *certain* – when you caught the edge of yourself in every shiny surface and tried to see some truth, reach for something your brain couldn't process – that couldn't be the path you stayed on. Could it? Who felt certain, really? About jobs, about family, about where to live? Wasn't life a series of questions, and deciding which ones you could leave unanswered? Wasn't life recognizing that the further down the road you walked, the more side streets you passed by?

'Oh my god,' Rosa said. 'I would pay for that. To *know* that I was definitely going to meet someone. You know, in say, four years' time. So I could just get on with my life and know it was going to happen. No more fear.'

Dee tutted. 'Fear? Really? Rosa, you're twenty-nine years

old. More to the point, it's the twenty-first fucking century.'

Rosa shrugged. 'I know. I *know*. But I also know what I feel, right? And I feel the fear. Dee, it's hard to meet someone. You know it is. And I – I don't want to be single for ever. That's scary. That's what the fear is.'

The parallel lines of Joe. The way she could breathe herself backward to being in his arms, breathe herself forward into his standing in a suit and a tender smile, a soft expression of admiration that was no longer directed at her. There was being single, and there was being single while Joe was not. And it was all overlaid with a ferocious awareness of her own wrongness – how pathetic this was, how ungenerous to the man she said she loved, once, how ungenerous to *herself* that she remained, now, caught in the cobwebs of someone who had treated her badly. *He cheated on me, and I still want him. I loved him, and I don't want him to be happy.*

'There's a different kind of fear,' Liv cut in. 'Being with someone, but not being sure.'

Dee and Rosa swung their faces towards her.

'I mean, things just being *slightly* not good enough,' Liv tried to explain. 'And then not knowing how you measure that anyway. Like, is it you? Is it them? No one's done anything awful, there's no big fight, no big breakup moment. They're still the same person you were when you met them, when you decided that you loved them. They haven't hurt you. God, they're doing everything they can *not* to hurt you. You're just not sure, and you know that not being sure isn't fair, to them, to you, to anyone.' She felt a soft slurring of her brain into the cocktail, and drank it up, while Dee and Rosa stared at her. 'Nothing's ever certain, that's the problem. Where you live, where you work. Who you love, who you fuck. Who you fuck over. Haha.'

'You're telling *me*,' Katie said, reappearing with two more glasses.

Dee raised hers. 'Philosophy of the second drink.'

'Okay, good,' Rosa said. 'Potential themes for this article: "crippling fear" and "nothing's ever certain". Which do you think is more uplifting?'

'You just need to throw yourself into it,' said Katie. 'Stop overthinking the digital thing, and just treat the apps like real life. Find a picture you like, get chatting, right?'

'Those,' Rosa said, 'are the words of someone who has never had to use a dating app in their life.'

Katie winced. 'But come on, isn't that the whole point of your column? Seeing the good? Seeing the *personal*? That's what Ty wants, right? Your whole spin on this process that too many people find – what, I don't know, *transactional*?'

'Nothing wrong with transactional,' Dee said. 'If everyone knows that's what they're getting.'

'You should write this for me,' Rosa said.

'It can't be that bad,' Katie said.

Rosa snorted. 'Believe me, Dee, Liv and I could *all* head out with someone from an app and there wouldn't be a scrap of The Last Romantic in it. Apps are – they're connection by numbers, and people only after one thing, and no one cares who you are or what you say.'

There was an unfamiliar bitterness to her voice, and her

friends caught each other's eyes. Katie was plaintive, and Liv was uncomfortable, and Dee, despite herself, felt a little stab of sympathy.

'Come on,' she said gently. 'That's not like you.'

Rosa shook her head sadly. *I don't feel like me. Since seeing Joe – since seeing Joe and her – something's changed. The Last Romantic? She was hopeful, and how can I feel hopeful, now?*

'Nikita and I met on an app,' Liv said, and Rosa sniffed.

'Well, you were one of the lucky ones. And I'm not feeling very lucky.'

'Okay, so what if we do the app thing too?' Dee said. 'Liv and I. I will prove to you that there's someone better than Salmon Man out there, right?'

Liv laughed into her glass, caught Dee's expression and hurried to agree. 'Okay, sure. Yes. Probably about time I got – ha – back on the horse. But I draw the line at men holding giant fish in their profile pictures. What is that?'

'And standing next to drugged tigers?'

'Right! And anyone – man or woman – who spells their life out in a series of emojis.'

'Or a series of demands.'

'Or who immediately segues into "Red hair, hey? Bet you're a fireball in bed".'

They clattered their glasses together and Katie gnawed on her lemon peel, tasting bitter astringency.

Fish in the Sea

Days? Weeks? Months? Minutes? Sometime, somehow, you will wonder about meeting someone else.

Is it a suppressor of your feelings, a way of covering up your pain? Is it to get back at the person who came before, to beat them in a competition you never imagined having? Is it an optimistic opening of your heart to the world, or a pessimistic search for protection against it?

How much do you miss the *person, and how much do you miss being with* a *person?*

Try to understand yourself. Take those tentative steps – am I ready? Who am I looking for? How will I find them? And what if I don't?

A new partner can never – should never – be a replacement for the old. You should not expect that of someone new, or place that burden on their shoulders, or be so dismissive of the person with whom you shared so much. But nor should you sink into a rejection of possibility because of the pain of the past.

Most of us date with a mixture of motivations. Simple and complex. Healthy and unhealthy. The simpler and healthier your motivations are, the better equipped you will be when dating goes wrong. And it will go wrong. You will not be compatible with everyone you meet. You will not fancy everyone you meet. You will not like everyone you meet. Navigating this minefield requires a heart that is simultaneously open, steely – and has a sense of humour.

Getting out there and meeting new people will likely help you navigate your heartbreak if it is a positive experience, a whirlwind of attractive and interesting and engaging people who remind you just how full the world is, how much potential your life holds.

Getting out there and meeting new people will likely intensify your heartbreak if it is a negative experience, one in which nobody seems as good as your ex, in which bad manners and bad jokes and bad chemistry abound.

And sorry, darling – there are no guarantees.

You can shift the odds in your favour. You can play the numbers game, knowing that the more people you meet, the more likely a click – and that even the clicks you don't want to take further can be fun, a giggly night out, an intriguing conversation, bodies that fit. You can tread lightly, counselling yourself that romance and flirtation and sex are just small parts of a full life. You can murmur que sera sera. The world is full of wonderful people, and mechanisms for meeting them. There are people out there who will tell you stories that make you laugh with utter abandon; people out there who will cook you the best breakfast you have ever had; people out there who will teach you things you didn't know you didn't know.

But. But. Many people will bandage your heartbreak by making promises they can't possibly guarantee. 'Of course you'll meet someone else.'

'Of course you won't end up alone.'

Maybe you will, maybe you won't. Falling in love with someone who falls in love with you is far more a matter of luck than people who are in relationships like to admit, and people who are not in relationships like to believe.

If you cannot comfort yourself by wrapping your own arms around your body; if you cannot take pleasure in sitting in solitude with a book or an ice cream or a drink; if you cannot understand the difference between 'alone' and 'lonely', then you will be buffeted and ravaged by so many more of the storms of your life.

Alone need not mean isolated. Alone can be independence, freedom, fierce joy. Alone can be a rediscovery of your own boundaries and your own wild breaking of them.

Chapter Eight

BREAKUP FILMS

'How're the drinks, Dee?'

'Thing of beauty,' she called from the kitchen. She was painstakingly pouring a chocolate-coloured liquid into four glasses. Guinness and Tia Maria. Katie's favourite, and this night in had been carefully constructed around her. Tomorrow they would pack up the flat. And while Dee had never done this herself, the thought of it made her heart ache.

Three years previously her grandmother, Mel's mum, had died. That in itself was not as sad as it sounded, Dee always rushed to tell people. She was old. She lived a good life, and she died a good death. Peaceful. It was time.

What she didn't talk about was the horror of going with her mother to pack up the flat afterwards. Filtering through the years. The photograph albums, yes – but also the Mickey Mouse cereal bowl Dee always had for raisins and chocolate-covered peanuts. The sticky blue ring binder stuffed with recipes torn out of decades of weekend newspaper supplements. The royal wedding biscuit tin, the crocheted cushion. The bit where the carpet had worn through to a pale plastic mesh, the indent on the sofa.

And worse still, her mother's childhood bedroom, which had then become her and Dee's shared bedroom for four tremulous, troubled, phoenix years. There was still box after box pushed under the bed. Books and clothes and tattered board games. Some of them had made her mother cry, and some of them she had just held very close to her chest, and throughout Dee had felt horrifyingly impotent. Packing up a home dredges up pain as it does dust. Nostalgia was the pain of returning; the agony of going back again. Dee looked at her mother, who looked like *her* mother, and she realized the appalling rupture. There was her mother *then*, bright smile and young hair saying do you want to go to Granny's today? And there was her mother *now*, grey with grief and a lost expression.

She took the drinks into the living room in pairs, and Katie made a warm noise of appreciation.

'I love you. This is perfect.'

I need a proper breakup film, she had said, and they had scrambled over each other to list ideas in the heartbreak handbook. Dee suggested a series of arthouse options; Liv favoured female friendship or female romance. Rosa, blushing, admitted to spending evenings under her duvet watching children's cartoons. Something about the safety of childhood, she said. In the end they chose a comedy in which three women enacted revenge on the man who had been cheating on them all simultaneously. It was ridiculous and glossy and crass and simple enough for them to talk over without losing track of the story.

'So how's the whole "here's how you do dating apps" thing going?' Katie asked, wondering how casual she sounded.

'I've been speaking to a few people. Celeste somebody. Freddie something,' Liv said.

'Let's have a look?'

Liv tossed her phone across and Katie examined these pictures of strangers: with a drink; on a bike; at the beach. She tried to imagine appraising Chris like this. What if, instead of catching his eye, spinning up to him with rum-and-Coke confidence and asking him what he was studying, she had done this? What would he have typed about himself, then? Prosaic, harmless: *Economics student, beer enthusiast, City 'til I die?* Or, more accurately: *Fiercely ambitious, push-ups before breakfast, inferiority complex?*

And what would he write now? Her stomach lurched as she imagined scrolling along, seeing the face that had breathed into her, moved above her, bestowed upon her the most private smiles and grimaces and winks over nine years. Chris presenting himself to the world now: single, successful, a flat with a balcony and a list of countries he wanted to travel to. *Looking for a partner in crime.* Yes, that would be it, she thought bitterly, a cliché he didn't realize was a cliché. Chris never loved words the way she did.

But oh, he loved her, and she loved him, and it didn't matter then, whether he read novels, or understood irony, or why the word *luscious* sounded so. The mortar of intimacy, built up through time, and the way it held together what looked recklessly incompatible in a stranger. How could she meet someone now, and tell whether the things that clashed with her were actually things that would make them closer? How could she do all that work again?

She threw the phone back to Liv. 'Nice. Are either of them as pretty as Felix, though?'

'No one is. This is a problem.'

'Have you made a date?'

Liv shrugged. 'I've vaguely said things about getting drinks. Leaving the ball in their courts. See who replies first.'

She felt very aware of her artificial breeziness, and added, 'Dee? Rosa?'

'All sorted,' Dee said crisply.

'Hold on a minute,' Rosa cut in, incredulously. 'What do you mean, *sorted*?'

'Just that,' Dee said, shrugging. 'He's called Isaac. Keeps making the same joke about hipsters. Works in something science-y. We're going for drinks. You know, if something doesn't come up. Here.'

She swiped through her phone, then threw it to Rosa, who caught it deftly and perused.

'Oh, he's cute.'

'Well, if the whole point is sex . . .'

'Point taken,' Rosa said, shaking her head. 'And I'm just juggling tired "how was your day?" conversations. You're making this look *easy*.'

'Well, it is,' Dee said. 'Just only up to a point.'

'What point?'

'Wanting it to be more than it is,' Dee said. 'There's millions of people in this city. It's easy to find someone who wants to go for a drink. It's easy to find someone who wants to fuck. You're looking for someone you – you know – *gel* with. That's harder.'

'See this – this – is why I hate dating apps. That's so bleak!' Rosa exclaimed.

'Thought you just said it was easy?'

'Well, yeah, but – Liv, help me out here.'

Liv looked aghast. 'Not sure I'm much use. I'm obsessing over someone I can't hook up with, remember? Plus, I don't even know if Felix and I – *gel*. It's totally a physical thing.'

As if to confirm the fact, somewhere south of her stomach turned and clenched flutteringly. The moment was broken by the doorbell, echoing hollowly through the living room. 'Pizza!' she said. 'I'll get it.'

She scrambled to her feet and trotted out into the communal hallway. The front door was solid – no glass – and so she had no time at all to process what was about to happen, to compose her features, even to turn around and run away. Liv opened the door and there she stood, looking appallingly familiar and yet different, like a photograph in which the colours were off. Even now, the contrasts between her and Felix were even more pronounced than she had suspected; the softness and gentleness where Felix was sardonic and knowing, and Liv hated herself for it, because god, Nikita had always looked like home.

She was crying before she started speaking. 'Liv. Livvy. I'm sorry for turning up here like this. I wanted to call first, but . . .'

She shook, putting a hand onto the doorframe to steady herself, and Liv stood frozen, before reflexively reaching out and gripping Nikita's arm. She was wearing a new coat, dripping wet in the gentle rain.

'Please,' she was saying then. 'I know – everything you said. But please. I love you so much, Liv. It's too hard.'

'I—' She stopped.

'Please. Please can we talk?'

She closed her eyes. *Talk.* Conversations were like tree roots, searching in the dark. And she knew what Nikita was looking for; the underground lake of a reconciliation, promises of together again. It would be easy, so very, very easy to offer her that.

She opened her eyes. Nikita's face was contorted.

'I . . .' she said again.

'Please. Can we just go for a walk maybe?'

She drew in a skeletal breath. 'Okay. Wait there.'

Afterwards, she would barely remember stumbling back into the flat, calling out Nikita's here, wants to talk, I know, I don't know. Pulling on the first pair of shoes she found, wrapping the weight of her big coat over her shoulders. Dee and Rosa and Katie would describe how pale her face had gone, how in shock she looked, the way the words poured out of her like sand. There was no protesting. She returned to the threshold, and Nikita, and she put her hand on her arm again and walked her out into the night. It was colder than before.

They began in silence. Liv looked sideways once, twice, and she felt that old fluttering. Nikita's skin glowed; her eyes glittered. The new coat – jade green and black – made her look taller. She was beautiful. She always was.

She remembered their meeting – that improbable ping-pong bar, shots of whisky. She remembered their first kiss – the smoking area, wires of fairy lights. How they played each other's bodies, fingertips and sweat and sweetness. Meet-cute; sex scene; breakdown; make up; shatter. The film reel of their shared past; the artificiality of choosing where to insert an ending.

Nikita stuttered, and said, 'I've been thinking about you so much,' and this was gorgeous, and horrible, and mirrored. Liv had no idea how to respond, so she made an *mm* noise. The easy answer was *I've been thinking about you, too*, and it was truthful, but not the whole truth. Liv had thought about Nikita as she thought about ending things with her; she had thought about her through layer upon layer of guilt; she had thought about her against Felix, and tried to use that as confirmation that she had made the right decision.

'I've thought about what you said – then,' Nikita tried again. She had sucked her crying back into her body, and was speaking in the precise way of someone trying very hard to be calm and measured, because the stakes of everything depend on it. 'I've thought about it a lot. How you didn't think we were – *compatible* – for the long term. And about me deserving someone – someone better.'

'Mm.' *Is that what I said?*

'I know I can be – you know – quieter. Not as assertive. D'you remember that restaurant, when you got cross because I didn't want to complain?'

'Mm.' *Maybe? I don't know, Nikita. It wasn't about one thing, was it? It wasn't about one event.*

'I've thought about it a lot. And you were right, you know. How I need to stand up for myself, that kind of thing. I mean – yeah! Twenty quid for cold ramen, right?'

'Mm.' *Maybe you don't. Maybe you're perfect just the way you are. Was I doing that cardinal thing you read about in women's magazines when you're still just imagining what it would be like to have a partner? Was I trying to change you? Was I focusing on your flaws instead of your strengths? Was it all my fault?*

'But the point is, I'm really changing. I – I guess I took it on board. I got a promotion, you know? My housemates are saying I'm different. More self-assured, they said.'

Liv looked across at her again, and wondered whether she could see it. Taller, yes – and stronger? A deliberation, a poise, she hadn't seen before?

'That's great,' she said. 'Congratulations.'

The words sounded like knocking on a locked door. It *was* great. Nikita held a fierce sense of loyalty to the green engineering company she worked for – loyalty was, of course, one of her most beautiful qualities – and she had given it late nights and weekends with a dogged patience.

Nikita's expression was tragically expectant, and Liv inhaled raggedly.

'Nik . . .'

Her trailing off spoke for itself, and Nikita reached across and grabbed her hand with an assertiveness that – yes – she might not have expected. The shape of her hand and the texture of her skin. They stopped on the pavement, and Liv was looking into her grey-green eyes, shiny with hope and heartbreak, and Nikita was saying, 'Liv, please hear me out. I'm already a different person. Things are going really well.

Work. I've been running again, you know? Confidence. I'm just asking you to give me – to give *us* – a second chance. Isn't it worth trying? We were together over a year – that doesn't just *happen*. There's so much that was good. Isn't it worth seeing if it can work again?'

Liv found herself swallowing and – was she nodding? Or just moving her head?

'Let's keep walking,' she said.

*

The film was still playing. Rosa tapped nervously on the edge of her glass. 'What do you think she wants?' she asked, knowing the answer. Dee snorted accordingly.

'It's Nikita, isn't it? She wants her back.'

Rosa grimaced. *She wants her back.* To be wanted; to want. To be wanting.

Katie was swirling her drink. 'Do you think she will?'

Dee snorted again. 'Not likely. She's the one who ended it, remember?'

'People change their minds, don't they?' Katie said, feeling her phone hot in her pocket, Chris's stream of businesslike messages as they agreed the arrangements for the coming weekend. His mind had changed – a flat with a balcony, space for a second sofa. And where was *her* mind, now?

'You can't undo stuff like that,' Dee said decisively. 'Getting back together after you've said all those things? Recipe for disaster.'

'Not always,' Rosa said reasonably. 'I've known people . . .'

'That's true,' Katie interjected. 'Like Frankie and Mo,

155

from uni. They broke up for six months. They're married now.'

'Okay, fine. Exceptions. But it's not like Liv and Nikita – I don't know – just drifted apart, is it? She ended it. Liv broke up with her. She told her she didn't want to be with her any more. How can you be in a relationship after that? Nikita'll be aware of what she said for ever.'

I just don't fancy you any more.

This isn't easy. Rosa – I'm so sorry, but – but I've met someone else.

Katie. I've been thinking. I've been thinking a lot. This isn't working, is it?

'So maybe it only works if the person who did the ending is the one who comes back,' Katie said.

'I'm glad you said it.'

Katie smiled weakly. 'I'm not holding out hope for Chris, don't worry,' she said, wondering if she was lying.

Rosa stared into her glass. *Holding out hope.* She imagined pulling open the door. She wouldn't be in her ratty pyjamas, of course – she would be in the green dress with the white flowers. Hair cascading over her shoulders. Joe would be in the brown leather jacket. Stubble. Cautious smile. An infinity of apologies, and his arms around her.

She blinked back an embarrassing and unexpected trickle of tears and hoped they hadn't noticed.

'Liv barely talks about her,' she said. 'Nikita, I mean.'

'I've noticed that,' Katie said. 'I wondered – before I was staying over – if she was talking about her here. But she doesn't.'

'It's Liv, isn't it?' Dee said. 'Quiet steel.'

'Poetic.'

'It's true though. Strength, but underneath the surface. That's Liv.'

'*Felix*, on the other hand . . .'

'Oh, Felix.'

'What do you reckon? Drinks after a meeting? Bit of a fling?'

'Nah. She sounds serious, all that stuff about not crossing a line with clients.'

'Well, maybe that's what'd take her over the edge with it. Make her quit, I mean.'

Katie and Dee fell silent at this, and looked hard at Rosa. She swallowed, and said, 'Well, we all know it, don't we? She's not – *fulfilled*, you'd say, right? All those jokes about the water coolers.'

'She's been there for years,' Katie said.

'Maybe that's the point,' Rosa said. 'You know. Stagnation, or something. I sound like a bitch.'

'No, you don't.'

Rosa inhaled deeply. 'I know – I know she would've studied journalism. I offered, did you know? Said she could come stay with my parents for the course, for internships.'

Katie and Dee shook their heads.

'She didn't want to put my parents out. I mean, I get it. There wouldn't have been much room. It's a long time, people you don't really know.'

Rosa trailed off, unsure of whether she was justifying herself or articulating a fuzzy sense of guilt.

'Don't be hard on yourself,' Dee said. 'Or take too much credit. Independence. Moving here, life in the city, away from home – *any* home. That's always meant a lot to Liv. She made her choices. Actively, I mean.'

'Yeah,' Rosa said, unconvinced.

'It's amazing you offered her that,' Katie said, and Rosa didn't smile.

'The thing is, I know how she feels. Liv. Because I don't even know if it's what *I* want, you know? Not always. It feels so pointless sometimes. And then I think – well, what feels point-*full*? And then I think you must feel that way, Katie? Point-full, I mean. What's more important than teaching kids?'

Katie smiled weakly. 'When it's good it's really good. When it's bad . . . Working in something the world thinks is a Good Thing doesn't insulate you from wanting to jack it all in sometimes. Or feeling bored. Loving your job doesn't stop you from hating it.'

The line sounded weirdly familiar in her mouth. She wondered if it was something she had seen in a film. Or something Chris had said to her.

'Cheers to *that*,' Dee said, raising her glass. Rosa echoed the gesture, biting her lip.

*

They walked in the way you don't in the city, zig-zagging and looping around the flat along roads which Liv knew well, but not in this order. They were mixing up multiple different routes – her paths to the shop, to the off-licence, to the Tube station, to the park – so that it felt like all her life was being layered into this half-hour, but in an order she couldn't fathom. The rain was milky under the street-lights, and she almost laughed at the references that rolled across her brain: the kiss turned dance with an umbrella; the kiss over a nameless cat; the kiss in the shower she ludicrously claimed she hadn't noticed; the kiss . . .

'So tell me about the promotion,' she said.

'Oh, it's just to senior engineer. But there's more responsibility, you know? We're hiring a graduate soon and I'm going to be doing mentoring and things.'

'That sounds good.'

'Yeah, I'm looking forward to it. How are things at the agency?'

'You know. Same old.'

'You'll be running it one day.'

It was a strange statement, she thought. A kind of compliment-by-numbers. The sentiment was genuine – with Nikita it always was – but there was a false simplicity to it which stirred a flash of familiar frustration in her. *But I don't want to be running it one day! Do I? Are you saying that because you see something in me that I don't, or because you refuse to see something in me that I do?*

'And how are your housemates?'

'Oh, they're good. Nai's moving in with her girlfriend so we're thinking about moving to a three-bed. A flat maybe?'

'Oh, good for them. And you, I mean. Could be fun having a change of scene.'

'Exactly. How are your parents?'

'Oh. Fine. Same old.'

She winced at her repetition, and hurriedly added, 'They ask after you, hope you're well and all that.'

'That's kind. Well, please send them my – tell them I said hi.'

'I will. They'll like to hear about the promotion. How are yours?'

'Yeah, they're good. Planning a trip to India this autumn, believe it or not.'

'Wow.'

'And the girls? Dee and Rosa and Katie, I mean?'

'The women,' Liv found herself insisting, and feeling false accordingly. 'Yep, they're all good. Rosa's column's still going.'

'Ah, that's great. She must be psyched.'

'Mmhmm.'

Nikita made a noise that might have been the beginning of a knowing laugh.

'What?'

'You know.'

'Okay, fine. I'm a twisted, bitter old hag, happy?'

'No!' Nikita grabbed her hand, and her skin felt unbearably familiar. 'Liv – you know I've never thought that, right?'

'Right. I'm just being facetious.' *Like always.*

'I just meant – come on. We talked about it, didn't we? Should you or shouldn't you? Career change, all that?'

'I guess we did.'

'And maybe, sometimes, seeing what other people are doing . . .'

'Mmhmm.'

'But, for what it's worth, I think you're doing the right thing for you.'

Liv laughed hollowly. 'You do, do you?'

'Yes,' Nikita said, earnestly. 'I really do. It's *you*, Liv, more than you think. Writing, yes, but also – also strategy, and numbers, and all that stuff. Figuring things out, how to make the stories work. You're brilliant, you know.'

They walked in silence for a few minutes.

'Oh, and Katie's staying with us. She and Chris broke up.'

'What?'

'Yeah. About three weeks ago.'

'Wow. How is she?'

'Okay. Considering. It's hard.'

'Who—' She broke off, and Liv knew the question she was refusing to ask.

'He did. Though it sounds like it had been building for a while.' She paused on the edge, and jumped. 'I think Katie gets it.'

Nikita didn't ask what 'it' was.

They walked in silence for a while, and then Nikita said, 'What are you thinking, Livvy?' and she nearly screamed.

I'm thinking about how good you were to me, and how safe and comfortable it feels to have someone love you. I'm thinking about what it would be like to wake up next to you tomorrow morning. I'm thinking about someone knocking on someone's door in the middle of the night to tell them they love them, and how that's romantic and joyful and awful. I'm thinking about how much it hurt to break your heart.

She stopped, and she looked at Nikita's face. 'I'm thinking about tomorrow. We're going to Katie's flat. Helping her move out.'

Nikita closed her eyes. Gently, like a child.

'I'm sorry,' Liv whispered.

'I know,' Nikita said.

'I'm glad you came.'

'Really?'

'Yes. It was the right thing to do.'

*

'Listen,' Katie said. The front door had opened.

'Come on,' Dee said. They scrambled quietly to the hallway and tried to make sense of the muffled voices. But there was just a closing sound.

Liv opened the door to the flat and saw the three most important women in the world. She fell sideways into the wall, and howled.

They took her arms and walked her into the living room. The film was still playing but its colours seemed muted, its sound dulled.

Breakup Films

Breakups demand escapism, absorption into other people's stories. Read them. Listen to them.

And watch them – because movie-watching can be made gorgeously communal, and your commune is your scaffolding.

So you need to know the two types of film to watch in the aftermath of a breakup: the right kind, and the wrong kind.

The right kind:

* *Belly-laugh films. Films where you laugh the drink out of your nose and cramp into your stomach.*
* *Old musicals.*
* *Films that you are quietly embarrassed to like so much, but which nevertheless lift you into a happy place, because you have seen them a million times. The cartoons from your childhood. The cult films from when you first moved out. The action films from Christmas Eve. Pixar animations. Disney cartoons. Shoddy comedies.*
* *Romantic films only where you know the central couple have that chip that you and they were missing, the chip you can imagine will be perfectly in place next time. The friendship of* When Harry Met Sally. *The sex of* Dirty Dancing. *The conversation of* Before Sunrise.

163

* *Romantic films where someone walks away – and you know, ultimately, that this is what is right.*
* *Romantic films which turn into revenge films. The insaner, the better.*

The wrong kind:

* *Love-against-all-the-odds films, which will leave you wondering whether you could have tried harder, should have tried harder, would have tried harder.*
* *Films you watched with them, so that every line comes packed with the sound of their laughter, the feeling of your head tucked into their collarbone, the way they breathed on your hair.*
* *Films with kissing in the rain.*
* The Notebook.

But above all, what matters in a breakup film is who you watch it with. Whether they are curled on the same sofa, or on the other end of your phone, keep your scaffolding close.

Chapter Nine

REMINDERS

K atie was kissing Chris; he was kissing her. She knew the shape and texture of his lips so precisely; the feeling of his hand in her hair; the shiver across her clavicle, like moths fluttering under her skin. He pulled softly backwards but left his hand on the back of her head, and his eyes met hers, and he smiled.

She snapped awake and was at first embarrassed to find herself hot and sticky, and then confused as to whether it was because she had had a nightmare, or something else.

Katie-and-Chris no longer exists.

Liv shifted next to her, and Katie looked at her sleeping face. There was a crease between her eyebrows, and her hand was balled up fiercely into a fist near her chin. What a gesture Nikita had made. And what a gesture Liv had made in return.

She tried to imagine Chris laying himself out like that. Naked; plaintive; open. It was ridiculous; it was agonizing.

Liv was stirring then, and she rolled over and squinted up at Katie. 'Morning, you. Coffee?'

'I'll make it.'

Liv rocked onto her back as Katie left the room. She was

lying in a pool of sunlight, which caught the ceiling and made the crack stand out like a line of lightning. Nikita was such a *good woman*, she repeated to herself. Her earnest expressions; her open heart. Only someone like Nikita could knock at a door and ask to reignite a relationship and do so with such clarity and grace; only someone like Nikita could hug her as she told her no.

So why don't I want her? And why, oh why am I fixated instead on a man who smirks like he's with a different woman every night, who laughs like he's trying to get me to say something I'll regret?

She rolled over violently and punched the pillow in frustration, as Katie re-entered with two mugs.

'Ouch. How are you doing?'

Liv took the coffee gratefully. 'I'll be fine. Anyway, how are *you* doing? The big day.'

Katie looked carefully at Liv, trying to calculate how much was deflection and how much was generosity.

'Did you think about it? Saying yes, I mean? Asking her to come back here? Being with Nikita again?'

Liv made a noise of greater exasperation than she intended. 'Christ, I've thought about variations of that ever since breaking up with her.'

Katie was staring at her. 'Really?'

'Of course. There's a – a *tail*, right? I mean, like, a long tail, after something like that happens. Not a story tale. Or maybe, that too. Haha.'

She felt as though she were wilting. Katie was scratching her mug with her fingernail.

'Look,' Liv continued. 'It's a headfuck, obviously. I guess – I know I've done the right thing. I just don't really understand *why* it's the right thing.'

'What do you mean?'

Liv fixed her eyes on the window, and knew that Katie's were on her.

'Nikita's great,' she said. 'Of course she's great. She's kind and thoughtful and the right amount of ambitious and she treated me with respect and – fuck, she calls her parents every Sunday to see how their week was. No wonder my parents bloody loved her. Never mind them having an issue with me liking girls as well as boys, I think my mum was ready to buy a hat for the wedding.'

'I'm trying to see what the "but" is here,' Katie said tightly.

'But it's not enough, is it? If you're not – not *feeling* it, somehow. And I don't mean sex . . .' She couldn't help but shivery-smile to herself. 'That was always great too.'

'Sure.'

'It's like – Nikita's fucking *perfect*, you know, but it's that bit you can't pin down.'

'Sure.'

'The clicking. The chemistry. It wasn't working. Or it was, but it wasn't going to. In the future. I thought. I mean – I *think*. I *know*. It wasn't working.'

Katie's breath caught rattlingly in her throat.

'I know I'm not explaining myself very well.'

'No. You are.'

'Look, just because I feel this way doesn't mean that—' Liv caught herself, as Katie's eyes flashed.

'Doesn't mean what?'

'Nothing. Look, forget I said anything. Today's about you, isn't it? Let's go to the living room.'

They entered at almost the same moment as Dee, glazed in sweat. Katie let out a noise somewhere between incredulity and admiration.

'You are a *machine*. We drank – how much last night?'

'Only did four miles,' she said, sinking onto the armchair and gulping water. 'It helps. Sweating it out, or something.'

'I'll take your word for it.'

Dee eyed Liv carefully and said, 'How are you feeling?'

Liv shrugged and threw herself onto the sofa. 'Was just talking to K. Shit. Guilty. Mess.'

'You've got nothing to feel guilty for.'

'I know. But I do.'

Dee nodded. 'Female socialization, right there. It's not your fault.'

'Thank you.'

'You've been honest with her. And that's more than a lot of people get.'

'Honesty can hurt,' Liv said pointedly.

Dee winced. 'Touché. But so long as you haven't told her she physically repulses you, I think you're golden.'

Liv smiled weakly. 'I didn't mean to – I'm sorry.'

'For what?'

'For the comparison. For – don't you wish Leo hadn't told you . . . what he told you?'

Dee pursed her lips. 'I wish I could forget it.'

'That makes sense.'

'Anyway. I'm going for a shower. Anyone seen Rosa yet?'

'I'll go wake her up,' Katie said.

But Rosa was already awake, standing in front of her open wardrobe and clutching the dress that had fallen from it. Green with white flowers. She pressed the fabric to her face and tried to inhale the past. Perfume; pubs; bonfire night; cooking lamb shawarma and pickling chillies. *What a woman*, Joe's flatmate had said, and she had known Dee and Liv would have rolled their eyes, and she had glowed all the same.

And then, and then. Standing, shaking at his front door. Her hair in pre-Raphaelite waves down her back. Joe always loved her hair and so that day her hair needed to look the best it ever had. There was a bag slung over her shoulder she was hoping desperately she would not have to fill. *Joe has met someone else but we must be able to rebuild from here. This cannot be it; this cannot be the end.*

But when Joe answered the door she knew before his first inhale that it was.

The dividing lines of our lives, the splits between *before* and *after*. The gradual breakers of our innocence, the tears that we carry. The livings and relivings.

A sniff, a shudder. Behind her, Katie wordlessly pressed her face into Rosa's shoulder.

Left alone, Liv pulled out her phone. She flicked to Nikita's name. Her photo was still the apple, shiny and glowing.

She had sent her a message when she got home. *Hey Livvy. I just wanted to say thank you for hearing me out. Please get in touch if you can. Love you always, Nikita xxx*

She made another noise of exasperation. It was beautiful, it was perfect. It was nonsensical. As if Nikita could promise always. As if you could commit to catching your feelings in time, an insect in amber. Wasn't staying the same a bad thing?

The thought gave her an idea, and she switched across to her dating app. Celeste's and Freddie's faces shone out at her. No, they weren't as intoxicating as Felix. No, she couldn't possibly ascertain that, not really, through a phone screen and a photo or two. Yes, the superficial judgement was of a type she didn't much like – or want to be subjected to.

She typed fast enough to send the messages before she could think about them. *Hey. About time we actually got that drink in, amirite? Free next weekend? Lxx*

Clicks and whooshes and they were sent, and she got up to shower. Today was for Katie.

*

The boxes they had collected from corner shops and supermarkets were stacked in the corner of the living room. The van they had rented was parked a couple of streets away; it was agreed that Liv and Rosa would collect it, while Katie and Dee would walk to the flat and begin packing. This took twenty minutes, and Dee was bouncy with energy while Katie was sombre and sunken. Something beat in her stomach like a drum.

Dee squeezed her hand. 'We'll be done in a few hours. You'll be unpacking at Rafee and Jack's and making your room how you want it and it's going to feel like – like looking ahead. I promise.'

Katie tried to smile, and she trusted her, but the mixture of anticipation and anxiety was making her feel sick. Chris wouldn't even be there! And that was meant to be a good thing, now.

Arriving at the block of flats brought a kaleidoscope of jagged memories. Meeting the estate agent – it wasn't even a year ago – and they were hand in hand, wrapped in the love and anticipation and, yes, smugness of this move *up* and *on*. The agent saying wait 'til you see the view from the balcony, right over the park, it's really special. Chris saying yeah, I play football there at the weekends, so convenient, and could you just confirm that the rent includes the service charge? His hand on the small of her back; the privacy of the touches no one else gave you.

But there was Dee's on her shoulder, and Dee was behind her as they walked into the lift. She remembered drunkenly leaning onto Chris's shoulder as they came back from some dinner, warm and full. Looking blurrily at their reflection in the mirrored walls and trying to place Chris's expression, love tempered with something else, far away. The pinging sound as the doors opened. She was moving out. She would never live here again.

And then they were at the door of the flat, and she turned the key for the last time, and they walked into what had been home.

It was immediately unnerving. Chris had moved things. The chair was on the other side of the living area. He had shifted the angle of the sofa, and a pillow and duvet were neatly folded at one end. There was a box on the floor next to the fridge and the toaster and the kettle and the blender in which he made his power smoothies (ugh) were neatly stacked inside. In a rush of wicked indignation, Katie pulled out the kettle and stood it violently on the counter. 'Tea?'

'I'll make it,' Dee said. 'Take a minute. Trust me.'

She watched as Katie drifted across the floor. The delicacy of the movement; the way she was holding herself together. There was, Dee thought, an unbearable echo of her mother in her grandmother's flat, as though Katie were made of the most fragile glass and would splinter into a million pieces if she stumbled.

Chris had tackled the shelves, too. There were odd gaps where he had taken out the few books he owned, and an unsettling space where his video games used to be. He had not, Katie noticed, touched the photos. Five of them: Katie-and-Chris on holiday in Spain; Katie-and-Chris on a night out in Manchester; Katie-and-Chris in a restaurant for his twenty-fifth birthday; Katie-and-Chris at a friend's wedding; Katie-and-Chris on a hike in the hills. Each in its own frame, as though that could hold them somewhere solid.

She took a raggedy breath, and walked into the bedroom. And there was another gap; a huge and horrible abyss where their bed used to be. In the place where they had held each other there was a white envelope, with *Katie* scrawled across it in Chris's unbearably familiar handwriting. *I've seen that in birthday cards and Valentine's cards for nine years. I've seen that with 'dear' and 'love' and 'always'*. Chris had sealed it, and as she ran her finger under the fold of paper she felt like she was touching his mouth.

Inside was a stack of twenty-pound notes. They were new and crisp; he had clearly gone to the ATM especially to get them. To pay her. There was no message. She felt something sharp and hot rising in her throat, and swallowed. A stiff, lumpy pain dragged itself down into her stomach.

'Tea's ready,' Dee called, and she walked lifelessly back into the main room, ludicrously aware she was holding a wad of money, and she was saying he messaged me about this, it's for the bed and the sofa, glad he didn't forget, and Dee nodded and turned to pour the tea, and Katie blinked back everything.

The buzzer sounded angrily, and Dee crossed purposefully to it. 'Heya. Come on up.' A few minutes, and then Liv and Rosa were there too, armfuls of boxes and bags, filling the space with humming love. Where's the best place to put these and ooh is that tea, I'll have one too. It was like they were all operating on one speed and Katie was on another, slower setting.

Later, when she tried to recall the following two or three hours, her overwhelming sensation was of her body becoming somehow translucent, so that everything around her also passed through her. Everything felt insubstantial and aloft, like a film of things floating in outer space. Dee and Liv and Rosa took brisk control, lifting books from the shelves, clothes from the wardrobe, boxes from the dresser, commenting oh I remember this from Manchester and oh my god as if you still have this. Because there had been homes before this one, and there had been love before Chris.

It was remarkable, really, how quickly you could dismantle your life. How much space the clothes and books and bits and pieces took up in her head; how little in the boxes. Belongings that she had dragged from place to place, trying to build the feelings they promised. Standing in the corner of the bedroom was a chunky cardboard tube of her prints and posters, and she realized it had been pushed out of sight under the bed before. Well, that was something. *I can have exactly what I like on the walls. No questions, no compromises.*

In the kitchen cupboards Chris had left no more or less than she had expected: her rainbow-coloured bowls; the set of champagne flutes her parents had given them when they first moved in together (and Chris had broken one, the bastard); three cookbooks; four pots and pans.

'Um, Katie?' Rosa was holding out one of the framed photos like a baby bird. 'These – there are five. Chris – I guess he hasn't packed them up?'

'Don't feel you need to take them,' Dee said.

'I've got an idea,' Liv said. Deftly, she swept up the pictures. In a few enormous moments she had prized them apart and extracted the photos in a neat stack. 'Pass me one of the books. Something you don't read often.'

Katie, processing the plan and smiling despite herself, passed her *Henry VIII and His Six Wives*. Liv grinned. 'Perfect. Now.' She tucked the photos inside the back cover and placed it back in the box. 'For when you're ready. And now the frames can just be for something new.'

Katie nodded slowly. 'Did you keep photos?'

'Of course. Packed away.' *But I look at her messages every week.*

'Rosa?'

Rosa pursed her lips. 'One or two. But again, packed away.' *Looking at them breaks me.*

'Dee?'

A snorting noise. *Erase it all.*

Katie sat delicately on the edge of the sofa. 'Can I tell you something?'

Yes, yes of course darling. Always. Tell us anything. Tell us everything.

'I'm looking at Chris all the time. Online, I mean. I mean, he's not a very social media-y sort of person. But there are bits. Pictures his friends put up. Or messages from his football team. His company website. If you know where to look you can put together all these different elements like a jigsaw, and then it feels like I'm still seeing into Chris's life the way I'm meant to. I mean, I know I'm not *meant* to, not any more. But that feels impossible. So I look, and I keep on looking. And I'm scared it's going to make it harder to move on, but I'm scared to not look at all.'

The room filled with the breath of agreement and empathy.

'It's the obvious thing to say – but you should try to stop,' Dee said. 'Masochism and all that. And you're right. It will make it harder to move on.'

'I know.'

'Delete the apps?' Liv suggested. 'Or your profiles? Try to put a pause on it until you've had more time?'

'Well, obviously I've tried that,' Katie said. A sharp intonation; raised eyebrows.

Liv opened her mouth to challenge and held her tongue in generosity. 'Okay,' she said.

'I just turn them back on again.' Katie laughed shortly at herself. 'How ridiculous.'

'What if—' Rosa broke off suddenly, and Katie looked at her.

'What if I see him with someone else?' she finished.

'Well . . .' Rosa trailed off unhappily. 'Sorry. But I know, you know?'

'Yeah.' *Natalya* and her photo and her flat thrummed. Katie wrapped her arms around her torso and pivoted on the spot, gazing around the room. 'We thought we were going to be so happy here.'

And we were, sometimes. We sat on that sofa eating risotto and laughing at stupid TV. We stood on that balcony drinking wine and talking about where we'd go on holiday. We lay in that bedroom and I felt safe but also wound up tight, like I was waiting for something to happen.

Her friends were standing wordlessly. They held out the black sketchbook – the heartbreak handbook – to her. Yes – perhaps the most important thing of all to take. The bridge between the old and the new. The scaffolding, the safety net. Are you ready?

'Let me just check the bathroom?'

It was a bland little box of a bathroom, the way those in new flats are. Chris had commented to the estate agent on the sleek sheet of glass around the shower: *Oh that'll be easy to keep clean.* As if you clean the fucking bathroom, she had wanted to scream, and she had hated that, because how did you end up amid these appallingly predictable structures when you knew them for exactly what they were?

She looked at herself in the mirror. Her face was grey and drawn, her eyes were swollen. She needed a haircut. Of course Chris doesn't want this any more. She felt her stomach tighten itself again, and she felt herself cry again. Guts. Tears. You think you've shut those doors behind you, and then they open again.

She thought of Nikita's knock at the door, and she thought of Liv's choices, and her crying too. Her jaw was clenched, her teeth pressing into each other and sending a tightness behind her eyes. What would it mean, to have a choice in any of this?

She walked back into the main room of the flat. Okay, let's go. And they filled the van with her life, and she locked the door, and held the heartbreak handbook close to her chest, and dropped the key into the postbox behind her.

Reminders

There will always be something.

Yes, the photos. Yes, the rooms and the buildings. Yes, the songs that you danced to, the place where you had your first kiss, the online footprints. You know this. You know to pack them away, to sit on your hands – and you know how hard it is.

But also the turn of phrase that someone throws in the pub, which stands out like hearing your own name through a crowd. The film, the book, the song you know they would have loved. The comment you know they would have made on an item on the news.

And then, just when you think you have washed them out of every tangible facet of your life, you will dream about them.

Because one of the grimmest elements of a relationship fallout is the parasitic way it worms itself into every single one of your thoughts. It's not as clean and simple as 'all day every day'; it's more painfully up and down than that. It's a jarring fingernails-down-the-blackboard re-realization over and over and over, so that your mind runs like a Richter scale.

Making your first coffee of the day? You'll remember how they drank theirs black, and how you thought that was impossibly attractive when you first met them, because you were eighteen and still training yourself to drink martinis without wincing and to roll cigarettes from YouTube videos.

Instructions for Heartbreak

Steadying your breath before an important meeting? You'll remember how you moaned to them about your work, how they told you that they believed in you, that you can do it, how they helped you practise asking for your pay rise and companionably joined in calling your boss a knobhead.

Sleeping, still, on your side of the bed? Let's not even go there.

When love has left its imprint on your heart, it leaves a thousand other traces too. How to meet these constant reminders?

Head on. Meet each, acknowledge, breathe, move.

Resist the urges to drive more knives into your heart. Staring at their pictures; reading and rereading their words; digging out every detail of where they might be living, what they might be doing, with whom they might be laughing – each of these will buoy you for an instant and then sink you.

Don't burn or bin things now that you might regret later. Pack them away, hide them. I promise there will come a time when you can look at them without those knives – there might even come a time when you want to look at them.

You might try writing a letter to yourself. You might try converting these strange acrobatics of emotion into something semi-concrete, some sentences that you can pack away with the photographs and return to later. You might be astonished, then, at the tearstains and the blood, the grief you thought would drown you.

But now is different. For now, you need to learn to live with them, without them.

Chapter Ten

BACKWARDS

The door opened before Katie got to it. Rafee and Jack poured onto the pavement, oh nice you got a van, shall we help, here are your keys by the way. The speed of it was at once reassuring and overwhelming, like she was bobbing over waves, kicking her legs away from the dark below. Unpacking the van felt the same way; six pairs of hands and chatter around and above her. Three boxes of books by the sofa; two boxes of kitchen things by the fridge. A box in the bathroom; a suitcase and two binbags of clothes on the bed. Shoes and handbags and a hair dryer and a tennis racket. The cardboard tube of prints and posters; the jewellery box; the tent and the sleeping bag; the laptop and speaker and the tangle of wires. This was it; this was a life.

Rafee and Jack disappeared tactfully downstairs and her friends clustered around her new bedroom door; there wasn't space for all four of them inside.

'Do you want to come back to the flat for the afternoon?' Rosa asked. 'I can do dinner.'

Katie opened her mouth, and found herself saying no. 'I think – I think I just want to sort things out here.

Should – it would be nice to hang out with Rafee and Jack, probably.'

They nodded agreement, and hugged her one by one. Katie followed them down the stairs, everything feeling overly crowded. The proportions of the house were different to the flat; lower ceilings; narrower spaces. Jack and Rafee were playing a video game, but they both jumped to their feet, and went through a polite ceremony of waves and smiles as Dee, Rosa and Liv left.

She shut the door behind them, and tried to process this new noise, the way it sent a slight reverberation into the room, the clack of metal and wood. This is the sound of my front door now. This is each morning on the way to work and this is home safe after a night out. The percussion bookending each day. It will become familiar. It will.

'I'm just going to – I'll just be unpacking, and things,' she said, pointlessly. Of course they knew that. She climbed back up the stairs, and shut the door, and sat cautiously on the edge of her new bed, and breathed.

The room seemed smaller and colder than it had when she first looked round. She noticed a grubbiness to the walls and a cobweb dangling from the top of the window. The awful involuntary comparison of the bedroom in the flat, with its view over the park and its mirrored wardrobe. Chris would be in something like it tomorrow, floor-to-ceiling windows and a gleaming ensuite. Another *up* and *on*. She felt a rush of nausea rising in her throat and leaned forward, cradling her head in her hands.

Oh, and you thought you were making your way through

these stages so neatly, didn't you? You thought you had dissolved the dread in your stomach and moved your eyes to a place where they didn't betray you without warning? You thought you could set a marker on the calendar for *dating* and the fizz of anticipation; you thought you could see his name in your phone, pass him on the street even, and smile, shrug quietly to yourself?

She picked up her phone and flicked to Chris's name. His painfully gorgeous picture, the reminder that he had been online twenty minutes ago. Who had he been speaking to? Not me, not me. *Hey. I'm all moved out now. Thanks for the money. Let me know if I've forgotten anything? Hope your move all goes well xxx*

So you try to inject some autonomy into the turbulence you cannot control; so you try to recreate the bright and breezy person he fell for, once. Because these are his choices, not mine – yes, *choices* – and how dare Liv refuse to recognize them, her extraordinary privilege, the pain she has the power to heal?

And so she flicked again, to Liv's name. Her achingly familiar picture, the reminder that she had been in this room five minutes ago. She sounded confused as she answered the call.

'What's up, K? Did we leave something behind?'

'Why don't you get it?' Katie demanded.

She could hear Liv stopping on the pavement, picture Dee and Rosa a few steps ahead, looking back quizzically.

'Why don't I get what?'

'Nikita. What it takes for someone to come back like that.

What it means when you say that she's great, she's brilliant, she's perfect, but *it wasn't working*.'

Liv, two streets away, watched by their friends, felt the blood heating up across her face. She spoke quietly, and slowly.

'Of course I get it. That's why I've thought about it obsessively, ever since ending things with her, and ever since last night.'

'Oh, you've *thought* about it.' Katie bit her lip, annoyed at her own petulance.

Liv's voice rose.

'Yes. Yes, I have. They're not mutually exclusive. You can love someone and you can know that . . . That it isn't working.'

'Oh my god, can you *hear* what that sounds like?'

A crackling pause.

'I know it doesn't sound like enough. I know it's vague. But it's the truth.' Liv laughed nervously. 'Come on, you know how indefinable these things are.'

'Indefinable? Don't you think Nikita deserves more than that?'

A sharp inhale; gritted teeth.

'Katie. I know you're upset about Chris—'

'*Upset?!*' She was embarrassed at the shrillness of her voice, but more than embarrassed, she was furious.

'I didn't mean to belittle – I know you're devastated.'

'Yes. I am. Devastated, destroyed, everything. Because you know what, when someone tells you it *isn't working*, when that's the only explanation they've got for tearing your life into pieces, that's pretty bloody hard to hear, you know?'

And now Liv's voice rose, too. 'I know. Of course I know.'

'Do you? Do you really? Because from here it looks just like you've treated Nikita exactly the same as Chris has treated me, and won't even give her the benefit of the doubt when—'

'The *benefit of the doubt*? Christ, Katie, can you hear yourself? Nikita didn't come round asking me – I don't know – what she should cook for dinner. She was asking me to be in a *fucking* relationship with her. What are you asking me to do, be with someone when I know it isn't right? Look, I'm sorry if I didn't use exactly the combination of words you would have, but you know nothing, *nothing* about me and Nik, nothing about how hard it was, nothing about what we talked about, nothing.'

'Yes, because you *tell us* nothing! God, Liv, you're so closed off!' Katie's speech was running into places she had never planned; her temples were throbbing. 'All Nikita wanted is a *chance*, and you can't even give her that, and—'

'What do you mean, a *chance*? It's my *responsibility* now, is it, to be Nikita's girlfriend?'

'Don't put words in my mouth, that's not what I said—'

'You know what, Katie? You need to stop projecting, and you need to work through what you're working through, and you need to keep yourself out of things that have nothing whatsoever to do with you. My god, just because you've needed to unpack the *minutiae* of you and Chris doesn't mean the rest of us have to do the same.'

Shouting; tears; hanging up. Katie slumped on the floor, knees to her chest and cried into her jeans, willing the noise of the game downstairs to swallow her.

So this was the spiralling, the agony. Liv had held her, and slept beside her, and stroked her, and betrayed her. Yes – betrayed her, as she had betrayed Nikita, as she had betrayed Katie-and-Chris, because none of it was enough, people needed narratives that made sense, and if there was the tiniest chance to stem the bleeding of a broken heart, surely you took it, even if you knew it wouldn't work, even if you knew it was wrong, because nothing was worse than the pain of *right now*.

She opened the heartbreak handbook and wrote.

Sarah Handyside

Backwards

Loop back, lie back, fall back.
Heartbreak is not linear.

Chapter Eleven

MUSIC

B *reathe. Breathe.*
Katie stood up, wiped her face and gritted her teeth. Small steps. Wasn't that something her friends had told her? *The three brightest girls, the three wisest women, and now one of them hates me.* Of course the room looked depressing, empty and simultaneously full, with the light off and the curtains drawn. Unpack. Build. Distract.

Yes. Yes yes yes. She opened a box and pulled out her speakers. Of course. How foolish to be trying to do all this in silence, her thoughts fighting each other like wasps.

She played Stevie Wonder and Beyoncé and the Rolling Stones and Prince. She walked on sunshine, she wanted to dance with somebody, she was feelin' good, she felt good as *hell.* There was nothing but flowers, she was putting on her red shoes, pickin' up good vibrations. I am not broken. This will not break me.

But there is a new pain now; the jagged edges of a damaged friendship.

She passed the heartbreak handbook from one hand to another. Gently, she placed it on the shelf above the bed. A new home; a new beginning. The words of my girls – my women.

Liv's have held me up, and now they are ringing in my ears.

She shook a bag of clothes onto the bed. These for the rail, these for the drawers. A wardrobe would be better. I used to have a wardrobe. But the rail makes the room look brighter. The drawers are smaller than before. I don't have enough space. I need to take these to the charity shop. That's the top I wore in Spain. We sat in that bar in the square. Chris was wearing his blue shirt. Get rid, get rid.

As she emptied the bed of clothes something else occurred to her. No duvet, no pillows. Her bed – *their* bed – had been dismantled and sold and Chris was sleeping on the sofa wrapped in what had wrapped them. She had a naked, plastic-encased mattress. It squeaked when she sat on it. An unsettling echo of childhood – of children.

So that was something else to do. For tonight, she would be in her sleeping bag – the sleeping bag which had seen her through European interrailing, summers in youth hostels in Cambodia and New Zealand, festivals and hikes and simple sleepovers – and which now had to see her through the hardest journey of all. A camper, a hitchhiker. The dislocation, the distraction. For tomorrow, yet another new thing to buy and build.

The opening beats of 'Raspberry Beret'. His drawl, his moves. He thinks he loves her. That's what I want, that's what I can find, is that how Chris felt when he first saw me, is that how he felt when he saw Nat? Will anyone feel that way again? Dance, dance, keep on dancing.

The opening piano of 'River'. I'm standing in my new bedroom on my own and Joni Mitchell's singing and I'm crying and I wish I could skate away I've lost the best baby I ever had and it sounds like Christmas – Christmas without Chris – Chris – Katie-and-Chris.

Peggy Lee is telling me about when she was a little girl, when she went to the circus, when she fell in love. She thought she would die, she didn't. So simple, so easy. Skeeter Davis is asking about the sun, the sea, the stars. The world is ending, but the world goes on. So impossible.

She was slumped on the floor again when there was a tentative knock. 'Katie? Just making a cup of tea. D'you want one?'

Katie leapt to her feet, wiped her eyes, come in, come in, that sounds great, thank you. Rafee stood slightly awkwardly in the doorway, hand in his hair. If he could tell she'd been crying he didn't mention it, and she was grateful.

'How d'you have it?'

'Um – strong and milky?'

'Got you! It's the only way, right?'

'Right! People don't get it, do they?'

'Tell me about it. You're getting sorted okay?'

'Oh yeah. Won't take me long. Hey, thanks for helping get everything up here.'

'No problem. You've got good taste in music. Love a bit of Prince.'

'Oh no, sorry, is it a bit loud?'

'No, not at all! We were thinking of getting a takeaway later, by the way. Fancy it?'

'That sounds great.'

'Cool. There's a decent Thai place if you're up for that?'

'Perfect.'

He left the door open and so did she.

Later, they sat together on the scuffed but soft blue furniture. Rafee played Prince albums, which was a sweetly nervous gesture, she thought. Jack decanted the takeaway onto plates and dishes and they shared spicy prawn soup and fried noodles and red curry and green papaya salad. The staccato conversation of people getting to know each other, which loosened and softened as they made their way through bottles of beer. So how long have you been a teacher and what exactly do you do in the NHS and what does your charity focus on shifted into where did you grow up and what did you think of that film and have you been to the pub quiz at the Crown? We should do it together, right?

'So how long were you with your boyfriend?' Rafee asked, then. His face was open and clear and casual and – she thought suddenly – very attractive, with a lopsided smile.

'Um. Nine years. We met at uni.'

'Wow!' Jack said good-naturedly. 'Pretty serious, then?'

'Yeah. I guess. It's the right thing, though.' She felt as though she was speaking something real. 'You said you're both single, right?'

They nodded. 'Yeah. Phil's moved in with his boyfriend, left us grappling with dating apps.'

'Though for women, in our case,' Rafee added quickly, and she smiled, to them and to herself.

'You'll have to come out with my friends sometime.'

'For sure. They seem great. Nice of them to help with the move.'

'They're the best.' It was the truth, and it hurt, and Liv's face swam in front of her.

Music

They say your sense of smell is the most evocative. And sure, if you get a waft of what they wore in these weeks and months afterwards then you will be shocked at how dramatically you are transported.

But music. Music.

There are two types of heartbreak music: the uplifting, joyful, rest of my life kind, and the mournful, indulgent, other people feel like me kind.

Both are important.

Create a playlist to be your ballast when you feel bad. The music to get you moving. Get obsessed with a song or two and play them constantly – they will always remind you, in the weeks and months and years to come, of your strength in these strange days.

Wallow in sad songs, the marshmallow of anguished ballads and the fireworks of furious tirades. Feel connected to every musician who ever felt like this, the savage humanity of a broken heart.

Some songs will always be associated with your ex. Don't torture yourself.

You will anyway. Do it knowingly.

Play music LOUD. Good speakers; good headphones; fill your head with music.

Chapter Twelve

BED

The first week at Rafee and Jack's (and Katie's now, she supposed) passed at a strange speed. Each day was enormous and yet lightning-fast. That first Sunday she woke groggy and disoriented, tight heat from being inside her sleeping bag and a cricked neck from using a sofa cushion as a pillow. But the light slanting through the window was bright and warm, and the clothes hanging on her rail were a reassuring reminder of the old layers of her life. I'm here now, I'm here.

There were messages on the group chat from Dee and Rosa, but Liv was conspicuously silent. When they arranged lunch she was unsurprised to find only Dee and Rosa at the table – but surprised to find how much it stung. Rosa, squirming in discomfort, explained that Liv was out with 'Carrie from work', while Dee, always more forthright, said you're going to sort this out soon, right? Katie tried to shrug defiantly, and said we need some space from each other, and felt like a cliché. Dee and Rosa eyed each other, and decided not to relay Liv's exasperation on their way home, her ranting at Katie's conflation, and interference, and obtuseness.

Back at the house Katie curled on the sofa with tea and a book, and Rafee and Jack, initially reticent but quickly relaxed, played a video game which seemed to involve magic spells and monsters. She found, to her surprise, that it operated as a soothing background, like sitting in a bustling cafe or in a railway station, watching the mechanics of the world roll in front of her.

It was only when she went to bed, adjusting to the motions of putting on pyjamas and wrapping herself modestly in a dressing gown to go to the bathroom, that she remembered the sleeping bag. She lay in it, thinking about where it had been and where it could go. Her brother, teaching on the other side of the world. That invitation to visit which seemed so much harder for Chris to accept than it should have done. Perhaps she could go to Argentina on her own.

Then she scrolled through shops on her phone, eventually finding a luxurious duvet and four pillows on special offer, which would be delivered the following weekend. It felt clean and full of promise.

Then there was work, five days of meetings and lessons and this kind of lateness is unacceptable and you're working at this grade but I think you can do even better and let's talk about the exams and your futures are all ahead of you. After a couple of days the new route to and from school settled into her brain and body. She learned which shops to stop at on the way home for onions and chicken and crisps and wine; she figured out the precise way of jiggling the key in the lock when it felt stiff. She slept in her old sleeping bag on her new bed and tried to wrap her arms around herself, testing out the space and silence she was left with. And she felt the additional gnawing ache of Liv's words, and her words back.

A mile away, Dee and Rosa and Liv likewise oscillated between offices and shops and bars and bedrooms and sofas, talking and wondering about their friend, painstakingly putting together these new pieces.

Dee drew and edited and adjusted colours and changed angles, and each time a glowing email from Margot arrived in her inbox she felt a little glow herself. The makeup business wanted to go ahead; Margot wanted her to lead on it. She revelled in her new responsibility, and she wondered about the differences between masking and amplifying. She phoned her mother in confusion, and Mel laughed comfortingly, and said you're doing wonderfully, I'm so proud of you, remember back in the day you'd have had to settle for shorthand typing and husband-hunting.

Rosa batted around ideas for her article, trying to trick herself into a personality that she was suddenly aware she didn't possess. The reams of articles for The Last Romantic that went before, that carousel of candyfloss. She had written the city sparkly and how childlike it all seemed, now. How had she managed to make romance sound so dizzy and fun, when now, she knew, Joe's cheating weighed like lead on her heart? There was an answer that she hated and it was Joe himself, the possibility of his eyes on her words, his speculation as to how she danced on from him. To be The Last Romantic was to live in hope, but had it only ever been the hope that he would come back to her?

Liv made phone calls and wrote press releases and sat in meetings and admired Carrie's outfits, and everything felt disconnected, impersonal, as though she were acting out something that she once would have imagined differently. It was as though she were walking along a road from which smaller routes kept branching off, and she knew they were there while also feeling an intangible impossibility of taking them. Nikita and Katie, anger and sadness, guilt and defiance were all tangled together in her head.

Back in the flat, she quietly thumbed through her phone, jumping between the last message from Nikita, her open promise of forever love, and the more recent one from Freddie. *This weekend sounds good. Saturday?* The first so tight with intimacy, the second so slack with possibility. Celeste had failed to reply altogether – that silence, then, was somewhere in between. Had she changed her mind since their first exchange, the sizing up of photos and one-liners? Had she met someone else – was she already caught in fire-works? Was she simply busy?

Rosa, too, quietly flicked through her own phone, the scraps of notes and ideas she was trying to draw together. Funny, uplifting, adventurous? The conversations she was trying to strike up through the apps each felt so staid and stilted, needling her with a comparison to the witty ease with which she had first got talking to Joe, two and a half years ago now. Was that real, or just how she imagined it from this distance?

There had been a smug joy she had never voiced in being able to tell people, *Oh, we met in an airport.* The serendipity of *right place, right time*, the astonishment that in this place of transience she had collided with someone who altered the entire shape of her life. Joe had reached for her bag – accidentally, he always insisted, though she had her doubts – and they had joked about the ribbon attached to it. They had entered a mannered exchange about football – the World Cup was on, and dominating her newsroom – and that had formed the basis for their first shared language, their first in-jokes. It has all been so *easy*. Or did it just seem that way, now?

'What you need to do,' Dee said, 'is grasp the nettle.'

'What?'

'Just – go for it. Stop overthinking. Who're you talking to?'

'Um. A guy called Marvin. A guy called Tom. Someone else.'

'Right. Marvin. Just ask him out. Saturday. A walk in the park. A pint in the pub. You know how this works. Either he says yes or he says no and then you send a message to Tom instead.'

'But. Okay. Yes. You're right. I know you're right. I just – it feels so *artificial*.'

'Nope. You're taking it too seriously.'

'Going with the tough love?'

'Too right.'

Dee was on the money, though. Marvin replied after a couple of hours, Saturday sounds good, you know the Dog and Bell? And Rosa felt a delicate flame of possibility.

*

Then it was the weekend. Four weeks to the day, Katie thought to herself, as she wandered around the shop. Four weeks since *We need to talk* and *This isn't working*. Four weeks of the gap between them widening, solidifying. He hadn't replied to her last message. The flat was gone.

She felt a hot tightness rising up her chest, and swallowed it back down, reaching out to touch a cushion, to re-anchor herself. The duvet and pillows had been delivered that morning but of course she had nothing to encase them in, and so here she was, in the sort of shop that smug couples wandered around building wedding lists. *Don't think about that.*

How many years since she had done this entirely for herself? How many years of beds that were only ever Katie-and-Chris's? *Don't think about that.*

Chris had insisted on absolutely plain bed linen in cold colours – stone grey, pale blue, brilliant white. Said he didn't like fuss and bother. But now . . . She picked up a willow-pattern design that was blue on white, like her parents' plates. Another with a bold geometric pattern in different shades of red. Another that was white but waffled, like a dressing gown in an expensive hotel. Mustard yellow. Teal green. Scallops. Stripes.

I can make my bedroom exactly how I want it. I can make my life exactly how I want it.

She allowed herself to drift around the shop, allowed herself to be drawn across different colours and textures. She stroked sheets, squeezed cushions. And by the end she had built a pile of ocean blue and dusty pink that felt so precisely *hers* she almost cried.

She added more – a vase, a set of picture frames. The bag was dragging on her arms and an ominous cramping was building in her stomach, but her head felt light.

'Good taste,' the assistant commented as he scanned her things.

'Oh – thanks!'

On the way home she passed a florist and bought a bunch of peonies. *They just die, Katie.* And at home she hung her precious prints, and arranged her flowers on her chest of drawers, and made her bed. She shook the duvet into its silky cover, opened the window and let a soft spring wind blow into the room. She plumped the pillows into gentle mountains, and then she lay back, cradled.

All smelled new, and felt safe. She placed her hands on her hardening abdomen, breathed through the growing crests of pain, and tried not to think about them.

But of course she did. First – Chris, and nine years of hot-water bottles and nervously proffered painkillers and *we're in it together.* Then – Liv, and the implicit understanding of a girl – a woman – who felt a lighter version of the same vice on her stomach and thighs, an echo of the way each month made you confront the future. And finally – that stark face of the last doctor. *I assume you'd like to have children*, he had said, and she had fought a vicious urge to leap from her chair and slap him round the face, because how dare you *assume*, how dare you dictate to me when I'm alone in front of you, twenty-nine years old and strong and free. Except actually I do want children, yes, and I don't think it's through lack of imagination, I think I really do, but I don't know when, and you're telling me that *when* needs shape, and planning, and conversation.

*

So Marvin had chosen the Dog and Bell for a first date. What did that say about him? It was a little bit overdone, Rosa thought – a lot of craft ales with names like Monkey Juggler and Dead Spider – the sort of place Joe would have picked. Marvin had messaged her before she arrived to ask what she wanted to drink, and so she saw him as soon as she entered, tucked into a corner table with a beer and a gin and tonic. That was a relief – she hated the awkward scanning of a bar, trying to match person to profile photo. Being able to walk purposefully over and slip into the seat opposite as though their relationship already had layers of familiarity – there was a comfort in that.

'Hello!' she said brightly. 'So this is the awkward bit, right?' He laughed appreciatively (and also nervously) and pushed the gin and tonic towards her.

'Good to meet you, Rosa. Cheers.'

It was a perfectly nice date. Marvin asked her questions about her work and where she lived and where she grew up. They took turns to buy rounds. The pub filled up around them, got darker and noisier, and this, combined with two drinks, then three, loosened them, lengthened their sentences, softened their laughter. But there was still a tightness to it, and the drumbeat in Rosa's skull was *you're not Joe, you're not Joe, you're not Joe.*

And then he asked, 'So how long have you been single, then?' She grimaced involuntarily, and he said, 'Ouch. Sorry. Bad breakup?'

'Oh no,' she said, breezily. 'A little over a year. Together a year and a half, you need to figure out whether it's going to be for the long haul, right?'

He nodded. 'Sounds familiar.'

'So what about you?'

'Pretty similar. With my ex about twelve months, had a conversation about moving in together, decided we weren't up for it, here I am.'

And was his lightness as artificial as hers, Rosa wondered. Was his mouth forming these words while his ex-girlfriend's face flitted in front of his eyes? Was he trying to speak breeziness into being?

This, at least, moved the conversation into more personal, less clinical terrain. But this stage still felt so much like an interview, didn't it? No matter how much you leaned into the *anything can happen*, there were still no in-jokes, no shared stories, no topics that no one else understands quite like us. No matter how much you hummed with *what might be*, the excitement was still cut with edginess. The comfort of where she and Joe had got to, that easy intimacy that she had taken so dramatically for granted. And that was where he was now, with his arm thrown casually over his new girlfriend's shoulder as they wandered around a farmers' market, probably making jokes about what a cliché they had become while privately revelling in it.

After four drinks they had arrived at the pivot on the

see-saw. 'Another?' Marvin asked. And yes would take them into a late-night drink, a we-stayed-until-closing drink, a next-date-is-a-definite drink, while no would take them into the stilted awkwardness of I had a really great time and I'd like to do it again and I'll message you. Along one line he would bring the fifth round back and sit a little closer to her, start looking at her with more intent; she would shuffle towards him, let her hand brush against his when she put down her glass. Along the other line they would put on their coats and go outside and there would be a point where they went in opposite directions and had to choose between a hug or a kiss and the narration around both.

'Actually,' she said. 'I need to be heading home. Getting up early for a thing tomorrow.'

'Cool,' he said. 'Shall we make a move?' And it was impossible to tell whether he was disappointed or relieved.

A new awkwardness arrived then, as they finished their drinks and put on their coats and walked to the door. Rosa pulled it open, stepping backwards with its weight and wondering if Marvin would put his hand on the small of her back to steady her. He didn't.

Outside, in the dark, she indicated the road she was planning to walk down. 'Yeah, I'm this way,' he said, pointing down the other. 'So . . .'

'I had a lovely time, thank you.'

'Yeah, it was great to meet you.'

'Yeah, and you.'

'So we'll be in touch?'

'Sounds good.'

They hugged stiffly, as though they were made of cardboard, and Rosa walked home with her hands in her pockets, trying to drown the images in her head. Joe and his new girlfriend in the pub round the corner from his flat, sitting on those leather bar stools so their legs pressed together. Joe leaning forward and placing his hand protectively on her thigh, her glassy laughter. Their short walk home, arm in arm. Joe's housemates at their girlfriends'; the raw, loud sex of an empty flat.

The door was still double-locked when she got home. Liv and Dee were having more successful dates, then. The flat was dark and cold and still. Rosa debated pouring a glass of wine, then washed the makeup off her face and put on her pyjamas. She felt shrunken, like a child.

She had changed her sheets earlier – a fit of optimism, perhaps, or something subconscious, and darker? They felt cool and fresh and fragrant, and it occurred to her that they would feel more so if she took off her pyjamas. But that felt somehow alienating, impossible.

Instead, she went to the kitchen and made toast. She spread the butter thickly, so that it not only melted but also sat on top, thick enough for tooth marks. She poured a glass of milk. She took the plate back to her bed and sat cross-legged, as at primary school.

Does he still have the same bed? Probably. You don't buy a whole new bed after a breakup, do you? And he still sleeps on the left-hand side, so she's lying where I lay, and she's put a delicate silver watch on the bedside table, and a glass of water that she knocks to the floor without noticing as he holds her wrists and moves inside her.

*

Liv looked at Freddie's face and tried to smile. They were onto the second bottle of wine and she hadn't eaten – what was with these 7 p.m. drinks, she thought blearily, which rolled on for hours without anyone acknowledging dinner? Freddie was telling a story about a holiday he had been on, somewhere down south – Cornwall, was it?

She tried to give herself an objective lecture. *You know that you don't want to be with Nikita. You know that you can't be with Felix. You don't even need to be here. You don't need to be with anyone. You've come here because you'd like to meet someone, because it's fun to meet people, it's fun to do the cut and thrust of flirtatious conversation with someone, it's fun to have sex, to move your body with someone else's. It's fun, too, to play with your future, to remind yourself that something new and different can be a text and a drink away.*

Fun, the promise of fun – is that what you tried to wish and will into a future with Nikita? Is that what you knew was missing? In which case, surely it was better to stumble around words like 'working'; surely it was better to soften things, and make the break with grace and love? What would Katie say?

She gave herself an imperceptible shake and tried to focus on what he was saying. On his face. Christ – Freddie was a good-looking man, wasn't he? The sort of cheekbones people tried to contour into their faces with makeup; big eyes.

He finished his story and she laughed at the right moment and he said, 'You have the cutest laugh,' and she carried on laughing, and he wouldn't know why.

'So anyway,' he said then. 'Your profile.'

She took a mental inhale. 'Yeah?'

'You go both ways, right?'

She coughed into her drink. 'I'm sorry?'

'You know. Interested in? Men, women?'

'Right?'

He was licking his lips. 'Sorry,' he said. 'I mean, you're bisexual, right? Or is it pansexual?'

'Bi, I'd call myself. If someone asked.' She looked hard at him. 'What *are* you asking?'

The swing of the pendulum, then – the possibility of 'So you've been with women?' with a lascivious glint in his eye, of the knowledge that she was ticking off some neat fetishized box in his head. But Freddie had the grace to at least look embarrassed, down at his drink, and say, 'Sorry if I've offended you,' and she softened slightly.

He was here, wasn't he, and he was hot? Yes, she could stare coolly at him, remind him that it was his responsibility to not be offensive, not hers to not take offence. He would finish his drink and later he would tell his friends grumpily about the cold bitch he went for a drink with. These fucking feminists. Or she could say look, this isn't important, right, do you want another drink? She could feel a vague irritation at her own pliability, while knowing that she, too, was appraising him in the shallowest of ways. The curve of a bicep under a T-shirt; the glimpse of a taut stomach, a line of dark hair.

Why was it so hard to pin down her own motivations, she wondered. Was it because they were moving, or simply because they were multiple?

He licked his lips again, and reached across the table and rubbed her thumb gently. 'You have amazing eyes.'

That made her laugh again, at the cliché but also at herself, because his fingers sliding back and forth on her thumb sent a flicker, a skitter of sensation up her arms and across her body. Bodies could exist separately from thoughts, couldn't they? Gently, she let her hand curl around his, a wordless signal, and then they were holding hands.

'So,' he said then, 'they've called last orders.'

'They have,' she repeated. Then she said, 'Do you want to come back for a drink?'

It was a fifteen-minute walk. They continued holding hands all the way, which Liv found faintly ridiculous. It felt like a weird imitation, an echo of what she knew before. Nikita always wanted to hold her hand, even on holidays in hot places where the sweat between their palms irritated her, or on paths that were really too narrow to accommodate them both. But there was a cosiness to it too; a reflexive ease. Freddie's hand was a different size and shape, and his skin was softer, and she knew almost nothing about him, and here they were.

'Who do you live with?' he asked.

'Friends. Two friends. Best friends.'

'Oh yeah? You braid each other's hair and have pillow fights, right?'

She laughed pityingly, and knew that Freddie thought it was genuine.

'Sure.'

'So how do you know each other?'

'Uni. We've lived together for years. There used to be four of us.'

She wasn't sure why she had added this, and willed Freddie not to pick up on it, but he said let me guess, gone off with her boyfriend, and she said that's very heteronormative of you and he said hetero-what? Forget it, she said, but yeah that's right.

'But the girls have more fun,' he said, and again she laughed at something far beyond his meaning.

The girls – the women. Yes, we have fun. We are bonded by so much more than you realize; we are tied together with tears and vulnerabilities and savage honesty – though that's broken now, isn't it, because Katie has said things she can't take back, Katie has attacked me for doing only the best I could, Katie has vocalized the worst things I think about myself – that I have been cruel to Nikita. That I have been unfair to Nikita. That I have broken Nikita's heart.

But then they were at the flat, and she said this is it, and he said wait a minute, and pulled her towards him. His face was faintly illuminated by the streetlight, and his eyes were dark brown. Still holding her hand, he dipped his head gently towards her.

So this is a kiss with someone who isn't Nikita she

207

thought. It wasn't bad – he was more fast and forceful with his tongue than she would have liked, but through a combination of pulling backwards and keeping her own mouth firm she was able to direct him to something softer and gentler. Though that was bizarre, too, because she was *managing* the kiss, as though she were calming down an agitated puppy perhaps, and wasn't it strange that she was thinking about it in this way, as though she were looking down on them both from above?

'So,' he said again.

'Come on in,' she said.

They made their way across the hallway and Liv unlocked the flat door. Single-locked – so Dee, or Rosa, or both, were already home. The lights were off, though, and the place was silent.

'So,' she said this time. 'Wine? Vodka? Gin?'

'Actually,' he said, 'I think your gorgeous smile is all I want.'

She nearly burst out laughing again. This sleazy and cliché man. Or was he perhaps a sweet and clumsy man? What was she feeling, really?

She was kicking off her shoes, then, and leading him into her bedroom, and he was sitting on her bed and pulling her towards him and they were kissing again.

I am going to have sex with Freddie, she thought. *I am going to have sex. I am having sex.*

This thought continued thumping at her throughout, as Freddie briskly rotated her through a series of positions as though he was following a recipe. *I am having sex.* And she *was* having, she *was* doing, this wasn't something that was happening to her, she was on top, she was rocking her body in that way she'd been afraid of messing up when she was a teenager, before it turned out to just be like – well, like riding . . .

You like that don't you, he kept saying, which was odd, really, because she thought she was being very quiet, aware of Rosa or Dee in the next rooms, and it was unsettling hearing that, like a line from a film, Christ, is this something people actually say in real life? And then he was saying I want to come on your tits, and that, *that* brought the absurdity to its peak. They both were so very many steps away from themselves, acting out something they had seen or read about.

Afterwards, she lay on her back and looked at the lightning-shard of the crack in the ceiling, jaggedly spinning out from the light fitting. Freddie had fallen asleep next to her. Someone else was in her bed again, and everything about it was different and peculiar. He smelled different to Nikita, and his breathing sounded different, and there was suddenly something so appalling about this stranger being here, next to her, in this place, that she had to get up, throw on her dressing gown and walk to the kitchen. She poured a glass of water and held it against her forehead.

*

Dee had a practised approach. Dress with long sleeves and a short hemline. Knee-high boots and a casual jacket – an outfit for a bus in the morning as much as a taxi tonight.

Toothbrush and comb in her bag – you could 'borrow' soap and shampoo, but toothbrush-sharing was strictly a long-term relationship thing.

She was five minutes early because she didn't care about being so, and she bought herself an overpriced negroni, and sat reading a book because that was more interesting than her phone. When Isaac arrived he commented on the book rather than the fact of her reading it – 'It's great, isn't it, where are you up to?' – before heading to the bar for his own cocktail.

Isaac made jokes about working in a science lab which Dee suspected he made with all new people – but he did ask two and a half engaged questions about her own work. He did not slip into casual racism or overt sexism – but he did comment on how many girls on dating apps were all about bodycon and pouting, and how great it was that Dee was not. They took turns buying rounds, and after the third he said the pizza here's great, if you're hungry? They shared two. He liked anchovies.

Then they ordered a bottle of wine, and Dee felt her head drifting into the good kind of drunkenness, the anticipatory swoops and flurries of a night with conversation flowing like hot butter and a man with high cheekbones and a sculpted jawline gradually shifting his body towards hers. He told her she had beautiful eyes and she smiled and told him yours aren't too bad yourself, and then she kissed him.

God, kissing was good. The way their lips pressed and pulled and pressed again; his tongue in her mouth feeling invasively alien and yet ferociously primal; the frissons of feeling shivering across her torso; her thighs squeezing together.

'So,' he said into her ear, and his breath was fast and hot. 'How far away's your place?'

'Nu-uh,' she said back. 'Let's go to yours?'

'Yeah?'

'Definitely.'

The taxi took twenty minutes and by the time they scrambled out at Isaac's the world was pulsating, dotted with stars. They did the fumbling dance to his front door, each pulling the other back, rotating in tandem, pushing into one another. Into the flat – my mate's at his girlfriend's, do you want a drink? Two whiskies and knowing looks. Dee said she liked the picture on the wall, bit Hockney-esque isn't it, and he said oh yes, 'A Bigger Splash', amazing blues, right? And then the whisky was gone and they were against each other again, he was pulling her to his bedroom, her dress was over her head, his T-shirt over his, shoes off, zips down.

His bed was neatly made and smelled like fabric conditioner. Dee smiled to herself as she pushed her face into the sheets. So he'd hoped, or planned, or known. He ran his fingers down her spine like the string of a harp, and then pressed the length of his body against hers. Hot skin on hot skin.

When they rolled onto their backs and lay in parallel stupor, Isaac said, 'I don't really *do* this, you know?'

'Do what?'

'You know. Sex on the first date.'

'You don't?' She was mocking him, but she didn't think he could tell. There was still a lingering scent of Cotton Fresh.

'Well. Not often.'

'Don't make a habit of it, hey?'

'What I mean is, this isn't – what I mean is, I'm not going to go AWOL tomorrow. I'd like to see you again.'

Dee paused.

'Oof,' he said. 'Silence is never good.'

'I didn't mean—' She stopped, and wondered what she wanted to tell him. Everything sounded like she had read it somewhere before. *I'm just not looking for a relationship right now. I'd like to keep things casual. Let's see what happens.*

'I meant – yes. Sounds good.'

But as they fell asleep in his bed she knew she wouldn't reply.

Bed

Your bed might just be the most intimate place you have.

Invest time and thought and energy in making your bed the best it can be. It is yours and only yours. Exhume traces and memories of your ex. Change the bedsheets; change your detergent; change the tone of your alarm clock; change the bedside lamp. Don't restrict yourself to a sad single pillow – cushion yourself on two, or three, or four. Nest. Luxuriate.

Make your bed explicitly about this new phase of your life. Whether you are alone in it or invite people to share it, your bed should take you forward.

Chapter Thirteen

MAKING CONTACT

Another week and early April had become Easter. Katie watched a particular date in her diary approach, build, threaten to swallow her – and then it was gone. No message from Chris, no acknowledgement. She complained animatedly over pizzas on which a nearby pub was running an irritating – but good value – 'hump day' deal – and for which Dee had been persuaded to abandon abs day at the gym. Liv was at a film screening with a group of current and former colleagues – a commitment detailed enough to sound like it had been planned for several weeks, but which nevertheless left Katie feeling an anxious sourness.

'I mean, I know there wasn't anything to talk about. Chris paid for the hotel, so he must have sorted out a refund or whatever. But just to not *mention* it?'

Dee and Rosa murmured their agreement.

'I guess – I guess maybe he's gone anyway,' Katie thought aloud. She pictured the little cliffside building, its terrace with views across the water, the bedrooms with their white muslin curtains and an idea of a sea breeze. 'No. That's ridiculous. France was *our* holiday. He wouldn't have gone with someone else.'

Her voice tripped up at the end, and there was a pregnant silence.

'Don't think about it,' Dee said briskly. Her phone chirped, and she glanced at it, made a noise of irritation and tossed it onto the seat beside her.

'Isaaaaaaac,' Rosa trilled, embracing the opportunity for a change in subject. Katie raised her eyebrows. 'He's *still* messaging you?'

'Every so often,' Dee said dismissively. 'You'd think he'd get the hint.'

'I don't get it,' Rosa said. 'He's a nice guy. You think he's hot. You had good sex. Why *don't* you want to see him again?'

There was a slight strain of annoyance to her voice, as she bit herself back from telling Dee how lucky she was. Of *course* Dee left a trail of men in her wake like this. She was compelling and carefree; looking at Dee was like looking at a very bright lightbulb – no, a mirror ball: something spark-ling and shifting and dancing far away.

Dee shrugged. 'I don't want the aggravation. I'm busy. And anyway, nice guy for an evening does not equal nice guy for the long haul.'

'God, you're depressing sometimes.'

'But it's true!' Dee hooted. 'Look at last week. Liv hooks up with Freddie – okay guy, we think – he treats her like a prop from his favourite porn. You *don't* hook up with Marvin because it turns out good chat on your phone doesn't equal zingy chemistry in person, and when you try to let him down gently he sends you a picture of his freshly shaved cock.'

'At least it inspired a decent article,' Rosa said. It *had* been a good piece – a meditation on digital flirting – enough for Ty to tell her to get started on another. A pity, Rosa thought, that writing about so-called modern romance made her want to bury herself in sand.

'Isn't it the balls that are freshly shaved?' Katie asked.

'Whatever,' Dee said. 'The point is, you'd be much happier if you chilled out a bit, lowered your expectations and just saw men as – you know, a bit of fun. Maybe, maybe not. *That* kind of attitude. Open. Easy.'

Rosa sighed. 'I know that's the theory. But it's not how I *feel.*'

Suddenly she slouched down in her seat, ludicrously attempting to hide behind the wine bottle. Katie and Dee followed her line of sight. Three couples of about their age had entered the pub, the men jostling and elbowing each other in friendly familiarity. They split between the bar and a table on the far side of the room.

'What is it?'

'It's – shit shit shit – that's two of Joe's housemates, and his friend Charlie. Shit. And their girlfriends. God, *why* didn't I remember they live near you, K?'

'I thought you liked Charlie?'

'I do! He's great. They're all great.'

'Even the girl with the pink scarf? Looks like a bit of a tosser to me.'

Rosa snorted more loudly than she intended, and sank lower.

'Seriously?' Dee said. 'Joe's not here. Chill out.'

'Joe's not here *yet*,' Rosa hissed.

'No, no,' Katie soothed. 'Look. Table of six. It's just them.'

And I used to be part of 'just them'. I used to do pub quizzes and Sunday walks and last-minute pizzas. I know that the drinks order will be three ales, a cider, a gin and tonic and a red wine. I know that the woman in the pink scarf – Cleo, she's called – looks stand-offish but has a brilliant sense of humour. I know that Charlie will be Joe's best man, and I'll never admit this but I used to imagine what he might say about me in his speech.

'Don't you want to go and say hello?' Katie asked.

Rosa stared at her. 'Are you joking?'

'Of course not! Just – well, like you said. They're great, right?'

'Yes. Doesn't mean I want to go over and be the poor pitied rejected ex-girlfriend. God! They'll *know* her, you know. They're probably all matey with her.'

Katie gazed at the table. The easy familiarity; the alluring togetherness. She pictured Chris's friends, imagined her own walk across the pub floor, tossing her hair. The relayed messages – saw Katie, she looks good, what *happened* there? Casting lines of intrigue and – yes – potential reconciliation. Was that what she wanted?

'Katie – swap places with me?'

'Oh, come on,' Dee began, but Katie had already slipped out of her seat and allowed Rosa to slink round.

'Okay. See? All better. And I look alright, right?'

'Of course. More than alright. You look stunning, you old hag.'

'Good. I mean thanks. Okay, carry on. K, how're you doing?'

Katie bobbed her head to non-existent music, shrugging, smiling, grimacing.

'I guess – I'm okay,' she said. 'Look at this.'

From her bag she produced the heartbreak handbook. Dee and Rosa affected quiet whooping as she placed it on the table, clinking their glasses in satisfaction.

'I'm serious,' Katie continued. 'Look. I've been adding to it myself. See? I made my bed all new, and I listened to music – I've been making a playlist, a kind of post-Chris, new me thing – and I wrote some things about feeling – feeling like things are going backwards, sometimes. It's good, it's helping. And I wanted to ask your advice, about something else to add.'

They looked at her expectantly.

'I've been thinking about emailing him,' she said.

Their faces shot to each other then back to her.

'Why?' Dee asked eventually.

'Because,' Katie said, the word soaked in a mixture of exasperation and confusion and – desperation? 'Because I can't stop thinking about him. About us. And I feel like there are things to say.'

'Should you say them?' Dee asked.

'What do you mean?'

'Well, look at Liv and Nikita,' Dee said.

Katie stirred her drink rapidly. Dee tried to catch Rosa's

eye; she bit off a too-large mouthful of pizza and chewed, looking at the table. Dee exhaled exasperatedly.

'You're going to need to sort this out sooner or later. You and Liv.'

'She could start by coming for dinner, couldn't she?'

'Fine, yep, or you could start by coming round to the flat, or she could start by messaging you, or you could start by calling her – the point is, Rosa and I can't carry on being stuck in the middle of your falling-out for ever. It's so – basic.'

'You heard what she said to me, didn't you?' Katie demanded. 'That bit about *minutiae*? I haven't been doing that, have I?'

'Oh, who cares if you have?' Rosa said. 'God knows I've bent your ear about Joe enough.'

Dee did a laugh which she turned into a cough.

'Anyway, what do you mean, look at Liv and Nikita?'

'I mean, was it fair of Nikita to do that?' Dee said.

'*Fair?*'

'Yeah. Turning up at your ex's place, out of the blue, asking to talk. I mean, imagine if Joe did that? Prick.'

Rosa smiled gratefully at Dee's defensiveness, and didn't say *I would love it if Joe did that.*

'Okay, but Joe's the one who – you know. Nikita's the *victim* here.' Katie regretted the word as soon as she said it, and Dee raised an eyebrow.

'Careful. Seriously, careful. Don't say that in front of Liv. That's out of line.'

Katie exhaled. 'Okay. I mean, yes. I know. I don't mean that. I mean – look – Chris is like Liv, right? As in, he's the one who did the breaking up. And so, maybe he feels – I don't know – maybe Liv feels – maybe Chris feels more of a *responsibility*, or whatever. Not to be in touch with me.'

There was a long silence, and the air felt hot and thick.

'So – go on then,' Rosa said. 'What *do* you want to say?'

It was a huge question. Katie sat and talked and tried to articulate the thoughts that had been swimming through her head, that she had spent hours writing and rewriting, and everything she said spoke of a million other things too. Katie-and-Chris were at the edge of everything she thought and everything she did. The breezy – or angsty – relationships she saw enacted every day at school, as teenagers kissed behind corners and messaged each other suggestively during class. Jack's nervous request for her to look at his dating app profile – *Would you mind? I'm never very good at this stuff . . . you know, female perspective and all?* Night after night in her new bed, blissful in soft pillows and a fragrant duvet but so quiet, so still, so buzzing with wonderings. Did we try hard enough? Did I try hard enough? I know all the things I've said – the clashes and resistances between us, the feelings of once entangled lines diverging – but also all the things I *haven't* said – the affection, the shared humour, the under-standing. Chris is one of a kind, isn't he – I mean isn't it *admirable* that he has the drive he does, that he clawed his way through that school and set his sights on what he wanted so firmly? Isn't it amazing that he learned about endometri-osis the way he did, that he took all that in his stride, stood by me, supported me, planned a future with me that took that into account? Am I really going to complain about a boyfriend leaping out of bed to play football on the weekends while I'm still dreaming, or planning ahead with a bit more detail than I do? What does that say about me? Couldn't I have let him be *him* more, and he let me be me?

They listened, and they thought, and Dee said, 'Do you want to get back together?'

Katie breathed enormously. 'Maybe,' she said.

Rosa tapped the side of her glass with a fluttering motion. 'I guess,' she said, 'if that's how you feel?'

'Right?' Katie said hurriedly.

'But going back to Nikita and Liv,' Dee continued. 'Liv said no. What if Chris says no?'

Katie swallowed a lump which rose sickeningly in her throat. 'What do you think?'

'I don't know how to say this kindly, so I'm just going to say it,' Dee said, and a smiling acknowledgement of her brusqueness bounced round the table. 'Are you sure this is wanting to get back together with Chris? Are you sure it's not just – you know – wanting to be with *someone*? And if it is—'

Katie blew out her cheeks. 'But even if that's true,' she said, 'what if Chris feels the same way? Wouldn't that give us, like, a head start? We know each other so well, right? Couldn't we – you know – build something good out of what we were? Isn't that easier, or better than trying to meet someone new? You know – start from scratch? You've just been saying yourself how hard it is to meet anyone! Freshly – freshly shaved *cocks* and all that. What's the point in trying to psych myself up in all those ways if it turns out Chris and I were right for each other after all? All that convincing

221

myself that there's someone better out there for me, and it really is all for the best, when maybe the point is that I haven't *fought* for us yet?'

Her voice got progressively higher and faster. Dee reached for the wine bottle and emptied it into her glass. 'It's an idea,' she said.

'Did you,' Katie said, breathing heavily, 'did you never think about getting back in touch with Leo?'

Dee pursed her lips. 'I guess I thought about what I'd say.'

Of course she had. Of course she had imagined what it would be like to bump into Leo on the street, to get a text or a phone call or – yes – an email or a knock at the door. The precise combination of words she could deploy to make him feel an iota of what *she* had felt, as he shattered something inside her. *I just don't fancy you any more.* Her body would be tighter and her skin would be clearer and her hair would be smoother. She would say something devastating but dignified, cool but cutting, something that would show Leo just how much she didn't care.

Something, then, that would be a lie.

'But,' Dee continued. 'I stopped myself. I deleted his number. Blocked him. It felt – I guess it felt too dangerous.'

She hadn't expected to use that word, and almost tried to undo it, but they were looking at her with softness.

And she knew, suddenly, where she had heard it before. The kitchen table at the bright beautiful home Mel had created for them both. Her mother sitting opposite in an orange jumper and with a blue scarf tied around her hair, serving them bowls of mussels cooked in white wine and butter. And Dee – thirteen, fourteen – asking, *Why did you stop trying to contact him?*

Mel looked at her in thoughtful silence; the sagacity of knowing when to stop and think.

'Your father,' she said.

'Yes. Why did you let him disappear?'

The viciousness, now, of those words. Of knowing that she could say anything and her mother would love her regardless; of knowing that she could be reckless and cruel and claim it as adolescent girlhood. Dee could hear the steadfast measurement in her mother's voice as she inhaled and exhaled and replied.

'You know that I didn't. *Let him.*'

'Maybe not when he first left. But later, when he stopped. When there weren't any more visits, birthday cards. You could have got angrier. You could have made him.'

The tiniest, wisest smile.

'You know that I couldn't, darling star. A person makes those decisions themselves.'

And the pain of hearing that. Of recognizing the choice that he had made.

'But even if I could,' Mel continued. 'Would you really have wanted me to make him?'

Dee scratched her fingernail across the wooden table top, leaving a pale scar behind.

'I did think about it, you know,' Mel continued. 'Many times. I thought about what I could say – about you, not me. About his fatherhood, not our relationship. But it would have been – dangerous, I think.'

223

'*Dangerous?*'

'Yes. One of my jobs is to protect you. From disappointment, from hurt. Opening up contact after he'd already showed us, told us, exactly where he stood? I couldn't bear the idea of you being let down.'

Dee stared into her bowl. 'I wish he had wanted to.'

'So do I.'

And had her mother been referencing a different kind of danger, one she would not voice to her daughter? The danger of opening up a gap of possibility – one which could be filled, oh yes, with hope and anguished optimism, but also with the most feared aspects of oneself. Desperation, perhaps, or aggression, or mortification. An image flashed across Dee's brain – her mother on her knees, her mother crying – and she felt a wave of dizziness.

'I think I know what you mean,' Rosa said slowly. 'There's – there's so much unpredictability, isn't there? Look.'

She picked up her phone and flicked to Joe's name. The last message she had sent him – nine months ago, now: *I miss you xxx*. And his reply: *I'm sorry, Rosa. But it's for the best. X*. And the messages above that, her ragged heart poured out over and over, the small luminous screen of the phone wildly unable to do justice to her pain, her depth, her longing.

She tossed the phone to Katie, who read and swallowed again. 'He replied to you,' she said.

'Yeah,' Rosa said. 'Briefly. But that last message – I realized that anything I send him, *she* probably sees. And that's weird and horrible.'

Weird and horrible. Yes – and so much more than that. The distinct, tight pain of knowing that a line of communication once so perfectly private is now open to someone else. When my name flashed up on Joe's phone, did he roll his eyes and say Fuck's sake, it's Rosa again? *Or was he softer, gentler?* Oh no. What do you think I should say? *Did she read over his shoulder, or did he read it out to her, or did he throw his phone to her like I did just now to Katie? Did they compose that message back to me together, condescendingly thoughtful, smugly generous? Did they laugh at me? Did they feel sorry for me? And which is worse?*

Katie considered this.

'I think,' Dee said, 'it just takes some getting used to. How someone who you used to speak to all the time just isn't there any more. I mean, that only otherwise happens if someone dies, right?'

'Right,' Katie repeated.

'And anything you write down,' Rosa added, 'is out there for ever. It's not like having a conversation or a phone call. You have to think – it'll be in his inbox for ever. He can go back to it. *You* can go back to it.'

She was communicating, she hoped, the squeamishness she knew she could reignite in a second, scrolling back to those loving exchanges with Joe. The ones she hadn't deleted, because of the exquisite combination of comfort and pain they brought her. The messages that took her back in time, that reassured her that she had been in love. That she had been deserving. That she had been who he'd wanted.

225

'Okay,' Katie said after a few minutes. 'All this makes sense.'

'So what are you going to do?'

Katie opened her draft email. 'I'm going to try,' she said.

Dear Chris

Isn't that weird, writing 'dear'? We put it in formal letters but also Valentine's cards. It's like it means two things at once.

I know that there's some selfishness here. I know that this is painful for you too, and getting a long email out of the blue might drag up feelings that hurt even more. I'm sorry.

But I've been thinking about you so much, and about us. Have you been thinking about me? It's been nearly six weeks. That feels like no time at all and also all the time. It feels like enough time to have got through the crying-all-day phase (did you have that?) and now there's more – perspective, or something.

I'm getting on okay in my new place. My new house-mates are lovely, and it's near Rosa and Dee and Liv. Only for six months though, and then the four of us are going to move in together again. So hard, isn't it, trying to figure all this out in such an expensive city? I know we talked about that a lot. Sometimes I wonder if that pressure was part of what went wrong for us, and if we could frame it differently then we could go back to how we used to be.

School is good too. Exams coming up, of course.

And my parents and brother are well. They miss you, I think.

I do too.

I'm glad there's been some space, though. It's given me the chance to think about how we were arguing, the stresses and the differences, all the things we talked about that Saturday, I suppose. But in a new kind of light.

I know I could be difficult but I feel like so much of it was outside us. It didn't mean that I loved you any less, that the good things had gone away. It was like there was a distraction, like a film of something had come down between us but now I can see clearly again.

Chris, there was so, so much that was good about us. Remember Albert King in the kitchen? Remember fillet steak and chocolate sauce? Remember the Lakes and seeaagulllll?! Remember teaching you how to plait? Remember 'it's just like riding a bike' and 'singing from the same hymn sheet'? Remember Christmas turkey in that ridiculous washing-up bowl?

Remember being an elephant and a lion?

I thought about you even more this week. That little hotel we found by the sea. I was looking forward to it so much. I wish I was there with you now.

Please, please, can we meet up and talk?

I still love you so very much.

Katie xxx

She felt Dee's and Rosa's eyes burning into her as she reread the words she had spent so long arranging. Her finger hovered, and she teetered for a moment. Was this something like Chris had felt, waiting in the flat for her to come back from shopping, trying out different ways of *We need to talk?* The knowledge that once you took that step, something irrevocable had changed, and no matter how the next minutes and hours and days panned out, you would never be able to undo the words you had put into the world? And the knowledge, too, that if you didn't, those words would still waltz in your brain, mapping out different possibilities, different pain?

She exhaled and pressed send, and the spark of hope and confusion soared away with an anticlimactic whooshing noise.

The phone, then, painstakingly by her side. Dee and Rosa were chatting quietly together about TV and books and a politician who had said something outrageous. It was Rosa who saw she had finished first, and who met her eyes with a gentle moment of solidarity.

And then there was second after minute after hour of feeling her hand fidget at her side, twitching and flinching to pick up the phone, click, scroll, check. Sometimes she resisted and sometimes she succumbed, and every time 'Checking for Mail' shifted to 'Updated Just Now' and there was nothing new, nothing there, no heart-fluttering beep or vibration. It was a grim mirroring, she realized, of those heady few weeks after she and Chris first met, willing herself not to check her phone *again* for messages and feeling the anticipatory swoop each time his name appeared on the screen. Putting her phone in Dee or Rosa or Liv's room to stop herself from checking or messaging him back too quickly; feeling the warmth of seeing that he had filled his text with questions, clearly keen to keep this effervescent dance of conversation skipping onwards. All then was light, and all now was heavy.

By the time they were climbing onto the bus home there was still no response, and she had to concede that Chris was unlikely to be checking his emails at ten thirty in the evening. But nothing appeared the following day either, or Friday – two irritable days of feeling her phone like a hot stone in her pocket and ignoring sarcastic calls of *Phones away, Miss!* as teenagers filed in and out of her classroom.

It wasn't until Saturday morning that his reply arrived, tucked innocuously between an email from a clothes shop and one from their old university. And as Katie read it she felt a prickly heat and nausea spread across her body that she had felt only once before, six weeks previously to the day, when he told her that he had been *thinking*.

Katie,

I appreciate that you apologize in your opening, but I'm still struck by your decision to send this email when you know I'm on holiday – and a holiday I've really needed, actually, to unwind from everything that's happened.

We both agreed that we had discussed everything that needed to be discussed, and I'm unsure what there is to gain from meeting up to rake it over further.

All the best,
Chris

Making Contact

How it plucks at the edges of your brain and makes your fingers twitch and flicker. How it raps a tattoo on your thoughts and makes you act out a future full of possibilities.

Should I get in touch with them? Should I pick up my phone, send an email, knock on their door?

One of the most discombobulating, disorientating, mindbending elements of a breakup is how, in an instant, the person who was everyone becomes a person who could be anyone.

The person you were naked with in all ways, the person whose body was next to your body, the person who was your closest confidante – and now you have to skitter and second-guess, question and re-question.

No formula, no rules – but there are some things that can be helpful to remember.

Remember that any contact you have may no longer be private. You no longer have the cast-iron ability to ask for an intimate one-to-one, a channel that is only for you. Depending on the circumstances of your breakup – and the aftermath – your contact might become a topic of conversation at the pub, an eye-rolling comment to colleagues, a shared joke with their new partner. Can you cope with that? Can your words stand up to that?

Remember that anything written down takes on a new history. Texts and emails and letters can be kept for ever, *and they will stay static as your story changes. This can be romantic and beautiful. Or it can induce shame, guilt, teeth-grinding discomfort. You will suddenly remember that letter four years from now, and cringe.*

Remember the emotional load attached to place. If you meet them, choose your location carefully. Their turf? Your turf? There are such things, now. And if your meeting turns out to be the last place you ever spoke to them – or the last place before you rekindled everything – remember that it will hold that significance for you for ever. Don't taint your favourite walk, or cafe, or park, or pub.

Remember this word: dignity. If the contact you make is inflected with dignity, if you maintain, however impossibly difficult it seems, a respect for them, and for you-and-them, and above all for yourself, then your contact will be made with grace. You will remain floating even if they sink. You will have offered kindness even if there is none in return. You will recognize that in the months and years and decades ahead, and you will be glad of it.

Chapter Fourteen

ANGER

How dare you. How fucking dare you.
*   My own fingernails digging into my own palms.*
What gives you the right? What gives you the audacity?
The heartbreak handbook hurled into the wall.
I hate you. I hate you.

Katie shifted to a different speed: her muscles throbbed; her blood spun; her head shrieked. She had spent exactly seven minutes sitting on the edge of her bed, reading and rereading the email and trying to calm the churning in her stomach. That hideous heaviness, that agonizing pounding! She had thought it was over but no, two sentences from Chris and her stomach was once again somewhere else, her heartbreak in her guts.

Then she pulled on her trainers, blind, mad. She put the vicious phone in her pocket and she fled. Away from the house, away from Rafee and Jack, away from anything that might seem normal, because she was spinning far, far away from normal, she was pulsating, vibrating and she felt as though she would shatter anything she came near. She was the shrill frequency that splintered glass; she was the lightning bolt that melted sand. She needed space to scream and you could never find that in a city, that was why they had gone to the countryside weeks before, because here there was a person every few metres, a building in every direction, so many thousands of eyes on her, seeing her, judging her.

There was *so much to be angry about*. She had expended so much time and thought and effort these past six weeks on keeping herself afloat, on tempering her savage undulations, on drying tear after tear, that she had not allowed herself the true wildness underneath. Chris had made this happen. Chris, with his infuriatingly folded arms and his maddening talk of *working*, always *working*, then *not working*. Chris was responsible for the pain in her stomach and her brain and her bruised, sodden heart; Chris was responsible for her distraction, the way she kept staring into the middle distance when she should be doing something else. Chris had upended everything, and he had done it without giving her the chance to protest, or negotiate – or do it first.

And Liv, too, with her accusations of *minutiae* and her incomprehension of her own good fortune. No one understood how lucky they were, to be navigating the world without this continuous background stab of *look what you have lost*, and Liv especially didn't understand how lucky she was, the recipient of warm unquestioning uncomplicated love – of course it was *fucking* uncomplicated, Nikita had stepped straight from a scene in a romance film.

The effort it took, to quell these rages, to be good and polite and thoughtful and kind! To pretend your body had not been tightened and wound and wounded, to pretend your breath was gentle and your blood cool. She thought of her classrooms and the vicious taunts of teenage boys – *Crazy bitch, time of the fucking month?* – she thought of her own grasping for composure as arguments began to escalate.

Calm down, you're getting hysterical. I can't talk to you when you're like this.

Well I am *like this, this is me, this is who you say you love.*

She pictured Chris in front of her and knew she would swing at him, slash at him. Her hands formed ferocious fists; her teeth tore at imaginary flesh. No one ever knew this violence, no one ever knew the work of placating it. Men threw punches and fired guns and waged wars and girls – women – pretended they wouldn't, swallowed their own fire. She pictured Liv in front of her and she was frightened of herself.

Anger

You are allowed to be angry.

Chapter Fifteen

DRINKING

'That,' Dee said, 'is absolutely outrageous.'

Katie had circuited the park three times. Simmering, boiling, overflowing, calming, simmering again. She had raked her hair and stamped the ground and scowled at strangers. She had ground her teeth until her mouth tasted chalky and a meaty hiss sounded in her ears. Then she had screenshotted the email and sent it to the group. Dee and Rosa immediately responded with a flurry of messages.

Nooooooo!!!!

What. The. Fuck.

Jesus.

And then there was Liv's name too: *God, that's savage. 'All the best' – what is he, your solicitor?*

Katie thought for a moment, broke for a moment. She gritted her teeth, and she breathed. Finally, she replied: *I know, right?*

It was banal but she hoped that Liv could sense that it was meant with peace – it meant *Thank you for understanding me* and *I'm sorry.*

The messages quickly evolved into an agreement that their

Saturday night needed to shift from pints in the pub to something rather more *extravagant*. And as Katie zipped up her favourite black dress and dried her hair upside-down and applied red lipstick she could almost imagine herself back there again, their Manchester house, readying them-selves for Big Nights Out with supermarket vodka and squash, pop music and the smell of hairspray and cheap perfume. It was all so free and easy then because it was so *immediate*, nothing to worry about beyond an alarm clock the next morning or an essay deadline the next week. *The rest of our lives* was always ahead of them, and huge.

As she made her way down the stairs she realized that Rafee was alone on the sofa – she had thought, or imagined, or assumed, that Jack was with him. He was reading a book and playing – she smiled quietly to herself – Prince.

'Hey,' she said. 'Oh – *Middlemarch*. I think I read that, years ago.'

'Aha. I'm reading it for my book group.'

She smiled again, something between surprise and endear-ment.

'Anyway, you look great,' he said. 'What's the plan for tonight?'

'Oh, I'm heading out with my friends – my old housemates. Cocktails at this bar that does a great sixties and Motown night. Think we all need to let off some steam.'

Did something flicker across his face when she said *my friends*?

'Where's Jack?' she asked, quickly.

'Oh, out with someone from that app. Looks like your edits worked!'

'Brill! Well, always happy to help!'

She had no idea why she said this, and immediately wished she could scoop the words back into her mouth. Rafee hesitated, swallowed and nodded. 'Well, have a great time anyway.' And then she hurried out of the front door, thoughts whirling in ways she couldn't quite define.

At the bar Liv was sitting alone at a table for four, sipping one of two cocktails. Dee and Rosa are just catching us up, she said, and this artificiality was so blatant Katie almost laughed. Liv pushed the glass delicately towards her.

'Thanks.'

'No problem. It's two for one, so . . .'

'What is it?'

'Lychee martini.'

'Yum.'

'You going to sit down, then?'

'Right.'

They looked hard at each other. Liv's mouth was set in a determined line. Katie inhaled and said, 'I'm sorry.'

Liv nodded tightly. Then she said, 'I'm sorry too.'

'I – they're separate. Chris and Nikita.'

'Yes, they are.'

'I shouldn't have said – of course you don't owe Nikita a second chance.'

'No.' Liv sipped her drink. 'But I understand why you said it. Because sometimes I think it.'

'Really?'

'Yes.'

From there, the re-mortaring of what they had scraped away was shockingly easy. Liv stammered her way around her broken thoughts, how much she had loved – still loved – Nikita, but how much, also, she knew herself. Katie tried to marry how she knew that Chris's words had not come from nowhere, how she knew that there had been that slow build-up of tension and arguments – with her longing, nevertheless, for the ease and safety he had given her. I want him to knock at the door like Nikita did, and I want to jump into his arms yes yes yes, and I know that it would be a huge mistake. *I've lost my lover*, they each thought, *I can't lose you too.*

Dee and Rosa arrived, and now Katie was tucked around a table with her friends, cradled and buttressed, and there were four cocktails and three loving faces and the bar was filling up around them, that Saturday-night electricity of *let loose* and *what if*, sinuous music and darkness and light overhead. And Chris had just come back from France.

'I'm glad you get it,' Katie said. 'I wondered – when I read it – was I being ridiculous?'

'No!' they chorused.

'Outrageous,' Dee repeated. 'And *fucking* unnecessary.'

'It's so – clinical,' Rosa said, reading the email again on her phone. Even Joe, she noted, had softened his last message more than that. *I'm sorry, Rosa. But it's for the best. X.* There was something exceptionally unsettling about seeing here, in black and white, how Katie-and-Chris had switched into something else, formal and cold.

'Right?' Katie exclaimed. 'I just – I don't get it. How you

239

can read someone – someone *pouring their heart* out like that . . .' Her voice cracked, and she steeled herself, and swallowed the rest of her cocktail.

The way it slid down her throat like oil, pooled across her torso like a smile. Oh it was *problematic*, wasn't it, the way alcohol burned off the hard edges of agony and replaced them with something bubbly and soft? Problematic, yes, but reliable too – a transportation and a lifting, as though she were filling with helium.

'How you can read an email like the one I sent him,' she continued, her voice steadier, 'and not be more – you know – *compassionate*?'

They nodded glumly.

'Maybe he thinks this *is* compassionate?' Liv ventured. 'You know – the tough love thing? He doesn't want to give you false hope, or something?'

'As a connoisseur of the tough love, I'm going to say that's too extreme,' Dee said.

'And it's just not like Chris, at all,' Katie said.

And that, *that* was the crystal at the centre of it all. What was 'like Chris' any more? He had slipped around the corner from her now; the door was closed. In those six weeks he could have been anywhere, done anything, become anyone. It was no longer her concern, *could* no longer be her concern, and that was what hurt most of all.

'So this is it,' she said, performatively decisive and putting her phone in her bag. 'Operation get-over-Chris. No looking back, or something. And it starts *now*. With another drink.'

'My round,' Dee said. 'Come and help carry, Liv?'

Rosa took Katie's hand. 'Sorry,' she said gently. Katie smiled in recognition.

'I know. But I mean it. Onwards! Talk to me about – hey, you're The Last Romantic, aren't you? Talk to me about meeting people, and flirting, and falling for people. All those things.'

Rosa tried to smile. 'That's the theory, isn't it? But seriously?' She scrolled through her phone to the messages with Marvin. The delicate dance of flirtation prior to their date. His tentative message *after* the date – want to go out again? Her attempt to be kind: *Hey Marvin. I had a really nice time too but I just don't think the chemistry was quite right. Sorry. Rx.* And his response: *I could show you a good time.* Followed by . . .

'I mean, it's not even a good picture, is it?' Katie said, tilting the phone left and right. 'What's with him just scooping it all out of the top of his jeans like that? And it's *blurry*.'

Rosa burst into laughter. 'Exactly. Aesthetics of the dick pic, hey? It's a bit *peekaboo*, isn't it?'

'What do you reckon makes for a good one?'

'Actually hard, obviously. Good lighting. It's all about the angles.' She reddened. 'Fuck, that's probably the sort of thing Ty wants me to write about.'

'You think?'

'Well, yeah. Funny, uplifting, adventurous, right? Some bright and breezy, woman about town persona. The person Dee tries to coach me to be, taking it easy, who cares, meet a man and move on. I know the theory. But . . .'

But it's not what I want. I resent being made to want it. She didn't describe the erratic thought processes she had gone through while crafting the feature. Because it would appear as a byline, wouldn't it – her name and her photo and her first-person narrative of how to make text and pictures have heart and soul. And maybe – just maybe – would Joe read it? And if he did, she wanted him to see her glowing, striding. She wanted him to think she was not thinking of him.

How absurd, then, that the article Ty brightly said would speak to Generation Z was intended in fact to speak only to her ex, to show him just how much she was dancing through her life without him.

'Do you want to be that person?'

Rosa exhaled deeply. 'Maybe. I mean – yes. Yes, of course I do. Dee has *fun*, right? She gets to meet interesting guys and have good sex and when she speaks to someone who's a creep she just laughs it off. There's advantages to the bright and breezy thing. And think how great it must be when you meet someone amazing, then! Like a brilliant surprise.'

Katie smiled gently. 'But that's the point, isn't it? You want to meet someone amazing. And there's nothing wrong with that.'

Rosa laughed shortly at herself.

'Mm. You know my friend Nina, her hen do's coming up? God – it's mortifying, but the way we used to chat about that when we were little. Who we'd meet. Who we'd end up with. Diet of too much Disney and old musicals. Anyway, you should see the phone chat, all these girls – yes, *girls* – organizing the weekend. It's so – *squealy*. It's all – bottles of *bubbles*, and colour schemes, and stupid games. It's like – is this seriously what matters most? But I think they mean it.

And I think Nina means it too. I think she's happy. And in some ways it must be nice, you know?'

'Mm,' Katie echoed. She picked up the phone again, scrutinizing the picture. 'It's weird, isn't it? I only saw one for nine years.'

Dee and Liv arrived, four more cocktails in hand and peals of laughter as soon as they saw what Katie was looking at.

'So, marks out of ten?'

'Oh, no more than four. If you can't even be bothered to put the thing in focus . . .'

'Maybe he was so excited his hand was shaking?'

'Christ.'

'And do you reckon he knew, when he sent it to you, that it would end up getting *dissected* like this?' Liv asked. 'Like, is the idea of a group looking at it all part of the turn-on? Or does he genuinely think that's going to entice you into a little back-and-forth?' Nikita swam into her head, and she smiled less secretly than she intended. They looked at her expectantly.

'Just – remembering.'

And they knew what she meant, and didn't ask her to elaborate, and she felt the quiet hot drumbeat they wouldn't know, couldn't know, of the lines of breasts and hips, shadows and light.

Then Katie suddenly formed an irrational smile, which became a giggle. Their faces swivelled to her.

'Sorry! Sorry. Oh god. I just – oh my god I just imagined Chris sending me a picture like that. I mean – Jesus.'

'What, you mean you never did the sexy pictures thing?' Dee asked, incredulous.

'Oh come on! Can you actually imagine straight, serious Chris getting his clothes off and figuring out the most erotic angle? When he knew I'd be coming home that night and stripping off and getting into bed with him anyway? He'd have found it – embarrassing, I reckon.'

The giggling became deep, boisterous, from-the-stomach laughter, bending and undulating in her seat, sweet pain across her torso, because it was ridiculous, wasn't it, to be sitting here discussing Chris in this insanely unerotic abstract? It was ridiculous that she would never see Chris's body like that again; it was ridiculous that she assumed Chris would never, could never – and yet how could she know, really? It was ridiculous that right now he could be turning this way and that in front of a mirror, performing for someone else in a way she had never known.

So her laughter was frantic but it was infectious too, and it took them all to a lighter, fizzier level. They drank the next round more quickly. Katie felt her head warm up and bubble, her body become more supple and springy, felt herself moving further and faster each time she threw her head back in laughter or placed a hand on her friend's arm for emphasis. She finished her drink while the others were halfway through theirs and skipped to the bar, feeling like she was levitating, sparkling. This was the magic, that the right women and the right music and the right drinks could hold you, lift you – that email from Chris was already seeming so much smaller, nearly inconsequential really, and certainly something she didn't have to think about now.

The conversation turned again, and they began discussing

the flat, and the living room without a window, and Katie's six-month tenancy with Rafee and Jack.

'You know,' she said, 'it really has worked out okay, hasn't it? Rafee and Jack. They are Nice Men.'

'Cheers to that!' Clinking, drinking, rolling thinking.

'But for the long haul. You're my loves. My *loves*.' She stretched her arms around Liv and Rosa, and Dee opposite leaned in for the embrace too.

'Four-bed could mean a house,' Dee said.

'True! House and garden and a white picket fence. Living the dream.'

'The dream of half our wages on rent!'

'Cheers!'

'Hey. I'm going optimistic. Six months – that's enough time for four promotions, right? Account director, senior designer, head of lifestyle, head of department?'

'Cheers to *that*!'

The music seemed louder and the bar seemed fuller and the night seemed *more*. Katie knew that they had come out because Chris had made her feel lead and stone but now she felt air and fire. People, so many people, jostling around their table and laughing and talking and bending to speak in people's ears with heat and hope. Her thoughts felt speeded up and loosened and lengthened, and then Liv was saying something, oh my god, don't look, oh my god.

They pushed their heads together conspiratorially, and Liv said, '*Felix* is here.'

'What? Seriously? Where?'

'Don't all look! Shh. Okay. Over by the bar, that pillar

with the mirrors. He's tall. Black shirt. And I told you – Marlon Brando.'

Attempting sober subtlety, they shifted their bodies and tilted their heads and saw him – yes – six foot four and dressed in black, broad-shouldered and chisel-cheekboned and scanning the bar in a hungry way. Dee whistled.

'Well, you weren't kidding. Hot and knows it.'

'I know. I know.' Liv sunk down in her chair. 'Just carry on talking. And don't tell me if you see him with someone. Or do. Maybe that's good. Yes, tell me. No, don't. Where were we? Rosa, what's your next byline going to be?'

'How about how to make hen dos an actual celebration of romance? Or do you think I'll just sound bitter?'

Rosa's half-wry, half-drunken amusement was matched by Dee and Katie, as Liv tried to cover her face with her hair and fanned herself and drained the rest of her drink.

'I'll go,' Rosa said. 'Help carry, Dee?'

It was busy enough now for Dee to wait behind Rosa rather than next to her, and as she swung her gaze back and forth across the crowd she suddenly found herself eye to eye with – well, someone. Someone who looked bizarrely out of place in his plaid shirt and scruffy hair, as though he should have been throwing hay bales around in a barn, or walking a dog along a clifftop. He grinned. 'Assessing the scene?' he asked.

'Something like that.'

'I genuinely just stopped myself from saying "Come here often?" What I mean is, has the Motown brought you here? Or just a pit stop on the way somewhere else?'

'We're here for the music. And the superfast bar service, obviously.'

'Of course. Who's "we"?'

'Friends.' Dee flicked her head to indicate Rosa.

'Well, me too. Heartbroken mate's been prescribed a lot of beer.'

Dee smiled despite herself. 'Sounds familiar.'

'Aha. But can I take it you're not the heartbroken one?'

'Nope. Heart of stone, me.'

He laughed, the kind of unselfconscious guffaw that should have been embarrassing but wasn't, because he wasn't. He extended a hand. 'I'm Josh.'

'Nice to meet you, Josh.'

'You know, traditionally this is when you tell me your name.'

A quick exhale. 'I'm Dee.'

'Dee. Nice. Short for . . . ?'

'Just Dee.'

'Cool. And what's the story of your life, Dee?'

'What?'

'You know. Who are you, what do you do, cats or dogs, political persuasion, going anywhere nice for your holidays this year?'

'Wow. That's – wow.'

He was looking expectantly at her though, and she rolled her eyes. 'That's a pretty deep dive for a bar with a sticky dancefloor and two-for-one cocktails.'

'Well, you know. Asking if I can get you a drink is stupid when you're clearly waiting for your friend, and I've already

247

tried to bypass the "Come here often?" thing. We could talk about music but given we've both come to the same night I think that's just going to be us agreeing with each other.'

'Fine. Cats, then.'

'Cats! Wow. See, that's a bold move for a meet-cute. Everyone loves dogs, but people who hate cats *really* hate cats.'

'Everyone does not love dogs,' Dee said. 'Everyone thinks they should *say* they love dogs because of the man's best friend, loyal and lovable thing.'

'Aha. Whereas you . . . ?'

'Dogs are obsessed with their owners no matter what. You basically feed it and walk it and it thinks you're god. Cats are independent. Aloof, even. So if your cat is into you, you really feel like you've earned it, you know?'

He laughed again, his eyes crinkling. 'I see your point. But do you actually have any?'

'Not in London.'

'But in . . . ?'

'Brighton.'

'Nice! So what are they called?'

'What?'

'The cats!'

'Oh. Audre and Simone. There was Betty as well, but she died.'

She looked hard at him. His eyes were still crinkled. 'Got it,' he said.

Rosa turned, first two drinks in hand, and passed them to Dee, processing the scene in a few seconds, and smiling.

'Have a good night, Josh,' Dee said.

'He was cute,' Rosa said as they walked back to the table. Dee shrugged. 'He was checking out the bar for the nearest person to hit on. Not the point of tonight, is it?'

Next round and the bar hit critical mass for dancing. Katie closed her eyes as she wound her body round and around the music. God, music was good. Dancing was good. Drinking was good. They were out because of something Chris had sent her, weren't they, but the more she moved and drank and moved and drank the less important that seemed. Oh, the way she floated and flew.

She opened her eyes and felt warmer still, the gorgeous familiarity of her friends, the ways they danced too. How well she recognized Rosa's bounce and Liv's sway – and oh, Dee was talking to someone, someone who looked bizarrely like he had been transplanted from a country pub, someone who was speaking into her ear, and she was rolling her eyes at him but also doing a small secret smile. The man took something out of his pocket and gave it to her before making his way back through the bodies.

'Who was that?!'

'This guy. Josh –' Dee looked at the card he had given her – 'Josh Clancy, apparently. Furniture designer.'

'That's cool!'

'What's not cool is giving someone your business card. What is this, 1995?' But she slipped it into her bag all the same.

They had moved away from rounds, now, and Liv was pushing and sliding her way through the crowd to the bar, what next, gin, tequila? She took a few seconds to process the hand that gripped her arm but then turned in furious indignation, and found herself face to face with a familiar smirking smile and a sudden need to act casual-surprised.

'Felix.'

'Liv. Fancy seeing you here.'

'Well, you know. Great minds think alike, or something?'

'Now I know you're not a smoker, but how about keeping me company for some unfresh air?'

She rolled her eyes and knew she was going to follow. Smoking or otherwise, Liv had always taken a perverse delight in the wall of contrast that hit you on exiting a bar or club. The winters in Manchester had been so cold, and their outfits so tiny, that going for a cigarette had sometimes felt like switching dimensions; the sudden blast of a different kind of air, the dramatic shift in volume and pitch. She liked the way clubs and bars sounded from just outside, muffled bass like heartbeats, and the way you felt simultaneously in and out.

She leaned against the wall, watching as Felix deftly rolled his cigarette, and as her brain undulated through several fiercely strong drinks she tried to lecture herself, repeat a mantra. *Felix is my client. I am a professional. I want to protect my job. Felix is my client. I am a professional. I want to protect my job.*

'So,' he said. 'Do you come here often?'

She burst into laughter, and he raised an eyebrow, smiling crookedly.

'Actually we do,' she said. 'My friends and I. I think it reminds us of nights out when we were younger.'

'Because you're truly ancient now?'

'Exactly. So anyway, how's it all going? We've got a meeting soon, right? Updates on the big research project?'

He rolled his eyes. 'I make a point of not discussing work at weekends.'

'Right. Well, we were talking about dick pics before, if you have an opinion on that instead?'

This time he raised an eyebrow, and his smile got smirkier, and Liv knew there was a voice somewhere in her head warning her, but another one giggling and spinning faster and faster.

'Yeah. You know, trying to figure out the appeal. When men send them to women they don't know. I mean, is it like a form of digital sexual assault? Like flashing? Is that seriously what does it for a lot of guys? Or do they really think it's going to lead to something more? And if so, where's the *foreplay*, you know? Women do this shit *much* better, let me tell you.'

'Well,' he said, 'I can't argue with that.'

The warning voice was getting louder but so was the spinning voice. *That job. That fucking job I've fallen into. Why aren't I writing columns about my life, seeing my name next to my photo? Rosa, bloody Rosa with her house in the suburbs and her unpaid internships while I had to get on a graduate scheme and rent a tiny bedroom and why do I think 'had' to, anyway, why do any of us 'have' to do anything? Why do I act like I don't have choices? Is this all there is, is this all there is?* The air was getting colder and Liv gave herself a shake which made her head ping and said I'd better head back inside, have a good night.

Back to the bar, vodka tonic please, thanks, back to my

friends, dancing dancing. She threw her arm around Rosa's shoulders and said I love you, you know, and I'm so proud of you, the writing you're doing. Oh thank you darling, that means a lot, I find it so hard, you know, don't want to be this dating anthropologist person, I love you too.

The world is shaking stars and popping lights. Everything is tipping backwards and forwards. A thousand conversations just out of earshot, a hot arm on my arm on your arm, sticky fabric scuffed shoes where's my coat? Taxi taxi time to get a taxi. Who's here? Liv's at a table with Felix, his hand is snaking up her top, her face his face oh they're kissing, oh she's smiling waving, come back to mine he's saying okay yes yes I will yes. Dee's got water from the bar, she's drinking a pint of water, good woman smart woman, but her head is pounding spinning swimming, business card in her purse, I'd like to go out with you sometime, haha who says that, no no, you're all the same, all the same he might be fun, bit of fun. Rosa's in the taxi got her phone out trying to focus, double triple, everything moving blurring where's Joe's name, Izzy Jan JOE yes yesss *Joe I misssyou love u sohad dancngs plea e xxxxzn*. Katie's out first, keys keys urgh this new door so stiff sometimes do the thing where it lifts in the lock okay yes yes be quiet boys sleeping men sleeping urgh stomach stomach going to be sick bathroom bathroom. Rafee's here, eeshk big night then you okay glass of water don't worry I can clean it up, no, NO, oh god I'm so sorry I'm so sorry I'm crying I'm sobbing.

Drinking

Are you a drinker? Booze can be nectar and venom. Alcohol can guide you through heartbreak like an old friend – and then it can trip you over so very dramatically.

I mean, you know the advice already. Know your limits, drink a glass of water between orders, don't mix your medicines. Failing that:

* *Leave a two-litre bottle of water by your bed before you go out (a pint glass is never enough and you'll knock it over when you're getting undressed anyway). Painkillers too.*
* *Make sure you have the following in the freezer: oven chips, potato waffles, smiley faces, hash browns – every frozen potato product you can muster. Coke in the fridge, Berocca in the cupboard.*
* *Write your ex's number on a piece of paper, and leave it tucked in the bottom of a drawer. Delete it from your phone until tomorrow.*
* *If you can't bring yourself to brush your teeth, gargle mouthwash and that will do. Wash your face before you go to sleep. Worst comes to worst, smear a baby wipe followed by the contents of a Vitamin E capsule over your face.*

Chapter Sixteen

SUNDAY AFTERNOONS

Liv opened one eye and winced. She was lying on her side, her arm pinned underneath her body so that her hand had gone numb, and she could feel a slightly sticky, slightly crusty texture running from the edge of her mouth and up her cheek into her hair. Her mouth felt unspeakably dry, and her skull was springing, pulsating. The high-pitched echo of last night's music was ringing in her ears.

Only then did she process that the view in front of her was not her own bedroom but an entirely different one, with a cold grey wall across which a sharp line of sunlight was being cast through a half-open black Roman blind. On the floor was her own sparkling sequined top and her black shorts though not her leather jacket, where could that be? And behind her . . . she squeezed her eye shut again. *Fuck.*

Felix made a generic sighing grumbling noise and rolled over, tugging the duvet from her shoulders. Liv felt horrifyingly naked. She tried to ascertain whether he was asleep. His breathing was the rumbly, sticky, hungover kind, but it seemed even enough. After a few minutes, holding her breath, she eased her arm out from under her body, biting her lip as the blood rushed back to her fingers. Then one leg, then the other. Painstakingly sliding herself out of – oh god oh god.

As she pulled herself up to sit on the edge of the bed, her head began throbbing even more powerfully. She desperately wanted – well, lots of things, but water first. There wasn't a glass to be seen.

Even now she didn't recognize the room particularly – partly because it was so generically chrome-and-grey-and-white-furniture – partly because her brain was still stretching and squeaking to try to recall . . . they'd got a taxi, hadn't they? She had vague memories of his hands on her thigh, up her top, pushing into each other, a frenetic kind of wrestling. She screwed up her eyes and swallowed once, twice. Saliva was pooling in her mouth. She swallowed again, and forced several large inhales and exhales.

She couldn't see her knickers anywhere so pulled on the shorts directly, wincing again as she buttoned. Everything around her crotch felt raw. She hadn't been wearing a bra, so pulled the sequined top straight back on. It looked incongruous in the morning light, like a Christmas tree in July. Then she stumbled through the half-open door, refusing to look back at the bed, and found her way into the main room of the flat.

Like the bedroom, it was grey and white and shiny and harsh. There was a long low sofa with chrome feet, Felix's black shirt from the night before strewn across the back of it and one of the cushions on the floor. There was a glass coffee table, also with chrome feet, two tumblers of whisky and an overflowing ashtray. She instantly connected the harsh crackle in the back of her throat and retched.

Sink. Glasses. Felix's cupboards were the bare kind she recognized of a certain type of man who lived alone and didn't particularly care about making the place homely. Three plates, two mugs. Felix was not a man who had people round for dinner. He was not a man who fed people. She picked up one of the whisky glasses, rinsed it as thoroughly as she could manage and poured and drank, poured and drank.

After three glasses of water she was feeling better enough to move on from a pounding head and nauseous stomach to a different kind of sickness, something deeper and more profound. What had she done?

Well, had sex with Felix, clearly – but what was this going to *mean*? The night was such a confusing mosaic in her mind, but she knew she had pulled him towards her in the taxi, pressing herself against his erection. She knew she had unbuttoned his shirt and lifted it over his head, and she knew she had pulled him frantically into his bedroom, and she knew she had bucked and rocked and moaned and oh god she was screwing her eyes shut again.

Time to go home. Definitely time to go home. What was missing? Handbag, jacket, shoes. And underwear. Fuck.

Her shoes – she breathed thanks to something that she had worn flats – were underneath the coffee table. Her handbag was dangling on the back of the chair and by some miracle her phone and keys and bank cards were still inside it. Her jacket was still nowhere to be seen. Had she left it in the bar? And as for her knickers, after feeling under the sofa cushion and retching again, she had to admit defeat.

'Morning,' made her jump and her stomach fold again, as Felix walked into the room. He half sauntered, half staggered to the kettle, and after switching it on turned to face her with an amused, almost quizzical expression. He had pulled on a pair of grey tracksuit bottoms and looked – well, *delicious* – but also excruciating. It was as though he had peeled off the upper layer of her skin. He had bitten on her nipple and she had scraped her fingernails down his back.

'Do you know where I put my jacket?'

'Hm. There's a hook by the front door. Not sure you had one, to be honest.'

'Okay. And – um.' She decided that asking if he had seen her knickers was impossible.

'I'd offer you breakfast, but.'

It was a 'but' that was intended to imply that he simply didn't have anything in, or had plans that he needed to head off to in half an hour, while really meaning, Liv decided, that he wanted her out of the flat so he could lie in bed with his laptop and possibly have a wank. Well, that was fine.

'Oh no, that's okay. I'm not a hangover breakfast person. I need to head home now.'

She scooped up her bag and held it against her stomach. 'So – er – I guess I'll see you soon?'

An expression of something approaching panic rolled across his face, and she internally rolled her eyes. 'I mean at work.'

'Right! Of course. The meeting. Absolutely.'

He walked towards her then, and put his hands on her

cheeks in a way that felt unbearably tender and out of place. It was a gesture of intimacy and affection. It was the sort of gesture Nikita would have made.

'So, thanks for the dick pic lesson, anyway,' he said, and she felt another wave of excruciation as she recalled encouraging him to stand, pose, *present* while she pretended to take photos with the air. *Click, click, click*. 'You've got my number. Your turn now?' He didn't kiss her. 'I think I need a few more hours. The front door'll lock behind you.'

'Cool. Thanks.'

Her jacket, as it turned out, was not on the hook by the door. She looked down at her sparkling top and short shorts, tiptoed back into the living room and whipped Felix's black shirt off the sofa. Buttoning it up she looked a little like an eccentric art student, but at least it covered the sequins. When she got home she could throw it in the bin.

*

Katie woke with an acrid sourness in her mouth, and a thumping anxiety in her chest. Her hair was smeared across her face, delicately fragranced with her own vomit. Her stomach twisted and pounded. She gingerly pulled herself into a seated position, and the world swam. Jesus. *Jesus*.

It was a hangover that took her back in time, leapfrogging Chris and transporting her to Manchester. Mornings after in a couple were companionable, if ever so slightly inflected with annoyance. A morning after in a new houseshare . . . she felt a nauseating combination of guilt, embarrassment and nostalgia. Eventually, she put on her baggiest hoodie and thickest socks and hobbled to the kitchen. Rafee was buttering toast, and gave her a remarkably understanding smile.

'Hey,' she croaked.

'Hey!' There was perhaps a slightly artificial brightness to his voice, she thought, and no wonder, poor guy, when she had first vomited and then sobbed in front of him – but he was also proffering a cup of tea, and asking her if she wanted toast, and when she shook her head he said, 'There are two kinds of hangover, right? The eat-through-it kind and the never-eating-again kind?'

'Absolutely. Listen – I'm really sorry.'

'Don't worry about it. We've all been there.'

'Well, maybe. Still don't think I've lived here long enough for you to have to – oh god.' She pulled a chair out from the little dining table, and buried her head in her hands.

After a few moments, to her surprise she felt a hand gently rubbing her back. 'Thank you,' she mumbled into her hands. 'That feels nice.'

'Ah, you can't see what I look like. Awkward central. Heterosexual man, physical contact – you know how it goes.'

She giggled gently.

'D'you want to watch TV?'

'Yes, please.'

Rafee took the armchair and Katie sprawled on the sofa and they aimlessly channel-hopped through cookery and gardening and politics. After a bit – as though he had been building up to it, perhaps – Rafee said, 'So was it an ex thing? Or just a too-much-to-drink thing?'

Katie picked at her sleeve. 'Both, I think.' She hesitated. 'I mean both, definitely. And they're related. Drinking makes you feel better and then it makes you feel worse, right?'

'Definitely. I got made redundant a few years ago. I was working for a smaller charity then and they lost some of their funding. Anyway, I came home with a six-pack and a bottle of whisky. Started off toasting how it was going to be the best thing that had ever happened to me, ended up at 3 a.m. wailing about how I'd wasted my life working in the third sector. Pretty bold take, given that I was twenty-three at the time.'

Katie giggled into her hoodie.

'And it all worked out.'

'What? Oh – yeah. New job three months later, and that's where I am now. I mean, I still worry I'm wasting my life, but doesn't everyone?'

'I don't think it's a waste, what you do. Far from it.'

'That's kind. We're at that point, aren't we, where the ones who did law and accountancy and management consulting have really taken off?'

'That's true,' Katie said and pictured Chris. Quickly she added, 'But that's just money. It's not soul.'

He looked at her in amusement. 'Did you always want to be a teacher, then?'

'Pretty much. I mean, I wasn't clever enough to be, like, a professional historian. And I like kids. Not that "kids" is really the right word for a bunch of sixteen-year-olds. But. They're funny, and they surprise you, and the cheesy line about making a difference to young lives is true.'

He nodded and smiled.

'Morning.' Jack had staggered into the room now, wearing a Pacman T-shirt and tracksuit bottoms, rubbing his eyes under his glasses. 'Hey, did Rafee tell you? Your edits to my profile worked like a charm!'

'I heard! How'd it go?'

'Good, I think. You know, nice chats and all. Stayed 'til closing. I asked if she'd like to go out again, she said yes – that all sounds promising, right?'

'Definitely.'

They settled from there into a comfortable lazy Sunday. Mugs of tea, sandwiches, slow conversation. Katie sent a series of green-faced emojis to the group chat – and Rosa responded with a list of suggested activities so precise that Katie carefully transcribed them into the heartbreak hand-book: music, good food, bad television. The food, in particular, came with a list of examples.

Rafee and Jack asked if they could commandeer the TV for a game. Of course, of course, Katie rushed to say, I want to read my book for a bit anyway, but her eyes kept falling off the end of sentences and she realized she had got to the bottom of the first page without taking in a single word.

And so she curled on the sofa scrolling through her phone, doing precisely what she knew she should not. She read and reread her email, and Chris's terse reply, and tried to swallow the rock that kept forming at the back of her throat. She visited the hotel website, the one she had alighted on after so many articles and forums and weighings-up, knowing that Chris would be picky about things like *quality* and *ratings* while she wanted a view that would make her heart sing and walks with waves crashing nearby. The same white muslin, the same two wine glasses on the terrace, the same apricot light across the water. She tried not to think about whether Chris had gone alone, but she was back on the company website now, back to Nat's picture, that easy confidence, that laughter.

Because there was a particular pain to this time of the week, now. That ragged breath between Saturday adrenaline and Monday bracing; that anxiety-ridden expanse in which there were so many possibilities for what one *could* be doing, and so many ways of imagining what *they* were doing. Sunday afternoons were for comfort, and familiarity, and bolstering – and the person who once offered all those things was gone.

So she rotated, so she agonized, until her phone flashed with another message from Rosa and, wild-eyed, she scrambled to her feet, explaining that she needed to go to her friends immediately.

*

Rosa had awoken feeling equally unwell, but cossetted by pyjamas, and her own soft empty bed, and the knowledge that she just had to slope through to the kitchen to get a pint of water and make a cup of tea. She pulled on her slippers and her dressing gown, and dragged the Hangover Blanket through with her. The flat was quiet and still. Of course – Liv had gone back with Felix. Dee's bedroom door was open, which meant she was out for a run. Machine.

Katie messaged while she was waiting for the kettle to

boil – a row of cartoon faces with progressively sicker expressions – and, smiling, she responded with a list of suggestions. Sunday hangover dishes was a food category she had perfected some years previously. Then, in a burst of horror and fear and shame and *please please let it not be that bad*, she realized that Joe's name had risen to the top of her messages. She clicked, she scrolled, oh no, oh no.

Joe I misssyou love u sohad dancngs plea e xxxxzn
Fuck.

She scanned it over and over and tried to imagine how it could possibly be read as anything other than what it was; a drunken, sloppy, messy pouring-out of unrequited everything. She made the tea and curled on the sofa like a small lost animal, and read it and read it. And then she processed the two blue ticks. So Joe had read it too.

She checked the timings. Message sent: 01:47. Message read: 08:35. Two hours ago. Long enough ago to suggest that he wasn't going to reply, especially as he was last online fifteen minutes ago – and then suddenly, shockingly, now.

She dropped the phone as if electrocuted. Ridiculous, she knew, particularly as there was no reason to suggest that Joe was looking at the same message at the same time, but somehow the possibility that he was felt viscerally sharp, like a needle joining them through space. As though he could see her bleary, swollen face through his own phone, and his expression would be full of pity.

And her. *Her.* Rosa was horribly aware of the things they had written into the heartbreak handbook. *Remember that any contact you have may no longer be private.* So. Had Joe woken, rolled his eyes, and passed his phone to *her* to read? Had she passed it back to him, shaking her head? *Maybe you need to block her.* Or *I just feel sorry for her. Come back to bed.*

She burrowed her way deeper into the sofa and the blanket, and turned on the television. This was how Dee found her twenty minutes later.

'Ouch. Head or stomach?'

'Both. And I've done a Bad Thing.'

'What . . . Oh! You were texting – in the taxi – shit, did you say you were messaging Joe?'

Rosa buried her head in the blanket. 'It's bad. It's so bad, Dee. And he's read it, and he hasn't replied, and now it's just *there*, out in the ether. You know when something's just *dangling*? I mean, at least if he sent me a really angry message then there'd be, like, a denouement to the thing. But – gah. Look.'

Dee read the message, head tilted to one side. 'Joe, I miss you, love you, so had? So *hard*? Dancing, please? Ouch.'

'It's not good, is it?'

'Well . . .' Dee sat down, considering. 'I mean, is it anything he doesn't already know?'

Rosa grimaced. 'I guess not.'

'I mean, big picture. He's the one who – who did the *actual* Bad Thing, right? He knows that he hurt you. Your message doesn't even attack him for that. It's just – love.'

This was true, but it was still unbearable. Rosa shook her head and tried not to cry. 'It just feels so . . .' She sighed. 'I don't want him to see me weak, you know?'

'I know. Believe me, I know.'

'What about you, anyway? Have you heard from the furniture dude?'

'What? Oh. No. I mean – he doesn't have my number.'

'But you're going to message him, right?'

'Oh, I don't know.'

'Why not?!' Rosa cried out passionately. 'Please, please give me some faith that there are still nice men to be met in bars?'

'He seemed almost *too* nice, you know?'

'Oh, come on! After all the lectures you give me about bright and light and see what happens! Please message him? For me?!'

After a brief face-off Dee shook her head in wry amusement and fetched both her phone and the neat little card. It was dark brown with white writing; unfussy but slightly unusual. Josh Clancy. Furniture Designer. 'Fine. *Hey Josh. This is Dee from last night. The cat lady, apparently.* That satisfy you?'

'Perfect. Now go and get your duvet. You're getting sucked into this hangover whether you like it or not.'

After another twenty minutes there was a scrabbling, rattling sound at the door and Liv walked into the room, dangling her bag from one hand, a black shirt from the other and with her hair and makeup magnificently dishevelled.

'Morning!'

'Is it? My phone died. I didn't even know where his flat *was*. I had to get two buses and then the Tube. Plenty of time to think about what a stupid, stupid mistake that was.'

Dee made a dismissive noise. 'Don't torture yourself. Men

have been doing this for ever. That's a pretty sexist double standard if you're saying Felix can have casual sex without consequences, and you can't.'

Liv considered. 'But that being the theory doesn't make it true,' she said. 'We've got a meeting in a couple of weeks. You know what it's like. There's going to be all this tension. I'm going to be sitting there thinking *you've seen me naked, you've seen me naked*, wondering if he's going to make some snide comment, some horrible joke – god, worrying that he's going to have said something to his colleague, even. Because feminism aside, we *know* that something like this is still a story he can show off about, like a fucking *conquest*, whereas I'm the one who's going to have crossed a line, been unprofessional, can't control myself. And it's going to make me nervous, and shit at my job, and this is our star client, *my* star client.'

Anxiety was buzzing in her stomach as she spoke, but so too was something else, something unexpected, something she only realized was true in the moment she said it. *Our star client. My star client. Yes, a client doing valuable research and telling interesting stories – stories that I'm helping to shape. It's good work, it's fun work, it's stimulating work – and I don't want to lose it.*

Was there such a thing as your work life flashing before you? She recalled that younger version of herself, sitting in interviews with a falsely enthusiastic expression and a cheap dress, knowing that this wasn't really *her*, that this was a stopgap, something to pay the rent amid tall buildings and crowded clubs. The promotions and pay rises that came like clockwork, each making something a little more concrete and something else a little more distant. How she had built up something between *me* and *my job* that she had always assumed was a guard – but had it been keeping her out of something instead of inside it?

She looked at Rosa, curled up as tightly as she could, tear streaks across her face, and felt a rush of love and sympathy. How she envied her; how she admired her. Then Felix's face flashed before her, his eyes shut, his mouth in something like a grimace, sweating. She tried to shake it from her head as she folded herself next to Rosa and stroked her face, you special woman, you brilliant friend.

They sank into the half-comfortable, half-anxious fug of Sunday afternoon, ate crisps and watched things which made them laugh. The air felt hot and heavy. The demands of the following morning began to cling to them as the sun sank.

Dee's phone vibrated – she read the message and rolled her eyes. Rosa, cackling, grabbed the phone from her and read the message from Josh aloud, but before they could dissect it, the phone was vibrating again. Mel's image filled the screen, hands meeting under her chin in mock posturing. Rosa passed it back to Dee, it's your mum calling.

She answered lightly, hey mama, what's up, and then she frowned, and Rosa and Liv were looking at her, mouthing everything okay? And she frowned some more, and stood up, and walked into the kitchen, sliding the glass behind her. Rosa and Liv watched her as she brought one hand to her waist, and then her head. She was walking, and then she was icy still.

Sunday Afternoons

Sunday afternoons are perhaps the most painful time of the week to be heartbroken. You will imagine that the rest of the world is cocooned on sofas with their other halves (and what a horrendous phrase that is), or else filling their days with more productivity, more adventure, more good deeds, more happiness. The Monday blues are creeping in and if you went out last night, you're feeling it.

Artificial uplifts include: Music (remember your Happy Songs playlist? Get it going). Good food.* Bad television. A walk. Painting your nails. A bath and a book.

If you make a list of what you want to do this Sunday before this Sunday then you can sidestep the paralysis of indecision, and gain the good vibes of 'I've done what I wanted to do'. This list does not need to include running a marathon or baking cookies.

Remember that the wide-open everything of your week-ends can, in fact, be one of the most liberating and glorious things about being single. You don't need to compromise your plans around somebody else. You can lie on the sofa eating instant noodles and reading cheap paperbacks. You can slouch round the park in your oldest, grubbiest, holiest leggings. You can listen to true crime podcasts about grisly murders. You can watch nineties sitcoms on repeat for the five millionth time. You can wander around an art gallery and mournfully remember how the TV shows of your youth promised you'd meet your spouse there (you won't). You can paddle in the sea. You can sing.

But above all: go to sleep. Tomorrow will feel different.

* *Rosa's failsafe hangover cures:*
- * *Two aspirin and a pint of Diet Coke.*
- * *Sparkling water and lime.*
- * *Cheese toasties with crispy chilli oil.*
- * *Stale croissants with melted ham and cheddar.*
- * *Instant noodles with kimchi and hot sauce.*
- * *Shakshuka.*
- * *Pickled onion crisps.*

Chapter Seventeen

THE UNEXPECTED

Dee would not remember, later, whether it was seconds or years between the phone call and the train to Brighton. It was dark and then it was light. If there was sleep she did not recall it. If there were dreams they would only have been of one thing. She packed her bags blind. She hugged her friends pale. She lived a thousand lives in the hour-long journey, Sussex in spring spitefully green and verdant outside the window.

Her mother teasing her hair with a pink plastic comb, her hands like an acorn's cup around her skull.

Her mother making fish finger sandwiches and swaying her hips in time with the radio.

Her mother walking with her, hand in hand, to school, then waving at her from the front door, then nodding to her over a coffee. The string that connected them pooling out as she grew – ever elastic, ever steel.

Her mother listening to her bubble about her job, and boil about Leo. Her mother telling her she was strong. Darling star, darling star.

Was this what it meant to see her life flashing before her

eyes? The vividness was astounding. Twenty-nine years of the tightest, fiercest, brightest love. Why had she not spent every second of every day with her mother? Why had she not drunk her in harder? Why had she never considered the possibility of her absence?

Her phone vibrated and she ignored it. There was nothing to be done. Either it was Katie, or Liv, or Rosa, offering her their thoughts, their affection, their love, more of everything they had wrapped her in the previous evening as she gasped on the floor. Or it was Simon, demanding to know why she wasn't at work, a barb undercut with quizzical concern. Or it was Josh, pleasantly inviting her for a drink, calm and clear and open, and of a bitterly different world.

Or it was her mother, checking her arrival time, trying to make things sound normal, when nothing could ever be normal again.

I didn't mention. I didn't want to worry you. But I've had a biopsy now. Darling, they've confirmed that it's cancer.

The white noise; the pins and needles that stabbed her forearms as she tried to hold onto the phone. The vague awareness that she had dropped it, that Rosa had slid the door open and was running in to catch her; that Liv was speaking to her mother and gripping her hand.

They think they've caught it quite early. They think it's quite aggressive.

'Quite.' A word used to denote lack of commitment, banality. A word intended here to make the outrageously appalling seem contained.

Dee screwed her eyes shut and imagined herself into the

previous day, the innocent purity of *before the phone call.* How foolish she had been, worrying about the lies Josh might tell, or how best to impress Margot, or how to shave a second or two off her mile pace. The ridiculousness of those concerns. Her life had been perfect, and she had never realized.

An eternal microsecond later the train pulled into Brighton, and she saw her mother before they stopped. She looked exactly the same. The crinkles at the edges of her eyes; the purple streak through her hair; the orange bangles. Dee realized with a horrible shock that she had been expecting the colours to be muted, her mother to somehow, already, look different, drained. But she was the rainbow she had always been.

They tumbled into one another's arms on the platform. Darling star, my darling, I'm sorry to have worried you, don't be stupid, you should have told me before the biopsy, I'm not leaving. I'm not leaving. Dee was horrified to feel a tingling at the corners of her eyes, and she blinked ferociously.

'We can walk, right?' she asked, and her mother cackled reassuringly.

'I'm not quite on my knees yet. Of course we can walk.'

It took forty minutes, as it always did, and Dee made her mother unpack every detail throughout. When did you notice the lump and does it hurt? How long did it take to get the appointment? What did the first doctor say? And the second?

'Let this be a lesson,' Mel said breezily. 'You do check your breasts, don't you darling?'

'Of course I do,' Dee lied.

'Well then. It was exactly as you'd expect. I noticed a lump a few weeks ago. In the shower, actually. Did you know that's one of the best places to do your check? Soap, water, slippery. Anyway. Booking in at the GP took a week or so, and they referred me to the hospital for the biopsy. It's all been very efficient, really. They called me in as soon as they got the results, and we discussed treatment straight away. And I called you, of course.'

'So what happens next?'

'A mastectomy,' her mother said. She managed, grotesquely, to laugh.

'A mastectomy?' Dee repeated, pathetically. The sun was shining.

'That's right. It's the only sensible option, apparently. But it should mean that afterwards, I'll be totally free of it.'

'Unless it comes back,' Dee said. She snapped her hand to her mouth, horrified. Her mother made a noise she couldn't place, and nodded slowly.

'Unless it comes back.'

Dee waited for her to continue, but she was gazing at the sky. 'What a lovely day.'

Dee wondered fleetingly when she had last left London, and remembered the walk in the countryside. An escape into space, that had been – a change of scene. How carefully Katie was moving through her pain.

'Okay,' she said. 'So when is the operation?'

'Two or three weeks, they said. Can you believe that? How quick it is?'

'It's amazing. And how long will recovery be?'

273

'Perhaps four to six weeks. I'm relatively young, of course. And strong. So they said it should be straightforward.'

'Okay. Well I'm not going anywhere.'

'Darling.'

'I mean it. I'll work from home. Your home. Our home. I'll call them. They can courier a computer or something. I'm not going back. I'm not leaving you.'

'That's completely unnecessary. Alicia next door knows everything that's happening. She's going to look after me. Yolande and Kim and Rachel – they're all ready to step up. I'm not going to be able to move for visitors and cups of tea and – and bloody *fruit* baskets. You don't need to put your life on hold around me. You should be with Liv and Rosa. And how's Katie, by the way? Breakups are difficult, aren't they?'

'Stop it!' Dee exclaimed. She stopped walking, and clapped her palm to her forehead. Her mother stopped a few paces along, and turned.

'Please,' Dee said. Her voice was hoarse. 'Please don't make things normal.'

Her mother stared at her for several minutes. Then she nodded, and placed her arm around her daughter's shoulder. 'Okay. Let's go home.'

Yes, Dee thought. *Please. Let me go home.*

The Unexpected

Can you protect yourself from heartbreak?

You can try. You can be strong; you can be steel. You can grit your teeth; you can rationalize. You can read about a thousand terrible heartbreaks and learn a lesson from each; the warning signs, the weaknesses.

You can hide yourself away; you can cut your strings. You can stand alone; you can stand apart.

But it will never be enough. There will always be something that can floor you.

All hearts can break.

Chapter Eighteen

NEW LOOKS

*A*re *you home? I need to come round RIGHT NOW. This is an emergency. Xxx*

The message arrived in a group without Dee, created to arrange her last birthday drinks and now horrifyingly repurposed. For the past few days it had flickered with nervous questions and suggestions and helplessness, links to pages about operation recovery times and luxury ready meals. Rosa replied: *I am. Liv's working late. What's happened? Xxx*

Twenty minutes later, frantic knocking. Rosa ran to answer, what's wrong, you didn't say, oh, *oh*. It was at once immediately apparent and so shocking she needed a moment to blink and process. Katie's glorious long mermaid hair had been replaced by what could only be described as a pixie cut.

For a moment, Rosa was speechless. The rest of them had experimented with their hair over the years, even if the multicoloured strips and undercuts had gradually been replaced with subtler highlights and dip-dye. But Katie's hair was her *thing*. Bouncy, beachy, bright blonde waves down her back since the day they met.

'It suits you,' Rosa said as she steered Katie onto the sofa. And she meant it; the feathery, boyish style accentuated Katie's cheekbones and suggested the sixties. But Katie was shaking her head.

'I cannot believe – I *cannot believe* I've done this. Get dumped, cut all my hair off. I may as well go cat shopping tomorrow.'

Rosa laughed and tried to turn it into a cough. 'So what was it – a spur-of-the-moment thing?'

'Kind of. There's one of those training salons near school. They're often looking for people to be models. And I just thought – well, why not? It'll make me feel good, right?' *It'll make me feel good to get an expensive haircut on the cheap, because I can't get Nat out of my head and I bet she gets a proper cut every six weeks and does a deep-conditioning treatment every weekend and is basically a paragon of aggravatingly expensive self-care.*

'Anyway, I started off thinking just a trim, you know, but then I thought Chris only ever knew me with this stupid long hair, why don't I just get rid of it, cut it off, new woman and all that. And then I was thinking a bob, and then there were all these pictures, and women there who looked like supermodels, and I think I just got caught up in it. You know how it is?' *Trying to make yourself into how you hope you could be. Trying to make myself more beautiful than Chris could ever have imagined.*

Rosa nodded. 'Oh, that all makes sense. Don't beat yourself up, honestly.'

'Seriously, what was I thinking? I need like, a chaperone.

Someone who signs off on my life decisions while my head's in a state.'

'God, don't. Nina's literally entrusted her maid of honour with something like this. All of these grandiose texts about how she's *there to keep my feet on the ground when my head's too wrapped up in table plans!!!* I think it's something she's seen in a film.'

'Oh that's right, the hen's next weekend, right?'

'*Bride tribe incoming,*' Rosa recited, feeling something between incredulity and pity.

Katie ran her hands aggressively through her hair. 'I can't *believe* I've done this,' she repeated.

'It'll be the change that's freaking you out, not the actual cut. It must feel so different.'

'You're telling me. I feel like I've lost about a stone. And it's *cold.*'

'You just need to get used to it.'

Katie met Rosa's anxious look. 'Oh, thank you for trying. But seriously? This was a huge mistake, right?'

Rosa was saved from having to answer by Liv's arrival, looking almost as dramatic. She was wearing a black blazer over a white shirt and a pair of billowing dark green palazzo pants, underneath which, judging by her height, was a pair of towering heels.

She took two steps into the room and froze. 'Oh my *god.* You look incredible!'

Katie managed a nervous smile. 'Thanks. You too.'

'Seriously!' Liv dropped her work bag and leapt across the room, holding Katie by the shoulders and turning her left and right with rough and tactile intimacy. 'I can't believe you didn't tell us beforehand! What a transformation!'

'I guess – it was a bit of an in-the-moment thing.'

'Well, I salute you. Great choice.'

Katie tried to nod.

'No, no, I get that it's a big change,' Liv said. 'You just need to get used to it.'

'That's what Rosa said. You don't think it's a raging cliché? Newly single, new hair?'

'Course it's a cliché. But for a reason! Shedding old skins and all that.'

Katie shook her head again. Could this be right? Chris had enjoyed her long hair, it was true. He had enjoyed scooping it on top of her head and letting it drop and swing; feeling the weight of it in his hands; twisting strands around each other (despite her efforts, he never learned to do a proper plait). There was something doll-like and protective, now that she thought about it, in the movements, the way he touched her. The thought gave her a strange, sinister thrill. She shivered.

'But I hate it. I love having long hair. *Loved*. It'll take years to grow back to how it was. I don't even know how to style this.'

'You'll probably find it's easier,' Rosa suggested. 'I mean, there's less of it, right?'

Katie ran her hands through it again. 'It feels so different. She put, like, wax in it or something. Tousled it all with her fingers. It feels like a *boy's* hair.'

Liv rolled her eyes. 'Come on.'

'Okay, it doesn't feel like *me*, then.'

And just how does that work, they all thought. We all look in the mirror from morning to night, but do we really see ourselves? If we passed a person on the street who looked exactly like us, would we recognize them? Would we see what we cannot see now; would we be more generous?

'Anyway, you look amazing,' Katie continued. 'What's going on, big meeting?'

Liv kicked off her shoes – they were, indeed, impressively high, with a block heel and a gold buckle.

'Something like that,' she said. 'I mean no, actually. The thing with Felix's company isn't for a couple of weeks.' She shuddered. 'But I've just been thinking – I should take it a bit more seriously, you know?'

'You do take it seriously,' Rosa said.

'Not really. I mean, I do my job, right? I do it *well*. But there's always been part of me that maybe didn't really care enough? Like, a bit of me was always thinking, *I won't be doing this for ever.*'

Rosa picked at the edge of the sofa.

'So I'd make jokes about it,' Liv continued. 'And tell myself it was all a bit of fun. But now – I guess the thing with Felix has changed my mind a bit. Or focused it, or something.'

They were nodding, and she hoped she was fully communicating what she meant. The thoughts had been percolating since the convoluted journey home from Felix's flat – a complex layering of regret and apprehension and annoyance – and then a gradual unpacking of their roots, a slow understanding that they started somewhere different than she had expected.

She would never actually tell her parents about sleeping with Felix, of course – that was for women who simpered *My mum's my best friend*, or else women like Dee, who poured sugar and shit alike into their mothers' ears, and cackled conspiratorially. But she would, she thought, give them a call and *catch them up with things* – she knew, with a frisson of discomfort, that such a phone call would be more significant for them than her, and that she would feel, afterwards, as though she had completed a good deed. Which made the entire thing selfish anyway, surely? But as her parents asked polite questions about her work and how the agency was growing and if she was working on any new accounts – and as she translated corporate public relations and the tech start-up industry and financial projections into language they would understand, she found herself feeling – Christ – *proud*. And, more than that – enjoying the pride they bounced back at her, the warmth in their voices, the soft cradle of their love.

Twenty-nine and living in London, twenty-nine and account manager at a PR agency which won awards and clients like lightning. The subtle shift from nervous newbie, flushing crimson when her manager underlined typos in red pen, to presenting her own segments at meetings, calling editors on numbers she knew by heart, feeling the soft thrum of satisfaction at the right stories in the right places.

'So I went shopping yesterday. Figured that I needed some more – professional clothes? Almost like a uniform. Or a costume? Haha, what's the difference, hey? Does this make any sense?'

She was smoothing down the fabric of her trousers as she spoke, a fabric that was thicker and heavier and more expensive than the past.

'Definitely,' Katie said. 'It's a big deal, what you wear.'

'Right. And I think I used to think that was, like a sexist double standard thing. But clothes are *expression*, too, right? I mean, I was thinking about high heels all the way home. How there's something dodgy in there, isn't there, when you know they're designed to make women look a certain way, and you can't run in them, and Christ knows I nearly broke my neck at uni sometimes, staggering around in cheap stilettos. But then today – walking into a room in the *right* shoes. You feel powerful, right?'

'Maybe that's it, then,' Rosa said to Katie. 'You need to let your hair make you feel powerful. Like, owning it or something.'

Katie tried to smile. Oh, when words were easy and action was impossible! She flattened her hands on her head and tried to make sense of what had happened – no, what she had *done*. How bizarre, how discombobulating that you could amputate part of yourself like this – and how over-dramatic, too, to be thinking of it as such. It's only hair, it'll grow back. But growing back takes years. I used to think I had them.

'Anyway, I feel horrible, making a big deal about this,' she said. 'I guess you haven't heard anything else from Dee?'

They shook their heads, and looked glumly at each other.

'It feels impossible . . .' Rosa began.

'To know what to do,' Liv finished.

They were trying – of course they were trying. The group chat was full of tender expressions of love and thought and *anything we can do* and knowledge that asking what needed doing was just one more burden.

'She'll get in touch when she can,' Liv said pointlessly, and they knew it was true, and had no idea what 'when she can' could possibly mean.

'You know she heard from Josh?' Rosa said. 'Right before her mum called.'

Liv tutted. 'As if that matters, now.'

'I know. But—' Rosa broke off as she recited the message in her head: *Trite, I know, but I can't get your face out of my mind, cat lady.*

Trite, yes – but gorgeous also. Because *she* was swimming across Rosa's skull too, her floral jacket and her chestnut hair, a pitying smile as she read a text message over Joe's shoulder, and him kissing her knuckles while telling her *I'm so much happier now*. She's beautiful, she's so very beautiful and he probably tells her so. And I shouldn't care, I shouldn't care, that's really not the kernel of pain at the heart of this, is it, that she has a good face and a good body and good clothes?

Katie dragged herself to her feet. 'Thanks for calming me down. I'd better go home. Need to figure out how to not look like a choirboy for school tomorrow.'

When she got to the house she paused on the doorstep for a moment, and wasn't quite sure why. The curtains were open; she could see Jack on the sofa and Rafee moving around further back, in the kitchen. A moment; a breath.

'Hey guys.'

'Hey.'

'Hey – oh, *hey*. New hair!'

'That's right. This is why you shouldn't make spur-of-the-moment decisions.'

'Oh well,' Jack said. 'It'll grow back, right?'

She burst into laughter. 'Yes. Yes it will.'

'And you can always borrow a hat,' Rafee added. His eyes were twinkling. 'I'm kidding. You look great. D'you want some soup?'

'That'd be great actually. I'm just going to take my stuff upstairs.'

And in her bedroom Katie stood in front of the mirror, examining the way the light was softer now in the setting sun. As she turned her head she noted the lack of weight, the way her hair no longer swung and moved without her, no longer fell like a screen across her face, a shield around her shoulders.

New Looks

Understand your motivations for wanting to transform your-self. Shedding old skins is good. The secret formula for winning back your ex is not. Health and happiness is good. Validation from others above yourself is not.

But let's face it – these qualities overlap and bleed into each other. When haven't we looked in a mirror and imagined how others might see us? When haven't we fantasized about how precisely earth-shattering we could look in that moment they saw us from the other side of the road?

It is all epidermis. You are you with hair spilling down your back and shaved off at your skull. You are you in your tatty trainers and your shiny high heels and your bare feet. You are you in ink and blood and sweat and cake. You are all that you need.

So spread your makeup across your bed and colour your eyelids the shade you never use. Scour the internet for the dress you thought about but never purchased. Show your hairdresser the picture that made you scared. There is joy, so much joy in experimenting with that epidermis, and nothing is as permanent as you think. Hair grows back. Piercings close over. Even tattoos can fade – or be finessed.

Rediscover the looks you thought summarized your personality at seventeen; explore the looks you aspire to now. Read 'Warning' by Jenny Joseph; read fashion magazines.

Remember that they were never with you purely for that

epidermis, and if they were you would have scorned them for it. A glorious haircut or a spectacular outfit or an extraordinary face of makeup is not the secret that will make them beg you back – but it might make you feel magic.

And if it doesn't – there are worse disasters.

You are always in transition. You are always in the process of transformation. You are always on your way to the new.

Chapter Nineteen

THE RACE

Her trainers were the only thing Dee remembered packing with any kind of forethought. If she had to face horror, she needed to run. Each morning she woke with the sunrise, a knot of anxiety buried in her torso, and each morning she ran to the seafront, and along, and back. She was chasing, always chasing a microsecond in which she thought of nothing but her breath and her body, and each one she caught flickered and died like the embers of a fire. The cats waited for her in the kitchen, and rubbed themselves against her sweaty legs.

She tried and failed to call Margot a dozen times. Margot was the crisp embodiment of everything she had once thought she was seeking. Now there was only one thing to seek, and it was as elusive as smoke. Instead she sent a disjointed text to Simon, and closed her messages before she read his reply. In her head, he could remain acerbic. His sympathy, his gentleness, could not be borne.

*

Rosa waited on the driveway as the taxi retreated, steeling herself against the trills of laughter she could already hear from inside the rented farmhouse. She had deliberately arrived late, so as to avoid as much of the excruciating 'welcome fizz and nibbles' as possible – but on the other hand, this meant arriving when everyone else was already either drunk or self-righteously discussing their pregnancies.

Eventually she rang the doorbell, bracing herself for one of Nina's friends aggressively brandishing her own engagement ring. Unexpectedly, Nina herself answered – garlanded, yes, with a 'bride' sash and a little white veil, but with a smile that whiplashed Rosa back to being ten years old. How strange it was, the way people's faces grew and roughened – but always retained an echo of their childhood.

'Ro-ro!' Nina squealed, and enveloped Rosa in a perfumed hug, spilling a trail of prosecco down her back.

'Ni-ni!' Rosa chirped back, and it was embarrassing and childish but comforting all the same. Trampolines and pillow-cases; sleepovers encrusted with gummy sweets and marsh-mallows; the tinny sounds of their doorbells and late-night confiding. As Nina pulled outwards from the hug, looking into Rosa's face with slightly bleary eyes, there was so much more between them than Rosa had expected. Nina's hair was cut through with predictable highlights – but it was hair that Rosa had brushed and braided. Nina couldn't help but thrust her engagement ring forward for Rosa to inspect – but as she obediently admired it, Rosa also remembered painting her fingernails. Turquoise and purple and glittery blue. Today they were a tastefully bland pink.

'I'm so glad you're here,' Nina said thickly.

'Me too. I'm sorry I'm late.'

'Oh! No. Come in, come in.'

There was a flurry of where to put her bags and then Nina steered her towards the laughter, rattling through an explanation of the other – urgh – *hens*. 'Gav's sister of course, the girls from university, and some from work. And half of our "couple friends", you know – Leonie's married to Gav's best man, Freya and Abby are more widows to the football team. You're the only one here from *home* home, but everyone's really nice, you'll fit right in.'

Rosa smile-grimaced, wondering which phrase she objected to most. She had a nasty feeling that some of Joe's friends' girlfriends might use similar language. But then, to her surprise and appreciation, Nina grasped her hand as she led her into the kitchen. She spoke with – yes – a certain amount of mannered ostentation, but also affection, as she introduced Rosa as her oldest friend. And even as Rosa took in the cluster of pastel-clad women, their blonde highlights and their French manicures, processed how different they all looked from her own three special girls – women – so she pressed her palm to Nina's, and felt a link in the chain. Oh, it was tedious in a thousand different ways, this celebration of luck and mundane normativity, undercut with savage competitiveness – but woven through it was love.

Rosa was presented to a cluster of four women who knew Nina from university and handed a glass of something bubbly and over-sweet. She answered their questions with as much lightness as she could muster – we grew up next door to each other – yes, I do have some funny stories for the maid of honour, I'll have to speak to her – yes, the venue looks beautiful – no, I'll be coming on my own, broke up with someone last year – a few different people, nothing serious. Then one of them asked her what she did for a living, and she described her work with relief and more than a little pride.

'Oh, wait a minute – I think I read something you wrote the other week? That art of –' the woman hunched conspiratorially over her glass as if about to announce the most atrocious swear word – '*sexting* article?'

Rosa smiled in what she hoped was a breezily worldly sort of way. 'That's right.'

'Oh my god, I *loved* it!'

Did you? Or did it just offer you a vicarious glimpse of something beyond your evenings on the sofa and your solitaire diamond, the opportunity to giggle wistfully about possibilities you don't really wish for at all? The Last Romantic sells hope, but it's the hope of ending up where you already are. Isn't it?

The other three women laughed shrilly and clustered closer, chattering about apps and dates and dancing. Each couldn't help but throw in an anecdote or two about how they met their partner – anecdotes Rosa suspected were less spontaneous than they seemed – while simultaneously pressing her for more views on what passed for foreplay these days. They really did believe people met at gallery openings and kept sex swings in their living rooms, she thought. A different kind of person – perhaps even the person she used to be – would feel pride and pity. Pride in her work and her optimism and her profile, pity for these women who were more concerned with how their relationships looked from the outside than how they felt. But something had changed. The work felt hollow, the optimism forced. And however cookie-cutter these women seemed, she knew that each had their own unique intimacies to go home to – the familiarity of another body, another voice – and they were intimacies that she ached for.

More than one of them insisted that they wished they were single, wished they could try out this whirlwind world of multiple men, expressed envy for Rosa's life of cocktails and coquetry. And of course Rosa smiled tightly, and tried to repress the vision of a racetrack, of these smug women gathered by the finishing line pointing at her as she tried to catch her breath. It was an image for the heartbreak handbook, she thought.

On the other side of the kitchen Nina let out a high-pitched giggle, and Rosa was startled to find herself automatically picking it out without looking, the way mothers recognized the cry of their own babies in a crowd. She and Nina were so very different, and so very the same. She could smell the roast chicken of Sunday lunch in Nina's house or her own – roast chicken which even now offered the most comfort after a difficult week. Nostalgia was a potent drug.

How strangely sad, then, that she knew that none of the rest of the weekend would reach the sacred levels of memory that their childhood friendship occupied. There was dinner (forgettable pasta) – there were prosaic games – there was a nearly naked 'butler' – there was another dinner (forgettable fish) – there was 'farewell breakfast' (forgettable eggs). She thought of Dee and Liv and Katie. Dee would archly critique the double standard of employing a pseudo-stripper. Liv would mix better drinks. Katie would turn up the music and make everybody dance.

On the final morning, as she zipped up her suitcase and checked under the bed for anything she had dropped, there was a knock on the open door.

'Ro-ro,' Nina said. She was wearing jeans and a pale pink rugby shirt; she looked alien and familiar and blissfully hungover. 'Just wanted to say thanks again, before you head off.'

'Oh!' Rosa said awkwardly. 'Wouldn't have missed it, Ni-ni. We probably planned this when we were twelve, right?'

'Right,' Nina smiled uncomfortably. They had planned for far more closeness than this, Rosa knew. In another universe she was Nina's maid of honour. In that universe, she had gathered the photographs to decorate the living room; she had interviewed Gav for *Mr and Mrs*, and her laughter when he told her about their favourite sex position was inexplicably genuine. In that universe, Joe had had his suit dry-cleaned ready to accompany her to the wedding, and Rosa pretended to roll her eyes as people said to her 'You're next!' In that universe, Joe's other woman did not exist.

'So, how do you feel now, then?' Rosa asked. 'Not long to go!' She felt ridiculously banal.

'I know,' Nina said. She smiled and shrugged, weakly. 'It can feel like it runs away from you, you know? I mean you don't know – I mean – I mean you're not engaged, but . . .' She trailed off. 'Sorry.'

Rosa smiled weakly too. 'I hear they – uh – take some planning. Weddings.'

'Right. Even just – I don't know, picking the menu. They made it take *weeks*.'

'What did you go for?'

'Um – chicken.' Unexpectedly, Nina blushed. 'Don't laugh at me, okay? Gav was teasing me for being boring. It's just – I don't know, chicken makes me think of family.'

Rosa felt a rush of warmth.

'I know what you mean. How are they?'

'Ha. My mum's got obsessed with hats. And my dad's been working on his speech for months.'

Was that pride, or embarrassment? Or both?

'Well, Gav's great,' Rosa offered, aware that she had met him precisely four times. He was a tall accountant who played football.

'Yes. He is.' Nina ran a hand self-consciously through her hair. 'I'm not sure I ever said, you know. How sorry I was. About you and Joe.'

Rosa startled for a moment and then arranged her face into what she hoped was nonchalance. Nina's save the date and actual wedding invitation had been bisected by the breakup, and there had been a particular kind of pain in receiving the first addressed to her *and* Joe, and the second to her alone. And, far from being unsure, Rosa knew exactly how much sorrow Nina had expressed – two voice notes, and five texts.

'Thanks. History now, isn't it?'

*

293

To her immense surprise (and equal relief), the advice that Katie just needed to get used to her new hair turned out to be true. Yes, walking into the classroom the next morning elicited a few whistles and shrieks, but she had expected that. Entering the staffroom, half of her colleagues appeared not to notice and the other half offered warm compliments, each of which unknotted her anxiety a little more, and helped solidify the connection between *me* and *this hair*. By the end of the first week she realized she was walking to and from work with her head held higher. It felt as though something else had been shed along with her hair; something heavy and from the past. A week after that and she was *Katie with short hair*. The tendrils around her neck had softened.

Saturday morning was the kind of green-and-yellow early May day which spoke of approaching sunshine, pints in beer gardens and outdoor music. She took her coffee into the tiny garden and there was a light wind; it moved her hair in a way it wouldn't have before. In a day or two, she knew, there would be the tightening vice on her torso, the sinister shuddering, the blood. But not yet. For now she felt bright and buoyant – and like she could hold it.

A conversation with Dee from their walk in the country-side weeks previously echoed into her head. *A perfect day for a run.* But Dee was miles away. Pangs of pity, sorrow, gratitude, guilt. A cloying sense of impotence, as she and Liv and Rosa continued grappling for the right things to say or do. They had organized the sending of flowers (Katie) and artisan brownies (Rosa) and a book of poetry (Liv) and each felt both necessary and wildly inadequate.

Liv, however, was keen, and they set a time and place over text. Katie pulled on her leggings and T-shirt with a breezy sensation she hadn't realized she was missing.

There was no sign of Liv around the park gates so she began doing some vague stretches. The air smelled like growing. Then she heard her name, inflected upwards, and spun, realizing only as she did so that it had been a man's voice, not Liv's. Standing in front of her was – what was his *name*? Mark? Mikey? A colleague of Chris's, anyway – someone she had sat next to in bars and probably included in rounds and chatted to with Chris's arm thrown carelessly across her shoulder, her hand on his knee.

'Oh – hey!' she managed. 'How are you doing?' She pushed a strand behind her ear nervously, and felt naked.

'Not bad, not bad. Keeping busy. What about you? Great hair, by the way. Wasn't sure if it was you.'

'Oh – thanks. I mean – I guess you know? Chris and I . . . ?'

'Yeah, yeah. Couple of months ago now, right?'

Katie paused as she processed. Yes – eight whole weeks. How quick and how everything. She processed, too, the casual tone of his voice, the way *eight weeks* was no longer a recent trauma to elicit sympathy, but a statement of fact, the clinical narrative of her life from the outside.

She felt as though she were standing on top of a ledge, and saw the jump that she could make but shouldn't, the leap she had known was there these past weeks but never looked directly at, never weighed up the distance and the windspeed because the moment she did she would fall. Go back inside, close the window. But it was so very tempting, and the clouds were spinning like candyfloss, so she said, 'He's moved in with someone else from your work, right? Nat?'

And as she had suspected, or predicted, or hoped, or feared, an expression of discomfort and awkwardness flashed across his face. An expression sitting over a thousand words.

'Um, yeah. That's right. Did you know – do you know her?'

'No, we've never met,' Katie said icily.

'I see. Well, it's good to see you, anyway. I'll let you get on with your run.'

And *he* ran then, speed over direction, hurrying to remove himself from something sticky and bitter. Katie watched his receding back and the detached, desolate thought sank into her skull. *Chris and Nat are together.*

A horrifying montage: Chris and Nat hand in hand; Chris and Nat at his work party; Chris and Nat walking by a French beach; Chris and Nat naked. All the smiles and winks and special phrases that had once been for her and her alone. The cluster of freckles on Chris's hipbone; the way he unconsciously clicked his tongue when he was watching the football; the way he said, 'Any more for any more?' when he cooked. All for her, all for *her*.

'K.' This time it *was* Liv, a curious expression mixed with concern. 'Who was that?'

'A friend of – this guy Chris works with.' She gazed after him. 'I think – I wonder.'

'Run and talk?'

'Okay.'

They started in silence. Katie felt her muscles seize and then relax, the strange undulations of running at first feeling like walking, then like agony, then like something that was, if not exactly a breeze, then at least like something she was built to do. As she settled into a rhythm she panted out I think Chris might be seeing her, the woman he moved in with.

There was a pause. The beat of their feet and the air moving into her, cold at first and then warmed by her lungs.

'How do you feel?' Liv asked.

'Shit.'

'Yeah?'

'Jealous.'

'Of her?'

'Maybe. Or of him? Of *them*.'

'Because?'

'Because they're together.'

'But you don't know if they are?'

'No. It's a feeling. Or a guess.'

Was their conversation stilted because they were running, or because Liv was trying not to be judgemental, or because she couldn't frame her words the way she wanted to?

When Katie had arrived in Manchester for freshers' week she had been so very afraid, and she had never spoken it. She had felt soft and light where everyone else was hard and sharp. They wore the right trainers and they listened to music she had never heard of. Dee was the most expressive nineteen-year-old Katie had ever met – for every politician pontificating on the news and every sunrise that sent petals

297

of pink light soaring across the sky, Dee had a story to tell. And Rosa could simply say *I'm from London* and pull people along in her wake, even if she never explained that her suburban version of the city meant something very far removed from what they were thinking.

Liv was something else again. She would roll her eyes and tell sneering stories about how the post office in her village thought garlic an exotic ingredient, but with her backcombing and Dr Martens and scorpion tattoo she looked considered, exact. Like she belonged, Katie thought, though Liv would have been surprised – and mollified – to hear it. Liv always seemed to be moving, away and onward.

Against all this Katie had felt so small, so ordinary, so unformed and simple. They scooped her up, those mosaics of personality and opinion and experience, when she still felt like a silhouette. They carried her with them, over the waves. Yet however far she got from the shore, she would always feel that Rosa and Dee and Liv were in a little deeper – and Liv was the deepest of all.

So her heart pounded through the nervousness of speaking the truth to one of her best friends, as she said I know it's none of my business, but it's weird that it's none of my business, you know? And whether he is or he isn't – the point is I feel like I want to be with someone before him. I want to win.

'It's not a race,' Liv said, reasonably.

'But it is,' Katie said. 'Or it feels like it, I mean.'

'Isn't that a bit of a cookies-and-aprons view of things? Finding yourself a – a *partner* isn't the be all and end all. It's not any all.'

'Yes. I know that. But . . .'

And they both knew how much was bound up in that word.

'I think Rosa feels the same,' Katie ventured. 'I mean, I know we know about Joe and where he's at. I know that's not a race either. But Rosa told me. She thinks the feelings about Joe will go away when she meets someone else.' She concentrated on the force as each of her feet met and left the ground. Solid to air and back again.

She didn't see, but Liv pursed her lips. 'Maybe.'

'You disagree? You think she needs to get over it.'

'I didn't say that. Don't paint me as the bitch here.'

Katie felt her stomach constrict. 'I'm sorry. I didn't mean—'

'It's okay.'

And Liv silently wondered if she meant it, if it *was* okay to be pushed into this position of critical coldness – or whether she pushed herself there. She thought of Nikita, and she thought of Felix.

'I'm going to try the app thing,' Katie said.

'Good plan. Don't let it get you down.'

'What do you mean?'

'You're a romantic, K. And apps aren't. Don't expect them to be, and you'll be alright. They're a catalyst, not the finish line.'

They looped back to the park gates, and Katie found herself casting around for – Chris's friend? Or Chris himself? The shadow at the edge of her field of vision, the always-possibility. She leaned into Liv for a brittle, sweaty hug, and was relieved to feel her friend's arms tighten around her. 'Thanks for this. I feel for good for it.'

'I'm glad. Maybe when Dee's back—' Liv broke off uncomfortably. They gazed into the nearly two weeks of their friend's – not silence; she had sent them messages, shaky updates and murmurings of gratitude – but her dilution, her diminishing. Dee had become a shadow – how could she not.

*

Later, Liv and Rosa perched on opposite sides of their dingy living room. Their laptops were open; a pot of coffee and several newspapers filled the floor between them. And while Liv flicked through spreadsheets and campaign plans she felt a quiet but delicious thrill, the gradually solidifying thought of *I like my job* and, more than that, *I'm building my career.*

How blinded she had been, all those years thinking outside instead of in! Perhaps this was growing up; the shift from ostensibly specific but in fact utterly abstract dreams like *ballerina* and *painter* and above all *writer*, to *how can* this *be more?* Future-gazing from a set of figures; finding satisfaction in what she once would have scorned. From the far side, she would have found the evolution sad. What did it mean that she didn't, now?

'Remember that godawful columnist – I mean, columnist is pushing it – in the student paper?' she said. 'He thought he was the first person ever to come up with an ironic moustache?'

'Oh my god. All those articles about gentrification *ripping the soul* out of places? Mate – look at yourself.'

'Exactly.' Liv paused. 'I was convinced that that was the kind of thing I'd be able to write, one day. I mean, what he thought he was writing. If that makes sense.'

Rosa looked nervously at her friend. 'Yeah?'

'Yeah. Kind of – political commentary without the politics degree. Or the family friends on editorial boards.' She laughed wryly and Rosa twisted her bracelet.

'But,' Liv added quickly. 'That's my issue, not yours. The chips on shoulders thing, I mean.'

'You don't have chips on your shoulder,' Rosa said with reflexive loyalty.

'That's kind. That's because you're my friend. But it's okay. I know – I know I found it hard, sometimes. Watching you do the things we talked about. But we did only talk about them, you know? You're the one who's actually done them.'

Rosa nodded weakly.

'And,' Liv continued, 'I didn't not do them because of some big wild factors I couldn't control. Not really. I mean – you offered, didn't you? I could have stayed with you, with your parents. I could have done the things you did, the course, the internships. And maybe I'd have got a job on a paper eventually too, or maybe – more likely – I'd have been another twenty-something freelancer, freaking out about the rent more than I do already, trying to explain to my parents why I don't have a pension. But the point is – we had choices. Both of us.'

'But they weren't the *same* choices,' Rosa insisted. 'It's one thing staying in your childhood bedroom when it's *your* childhood bedroom. I totally get why you couldn't – why you didn't – and it wasn't just the house either, was it? My parents helped me pay for the training, I didn't have to buy any food that year. I . . .'

She was wringing her hands pathetically, and Liv's face was etched with something like love. 'I know all that,' she said carefully. 'I'm saying – sorry, I guess. For not always being able to be as happy for you as I should have been.'

Liv swallowed, and Rosa laughed generously. It was the best thing she could have done. It shattered something tense, and Liv laughed too.

'I know you're willing me not to deny it,' Rosa said.

'Damn right,' Liv said. 'Dee would too. Female socialization, right? Don't apologize; don't deny it when someone's treated you badly.'

'Okay – *that's* a bit strong. You never treated me badly. You just – felt some things.'

'Yes. But now . . . I mean – and believe me, no one is more surprised about this than me – but I think I'm doing the right thing. For me. My work, I mean. It feels more – open – somehow, than it used to. Like there's all these different directions I can go in, but that's liberating, not constricting.'

Rosa exhaled deeply. 'That's nice. That's *wonderful*. I'm really glad for you.'

'Thanks. And I am for you. I mean, these columns. It's such an accolade, your editor wanting you to write like that. It sounds like the start of something exciting.'

'Mm,' Rosa said, and picked at a hangnail.

'Go on,' Liv said encouragingly – and this allowed it to pour out like a river.

'Oh Liv, I just find it so *difficult*. It used to be fun, I think. Looking for the good in places, in people. Taking readers along with me, you know? But since Joe – it's changed. I feel like he's reading my column even if he isn't. I feel like I'm forcing hope. And god, that whole dick pic thing – making it sound like I'm so *chilled*, like I'm just so *relaxed* about this horrible dimension of meeting people – meeting *men* – that we just have to put up with now, like it's just part of the *scene*, just what men *do*, let's all *laugh* about it. I hate that so-called progressive people would call me a prude for saying that. But I don't want that, do I? I want – bloody hell I sound like Katie here – but I just want a nice average boyfriend, and a nice average relationship, and not all this acting all the time. I want – I want what Joe has now. I want what Nina and all those women from last weekend have. And I want it privately, not – *constructed*.'

Not constructed, and not relayed to an audience, either. Rosa had been reflecting, recently, on the history of The Last Romantic. A slow burn rather than a flash of lightning. She had joined the paper like myriad other wide-eyed graduates privileged enough to be able to subsist on work experience and internships. *Yes, of course I can get you another coffee* and *Oh I'd be delighted to write about that*. She had pieced together articles from PR emails and events where everyone was better dressed than she was, and every piece of writing felt so formulaic, so far removed from the earnest way she had crafted *personality* and *voice* into her now mercifully deleted blog that she quickly found herself wondering whether journalism hadn't been a horrible mistake.

Then she was sent to report on a dating event tacked on to the launch of some new bar dozens of floors up in a shiny skyscraper, and Ty found the way she described the part-earnest, part-contrived setup 'charming'. Unexpectedly, readers did too. So he pushed her to another dating event, and then another, gradually coaxing and coaching her into this wide-eyed – well, what was she, really? Was The Last Romantic merely *her*, a version of Rosa tweaked and amplified for hopeful, hungry readers? Or was she a performance Rosa had now been living for so long that it was impossible to determine its boundaries?

She had even, recently, found herself opening an old folder on her laptop. 'The Greasy Spoon Gourmet' – *god*. Certainly she had no intention of resurrecting the blog, or even of repurposing the features she had carefully filed before wiping from the internet – but there was a sweet nostalgia, something touching, in reading herself back to twenty-one, twenty-two. In trying to understand who she had been, what she wanted. The gaps that had opened up since.

For here she was, now, carefully assembling a version of the previous weekend's hen to relay to Katie and Liv, picking out the most obnoxiously married of Nina's friends and embellishing them into caricature. The endless conversations about their own weddings honed in, in Rosa's retelling, on obsessions with the most banal napkin colours, social media hashtags and hackneyed poetry choices. The tedious questioning – do you have a boyfriend then? – morphed into tone-deaf tirades of well it's not too late and when you least expect it, that's when you'll meet someone special. It had felt simultaneously a betrayal of The Last Romantic's hope-fulness and wonderfully refreshing to lean into.

'I don't know,' Rosa said slowly, 'whether I'm the right person for this Last Romantic stuff any more. Or if I ever was.'

Liv formed a ball with her cheeks and blew out through her pursed lips. A slight whistle.

'Do you think I'm ungrateful?' Rosa finished.

Liv shook her head. 'No. Just honest.'

*

Not dissimilar thoughts were circulating in Katie's head as she sat gingerly on her bed, holding her phone at different angles and wondering what a particular facial expression would say about her. During Katie-and-Chris, she had quietly scorned the taking of selfies, it's all a bit narcissistic isn't it, and everyone looks like a tit when they're pulling faces at their own phone screen. But, she had realized with a nasty jolt, her camera roll remained stuffed with images of herself – pictures she had asked Chris to take, or pictures of her and Chris that she had asked someone *else* to take – because that was another little fragment of couple privilege, wasn't it? No one sneered when a *couple* wanted to mark a moment with a photograph, and no one knew when you asked your partner to take fifteen versions from slightly different angles.

Helping Jack refine his own profile had given her a sneak preview of what – and she hated herself for thinking this – she supposed was the *competition*. The first few photos she scrolled through were bodycon and fake eyelashes and pouting – and there was an unpleasant comfort in that, because wasn't she

305

something different – oh come on, Katie, own what you mean – wasn't she something *better*? But then there were others, so many others, who looked fun and interesting and clever and special – who looked like Dee and Liv and Rosa – who looked like *Nat*. There were pithy sentences about books and politics, wry descriptions of jobs, one-liners that didn't sound contrived or copied but rather that their authors would be *fun*.

Katie had sat in enough pubs with Chris and his friends to have developed a detailed understanding of what 'fun' meant. When you were still at school and your parents described one of your friends as such, they meant something skating close to the edge. *Oh she's so bubbly, quite the character, but just take care, darling, that she isn't a bad influence.* In adulthood, 'fun' morphed into something the same but different. It meant the girls – the women – who sat happily in pubs drinking pints and cheering at the football. Who told funny stories about their jobs without ever getting stressed about them. Who danced the perfect tightrope between stripper and *The Sound of Music*. Who didn't talk about their feminism, and who always stayed out late.

And Nat's fun, isn't she? Nat hides away the work – the gym and the app she uses to count her calories and the flat deposit her parents gifted her and the single fingernail she allows herself to bite when her job gets too much. Nat laughs easily, and cries only at sad films and adverts for children's charities and never, ever because of men.

Katie's own fingernails, she realized, were digging violently into her palm. The old foreboding tugging at the edge of her stomach. Her hand was easier to relax than her thoughts.

You can't know this. You can't know any of this. You've never even met Nat.

But I've met Chris. I've been with Chris. I've loved Chris. I know what he's like. I know what he likes.

Are you sure? You've broken up now. Evidently, he doesn't like you in the same way any more.

Bit harsh.

Well, you don't like him in the same way any more either.

No, but . . .

Why does it matter anyway? Why do you care?

Because.

You loved Chris. Don't you want him to be happy?

Maybe. But not before me.

Her heart drummed as she smiled, and she felt her new hair feather about her ears. Eventually she had a photo which looked, she hoped, approachable and intelligent – and oh, let's be honest – attractive. Fit. Hot. How much harsher it felt than preening in the mirror before a big night out, batting your eyes at a stranger across a room – and yet, how exactly the same.

The heartbreak handbook was open on her bed. In between photos she scribbled into it in Dee's voice, Rosa's voice, Liv's voice, her own voice, and each sentence made her heart skitter. *It's not a race. It's not a race.* She could feel Liv's hug from the park around her, and she could see Chris in her mind, a flirtatious smile, an invitation in.

She followed the new selfie with three further pictures from her camera roll: one in a bar; one on a hilltop; one at the beach. She had to crop Liv out of the first, and was horribly aware that Chris had taken the other two, and the long hair in each made her throat seize up, but as a trio they seemed to tell the right story. *Photo one shows what I look like when I dress up and wear lipstick – red lipstick – are you going to think that's classic, or over the top? Okay, photo two proves that I don't wear makeup all the time, don't even care about being dressed up all the time – look! I like to walk, and be outside! Photo three – I'm happy. Always, always happy.*

The absurdity of this window-dressing! The preposterousness that some man – *lots* of men – were going to look at this carefully curated version of herself, this cut-out of a life, and decide in a fraction of a second whether they wanted to meet her. Whether they wanted to fuck her. Whether they wanted to fuck her over.

Writing a caption to sit underneath the photos was even more difficult. Emojis felt childish; puns about history or teaching fell flat; saying that she liked travelling or music or food was ridiculous. Writing too little was an acknowledgement that all that mattered was her face; writing too much tickled the edges of desperation. Eventually she settled on *Lapsed ballet dancer, actual history teacher. Mine's a Guinness and Tia Maria*, and hit 'post' before she could change her mind.

Downstairs, Rafee and Jack, game controllers in hand, were navigating a series of obstacles on the TV screen. Jack was concentrating with incredible precision, while Rafee glanced up and said, 'Hey, how's things?'

'Ah, well. I'm – I've decided to figure out this dating app thing. Hey, I got it working for Jack, right?'

'Like a charm!' Jack said, without looking up.

Was it her imagination, or did a flicker of something pass across Rafee's face? He opened his mouth to speak, but there was a hesitation before he said, 'Nice one. It's a circus, mind.'

The phrase jolted something in her memory; the laughter of her friends. An elephant and a lion. The before.

'So I've heard.'

'Don't include your star sign in your bio,' Rafee said. 'Especially not with "typical" next to it. Always throws me.'

'Good advice.'

And as she curled on the sofa, suddenly, there they were in her hand, what felt like millions of men, an enormous landscape of horror and possibility. She swiped and grimaced and occasionally smiled; she frowned at improbably large fish and dopey tigers; she wondered why some had chosen to post photos of groups, or if others had cropped a girlfriend out of the frame; she puzzled over usernames like Johnandtherese or Jacobandmarie until she flicked to the descriptions and realized they were searching for a third; she winced at her own blandness, and wondered if she should be open to threesomes. Young, free and single in the city, right? She tried to sparkle into another version of herself; she imagined Chris and Nat curled on the sofa – *their* sofa – and blinked furiously.

More impressed by the breadth of a spirit than the size of a bra.

Christ.

Looking for someone who doesn't take themselves too seriously.

Christ.

Unashamedly sapiosexual.

Christ.

It took a shockingly short amount of time for the motion of quick scan; scroll if attractive; swipe yes if mildly interesting bio to feel reflexive, almost mechanical. An automaton of potential partners; a menu of men – or rather, sex – because the thing was saturated in it. Men in mirrors with their trousers pulled down to *just* above their pubic hair; men with winks and tongues and aubergines and water droplets splattered across their bios; men with euphemistic references to fun, fun, *fun*.

And as she swiped, so the tugging in her stomach morphed into a clenching – a clenching which sent her back to her bedroom for painkillers, and encouraged a sweetly innocent enquiry from Rafee – you okay? Yes, fine, she said, and hated her reduction of it, because if she wasn't explaining it to this kind, straightforward man she was sharing a home with, how would she explain it to this multitude of men she might share so much else with? She remembered Chris's navy-blue hot-water bottle, his insistence on co-codamol, his allyship borne of years of intimacy, and she remembered the last doctor, and she grimaced.

It was a matter of minutes before the first message pinged onto her screen: *Alright bbz?*

The Race

It was never meant to be a competition. You never imagined, did you, how love and intimacy would dance arm in arm with something snake-like and shameful, something you don't want to think, let alone speak?

You never thought there would be a hierarchy of your happinesses, a world in which your hopes for them would always be tempered by bigger ones for yourself. You never thought that Schadenfreude would creep around your heart, however much you claim, 'I just want them to be okay.'

It's not a race, people told us, when they worried that we would trip over our own feet, stumble in our eagerness to get somewhere else. It's not a race, people told us, when they wanted us to cradle ourselves rather than compare ourselves to others. It's not a race, people tell us, when we convince ourselves that the only cure for heartbreak is someone new to take their place; that their more rapid moving-on is a whole new shattering.

But a race, so often, is precisely how it feels.

If you travel through your heartbreak without a desire to win this new and savage competition, congratulations. If not – you are not alone.

But the race is a trickster. It makes you project imaginings and untruths onto new people. It makes you reshape mediocrity and mismatches into desperate hopefulness; convinces you that someone could be the one.

Here's how to win a better kind of race:

* *For the love of god, limit the spectre of comparison. Yes, this is hard in the age of the internet, and harder still if they remain close to – or entangled with – your life. But there are always blocking tools, always statements of 'please don't tell me about them', always small pieces of armoury you can deploy.*
* *You're under no obligation to tell the people you meet about the person who came before. But try to imagine doing so. If the idea makes you feel sick, or tearful, or in any way appalling . . . you might be forcing this race thing a little too much.*
* *Consider the future anniversaries of this catastrophe. One year since your heartbreak – two, three. What do you want for you? How do you want to be? This is a beautiful chance to map out a destination – if not a pathway – that is purely and entirely about yourself. Lift a heavier weight. Read* Middlemarch. *Quit your job. Learn to make the perfect fucking soufflé.*
* *Race towards your new truly personal best – feel your own power.*

(We'll stop talking like PE teachers now.)

Chapter Twenty

PASSION

After each run, Dee ate breakfast with her mother. It was an echo of earlier life and an act of unity. They ate yoghurt and fruit – mango, apples, grapes. One day Dee bought a pomegranate and tapped the seeds out like gemstones. They faced each other across the table and talked – some days about the cancer and some days around the cancer. They talked about the mastectomy – though they never used that word, which tripped on the tongue and caught on the teeth; it was simply the *op*. A short sound, bubbly, weirdly playful.

Dee stared at her mother's chest, veiled in jewel colours, draped in scarves and necklaces. She stared at her own, naked, in the bathroom mirror. She pushed her fingers into her flesh like dough.

She read, every day, everything she could find about breast cancer research, breast cancer treatment, breast cancer statistics, breast cancer recovery. The very words *breast* and *cancer* had started to appear strange, spelled incorrectly, arranged oddly, as though the letters were shimmering in front of her eyes. As everything shifted and slid she felt as though she were grasping for solid in the middle of the fog, suggestions of *75 per cent* and *outlook is positive*, which held so much promise but such huge yawning chasms too. For every ladder that she grasped there was darkness at all sides.

A monitor arrived from Dee's office. The courier was chewing gum, and did not meet her eye as she awkwardly inputted a digital signature on his tablet. *Fuck you*, she screamed silently. *Can't you feel the weight of this house?*

Amid the protective packaging, there was a card in a pink envelope, and Margot's loopy, elegant handwriting.

> *Dee*
> *I wanted to let you know personally how sorry I was to hear about your mum. Illness in the family can hit you like a gut punch – believe me, I know. We'll do everything we can to support you through this. Work only when you can and when you want to, and from Brighton as long as you need – keep in touch with Simon and he'll relay things this end. Here's my personal phone number if you need to talk.*
>
> *Looking forward to welcoming you back when you're up to it. You're already missed.*
>
> *Margot*

'Good woman,' Mel said.

'Yes. Like you. All that strong woman stuff.'

'I'm very proud of you, you know. Your work, how well you're doing.'

'Don't.'

'What?'

'Make things sound like you're saying goodbye.'

Mel spooned yoghurt silently into her mouth.

'I mean,' Dee faltered. 'Thanks. I'm glad.'

'I remember you calling me when you got it. You were so excited. Not just for the job, but for her.'

'Yes. She's both things, I guess. Great designer, great mentor.'

Her phone chirped, then, and she tutted as she looked at the screen. Her mother raised an eyebrow. There was no question of being coy; Dee told her mother everything. This man gave me his number on a night out – no, wait, his business card. Who does that, right, and I didn't think that happened any more.

'It's good to be surprised. Was he nice?'

Dee hesitated, the doubling of 'nice' – too gentle, too insipid, versus genuine and good – swinging like a pendulum. 'I think so. Inasmuch as you can tell from five minutes at a bar. He seemed – wholesome.'

'Nothing wrong with that, my darling.'

'I guess not.'

'So, what's he saying?'

Dee pushed the phone across the table and her mother read it aloud.

'*Last try, I promise, and I'll get the message.* What, you're not replying?'

Dee gave her mother a solid look. 'As if that's important, now.'

Mel gave her daughter an equally solid look. 'Darling, not everyone is going to be like Leo, you know.'

315

Dee bristled. 'Of course I know. Don't bring him into anything. He's the past.'

'Mm. Prologue.'

'Don't. Seriously.'

Mel exhaled gently. 'And darling, not everyone is going to be like your father.'

Dee's mouth formed a stony line. 'What's that supposed to mean?'

She was taut, ready for a disagreement, verbal sparring. There was an exquisite pain, then, in her mother's shoulders dropping, her defeated exhale, her tiredness.

'I mean—' Mel broke off, and she almost looked tearful. 'There are good people in the world. Loyal people. And as long as you're staying here – and yes, of course I'm glad that you're here – I don't think you should remove yourself from your life completely. So maybe you should get in touch. Distract yourself.'

'I'm not removing myself from my life,' Dee retorted reflexively, and Mel sighed.

Later, Dee lay in the bedroom in which her mother had nursed her through chicken pox and tonsillitis, school upsets and disappointments, and she read them again.

Trite, I know, but I can't get your face out of my mind, cat lady.

Too much? What I meant was – do you fancy going for a drink sometime?

Last try, I promise, and I'll get the message.

Her hands hovered, and her head skittered. *I'm not removing myself from my life.* Seven different words echoed hollowly. *I'm not removing myself from my life.* Her mother's footsteps downstairs. *I'm not removing myself from my life.* The sheaf of letters from the hospital, the date of the operation scrawled jaggedly on the calendar. She typed:

Sorry for going awol. I'm actually back in Brighton, with my mum. Family stuff.

And that would be it, she told herself – convinced herself? – as she prowled from room to room throughout the tiny house.

But he replied. Three hours later – an amount of time Dee was irritated with herself for analysing – her phone lit up: *Sorry to hear that. Hope your mum's okay. Maybe when you're back? I'd picked out my cat T-shirt and everything.*

She frowned. Another three hours later, she went back to her bedroom. The cats joined her on the bed, one nestled at her feet, the other curled like a baby in the curve of her chest. Warm breath. She replied: *You own a T-shirt with a cat on it?*

This time, the reply came almost immediately: *Correct.*

What colour is the cat?

Striped. Orange and black.

Dee narrowed her eyes. This time Josh added a second message: *Don't believe me?*

I just don't believe any man in his thirties actually owns a T-shirt with a cat on it. I think you're trying to be cute.

Haven't you ever heard of Garfield?

Of course I've heard of Garfield.

Well. I liked Garfield as a kid. For a while. And you know how when extended family pick up on a scrap of something you're into, and it becomes the focus of every birthday and Christmas present for evermore? Hence, a Garfield T-shirt.

Okay. You've convinced me.

So what was it for you?

What?

The childhood passion that shapes every ongoing gift from people who don't know you very well.

Dee cast her eyes from wall to wall. She had been six when they moved in, her mother glowing with relief and pride and anticipation as they left behind *her* mother's. These walls and windows, these doors and roof tiles, they're all ours, darling star. A room of your own at last, and what colour would you like to paint it? Lime green and orange – done.

Dee had requested two more iterations before leaving home – pubescent pink and purple, then a teenage stripping back to one teal wall offset by three white, plastered with posters and magazine cut-outs. Each time her mother had delighted in overalls, rollers and brushes. Shouldn't we turn it into something else, now, Dee had asked more recently – a studio for you, or a lovely guest bedroom – and her mother said but it *is* the loveliest guest bedroom it could be, because it's still so very you. The cut-outs had been replaced with a series of framed prints of Dee's best work projects, and the ceiling was still scattered with glow-in-the-dark stars.

Um. Drawing, I guess. Coloured pencils, sketchbooks, all that kind of thing. I'm a graphic designer.

Aha. Doesn't count, then. If you've actually turned said

childhood passion into a meaningful career. (Promise I'll ask
more about it, though.) This needs to be much more obscure.

Dee rolled her eyes as if someone were watching, and
caught herself.

Fine. I told my mum I thought foxes were cool, one year.
I got a fuck ton of bizarre fox merchandise.

Perfect.

Yeah. Pencil case, candle holders, fridge magnet. It was
unlike her, actually. My mum's usually great at presents. She's
the best.

Are you close to your folks?

My mum, yes. Very.

You're leaving an obvious gap, there.

She made a noise of exasperation, and dropped the phone
to the bed. One of the cats purred. She tried to remember
what Josh looked like. Somehow – *woodsy* – she thought.
Taut and gnarled in a way men in their thirties weren't
usually – hair that looked sea salted, hands that looked like
the furniture maker he claimed he was. Yes, claimed – because
what could you ever really know or believe about people
– men – that you met for these tiny fragments of time, who
spoke to you in bars because they liked the look of your
makeup or the line of your body, and nothing more?

Leo had complimented her on her rucksack rather than
her face, and that had felt like a superior kind of meet-
cute, an acknowledgement from the outset of shared taste.
But what good was it, in the end, when it collapsed into
those vicious seven words? Leo had played the guitar to
her, and ridden bicycles with her, and taken photographs

of her, and it all meant nothing, ultimately, just as it had twenty-seven years ago when her mother cried and asked her father not to leave.

Her phone glowed again. *Sorry. Bit intense for a text?*

Her heart drummed, and she heard her mother coughing from the next room.

*

Liv and Carrie were sharing a table in a room that the agency called 'intimate' for external meetings, and 'cramped' for internal ones. It felt like they were breathing each other's air. Carrie appeared to be deep in thought, gazing intently at her laptop screen, her perfectly crimson mouth slightly parted.

Startlingly, Carrie looked up and caught Liv's eye before she could snap away. 'What?'

'Oh. I was just – thinking.'

'Right. Well, that's what we're here for. What do you think of this for the opening?'

Liv scrambled round to Carrie's side of the table, trying to avoid kicking her chair. She was wearing another new outfit – a black-and-white houndstooth dress and patent penny loafers – and while on the office floor it had made her feel polished and powerful, in here it seemed somehow restrictive, too tight. Carrie's silky shirt was emerald green.

'So I'll do these slides,' Carrie said, clicking. 'Financial coverage, past twelve months. And here's where you'll take over. Corporate coverage. And then we'll hand over to Zachary for the coming year.'

'Subtext, please don't fire us,' Liv murmured.

'What makes you think they're going to fire us?' Carrie asked sharply. 'We've beaten every target we had, and then some. They've just secured a new funding round. Things are going *well.*'

'I know.'

'Well then. Don't go all *wilty* on me.'

'Wilty isn't a word.'

Carrie's eyed fixed on Liv's. Her expression was concrete.

'Touché,' she said. 'But you know what I mean. It's an opportunity, Zachary asking us to lead on this. Let's not fuck it up?'

Liv stared down at their notes. It was true, she thought. It had taken years, but the increments added up. How far they had come.

Two days to go. Annual review with Felix's company – no, not *Felix's* company, Felix was irrelevant. He would arrive, one of four. Not even the most senior – certainly not the lead decision-maker. They would sit on one side of the boardroom and she on the other, buttressed by her colleagues.

'Carrie,' she said.

'Mm?'

'Did you always want to do this?'

Carrie snorted pityingly. 'The idea of a job as the culmination of a childhood dream is the epitome of privilege. It's something rich people say to obscure that their parents gifted them a house deposit and that an inheritance will make up for the fact that they never paid into a pension.'

Liv inhaled.

Chris in a straw hat and a misshapen blazer. *Second-hand, obviously, from the fund for scholarship kids*, he slurred one evening over too many tequilas.

Where did you go to school, then?

Rosa's parents' home, her paid-for phone bill and dinner in the oven.

Mel. Do you think money can make you happy?

The ways one projected oneself forward at fourteen, at twenty-one, at twenty-nine.

'Do you know what word I hate?' she said. '"Help." "My family are going to help." "His parents gave us some help." People crack it out to feel good about being open, but it's deliberately vague. No one ever actually gives a number. And so the huge financial help they get looks the same from the outside as help that meant a train ticket, or a suitcase, or a hug, and what's made out to be radical transparency actually goes to embed all these invisible chasms between people.'

'People with money never want to believe they have money,' Carrie said. 'I mean, do you, now?'

Liv opened her mouth and closed it again.

'So, no. I didn't always want to do this. I wanted to be cabin crew, and a vet, and a talent scout, and a fucking circus performer. Because I was a kid, and the only jobs I'd heard of were in stories or on TV. Then I got older, and I wanted reliability, and scope, and to use my brain. I'm good at writing, and I'm interested in business. Corporate comms, it's a good blend. I'll stay here for a few years, then go client-side. Maybe do an MBA first. Big company, board-level position. With the right experience, that's achievable.'

She was cool and calm and utterly convincing.

'I'm good at writing too,' Liv said unnecessarily, and felt like a child.

'I know. You're also good at numbers, and people, and imagining ahead.'

'Thanks.'

Carrie clicked her tongue impatiently, but not unkindly.

'I know you think you've got a novel in you, Liv. We all do, right? And sure, maybe you'll write one, one day, if you get bored of going out all the time, or you marry a million-aire. But just because it's the only thing you could imagine doing when you were younger doesn't mean it's the only interesting thing to do now.'

The word *interesting* reverberated like a fingernail on glass.

Liv gazed at the notes again. Their first slide was projected onto the shared screen. There were so many tomorrows. She would stand tall. She would speak with clarity and passion. She would show them how they shone.

*

In another office – specifically, the toilets in another office – Rosa was staring at her reflection. Her hair was wound into a tight ball on top of her head, an attempt to steel her. *I can do this. This is not difficult. The worst that can happen is 'no'.*

But oh, how horrendous 'no' could be! Wasn't that precisely what Joe had told her – so, *so* long ago, now? Hadn't he told her 'no' when she wanted 'yes', and hadn't that shattered her into pieces that she was still unable to repair? Wasn't *she* a constant ghost in her mind, that floral jacket, that dark hair, Joe's casual arm across her shoulder?

No, no. This is not about Joe. This is not about *men*. This is me, me, me.

This was the mantra as she made her way back into the office, scanned for Ty's, walked – no, *marched* – towards him.

'Ty? Could I have a word?'

'Rosa,' he said distractedly. He looked harassed in an endearing sort of way. 'What is it?'

'I've had an idea.'

'Romance for the twenty-first century? Remember: acerbic, good; bitter, bad. Last one was a bit too close to the edge.'

'No – actually . . .'

He looked up from his screen. 'Are you okay? It's not personal, you know. I don't *actually* think you're bitter. You're the woman who wrote me six hundred words on building sandcastles with your partner, for goodness' sake.'

'Actually – I – I had an idea for a food piece. Well, a cooking piece.'

'Cooking?'

'Yes. I mean, cooking *and* dating. Like, easy but impressive dinners. What different dishes say about you. That kind of thing. Not recipes, exactly – more like – ideas? Food and relationships. I'm really interested in food, you see – and I think I can write about it well – you might remember when I first applied here, actually, I had this blog . . . Anyway, I mean obviously it's a real skill, I'm not saying I'm like, a restaurant critic, but I think, and . . .'

She was floundering, and felt it. Her face was getting hot, and felt translucent, as though he could see her insides. He swivelled his chair back to his computer.

'Sure. If you think – I trust you, okay. Write, file and we'll talk.'

Write and file, write and file. Rosa walked back to her own desk, breathing hard. Okay. Bring it on.

*

Katie had made a spot on the sofa hers. Rafee at the other end; Jack in the armchair. They had fallen into a weeknight routine when they were all in together; eating out of bowls and watching quiz shows. It felt simultaneously safe and extraordinary; so astoundingly different from what had been *home* just a couple of months before. On Tuesday, Jack headed out for what he nervously, grinningly explained was his third date with Amelie – and Katie noted that Rafee remained on the sofa, rather than taking Jack's spot on the chair. Her legs were curled up, neatly folded on *her* half. A polite ocean of space between them.

The heartbreak handbook rested on her lap. After initial embarrassment she had taken to writing in it – and reading it back to herself – while in the living room. If Jack had noticed it he hadn't said so, but Rafee had voiced careful intrigue. A project with my girls – my women – she had said.

Rafee was reading a book, and her phone felt like lightning in her hand. She was flicking – and how she hated herself for it – backwards and forwards between Chris's social media profiles and the dating app. Searching for Chris's present; searching for her future. Why were they still so entwined?

Chris, never an enthusiastic user of social media, had made only the lightest of changes over the past couple of months, but each was a shot of poison. The quiet removal of 'relationship status'. The replacement profile photo – no longer the two of them, laughing, loving, but Chris alone, smiling over a pint. The vicious irony, of course, was that she had taken that photo. So she was still there, a ghost just outside of the frame.

There was the merest scattering of new pictures, but each brought the pain of an annual inflection she was now locked out of. For just as the school year formed a background rhythm to time passing, so too did the dates you learned over years with the same person. March – his best friend Charlie's birthday. April – his group night out to mark the beginning of the cricket season. How tedious and generic and comforting it had all been – how appalling that it carried on without her.

When they were younger, she would have been able to harvest so many clues from a sweep like this. Then, they chattered across each other's digital spaces, leaving strings of sentence for others to unpack. The unselfconsciousness – or ostentatiousness – of another era. Now, there was nothing to indicate whether Chris had spent the past eight weeks wallowing on the floor, or sweating through weights at the gym, or fucking Nat in white sheets.

Yet just a swipe away were hundreds – no, thousands – of men, all with pictures and words selected, it seemed, to draw her in, whether for a night or a lifetime. Yes, she hadn't expected it, but there were men here who wrote plaintive lines like *looking for my lobster* or *want to find someone I'll delete this app for*, and she hated herself for finding them tragic while wishing for an echo of their desires. It was so *conflicting*, holding this explosive potential, this menu of men, this *possibility* which fizzed and popped with the energy that, she now saw, had slowly leaked away from Katie-and-Chris over those nine years. That energy was what had died, and yet grasping for it felt like plunging her hands into a shoal of fish, darting and silvering away from her fingers.

Because each of the men she started messaging was a reminder of precisely how much intimacy you gained over nine years. Jokes felt flat, stilted, when she didn't know what their laughter sounded like. Bland statements about *what do you do?* and *what are you up to this weekend?* felt unbearably tedious, surface-level wittering. Immediate requests for her to send pictures were impressive in their boldness, but ultimately sordid and depressing. Two months ago, she was living with a man who kissed her clavicles and washed her underwear and made her scrambled eggs.

A new message arrived. Two words – *Free tonight?* – followed by a winking emoji.

It was from a man called TJ, with whom she had exchanged precisely three messages so far. According to his photos he was dark-haired, muscular and knew it, and according to his bio he enjoyed climbing, ramen and techno.

She glanced across at Rafee, who was biting his lip in deep concentration.

'Enjoying it?'

'What? Oh – yeah.' He tipped the book forward and looked at the cover, as if to remind himself what he was reading. '*Girl, Woman, Other*. It's interesting.'

'Is it for your book group?'

'That's right.'

'*Middlemarch* and now this?'

'Yeah – it's deliberate. One month an old classic, one month a future one. As in, a big recent prize-winner, zeitgeist-y whatever. *Forwards, Backwards* – that's the theme.'

'That sounds cool.'

'It is.' He looked carefully at her. 'You should come, if you fancy it? It's a nice crowd, too.'

The phone was still hot in her hand, and Rafee looked calm and cool. Somewhere, years ago, there was a version of Katie which would have rolled her eyes at book groups, at the idea of people clustering together to earnestly discuss – what, *art*? People who needed a club and a date in the diary to do something pleasurable – who needed a structure for their passions. She felt a soft squeeze of pleasure in such scorn being left behind.

'You know what, that sounds great.'

'Great!'

Then she scrolled back to her messages. She typed in a flutter, pressed send before she could think herself into a different decision. Two words – *Sure thing* – and a kissing emoji.

Passion

Love is passion; heartbreak is passion with nowhere to go. Passion drives us, fires us, breaks us.

But there are so many more kinds of passion than you thought of when you were falling in or out of love.

Heartbreak can operate as rocket fuel for different kinds of passion. Embrace those sparks, those catalysts. You were made to love so much more than people. You were made to love jam running down your chin and juice staining your fingers. You were made to love dancing and jumping in puddles and climbing mountains. You were made to love stretching and pushing and succeeding; you were made to love slowing down and resting and breathing. You were made to love painting the walls of your life.

Throwing yourself into your gloriously selfish passions can be truly joyful and world-expanding in the midst and the beyond of heartbreak. Bring yourself back to yourself. Remember yourself; keep yourself.

Chapter Twenty-One

SEX

The next morning was caramel-clear. Katie had set an alarm, astounded at herself for staying over on a school night, but woke up long before it, with the sunrise. She decided to walk home rather than cramming herself into a bus or a Tube carriage – she wanted air, and space. There was a raw ache between her legs, and a slick across her skin. TJ offered her a shower and a coffee and she declined both – not quite out of embarrassment, but of a desire for something else.

As she walked, she replayed the evening in exquisite detail. Eight p.m. – the time she and Chris would generally cook for each other, or book for dinner in restaurants. Dating performances, domestic routines. The normality, the *banality*. And here she was, knocking at the door of a flat she had never visited, willing a fast-forward through those first seconds after TJ opened the door – the seconds in which he could transition from *stranger* to, at least, a face that she recognized in the flesh.

Yes – flesh. The *reassurance*, the *concretization* at seeing bland messages and generic photos translated into something multi-dimensional! TJ was at once less attractive and more magnetic than his profile on the app – his face was wonkier, his body softer – and yet he was *there*. He was real.

'Hey, Katie.'

'Hey, TJ.'

'Want to come in?'

'Sure thing.' *Sure thing?! Again?*

She had chosen not to tell Rafee where she was going, and had chosen not to think too carefully about why. Going to hang out with the girls – the women. But she had messaged them on the way, and copied across TJ's address, and also chosen not to think too carefully about the morbid subtext to this. TJ was wearing grey tracksuit bottoms, and a blue jumper, and a smile. He looked safe. But a stranger, too.

He offered her a beer, or wine, or rum. She started asking for a glass of wine and changed it in the moment of speaking to a rum and Coke. Burnt sugar and ice. It tasted like birthday parties and the past. TJ explained that his housemate was out for the evening, so they could chill in the living room. He played music that reminded her of Manchester, and talked to her about rock climbing.

Chris was there throughout; a shadow, a ghost. He stood in the corner of the room sneering at the posters and sniffing at the lack of balcony. Chris wore his self-assurance differently to TJ; where TJ was feline and sardonic, Chris was statuesque and concise. He was brittle, too – but was that brittleness visible to everyone else, or only Katie? And had it been there from the beginning, or only in time?

What are you doing here? Chris asked her.

I'm here for something new. Just like you.

Just like me?

You and Nat. You and anyone. You were with me and now you'll be with someone else, anyone else, everyone else. The world is open and the world is changed.

After three drinks she and TJ were lying on the floor, cushions pulled off the sofa, taking turns to play music. The room felt hot and muggy. She took his phone to change the track, and he let his fingers drag across the back of her hand. Her skin crackled.

Her first kiss with Chris. A costume; a party; crowds of people. Throbbing basslines; cheap beer. No moment where the world shifted, and yet a moment where everything was altered. The opening bars of nine years. Lips on lips so many thousands of times.

As her mouth met TJ's, she noticed a million ways in which his was different to Chris's. Narrower; softer. As TJ's tongue flickered on hers, she noticed how utterly bizarre it was, this primal dance, this sharing. His fingers tickled the soft hairs on the back of her neck, newly naked. Lightning flashed down her spine. He moved his lips gently from the corner of her mouth, down her neck and across her collarbone, and she tried to process how what was an expression of sacred intimacy just a few weeks previously was here, now, so surface and yet so spectacular. TJ did not know how she liked to curl up in pyjamas with a mug of tomato soup, or that she bit her nails until she was twenty-two, or what her voice sounded like when she said *I love you*. There was not love here, but there was something else. She was undoing buttons and pulling clothes; her body was warming and rocking.

TJ's body was both the reverse of Chris's and the same – the negative of a photo, a reflection in the water. Just as her body was both the same as it had been with Chris and changed – short hair, yes, but also something intangible, a hardening, a knowing. As she lowered herself onto TJ, she felt how each distance was slightly different: the pliant crease at the top of her thigh which Chris would bury his fingers in and TJ could not reach; the different point at which her calves crossed around his back. The music was a heartbeat and she heard herself moaning. TJ pushed her back onto the floor and clasped her slippery hand in his, and as she shuddered under him, she wondered if that – palm to palm, fingers interlocked – was the most intimately bizarre, bizarrely intimate feeling of all.

*

Carrie and Liv had been tasked with setting up for the meeting. Pastries; fruit; tea; coffee. A jug of iced water, which nearly slipped from Liv's grasp as she lowered it to the table. A sharp, hard reverberation rang out, and Carrie glared at her. 'Careful.'

Liv pressed her palm against the cold side of the jug, bringing herself back into the room. They would be here in ten minutes.

'What's *with* you?'

'What do you mean?'

'You're all – it's like you're *nervous*.'

Was there a hint of scorn in Carrie's tone? Liv drew herself taller.

'Nope. Just making sure I'm clear on the narrative.'

Carrie narrowed her eyes. 'Right then.'

Not for the first time, Liv wished fervently that saying something could will it into being. Her heart skittered, and her skull thrummed with frustration. There was *nothing to be nervous about*. She had *done nothing wrong*. She did *not believe in this bullshit*.

And so, when Felix and his colleagues walked into the room, flanked by Zachary and two more of her and Carrie's directors, she walked forward purposefully, smiled warmly, shook hands firmly. Great to see you again and how are you doing. She met their eyes. She gave Felix no more or less attention than any of the others.

But as he took her hand he squeezed it slightly too tightly, so that his fingernail scratched her palm. He leaned forward, as though to kiss her on the cheek, and whispered.

'*I have your knickers in my pocket.*'

It seemed unbelievable, then, that the entire room could not hear her heartbeat, count her frantic breaths, watch crimson spreading across her face. A montage of that night was projected onto the wall of the room. She felt hot and cold and far too fast, and snatched her hand away. A crooked smile was playing across Felix's face.

'Right, shall we get started?' Zachary led the room in sitting down. 'Liv and Carrie will be taking us through the retrospective, and then we'll move on to a proposal for the next twelve months.'

'Excellent,' Felix said, slightly too loudly. Zachary glanced curiously at him, and Liv flinched. There was a horrible pause.

'Okay then,' Carrie said briskly, and launched into the presentation with the perfect balance of enthusiasm and poise. Liv stood in what she hoped look like relaxed and supportive silence, looking at Carrie, looking at Zachary, looking at Felix's colleagues, looking absolutely everywhere except at Felix himself, convinced his eyes were boring into her.

And why does it matter anyway? I've done nothing wrong. I'm a twenty-nine-year-old woman who had casual sex with someone. I consented. We used a condom. And didn't I have fun? Didn't I enjoy it? Take some fucking ownership, Liv.

'Liv?' Carrie hissed.

Liv jerked herself back into the room. All eyes on her. The clients were eager; Carrie and Zachary were on the edge of annoyed. She grappled for her place in the presentation, garbled her words. Somehow, she gave voice to the things they had done: the profile of the research project in a major publication; the CEO on a primetime news show; the head of R&D on a key seminar panel. Each had been her sweat and grit and adrenaline, and each felt weak and fluttery, wilting under the lights, and their faces, and Felix. She felt as though her clothes had melted away; she felt as though she were posing, just as she had done a week ago, or was it two, or three. Scene after scene was replaying in her mind, so vivid that she had to check her stillness, convinced that she was repeating those twirls, stretches, carnival thrusts.

She could hear her own moans, feel Felix's hands on her wrists. It was a squeeze and a punch and fingernails down a blackboard and it made her feel a dozen different layers of shame and hatred.

'Right, thank you, Liv,' Zachary said at some point. There was a pointed cough, and Carrie steered her to an empty seat. The meeting moved on, and Zachary pulled affable laughter from their throats, and they nodded and stroked their chins thoughtfully at graphs and tables, and by the end there were more handshakes and agreements and smiles. It had gone well, Liv supposed. She felt as though she were behind a sheet of frosted glass, everything slightly muffled and out of reach, and everywhere she shifted to in the room she felt Felix watching her.

After fifty years or fifteen minutes she managed to excuse herself, and made her way to the bathroom. It was mercifully empty. She leaned towards the glass and tried to understand herself.

The door opened, and she snapped back from the mirror, and turned to face Carrie. Her arms were folded and her eyes were narrowed, but there was something sympathetic in the curve of her mouth.

'What's going on?'

'What do you mean?'

'Don't bullshit me.'

Liv hesitated for a moment. Carrie shifted her weight from one foot to the other. 'Come the fuck on. It's blatantly obvious that something's rattled you. Is it to do with them? Or something personal?'

Liv wondered wryly whether announcing that someone had died would coax a more sympathetic tone. Yet there was something galvanizing in Carrie's crispness. She inhaled and said, 'It's Felix.'

'What about Felix?'

'We – you know.'

Carrie pursed her lips. 'Don't pussyfoot.'

'Fine. We had sex.'

'When?'

'Um. A few weeks ago.'

'And it was just sex? You're not dating him?'

'No. Just sex. It was stupid.'

'Why?'

Liv stared at her. Carrie stared back, then shrugged and soared towards the sink, where she began applying a fresh coat of lipstick. Somehow, she managed to watch Liv's reflection while creating a perfect cupid's bow.

'Well,' Liv began. 'Because it's *there* now, isn't it? You know what he's like. All double entendre and sex eyes. It's distracting. You saw what a mess I was in there. And if Zachary and the others find out, they'll think I'm jeopardizing the account, or I'm using sex to get ahead. And even if they *don't* find out, now there's that extra layer on top of everything. It's another thing to think about, just when I'm trying to think about – coverage, and figures, and quotes and things. Every time he compliments me, or says something's a decent job. It's this – distraction.'

Carrie snorted. 'Felix isn't that important, Liv,' she said. 'Head of one division out of four – and the worst performing division at that. He's good at a witty comment or an obvious interjection, but there's no real substance there.'

'Ouch.'

'Well, it's true. I mean, don't get me wrong, he's nice to look at, but that's about it. Don't let someone like that derail you, for god's sake.'

Liv processed this. 'I guess.'

'Well,' Carrie continued, 'you're the one who called it "just sex". Maybe it's a bigger deal than you're letting on.'

'Definitely not,' Liv cut in quickly. 'Felix is – he's not someone I – I don't want anything else from him.'

'I don't mean him. I mean the sex part. Pass me some toilet paper?'

Liv did so, and Carrie blotted expertly.

'I mean, maybe you don't want to do "just sex", full stop.'

Liv bristled. 'I'm not some hopeless romantic – I don't think sex has to be all flowers and candles, you know.'

Carrie shrugged nonchalantly. 'There's a spectrum, right? No-holds-barred casual everything through to no holding hands before marriage. Maybe you want something more committed than you think.'

'No . . .' Liv began. She imagined Nikita's plaintive face.

Carrie shrugged. 'I'm not judging. It's all good, right? Just got to know yourself.'

And Liv couldn't help but give a short laugh in response. That was the kernel, that was the core. Know yourself, understand your own multitudes. So simple, so impossible.

'You broke up with Nikita, didn't you?' Carrie said, and Liv flinched. The emphasis was on 'you' rather than 'Nikita'.

'That's right.'

'How d'you feel about it now?'

They watched each other in the glass. 'A mixture,' Liv said. 'Guilt. Relief. Regret. But not *really* regret. All at once.'

Carrie nodded. 'That sounds about right.'

'What do you mean?'

'Just that. Breaking up with someone's *hard*, right? Especially when there isn't a huge fanfare, explosion, whatever. You know, when it's just – over. That's a difficult thing to tell someone. It's a difficult thing to tell *yourself*.'

'Yes,' Liv said. 'Yes.' She meant it a thousand times over. 'So you . . . ?'

'Two years ago,' Carrie said shortly. 'It's fine. Come on. We've got work to do.'

*

Write and file, write and file. Rosa had repeated it to herself through the week, each time she was struggling for the right way to describe poached eggs or toast or orange juice. The slightest resistance beneath the teeth before breaking into the flood of sunshine; the gradient of texture from buttery top to crisp bottom; the oscillation between sweet and bitter. Writing about food was at once far harder than anything she had done before and a delight: the fierce concentration on something she cared about; the conversion of something she truly loved into words. Framed around 'the second-best thing about sleepovers' the piece was, she decided, still comfortably within the realms of dating, but there was not a moan about app etiquette, nor a discussion of modern masculinity in sight. Each reread and edit was like dragging a comb through her hair; a smoothing here, a sharpening there – and when she finally clicked send she felt, if not a sense of certainty, then a soft bubble of hope and happiness.

It was only then she realized that, for the first time, Joe had not stalked her through the writing of the article. Each that had come before – digital flirting, online icebreakers, choosing the right set of profile pictures – had been written with the horrible consciousness of Joe as her first and foremost reader. Joe, whom she wanted to think of her as ricocheting around the city on a thousand impossibly exciting dates – Joe, whom she *didn't* want to think of arm in arm, hand in hand with a beautiful brunette wrapped in flowers. This time, he was relegated to the margins, a shapeless face in the crowd. She didn't care what he thought. She didn't care whether he thought at all. It was gloriously freeing.

Later, she clustered with Liv and Katie around a pub table, soaking up the cosy optimistic hubbub of a Friday evening. She and Liv rattled off debriefs of their days in quick succession and were now looking encouragingly, expectantly at Katie, who was smiling coyly. She had brought the heartbreak handbook with her and opened it on the table, asking them about passion and about sex. How did you feel after Nikita, after Joe? Rosa retold the dates she had attempted since breaking up with Joe, the wearying dynamics of strangers trying to become less so.

Liv winced through Freddie and Felix, and wondered aloud if Celeste had responded instead, if things might have been different, and how. She thought of how different bodies looked in photographs, and how power slipped and slid. But she thought, too, of Carrie's calm steel, of *Felix isn't that important, Liv*. There was so much more that mattered.

Katie told them the version of her night with TJ that she thought would sound best. She omitted the frantic scuttling in her chest as she walked to his flat; she painted TJ taller and cooler. 'I realized that for the first time in nine years I could have sex with someone – anyone. I could do *just sex*. I could text someone, and, like, *make an arrangement*. Brave new world! I would never, *ever* have thought I would do that. I always thought about sex in such a different way, right? I mean you have to, don't you? In a relationship? It has to be – *elevated* – otherwise what's the point?'

'I think Dee would say the hottest sex she ever had was with someone she met three hours earlier,' Rosa said.

'Well – right,' Katie continued. 'So – it *was* hot. It was good. It was great.'

She briefly wondered whether she was capable of articulating further physical detail to her friends, and felt an internal shudder. Chris's body had been intensely private; describing to her friends the expressions on his face in those most intimate moments, or commenting on the shape of his legs, the wonky line his hair made from navel to groin, would have felt horrifyingly intrusive. Yet surely, all those years ago, she had waved him off from that Manchester doorstep and thrown herself gigglingly onto the sofa, unpacking the night before in minute detail?

'I mean, it was strange, too,' she said. 'Great, but strange.'

341

'Of course it was,' Rosa said. 'Nine years with one man. How could it not be?'

'Like riding a bike,' Liv said, and Katie laughed shortly. 'Anyway,' she said. 'Rosa. How's the new article? Did you get it in?'

'I'm pleased with it,' Rosa said, eyes shining. 'I mean, we'll see what he says. There'll be edits, obviously. But it feels like *me*, you know?'

They nodded and clinked and began talking about future possibilities, how the food and relationships theme could morph into food alone, how Rosa might transform herself into a recipe writer perhaps, or even a restaurant critic. Rosa shook back her hair and laughed hopefully with her friends, and she felt light and free.

*

That would be the end of the exchange with Josh, Dee thought. He wouldn't put up with another unanswered message, another sudden disappearance. *Sorry. Bit intense for a text? Just enjoying the chat, you know.* Yes – and she had ended the chat right there, buried her phone under her pillow, because how could she possibly explain her father's absence over a text message – and why would she want to – and why was Josh interested, anyway?

But the next day her phone pinged again, and Josh had written *So my family are like the Waltons. I mean, I don't actually know what the Waltons are. But that's how people describe these tight, shiny happy units, right? My parents are really into each other. I used to think it was grim, when I was a teenager. You know – Muuuum! Daaaad! Cut it out! – when they were hugging each other in front of my mates. But now, I realize how lucky I am.*

And, astonished at herself, Dee replied.

That sounds special. I'm not close to my dad. He left when I was two. I don't see him.

Josh's reply came just moments later: *Sorry. That's heavy.* Somehow, he managed to avoid it sounding like a cliché. *So did he try?* he added. *To see you, I mean.*

These are very intense questions for a text exchange.

Yeah, I know. Beats talking about the weather, doesn't it?

It did, she thought. Swallowing, she constructed a more honest reply than she would have ever expected – honest not merely in its truthfulness, but in its detail. *Nope. At least, not past the first few months. My mum has this quiet, seething rage about it. She could deal, in the end, with him leaving her, but not him leaving me. I looked him up online once – social media, you know. I think he lives in London. But I'm not interested. I can deal with him leaving me, but not him leaving her.*

She pursed her lips and added, *Enough detail for you?*

Plenty, he replied. *I'm sorry. But it sounds like you and your mum are tighter for it.*

And throughout the week, as Dee ran faster and faster, and drew salty air into her lungs, and imagined it dissipating throughout her body, antiseptic and crystalline, she continued exchanging messages with this strangely warm and open man, miles and miles away.

Josh asked the type of probing questions which Dee wanted

to find contrived and yet he managed to deliver them with warm sincerity. And just as she wanted to characterize him as the type of person who forced long messages out of the other so as to expose nothing of himself, so he tilted the conversation back and revealed more. He answered questions thoughtfully, and he followed her answers with comments or questions which suggested he was reading them carefully.

He had grown up in Sheffield with two sisters and a brother. He liked art and history at school – though not woodwork, weirdly. Dee found herself smiling at the discussions of his siblings and writing, *My mum worried about only child syndrome, there were always masses of friends with kids round at ours when I was growing up. Forcing me to learn how to share.*

Oh you don't necessarily learn to share with three siblings, and you eat fucking fast, he replied.

He hadn't known what to do with himself after school, and got a working visa to Australia. Not a gap yah, right – he did stints in farming, and cheffing, and labouring before he realized that he liked carpentry, liked the combination of building things with his hands and designing things with his head. He liked the outdoorsiness of Australia and learned to surf without falling over, but he missed his friends and family and also the very particular atmosphere of pubs with sticky carpets and pool tables and dartboards.

His friends from Sheffield were split between those who had stayed and those who had relocated and were always talking about moving back. And yes, he probably would, one day, London's fantastic but I'll never buy a place here, will I – not that buying a place is the be all and end all, eighteen-year-old me would probably think I'm a right boring fucker, but there's something about putting down roots, isn't there?

I know the feeling, Dee wrote.

So you're not wedded to the big city for evermore?

She exhaled. *I don't know. I don't really think much about evermore, to be honest. I'll want to be there for my mum as she gets older. Maybe London, maybe here in Brighton. Maybe we'll live together in a cottage somewhere with fifty cats, you know?*

The words stung as she pressed send. Their breeziness, their certainty of the future. But all that was solid had crumbled. *As she gets older.* She will. She must. She might not. There was something solid and jagged in her throat, something sharp and bitter behind her eyes – but she didn't cry. Dee did not cry.

Of course, can't forget the cats, Josh replied. *That's good closeness, knowing you'd happily live with your mum again. Special kind of intimacy, living together.*

True. I mean, we'd drive each other crazy. But she's fantastic.

How so?

Dee stared at her phone. How was her mother special? How was her mother extraordinary?

Well, I mean. In so many ways. She's really youthful, but not contrived. Like, I was never embarrassed, or felt like she was trying to, I don't know, 'recapture' something. It's more that she never faded out the way some women do in middle age, baggy T-shirts and forgetting how to dance. She's always dressed amazingly, these incredible colours, and she's always read, and painted, and she does this feminist book group, and soup kitchen, and fucking pottery – *and even then she made a joke about Mad Middle Aged Potter Mother. She's just* fire. *There are people round every weekend, she does these amazing dinners – it's like, she's squeezing everything out of life, you know?*

Dee was unsure, as she typed, whether she was trying to challenge Josh, to lay down a gauntlet and dare him to think of her as obsessive, as a crank, as difficult – or whether she was expressing a flood that so many other men compelled her to hold back. There was something about the distance, here, the fact that his face was not in front of hers, that he was not scrutinizing her. There was something about the words on a screen rather than in her mouth; about the concretization of her love, and the fear that always sat within it.

She sounds pretty amazing, he replied.

She is. My hero.

Who do you live with now?

Friends. Two friends. They're great, too.

The ones from the bar? Drowning heartbreak?

That's right. How's your friend doing?

Better, thanks. He's the one who ended it. I don't know if that makes it easier or not.

Dee hesitated.

How's yours? Josh added.

Also better, I think. I haven't seen her for a few weeks, obviously.

They kept skirting around the precise reason for her being in Brighton. Somehow Josh – Josh who thought nothing of querying her on her absent father – had sensed that this was special territory.

Dee added: *She messaged me the other day, told me she'd gone for a run. Felt good for it. She seemed – up, somewhere, somehow. If a bit frenetic.*

Do you like running? I got dragged into a half marathon a couple of years back. All that bullshit about 'this is what humans are built for'. I nearly died.

Dee laughed shortly. *Yeah, I love running. Exercising in general.*

Sporty kid at school?

No. It's been more of an adult thing. She paused. And, barely believing the words as they appeared on the screen, soberly and in the sunshine, unprompted and open, she added: *A few years ago I had, I guess, a bit of a crisis of confidence. Exercising, getting fit – it helped.*

That's pretty impressive. The self-awareness, I mean. Pretty sure my own crises of confidence have been met with too much beer and the odd tattoo.

Thanks, she messaged back, and it seemed extraordinarily inadequate.

My mum always used to say this thing to me. 'Be strong'. And she called me 'star'. I mean that's not important. But 'be strong, be strong'. It was like this mantra. If you're strong, then you can take on anything. No one can break you; the world can't break you. And my mum's fucking incredible. You wouldn't believe how hard she worked when

I was little, not just to keep things going, but to make things sparkle.

And so I tell myself that running, going to the gym – all that's about being strong. And that's what I believe, right? That's what I want to be true. But then, there's also something about what I see in the mirror. I want to be doing it entirely because I want to be strong, but I know that I'm also doing it partly because I want to look a certain way.

There it was. There was the truth she saw in the mirror, the truth she saw as she squeezed her flesh between her fingers, the truth that, had Josh been sitting in front of her, she would never, ever have exposed. There would have been the crackling potential of sex between them, the coy duel, his eagerness and her armour.

The ticks on her phone screen turned blue, and then there was an atrocious silence. Dee's stomach somersaulted.

But Josh replied. *I think that sounds normal. Multitudes, right?*

Right, she wrote back. Something more than relief was flooding her body. And then Josh wrote again.

So when are you coming back to London?

Dee bit her lip. Coming back. *Going* back. It was impossible. Her mother's operation was two days away, and London was a lifetime away. Elsewhere, elsetime.

She flicked to the group with Liv and Rosa and Katie. Each day, they sent sweet, subdued messages of support. Each day Dee tried to reply. Each day the subtext of *when will we see you again?* went unanswered.

'I've been to the fish shop. Mussels. Thought you'd like

that. Remember when I taught you how to eat them? You must have only been about six or seven. Always up for something a bit squeamish.'

Dee looked up blearily. Her mother was carrying a weighty brown paper bag and wearing denim dungarees. She was smiling.

'What are you doing on your phone? Is this the famous Josh?'

Dee pocketed the phone. 'Sounds good. I'll help you make them.'

They moved in the practised way borne of time and love. Dee washed the mussels; Mel chopped shallots. Dee sliced crusty bread; Mel stirred butter and wine. Silence clung to them; a silence crusted around a date in the calendar, a letter from the hospital, an anaesthetic mask and a scalpel. Dee stole sideways glances at her mother's dungarees, the way they hung gently from her chest. Her mother had worn dungarees pregnant, nursing. Her own lips on her mother's flesh.

As they sat opposite one another on the same scrubbed table where Dee had eaten birthday cake and fish fingers and spaghetti hoops, and Dee's heart burned with fierce love, she said what did you see in him, my father?

Her mother stared at her, and swirled her fingers through the bowl of lemon water.

'Different things,' she said finally. 'He made me laugh. We used to have a great night out. But mostly I just fancied the pants off him.'

Dee stared back, and clicked a mussel shell like castanets. Her mother was smiling – a private, nostalgic kind of smile.

'It wasn't exactly what he looked like,' Mel continued. 'I mean, you've seen photos. He was nice-looking, for sure, but not – you wouldn't spot him from across the room and say there's the best-looking man here. But there was something about – his *essence*. It felt like our bones were drawn to each other. It was primal. Magnetic.'

'Wow,' Dee said.

'Yes. I know he was bad, in the end. But you came out of something good.'

Sex

An hour? A week? A month? A year? A whole new era or never again?

The first sex on the other side of your heartbreak might make the world move, or it might be something you'd rather forget. It might be a glorious opening up; it might be utterly banal. It might be odd. Sex is often odd.

If you have built up months or years of sex with one person, one person who saw and, more than that, helped create those most intimate dimensions of you, then you will likely notice that loss, that dislocation. You will notice a million differences in the next person – the shape of their body, the clustering of their freckles, their voice and their breath. It is strange and it is spectacular.

There is a difference between carrying something with you and having it overwhelm you. Those somethings are not of different weights – the shoulders that carry them are of different shapes. Stand tall.

Do not conflate sex with passion, or sex with intimacy, or sex with love. Sex can stand alone, fire and sweat. And that is wonderful.

Chapter Twenty-Two

TIME BENDS

*C*ount backwards from ten to one.

*

The ticking clock, the heartbeat.
  Inhale, exhale.
  Loop back, lie back, fall back.
  Heartbeak is not linear.

*

Dee sits in a corridor which smells of disinfectant and tension. Faraway sounds of joy and despair. Gratitude and devastation. *The operation should last around ninety minutes. You should be able to go home tomorrow. Recovery should take four to six weeks.*

Should; should.

She stares at the clock opposite. She can hear it ticking. She cannot see it moving. Her senses are contradicting each other, like the game her mother showed her as a child. One hand in icy water, one in hot, then both in tepid.

Time is its own uncanny in a hospital. Time begins and ends and freezes and floats here.

An hour and a half; a life and a half.

*

In London, Rosa and Liv and Katie keep their phones close. How can the future *be*, without Dee's mother in it? Mel has been here for as long as Dee has been here; they come together, go together.

Their first meeting with Mel: Manchester, their newly created houseshare at the beginning of second year. She drove Dee up in a battered red hatchback replete with ironic fluffy dice – or rather, they drove each other up, swapping shifts and boiled sweets and soundtrack requests as they broke down the hours.

Her first words to them: 'So this is the palace,' breezy and amused. But they knew she wasn't laughing at them – no, she knew a palace was precisely how it felt, with its eclectic carpets and pale yellow walls and condensation inside the windows.

She toured the house seriously, not pursing her lips or clutching at her wrists; she neither disapproved nor feared for them. She knew that they would walk home from the night bus in conspiratorial – but safety-conscious – pairs, laughing into the freezing dark and scattering chips along the pavement. She knew that they would throw parties at which more cracks and bruises would be added to the house and chipped away from their deposits, and she knew that it was all perfect.

She helped them stick posters and hang lights and later, when the pickle-jar cocktail shaker was revealed, she cackled at it and showed them how to make the best margaritas they had ever tasted. They danced with her in the kitchen and she seemed like an impossible combination of sophistication and freedom, youth and experience.

How different, they each thought, they each think, from my parents. Their conventionality, their distance. Mel is like a friend or a sister without it being contrived; she is not interested in reliving her youth or wishing herself younger. She wears the creases in her skin proudly, and they sing with the purple in her hair.

And was it there then, the imperfect cell, the cluster? Were the foundations of this day already in place all those years before, the division of Dee's life into *before* and *after*? Could she have lifted up her mother's skin and scooped out those beginnings, that whisper of a future horror? What could have been done?

*

Rosa is reading and holding her breath. Her column is live; the comments are open. There's the usual veneer of misogyny, of course – the *Why does this paper publish this woman's drivel?* And *I know what I'd like to do to Rosa the morning after*. But there are compliments, too. There are smiling acknowledgements of the awkwardness of the first morning together, confessions of waking early to apply makeup and brush hair before the other stirs. *You look so gorgeous in the morning*. There are shared recipes for scrambled eggs and notes on the best places to buy bread. *God, this is just the perfect articulation of the dualism after you've stayed over for the first time,* writes one. *You've broken the seal, you've made things that much more intimate – and yet you also feel more exposed than ever.*

Rosa feels a delightful spark ignite and spread through her torso. These comments are not only good – there are lots of them. Her article is one of the three leads on the lifestyle page – which means it is one of the three most read on the lifestyle page. As she scrolls again a fresh comment appears – *Great take on the dating column* – and she finds herself smiling. Yes, she thinks, yes. That is *exactly* what I wanted. Finally, finally, something is working.

And as she thinks this, she feels a lurch towards Dee. Dee, who just a few weeks ago was encouraging her, pushing her, helping her – and who, were it not for this spike of news, would be here now, hugging her perhaps, or raising a glass, or simply shouting YES! Ballsy, bright, beautiful Dee, who is the strongest woman in the world, but how can even that make a difference, when faced with this?

*

Liv's parents have come to London. A weekend away; a museum and the theatre. Their hotel is a budget chain near the station, bland and uninspiring, and she resists the urge to tell them that if you'd only asked me, I could have helped you find somewhere better.

They ask her to choose somewhere for dinner and she asks Rosa for advice; a tiny tapas restaurant with flickering candles and dozens of sherries listed on a blackboard. It is unpretentious and delicious; it is perfect.

They ask her about her friends and they ask her about her work. They ask her, gently, about Nikita. Liv stumbles and gradually settles. She describes the oscillations of these last months, the agony of uncertainty, the confusion of her own contradictions.

Her mother reaches across the table and strokes her hand, as she stroked her bruised knees and tree-scratched arms. And together they talk – not just about Liv's life now, but Liv's life then. They laugh together at the stacks of books she would bring home from the library, the times she waded into the river too far and muddy water spilled over her wellies, the colours she dyed her hair. They remind her of how she fought ferociously with her brother and sister – and how she curled up with them under a blanket on the sofa to watch cartoons.

They talk about the village, its soft rhythms and familiar faces, the way a particular tree looked sure to fall in the last storm but did not. They recall the times the river burst its banks, the times snowstorms cut off the electricity, the times heatwaves turned the fields from green to brown.

And as they talk, Liv looks out of the window over her father's shoulder, watches double decker buses and car head-lights and people in twos and threes and fours. She watches the buzz and anonymity and potential of the city at night, and she feels the old thrill.

She remembers being eighteen and leaving home, packing her belongings in binbags and a suitcase and a rucksack, and meticulously dressing herself in ripped black jeans and a vintage jumper and gold hoop earrings. Backcombed hair and shadow the colour of emeralds across her eyelids. She remembers being so very, very ready to leave that village.

Her father went to start the car before they left, because that is what he always did. Just checking in, he said. And as she and her mother stood on the doorstep, watching him with a kind of wry amusement, her mother put her arm around her shoulders, and squeezed her gently. We're very proud of you, darling, she said. You're going to have a wonderful time.

And she sees, now, the beautiful tension of those words, the ways in which her parents offer safety but not restriction, openness but not obligation. She doesn't know quite how much they know – her scratching restlessness, her violent hunger to be somewhere bigger, bolder, louder – but she feels the soft support of the cord looping back to them, regardless. She knows that her parents love her.

Because she is all of these. She is Olivia and Liv. She eats Heinz tomato soup with cheese on toast, and she eats char-grilled octopus with manzanilla. She wears wellies and Dr Martens and towering platforms. She loved Nikita in one way and she loves her in another. She can let her go, and she can forgive herself.

*

Katie has begun walking to and from work. It takes an hour and a half each way. Vaguely, she wonders if this is a waste of time, or a perfect use of time. She wonders if those wonderings are nonsense.

There is a point, on the route, where she knows that she is closest to the flats that Chris has moved to. She wishes she were not aware of this. She wishes that she could wipe a sponge over the map she carries in her mind, expunge Chris from the places where his echo reaches. But he is there, every time. Coffee with Nat before work; a glass of wine with Nat after work.

She doesn't wonder if Chris thinks of her, and so she doesn't wonder if this one-sidedness is strange.

She notices one day, one minute, that Katie-and-Chris has slipped from two months ago to three. May has morphed into June. Summer is whispering. She notices, too, how Katie-and-Chris remains astonishingly vivid. She can feel her arms around him. Her finger twitches to his name when she opens her phone.

She spends more time than she would like scrolling through digital traces of him. He updates little, and she is both grateful for this, and angry about it. She wants ferocious evidence: a picture of him and Nat; a picture of him looking miserable, pining for Katie and realizing his mistake; a picture of him embracing the delight of a happier life, better than hers in a thousand ways. But there is so little. She finds herself on ludicrous websites, reading his career history, the first line of his postcode, his exam results over a decade ago.

That gives her another idea, and she visits the website of his old school, staring at its Latin motto and bizarre straw hats. She feels layers of guilt, and envy, and anger. She pictures the eleven-year-old Chris, wide-eyed and frightened. She tries to imagine the names the older boys called him, and feels ashamed that she never asked.

And all the while she is doing this she thinks of Dee, and Mel, and hates herself. How heartbroken she thought she was, and how little she understood. Dee's mother might die. Dee's mother might leave her, not through *this isn't working* or *we've grown apart* but through blood, and pain, and fear. A kind of loss she is so cossetted from; a kind of loss that is terrifying in its uncertainty.

She knows what Dee would say to this. Don't be stupid. There aren't hierarchies of grief, K. That *there are starving children* never made you finish your vegetables, did it?

And she knows this, and she doesn't know it. She knows so little.

*

The operation is tomorrow and Dee is furious. So angry, so incensed at everyone in the world who is not living through this. How dare they, that couple from a few doors down, stroll up the pavement, holding hands as though they are *happy*? How dare they, that child on a scooter, whizz past in the opposite direction, giggling like spring rain? How dare they, Liv and Katie and Rosa, fill her phone with messages of love and support and promises, when all this shows is that nothing can be promised, nothing can be made certain, nothing can be scaffolded against these storms?

She thinks of Leo, and that is most appalling of all. Leo, that *speck*, that *nothing*, who had the gall to kiss her and fuck her and hold her and then tell her that actually, after all, he no longer saw her in that heated, special way. How dare he worm his way here, into this most red and raw and bleeding place?

The operation is tomorrow and Dee will not sleep. She feels as though she will never sleep again. She has forgotten how to dream.

*

Katie tucks *Great Expectations* into her bag. She can't remember whether she read it at school or not – which is ridiculous, of course, and a little embarrassing. But she has soaked it up (again?) these past weeks like a warm bath, and now she and Rafee are going to the book group together. She wonders who she will meet, and what she will say. She has been trying to articulate something about expectation, but the words have crumpled in her mouth.

She feels something anticipatory and light, like a bottle of pop that has been shaken but not opened. Rafee is waiting at the bottom of the stairs.

*

The operation was yesterday and her mother is in bed. Dee has made her a cup of tea but it sits, cool, on the bedside table, tannic skins forming on its surface. A knock on the door. Dee expects Yolande or Kim or Rachel, but it is a man she doesn't know, dark hair streaked with silver and a pinprick in his lip from a long-ago piercing.

For one appalling, ridiculous, insane fraction of a second she thinks it is her father.

Hello, he says, I'm Ad, I live over the road.

She feels her shoulders tensing, her back straightening. An old posture of strength and defiance.

He is holding out Tupperware boxes, and explaining it's a lasagne, and a dhal, and a sort of vegetably lentilly thing, anyway I know what it's like, times like this, it's difficult to cook isn't it? So these are for you, and if you need anything else, just pop over.

She's searching his face for something to be suspicious of. She's wondering what he wants, what he thinks, what he is about to shatter. But he's just smiling, this cautious sad smile, and as she takes the boxes he nods at her, and she stammers out a thank you for this act of kindness, this gesture that is just what it is, this man who is simply being thoughtful and compassionate.

And when she closes the door, Dee is shocked to find herself crying. So this is what it feels like, tears and sticky skin and scratches down her throat. This is what it feels like to make an animal noise, to scramble her face like a mask, to slide down the wall and hug her knees to her chest. Huge, heaving, gasping sobs, from the very roots of her lungs. She feels wrapped in something she hadn't realized she had, just as that which she always took for granted is slipping through her fingers.

The operation was yesterday and nothing will ever be certain.

*

Liv has been called into a meeting with Zachary. Her heart is beating horribly quickly. She is imagining a chain of possibilities, all of which circle around the meeting with Felix, and she is afraid, above all, of crying. Carrie glides out of the meeting room before her and catches her eye – her expression is impassive. Liv tries to make hers so. But she is furious with Felix, furious with herself, and she tries to wipe her clammy hands surreptitiously on her trousers as Zachary speaks.

Except his words are different – he is talking about *performance uplift* and *change in attitude* and *very impressed* – and he is describing a new title, a new role, a new number. She is shaking his hand and her eyes are level with his. Dee will be psyched, she thinks, this making the world how we want it to be. And then she feels a stab of guilt, because of course Dee's world is whirling out of her control.

*

We should go away, says Katie. No, I don't mean running away. We should take Dee on holiday. Somewhere in the sunshine. With water. We should have barbecues and make sangria and swim.

That sounds amazing. But she's in Brighton. She's been hiding there for weeks. She won't say when she's coming back.

Mel will want her to come. Mel will want her to live her life.

It won't be enough. Dee won't want to leave her side.

Mel will help us. Mel will tell her to. She's better, she's brighter.

I've got another idea. Something that will help to bring her back.

Katie opens the heartbreak handbook and together they pour everything they can think of onto its pages. All they have learned, all they have lost, all they have loved. Rosa writes recipes for the dishes Dee loves best: fried rice; noodle soup; prawns with chilli. Liv transcribes poems: Robert Frost; e. e. cummings; Elizabeth Barrett Browning. Katie writes a message on a postcard. The image on the card is a stylized Victorian circus scene: acrobats, lions, elephants, clowns. In the centre is the ringmaster; top hat, red tails, whip.

She tucks the postcard inside the cover of the heartbreak handbook, which she wraps in brown paper. She writes Mel's address – or Mel's and Dee's address – on the outside, and takes it to the post office. She wishes into the ether.

*

A package drops onto the doormat. Dee drifts to it as she has drifted through the house since the operation. The air feels thick and cold. There should be joy in her mother bandaged in bed, cleansed – cured? – but it is tempered with fear.

Uneasily, Dee has come to realize that this fear will never go away. The Dee who never felt an anxious weight when her mother's face flashed up on her phone is gone for ever. And this means that the Dee who met Josh in a London bar, who batted back his questions with light acerbity, is gone for ever too. So she has not told him when she will return to London. She cannot.

Her mother is asking about him again, gently but also ridiculously, because god knows her mother has never been the type to elevate relationships to the most important thing about her daughter's life. And so this is infuriating, this idea that Josh might somehow be granted a window into this place, this time, where everything feels like poison.

She weighs the brown paper package in her hand and she knows what it is without opening it. How many hours did they spend, she and Liv and Rosa, writing their heartbreaks into a form for Katie to grasp onto?

But when she finally slides a finger under the wrapping and lets the book fall open in her arms, she finds the pages far fuller than she remembers. Katie has taken it up and on; she has written about drinking, about hangovers, about remaking herself. There are torn pages from where the book has been thrown into a wall; there are ferocious, furious scribblings. The rage she feels in her blood burns in recognition.

Rosa and Liv are there too; quotes and scraps of conversation, fragments of their friendship like pressed flowers. Everywhere there is permission; permission to feel agony and elation and anger and everything that is extraordinary and appalling – because this is appalling.

A postcard, and Katie's handwriting. *Darling Dee. I hope this helps you like it is helping me. We have a plan, when you're ready. Love always.*

*

The operation is now and Dee bites each fingernail down to the meaty pink flesh of her fingertips while her mother is in theatre. Something about exposing that skin which is meant to be hidden, the white sting of air and blood, keeps her in the world. The hospital is saturated with antiseptic and blood and tears. Somewhere nearby, babies are being born.

A doctor walks towards her and Dee shakes. The world is turning sideways.

But she is saying it went well, we have removed the breast, there was no sign of spread.

The breast. The horrifying distances within oneself. Betrayals within a body.

The doctor's hand is on Dee's shoulder. A slight pressure on the strap of her bra. We'll have to do further checks, of course, she is saying. Of course, of course. She's groggy but you can see her.

Her mother looks older and thinner than she ever has before. The purple of her hair no longer looks like a party; it looks like a bruise. There are layers of green and white fabric and gauze. Dee realizes she was expecting to see an absence, an excavation, but of course her mother is swaddled, like a child.

She feels as though she is going to be sick, and she feels elated. The cancer has been extracted from her mother's body and incinerated. She tries to screw her mind shut against the imaginings of microscopic cells evading the scalpel, dancing into a stream of blood. She holds her mother's hand. I'm going to take care of you. We're going to go home.

*

An hour and a half; a life and a half.

Dee reads Katie's words, and shakes:

Loop back, lie back, fall back.

Heartbreak is not linear.

Chapter Twenty-Three

AWAY

The house felt like a secret. The track had taken them miles from the main road, winding through trees which embraced above the car, creating a shadowy tunnel. It was like driving backwards through time. Yet when they reached the end, the landscape opened up like a pair of wings, a mosaic of brown and green before them, crickets and the background haze of Mediterranean summertime. The swimming pool glittered like a gemstone and the table next to it quickly acquired the dreamy detritus of a holiday with the closest of friends: stubby beer bottles and sangria jugs; leftover crisp packets weighed down with stones; battered paperback books and sticky-sided sun cream bottles.

The countryside nearby was sprinkled with tourist attractions: medieval towns and ruined castles; glorious viewpoints and charming markets – and they ignored them all. Each morning Rosa drove into the village and came back weighed down with a new kind of cheese, or a fresh bag of prawns, or golden-brown bread – and always, always alcohol – but the house was their kingdom. It was both utterly domestic and a magic wonderland, dislocated from every trivial and traumatic concern of their lives.

Their conversations looked backwards more than forwards, and in this way they acted as a re-pointing of their friendship, a close examination and refurbishing of its bricks and mortar. They reminisced about their meeting and first impressions, how Katie had seemed softer than they later found her to be, and Dee harder. They exchanged memories of the speech bubbles Dee added to the women on the bar's sticky walls, and the kebab shops they favoured for chips for the night bus. They repeated their complex layer of in-jokes, the kind that can only be built up through observing each other's laundry, and hangovers, and frantic deadlines, and bad dates. In the evenings they recreated a calmer, slower, sun-dazed version of every club they had ever visited, turning up the speaker by the pool and dancing as the sun turned the sky nectarine and plum. Katie's holiday idea, they acknowledged within the first five minutes, and repeatedly thereafter, had been absolutely perfect.

Quietly, Katie thought of it as an idea for herself as much as for Dee. Dee, who to everyone's quiet surprise had left her trainers and leggings out of her suitcase, who slept late each morning through an undulating mixture of peace and anxiety. Each morning, then, Katie got up before the others, catching the sun just as it crept above the distant horizon. She climbed over the fence at the bottom of the weather-bleached garden and followed a line of olive trees down to the bottom of the field. There, she met a tiny stream bed, reduced to a trickle in the July heat, and followed its meandering path as the hum and buzz of daytime gradually increased. She jumped from rock to rock, and dry twigs scratched at her calves.

Eventually the stream brought her back round to the end of the track and there she began to run, taking the final two miles in alternating gentle jogs and flat-out sprints, running as she hadn't run in years, running like a child, limbs flailing, muscles squeezing, so that the blood boiled in her ears and she was aware of nothing, nothing except the dust flying up from her feet, and the already muggy air, and her body.

This morning ritual took her into herself and then out of herself. The first part of the journey was all thought, the second part no thought at all. The first part of the journey was a meticulous picking of a route across the dusty ground, navigating precisely, wondering if Chris was going on holiday this summer and where, and who with, and if he had got that promotion yet, and whether Pete and Fiona had asked after her, and if he would send her a birthday card, and no that was ridiculous, but what would he say about her hair, and how did he feel about their breakup now, and how did *she* feel about their breakup now, and how could a relationship be falling to pieces but also joyful, and would another relationship be better, and if it was going to be, couldn't she jump there now, please, and above all, *was Chris thinking of her?* It was exhausting, and the holiday was making it all seem bigger as well as smaller. Smaller because he was so distant, literally another country – bigger because he had followed her even here.

She traced a line from the Chris she met at the circus party, beer in hand and adorable elephant costume, to the

Chris that March Saturday, bracing himself against the kitchen counter, selecting each word with unbearable precision. The bookends of the Chris she had known, the Chris who had loved her, the Chris whom she had counselled, and yelled at, and wrapped her limbs around.

Those months of *getting to know you*, as they compared notes on market town teenagerhood – weird isn't it, that we name those towns for that rhythm of life that's so irrelevant these days? As they mooned over Manchester and mountains, as they scratched at the edges of *life after here* and what it might mean, what it should mean. As he described the tightly wound, pursed lips of the Home Counties, those rigid implications of a good degree and a move to the big city and a salary that would buy three bedrooms but ideally four. As she described teaching, and worrying about the naivety of *because I like children*, and about the far more personal uncertainty bound up in that, and the pushes and pulls of concrete and fields, and being blasé about mortgages but that's because it was different for our parents, wasn't it? Trying to distinguish between *being carefree* and *burying your head in the sand*, and it's all ridiculous isn't it, life is for living, life is for laughter, don't worry about it, chill out. Well, yes, Katie, but it's a hell of a lot easier to chill out when you're not worried about how to pay the bills, and your body means that children are ungraspable, like oil in water. She tried to draw clear lines between *privilege* and *obsession* and *realism* and *romance*, and every day they collapsed in on each other.

The second part of the journey was a stretch and push of everything, finding her limit and sliding beyond. There, she took herself to a place of no more or less than her body – not her body's scars and instability and uncertainty, but her body *now*, its movement and its pure burning – and it was blissful. The world was muscle and sweat and breath alone. But each time she arrived back at the house, rivulets down her arms and back, face throbbing, her thoughts came back.

Four months. Such a neat package of time – sixteen weeks, or a third of a year – and yet also the most surreally meandering *passage*; yes, how she understood the meaning of *that* word, now. Four months of journeying, trying to find her way in the dark, lost without a map, leaping ahead and looping back. She thought of TJ, and the heat of his skin, and the glory of being young, and rum, and sex, and skipping home with no framework, no demands but her own. She thought of Chris's parents' house, and their gentle welcoming, their yellow and orange mugs, and the close cocoon of a future that looked solid. And she thought of Dee, and Mel, and the visceral horror of her illness and her operation, the idea of Mel floating from room to room in Dee's childhood home while Dee herself lay on a sun lounger and tried to daydream. Because when your life was ripped from under you, the loss of daydreaming was something no one mentioned but should – how impossible it was to drift from second to second, minute to minute, without the continual reminder of *this dreadful thing has happened*.

'Do you want to talk about it?' had been implicit and explicit, from the moment they met Dee in the airport, to the first arrangement of the sun loungers, to the last sip and goodnight kiss each evening. Sometimes Dee tightened her lips and shook her head, and sometimes she described something: how small and pale her mother had looked immediately after the operation; how much soup – fucking *soup*! – she had made; how breast cancer survival had improved over recent years, but how you couldn't know, not really, not ever. They were fragments rather than conversations – pieces of reflection she set around herself like shards of glass – and her friends collected them up so they couldn't cut her, and stroked her hair, and tried to make sense.

'Your mum sounds like she's been so strong,' Rosa said, one day. Her voice was inflected with admiration and near disbelief. Dee lay flat on her sun lounger, looking at the sky.

'Yes. She always is, right?' Dee shook herself slightly, as though an insect had brushed against her skin. 'I tried to get her to talk – do you know, she never cried? Not once? And then a week or two ago – I'd gone out for a walk, and her friend Yolande came round – lives on our street, I've known her for years. Anyway, I came back, and they mustn't have heard the door, and I stood in the hallway and I heard her *sobbing*. Really, sobbing. She was saying she was scared. But she's never said that to me.'

They looked at each other.

'What did you do?' Liv asked.

'I went back outside. I walked for another twenty minutes and when I got back again they were in the kitchen making tea. Yolande asked me about Josh. Josh! Someone I met in a bar fucking *weeks* ago. It was tedious.' Her eyes were inscrutable behind her sunglasses.

'I guess – I suppose she doesn't want to upset you,' Katie said.

'Course she doesn't want to upset me. She's always protected me, from everything. It's stupid.'

'Is it?' Rosa asked quietly. Dee said nothing, but as she brought her chin towards her chest, it was trembling. The swimming pool shimmered.

'Yolande already lived there when we moved in, after my dad left. She had two kids, a bit older than me. She used to tell my mum, when I was screaming, "Put her in water or take her outside." My mum would do both at once. Take me down to the sea. As soon as I was big enough to paddle, I'd be in. And it's carried on, you know. All through school, all through trips back from Manchester, if I was in a funk about something, she'd say "Vitamin sea" and we'd head straight down to the beach.'

'Therapeutic.'

'Yeah. The sea makes me feel the right size. Small but also safe.'

'That's lovely.'

'That's like the heartbreak handbook,' Katie said. 'Do you remember? Months ago, when we went for that walk in the country. We wrote about being outside, and space and things. How looking at the sky makes you feel . . .' She trailed off, suddenly aware that she had been about to say *like your problems are smaller. Like you're reminded of how insignificant you are*, and aware, too, that that was horrific. Was that what she had meant? Chris walked across her field of vision, and smiled pityingly at her.

'Yes,' Dee said. 'I ran every day in Brighton. When you sent me the book, I realized why.'

The heartbreak handbook sat, now, on the golden stones between them. It had been the first thing Dee packed, and the first thing she showed them when they arrived. They hugged around it like a talisman, and Dee reverently placed it into Katie's hands. Thank you, thank you. It's yours to take back, now.

'So the first few days after the operation, Mum was in bed a lot,' Dee continued. 'But as soon as she was up for it, that's what I said to her. *Vitamin sea*. And I held her hand as we walked down. I mean, we hold hands a lot, but this time I was really holding *her* hand, you know?'

They knew.

'Could you tell her?' Liv asked eventually. 'That you heard her crying, I mean? Could that open – I don't know – open it up?' Even as she spoke she felt a violent impossibility, the idea of sitting across from her own mother, taking her hand perhaps, asking her if she wanted a cup of tea.

Dee was silent for a long time. 'I don't know if I want to,' she said. And it was the truth, she thought, feeling herself swing one way and then back. She tried to picture her mother's face as she said – what would she say, anyway? Would she be blunt, tell her *I know you're frightened, stop pretending*? Would she circle it gently, tell her how she herself had broken down at Ad's delivery of food, how crying for the first time in so long had felt therapeutic, yes, but also excruciating? A relief and a noose.

And then would she confess her fears, her prickling

realization that no doctor's reassurances would ever be enough? We cannot see any cancer *now*. But that makes no guarantee for *then*. And this is how we must live now, for ever.

'Ty, my editor, said something once,' Rosa said suddenly. 'We'd done a piece about people going back to visit the places where they'd grown up, the power of nostalgia and all that. The pain of going home again, that's literally what nostalgia means, did you know that? And he said wait until you get into your thirties, that's when the switch starts to happen, that's when you'll have friends who are starting to care for their parents instead of the other way around. And he said he always visualized it like a see-saw, this very specific red-and-blue see-saw in the park when he was a kid. How it always rested one way and then it swings back.'

She thought of her own childhood garden as she spoke, and Nina waving over the fence. The wedding was just two weeks away. A country house half an hour from the city; a place where they would play-act at wealth from years past.

Dee peeled herself upwards, wincing as her skin lifted from the plastic. She took off her sunglasses without meeting their gazes. 'I'm sweltering.' She walked and dived into the pool in a single sinuous movement, quicksilver, magical. Liv and Rosa and Katie deliberated without speaking, then one by one jumped in after her, splashing and shrieking. Something hanging low in the air shattered into laughter.

'So I've been thinking,' Rosa said, as they floated. 'I'm going to quit my job.'

Liv kicked her feet onto the bottom and stared at her. 'You're what?'

'Yes. I'm going to retrain.' Rosa felt a delicious thrill as she said it aloud.

'In what?'

Beside the pool, the heartbreak handbook's pages flickered in the breeze.

'In food. In cooking, I mean. The shift in my dating pieces – it's been great, I've loved it – but I've realized *why* I love it, you know? I don't want to be messing around writing about food, I want to be doing it. I don't want to be one layer removed – I want to be a cook. A chef.'

A flutter of imagined sensations; smoke and steam, metal on metal, fizzing and spitting.

She caught Liv's eye and swallowed. 'And I know it'll be a massive thing, financially. My family – there's maybe something my grandma was going to give me, which will help. And I'm going to freelance while I'm doing it. So I guess – you know, that means the journalism will still be useful, for now. And maybe it's crazy, after the training I've already done. But it feels like the right thing.'

Liv swirled water around her body. 'Wow,' she said eventually.

'Yeah.'

Dee and Katie glanced at each other, shared a skittery inhale.

'Where . . . ?' Katie began.

'A college. It's not far from the flat, actually. I mean, it'll probably be full of teenagers.'

'Your weekends'll never be the same,' Dee said.

'I know.'

'The pay . . .'

'I know.'

Rosa was biting her lip and watching Liv.

'Look, I don't – I don't think I'd have made this decision when I was twenty. For all kinds of reasons.'

Liv was nodding slowly. 'You don't need to be the same person now that you were then,' she said, and she meant it.

Sometime else, a younger Liv and Rosa clinked their mugs of wine together over pages of annotated poetry, highlighted novels.

'Thank you,' Rosa said.

Liv nodded again. 'I'm happy for you.'

The pool glittered, and they all breathed out. This is great, this is exciting, how long will it take, where will you go. Rosa shyly explained what she could, the things she needed to learn, the experience she needed to get, gave shape to this new ambition. Her friends listened and asked questions and listened again, and all of them noticed the distance between *then* and *now*. A time when everything was ahead of them and yet everything, also, seemed so final.

Katie turned to Dee. 'So your mum's been telling her friends about Josh?'

'That's right. Yet more stupidity, right? She's never been like this about anyone before. Even when I first met Leo. And the thing is, it's not like I've even told her anything about him. I mean, there's nothing to tell. We've messaged each other a bit, but that's it. And it's like she's *fixated*.'

'You've been messaging him?'

'Well. Yes. For a while.'

Golden flecks sparkled in the sunbeams above the water. 'And what *do* you think about Josh?' Rosa asked.

'Come on. It's been weeks. *Months.* The messaging – it was just for a while, when I was in Brighton. Then he asked me when I was coming back to London, and I ignored him. I think he'll have taken that as a pretty classic ghosting. What?' This was directed at Rosa, who could not hide her smile.

'Nothing. It's just – well, aren't you avoiding the question?'

Dee floated onto her back and looked at the sky. 'I don't know what you mean.'

'Come on. Doesn't matter that you ghosted him. Doesn't matter if you never see him again. What do you *think* about him?'

Another long pause.

'I think – I think he seems different. I don't think I've met someone like him before.'

'That's pretty special,' Katie said.

'Well. Special or not. It's done, now. How are you doing anyway, K?'

Katie was leaning against the edge of the pool, resting her arms on the hot stone. Behind her, a paperback copy of *No One Is Talking About This* sat damply, page folded down midway. A note from Rafee was scrawled inside the front cover: *I know you'll miss this, being away, but thought we could talk about it anyway. x*

She gazed down the garden towards the treeline of the stream. Beyond, the sky was shifting from blue to pink.

'I don't know,' she said. 'Time – time feels very strange. I can't work out if Chris and I feels like five minutes ago, or five years. Sometimes it's like I can reach out and touch him. You've probably moved on from it all, but working in a school, you never really get away from that rhythm of the years, you know? The summer feels like this *gap*, this dislocation between the past and the future. The new year isn't December–January, it's *now* – it's July–August, and it's all stretched out and – *languid*, somehow. There's so much time to think. September should be all fresh and different, shiny shoes and a new pencil case. For now – the year is over, but it hasn't begun.'

'That's how Manchester used to feel,' Liv said. 'I hated going home in the holidays. Everything felt so small and quiet. And I missed you all so much.'

'Yes. I did, too.'

They echoed, and smiled.

'We were so lucky to find each other.'

'*Find* each other? Jesus, Rosa.'

'You know what I mean!'

'Sure, sure.'

'We had an amazing time, didn't we?'

'Oh, don't get all melancholy. We're twenty-nine, this isn't the twilight of our youth or something.'

'God, we were young then though.'

'We're young now, you lunatic.'

'Older and wiser.'

'Something like that.'

'Would you live in it again? The Manchester house?'

'Fuck. Only if they did some serious damp-proofing. Remember those snails we used to get in the kitchen?'

'That mould on the living-room wall? I'm sure I've seen, kind of, sober investigative news clips about how dodgy that is.'

'At least we had a living-room window.'

'That's true. We were babies, though.'

'We're babies now!'

'We're *women* now.'

'Oh please. I still look around in a panic if someone tells their kid to let the lady past.'

'I'm pleased if I get ID'd.'

'It was great though. The four of us together.'

'Well. In a few months. Take two.'

They floated past each other as the sun sank, kicking droplets which shimmered like diamonds. They brushed fingertips, sweat and water.

'I've had an idea,' Rosa said.

'Go on.'

'The four of us. Living together.'

'Yes?'

'Well – what if we *bought* somewhere?'

They floated further. The music undulating through the speakers seemed louder. A fairground ride, a nightclub from the queue outside, the beginnings of a party.

'Do you think we could?' Katie asked, doubtfully.

'Why not? I know we could never do it individually, or even in a couple, not without a lot of help – but four of us?'

'They'll lend you four times what you earn, I think,' Dee said. 'Give or take.'

'Well then. Four times four salaries. And I know we'd

need a deposit, but we've each got bits and pieces of savings, haven't we?'

'Ten per cent of a lot is still a lot,' Liv said.

'Of course. I mean, maybe we can't do it in a few months. Maybe we rent together first again. I don't know, I guess we'd need to speak to an adviser or whatever. But the point is, *this* is what we could work to next. Somewhere of our own. Somewhere we can, I don't know, paint, and furnish, and build on. A fucking *home*.'

Dee circled her hands in the water so her body gently rotated like the hand of a clock. She thought of her mother. *A roof I could keep on paying for, food in the fridge. Confidence in the next month, and the month after that. That's the basis, that's the* foundation. *And it's a huge bloody privilege.*

As if they were inside her skull, Liv and Katie and Rosa caught her eye. Mel – your mum – she got it, didn't she?

'I think it's brilliant,' Dee said.

'Really?'

'Yeah. I don't know why we haven't thought of it before.'

'I guess – I guess we thought the future might look different,' Katie said. She wasn't sure if she felt mournful or not.

'It still might, K! This isn't about tying ourselves up for ever, starting up the cat sanctuary early! This is about – roots, and, and – security, and – fuck it – *investment*. In ourselves. In what's next. In *our* futures, right?'

'We could build that into it,' Liv said. 'An agreement, I mean. If, in the future, one of us met someone, and wanted to move out, or them to move in. We could plan for all of that.' She looked at Rosa and grinned. 'I think it's brilliant too.'

The sun had nearly set. Katie looked at the orange-pink clouds, and stretched out her arms so her fingers tickled the water's surface like a pond skater. She thought of the previous summer, and finding the flat with Chris. She thought of how she had felt, sturdy and safe. She thought of their moving day and its fractious tension, the growing awareness that something was wrong and the fear of facing it. She thought of warmth and calm.

'It is,' she said.

Away

Distance from your heartbreak can mean space as well as time. You cannot run away from your heartbreak, but you can leave it somewhere else for a while. You cannot escape your life, but you can look at it from a different angle.

And there are so very many other countries out there. You needn't cross borders to reach them. Walk around the park in the opposite direction. Buy your coffee from a new place. Visit the seaside and stare at the ocean – and then throw yourself into it, because icy saltwater is medicine for everything.

Distance from your heartbreak can enable you to be more generous, and less. It can enable you to pinpoint the ways in which they were wrong, and decide precisely how much sympathy you have for them. It can enable you to examine the places where your threads have been cut, and remind yourself that they have simply restarted somewhere else. It can be a pause, a break, a rest and a reset.

Going away need not mean running away – although is there really anything wrong with that?

Going away can be the best way of going towards. Towards all that you are going to be. Towards the new wild. Towards the rest of your bright, beautiful life.

Chapter Twenty-Four

BACK

L ondon in high summer: sticky heat and the smell of
barbecues; throbbing music and rhythmic rollerblades;
the crunch of beer cans and the slip of ice lollies. They
returned in a mixture of refreshment and excitement, chilled
out and spun out, unknowing but hopeful, and deliciously
aware that, even now, so many years after meeting, they
had found something new to share. For batting around the
idea for the rest of the holiday had, of course, involved
sharing salaries and savings figures and approaches to
investing – and this, they said in wonder to each other, was
something they had never talked about before, not really,
not like this.

Katie went first, I'm going to be obvious, aren't I, teachers'
salaries are public knowledge, and Dee said briskly well I've
got nothing to hide, and Rosa and Liv caught each other's
eyes, wondering how to temper, and qualify, and how the
other would react, and spoke at the same time. Liv explained
how her promotion and her bonus worked, and Rosa
described the gift her grandmother had promised her, and
what might be left over after her retraining, and gradually

their embarrassment dissipated, and they listed out what they had, and gazed at the possibility it added up to.

That glowing ember nestled in each of them throughout the flight home, the muggy Underground back to their pocket of the city, the dragging of their bags into bedrooms. Dee sat gently on the edge of her bed, so empty for so many of the recent weeks, looking at herself in the wardrobe mirror. Her skin had the darkened sheen of holiday, and she tried to smile at herself. She called her mother.

'Darling. How was the trip?'

'It was good. It was *great*. Feels ridiculous saying this to you, but I felt like I needed it.'

'Of course you did. And I'm delighted to say I have my own lined up too, now. A week in Greece, first week of September. Just me and the girls – the women.'

'Well, that sounds perfect.'

'Doesn't it? I'm going swimsuit shopping with Kim this weekend. Taking the scar out for a spin.'

Dee swallowed. This kind of cheerful ghoulishness had become a particular trait of Mel's over the past few months. Dee thought she understood its intention – related to it, even – that desire to bring the very darkest possibilities into the daylight, to demonstrate precisely how unconcerning they were, and above all, to derail pity before it began – but seeing her mother deploy the same tactics she knew of herself felt harsh and painful.

'And how are you feeling? How is everything? What happened at your check-up?'

She could sense her mother smiling wearily down the phone

as she explained that she really was feeling okay, tired obviously, but otherwise okay, very little pain, next doctor's appointment coming up, you know I'll tell you if anything changes.

If anything changes, Dee's brain repeated.

She remembered something Katie had said. Was it something Chris had said to her? Something that seemed darkly absurd in its casualness. Nothing stays the same. So what do you do, then? How do you brace yourself against this, and everything else?

'So, I hope you can relax back into your London life a bit, now,' her mother continued.

'My "London life". You sound like some online influencer.'

'Darling. I mean it. You've done a lot the past couple of months.'

'It was nothing,' Dee said fiercely. 'I mean – I don't mean nothing. I mean, it wasn't a question.' She flicked her finger against the glass. The sound echoed – toasts at parties, her toothbrush against the bathroom mirror, her hand on her mother's front door. Our front door. Home. 'Are you scared?' she asked.

There was a long silence. When her mother finally spoke, there was a strange inflection in her voice. 'Darling star, of course I'm scared. But whoever said life wasn't scary?'

Dee nodded silently down the phone, and felt liquid pool in her eyes.

'I had an idea, as well. Something you can help with.'

'Okay?'

Her mother laughed gently. 'Don't sound so worried! I was reading some things – interviews and so on – women who've had the op, you know? And the decisions they make around reconstruction, inserts, all that.'

'Okay.'

'And – drumroll – did you know that people get tattoos over their scars?'

'Okay. I mean – yes. Yes, I guess.'

'All sorts. I mean, you can imagine. Lots of flowers, lots of feathers, lots of wings. But I was thinking – well, I've got the most extraordinarily talented daughter, who designs beautiful things for a living. So it would be a *waste*, really, wouldn't it, not to ask you . . .'

Dee swallowed a flood of agony and adoration.

'Darling? Did you hear me?'

'Yes – yes. I heard you.'

'And?'

'Mum – of course. I'd be honoured. Of course I will.'

'And I don't mean to mask it, you know? Scars are strength, right? I mean to *celebrate*. I'll leave the details down to you, but I was thinking – well, of course I was thinking stars.'

Yes, stars. A constellation; a galaxy. To look at stars is to look back in time; the passage of light across distance; the persistence. I will shower your skin in stars. I will make you glow. I will keep you with me.

*

Rafee was cooking when Katie got in; the entire ground floor of the little house was filled with smells of spice and lime. He called to her with pleasing enthusiasm, hey, how are you, how was the trip, you're really tanned, want some wine?

She left her bag by the sofa, the heartbreak handbook nestled at the top, and took the glass gratefully.

'What a welcome. Thanks. Where's Jack?'

'Oh, he's over at Amelie's. Think they've really hit it off.'

'That's great.'

'Yeah, it is. He's a good guy, you know? Deserves to be with someone decent.'

Katie nodded and sipped. 'It's simple really, isn't it? Good people should be with good people.'

Rafee laughed. 'You put the world to rights by the swimming pool, then?'

She laughed too. 'Every night.'

'And how's your friend doing? Dee? And her mum?'

'Mm. She's okay, I think. Both of them, I mean. It sounds like the operation went well, and she's had some radiotherapy which has made her very tired. And now it's check-ups and scans I suppose, for the rest of her life.'

She paused, allowing 'the rest of her life' to flood them. Dee would never not fear her mother dying. She would never not be Katie from Katie-and-Chris.

'I think – I think there's a reasonable chance of it recurring. "Reasonable chance". That sounds awful, doesn't it? I talk about the kids having reasonable chances of getting decent grades. What I mean is, it's not over. It won't ever be over. And I don't know how you make sense of that. Dee – she's always got things very under control. One of those people who just seems – it's like the world fits around her, not the other way around. And this just smashes all of that, doesn't it?'

'For sure. Illness is a pretty intense thing at the best of times, never mind when it's just the two of them.'

'Exactly.' Katie was startled with a mental image of Chris in a doctor's waiting room.

'You know,' she said. 'I have this – this condition. God – nothing like Dee's mum, I don't really know why I'm saying this now. But it's – it might affect things to do with children, later on. If I want to have them. If I try to have them.'

'Oh, right,' said Rafee. 'You mean like PCOS? My sister has that. Sorry, that's very personal, isn't it? What I mean is, I get that, the whole will it, won't it, maybe you need to think about this earlier than you'd like thing. It's a headfuck.'

His tone was light and airy. She felt an echo of something months previously, meeting Jack and Rafee for the first time. *A right hassle.* How people beyond yourself could make the heavy seem casual, could remind you how differently it looked from another angle.

She nodded slowly. 'Not quite, but similar.'

'Well, sorry, anyway.'

'Thanks. And how have the past couple of weeks been for you?'

'Yeah, good. Not quite Mediterranean but good beers-in-the-park weather. We missed you at book group, of course.'

'Yes! I'm looking forward to the next one. Remind me what we're reading?'

'*Rebecca.*'

'Right! I actually first read that when I was about thirteen. I found it *so* romantic. And scary, of course.' She added this after a beat in which Rafee caught her eye, and she felt her skin flushing.

'Aha,' he said. 'Well, it's a new one for me, but romantic and scary sounds like a – a good combination.' Was he blushing?

*

Welcome back, account director. Drink this week? We've got planning to do.

Liv allowed the message from Carrie to marinate for a few minutes before replying: *Yes, definitely.* Ally; adviser; competitor; confidante. How lucky she was to know these multitudes. She turned to Rosa and Dee. 'Want to go out for dinner tonight?'

Dee shook her head, gnawing at her fingernail, while Rosa simultaneously nodded enthusiastically.

'Oh. We can stay in, hang out.'

'No. No. You both head out. I feel like being – quiet, I guess.'

'You sure?'

'Yeah, definitely.' And she meant it, Dee thought, as she tried to repress the circling. A walk around the park, perhaps, and then an evening on the sofa. These little pieces of certainty when the world was stormy. *Whoever said life wasn't scary?* The sun will set late, tonight. The hazy arc from midsummer to autumn. Candyfloss and Coke. *Whoever said life wasn't scary?*

'What do you fancy?' Rosa asked.

'Let's go to that Colombian place. Empanadas!'

'Sounds good.'

*

The two friends sat opposite each other on a rickety picnic bench as the sunset licked over the buildings, and they clinked glasses of cheap red wine.

'What shall we toast?' Rosa asked.

'We've been toasting all fortnight,' Liv said. 'Not sure there's any part of us we haven't celebrated.'

'It has been pretty saturated in narcissism.'

'I think a good dose of self-celebration was needed. At least, for Katie and Dee. And it'd be rude not to join in, right?'

'Right.' Rosa sipped her wine. 'And we have our plan, now.' She tested out the words, back in their own neighbourhood, seeing how they tasted, checking how they stood up.

'We do.' Liv mirrored her motions. 'It really is a good idea, you know.'

'You honestly think so? Not just drunken holiday me-anderings?'

'Well, that too. But yes, I honestly think so. I mean, all those assumptions that you have to wait until you meet someone and set up a joint account, and we forgot that we were family all along.'

Rosa smiled into her drink. 'I'm glad you feel the same way.'

'I do.'

They breathed the same unspoken weight beneath the words, the joy and the tension of finding yourself so echoed in someone else.

'So,' said Liv. 'We should toast *your* plan. This time next year, maybe?'

'Maybe. I mean, I'll be sweating in the kitchen instead of out here cheers-ing.'

Her eyes were shining, and Liv laughed. 'I'd say I can't believe it, but actually I can. I'm happy for you, you know.'

'You don't think it's a huge waste of the past few years?'

Liv took a deep breath. 'I really don't. We can be one thing and then another and then another. It's all authentic. It's all *real*. I think that's what I've finally figured out.'

Inside her head, Carrie smiled at her. So, gently, did Nikita.

And around them both swam myriad other figures – Freddie, performing an idea of connection he had seen elsewhere, and Felix, all smirk and swagger, and Celeste, a still-unknown shadow on the other side of a dating app, and every other person she had ever slept with, or flirted with, or lusted after. It was joyful and glorious and confounding. There was the Liv who wrapped her body around a different other every night and never saw them again; there was the Liv who dedicated herself to Nikita and grew a gorgeous intimacy step by special step. There was the Liv who wanted one thing and then another and all were true, all were real, even as some were consigned to the past, pieces of her growing up.

Rosa nodded slowly. 'I love you for saying that. A few years ago – god, even six months ago, it would have terrified me, I think. Going back to the start. But it's not, is it? It's just – a different set of rails.'

'I do have a new idea for a toast,' Liv said.

'Yeah?'

'Yeah.' She raised her glass, and it glittered. 'I think we should toast Nikita and Joe.'

Rosa swallowed. 'You do?'

'Yes. I think we should toast that they were good, for a while, and we were happy, for a while. And I think we should toast that they're in the past.'

Rosa nodded, and raised her glass into the same light. 'Okay. To Nikita and Joe. For some good things. And for being done.' Glass on glass, eye to eye, reflected smiles.

*

Dee prowled the flat like a cat. She had changed into leggings and a cropped top, vague thoughts of doing some circuits, working up a sweat to voiceless music, but something hadn't seemed quite right. She had tried to curl on the sofa and switch from channel to channel, but something hadn't seemed quite right there, either. Outside or inside? Movement or stillness?

Eventually, she followed the tug at the edge of her brain, walked back into her bedroom and sat on her bed. She picked up her phone, and she felt her hands turn slightly clammy. She put down the phone again. This was ridiculous. She got up and walked.

And so it continued, for ten minutes, and half an hour, until she was back on the bed again, phone in hand, breathing deeply, and telling herself, if not to be afraid, then to be okay with being afraid.

She found Josh's name. Their reams and reams of messages, their gradual unpacking of each other. The hopeful beginnings of something, the opening chapter which trailed away. She hesitated a few moments more, and then she pressed the call button.

Her heart leapt somewhere up to her throat as she pressed the little device to her ear, hard and hot. When was the last time she had phoned someone who wasn't her mother, or her best friends, or perhaps a client? How did a phone call work? Surely he wouldn't answer, anyway? But then, should she leave a voice message? What should that say? And shouldn't she have thought of this before?

But then the ringing stopped and it was Josh's warm, quizzical voice, an uplift as he said simply, 'Hello?'

'Hello,' she croaked, and cleared her throat, blushing. 'I mean, hello. Hi.'

'Hi's good, isn't it? Bit more casual. Less weighty.'

She laughed hurriedly, to show him that she thought he was funny, and to suggest that she was breezy, and to try to quell the jumping in her chest. 'So – yes. I wanted to say hello. To say hi.'

'Slightly unexpected, but definitely not unwelcome.'

'Yes. I mean, to the unexpected. I guess you didn't think you'd hear from me.'

'Well. You'd already vanished and reappeared once. I held out hope.'

She bit her lip. 'I mean, obviously I should have replied.'

'You said you had family stuff. I figured it was important.'

'You're being very reasonable.'

'Oh, don't worry. I moaned about you over a few pints. Finally meet an interesting one, and she disappears, that kind of thing.'

'I didn't mean to disappear.'

'You didn't, huh?'

'That sounded very American,' she said, and bit her lip again. But Josh was laughing. Her chest loosened slightly.

'I mean, I didn't mean to – to just leave it like that. I should have replied. It's been – it's been a difficult few months.'

'D'you wanna talk about it?'

'Um. Not really. But also, yes.'

'I don't mean here and now. I mean, say, over a pint.'

'Okay.'

'Come on, Dee. Sudden vanishing, phone call out of the blue. I need a bit more commitment than that.' His tone was still warm.

'Okay. I mean – yes. I'd like that a lot.'

'Brilliant. Pub by the park, tomorrow, afternoon, six-ish?'

'I'll see you there.'

Back

You can run from your heartbreak for a little while, but you will always have to come back. You can look at your life from an elsewhere, but you cannot escape it. This is how things should be.

What are you if not your past? You passed through your tears and torments and you stayed alive. You are strong, darling star, you are strong.

Chapter Twenty-Five

CLOSURE?

Katie was teaching a new class on Elizabeth I in September. Sixth-formers, supposed history enthusiasts – at the very least, a group who would have chosen to be there, rather than been compelled. The thought filled her with a pleasant glow of anticipation. Her undergraduate dissertation had centred on the great red-headed queen, that fierce and steadfast heir her father had so badly wanted but assumed would come in the shape of his son. She was excited, already, at igniting a similar passion in these teenagers, inviting them to trace a line from Elizabeth's extraordinary mother, those bold and brilliant women so many years ago.

So she pulled each book on Tudor history from her shelves, and laid them out across her bed in preparation for an afternoon of planning – and as she did so, a page fluttered, a breath, a gasp, and five photographs scattered across the duvet.

Her heart leapt into her throat, and then plummeted to the depths of her stomach. That weight, that *punch* – how she hadn't noticed its passing, and how suddenly it came back! *Heartbreak is not linear*, she thought. Because there he was – there *they* were. Katie-and-Chris. A life, a love.

She manoeuvred herself gingerly onto the bed. Outside, a cloud shifted and a line of yellow light slid across the room. Promise, and optimism, and illumination. She shivered, took a lifetime's breath, and picked up the photographs.

And they were so much more than – and nothing other than – photographs. The Manchester photo – oh, she could feel herself *straight* back into that bar, the jazz and blues it played which made them feel sophisticated even as they rushed for two-for-one cocktails and their shoes stuck to the floor. His arm was thrown casually over her shoulder and her head was flung back in easy laughter. It was just a few months after they met, the magical window between the circus party and their final exams, where they sucked the marrow out of the bones of that glorious city, and drank, and danced, and every bar was filled with dozens of faces that they knew.

Had it ever been better than that, she wondered? Of course life had gradually made more sense; of course they had placed the jigsaw pieces in increasing order – but that window seemed to exist out of place and time. How extraordinary it had felt, to be on the cusp of everything, to be falling in love for the first time and not yet fearful, to know that all those millions of divergent paths were still open – and how little they had been aware of it. She scrutinized Chris's face and he in turn scrutinized hers – then, not now – and his eyes were full of wonder. He was feeling joy and anticipation. Soon, he would tell her he loved her for the first time, outside, as they walked home from a club just as the sun was rising. She would nestle her head into his shoulder and laugh, and say I love you too, of course. How easy, how easy.

The Spain photo: the end of a month of interrailing between Manchester and the move to London. They hopped from hostel to hostel, staying in the cheapest places they could find and living off bread and cheese, and as the years went by they could afford further flights and better hotels, so it was uphill from there, she supposed, or was it downhill? Her skin was burnt brown and there was a knotted bracelet of coloured threads on her wrist. They were both sitting on their rucksacks, and she could immediately feel the weight of hers on her back, the way it rubbed two ovals of shiny, then flaky skin above her hips. A small but persistent discomfort; a sacrifice worth making for turquoise seas and shimmering heat.

Chris's twenty-fifth birthday: the restaurant he had mentioned for months previously because it, in turn, was being mentioned by his colleagues and clients. She had asked the couple at the next table to take the picture, caught between embarrassment at interrupting their display of intimacy and knowing that she wanted a record of their own. They were both glowing with health, Chris's muscles taut under his shirt and her favourite necklace glittering at her neck. They held hands above the tablecloth and there was a bottle which might have been champagne at the edge of the shot.

A year or so later and a picture of them at a friend's wedding: the first of Chris's close friends to get married and one whom, Katie knew with a jolt, she had been hoping might inspire Chris. It had been a typically performative twenty-something wedding; a church ceremony in spite of the fact that neither of the couple believed in god, and a country house reception paid for by the parents. A series of choices imagined over the previous year as carrying the most memorable weight: flowers to perfectly communicate the couple's sensibilities; tablecloths selected to complement the bridesmaids' dresses; favours for the guests to treasure always. Katie could remember none of them. She wondered if she were bitter. And she wondered what she had really wanted from Chris, even then. A proposal because she wanted it for herself, or a proposal because she wanted other people to see her with one? A proposal because that was what people did after three, or four, or five years together?

And finally, a rare selfie she had taken of the two of them on a climb up a Scottish mountain whose name she had since forgotten. Isolated from other people, Chris had permitted himself to beam at the camera, and they both looked happy and free, clouds scudding far above. And what she remembered, now, was the argument that followed, when she asked Chris why he so rarely posted such a picture online. Give me a break, he had said, and she had laughed at him, what kind of a line is that? And then he had been grimly silent for half an hour, for Chris never, ever liked to be embarrassed. Even by her, even when they were the only two people for miles, caught between heather and sky.

It was the most recent photo of the five, though still at least two years old. Had she stopped taking photos, or stopped printing them? And was it because she had come to feel a security, a sense that their relationship was no longer something she needed to knowingly celebrate or prove – or because their relationship had become so much the background furniture of her life?

She flicked through them again. She placed a hand on her stomach, testing for that pain, but it had faded away. She closed her eyes experimentally, wondering if tears were threatening, but none came. Katie-and-Chris lasted for nine years, she thought. Our relationship was nine years long. No more, no less. How special, how sparkling.

Something less than an image – a collection of sensations – drifted through her head. Movement towards bright horizons; thresholds; gentle closings. She recalled some far-off questionings of precisely how long it would take for change to occur, and smiled at herself.

She crossed her legs and scattered the photos like leaves in the triangle formed by her body. She took out her phone and took a picture. It was illuminated gorgeously by the sunbeam; every place where the photos caught the light glittered silver, a stack of jewels. She captioned the picture *Memories* and sent it to Dee, Liv and Rosa. Then, she picked up her bag, hesitated, and slipped the heartbreak handbook into it. She skipped down the stairs and out into the sunshine.

Messages began pinging back to her phone as she walked. *Glad you kept them?* asked Rosa.

Yes, she replied. *Who'd have thought?*

He was a fucking lucky man, Dee wrote.

Yes, she replied again. *I think I was probably a fucking lucky woman, too.*

Wise words, Liv wrote. *I just got a rush of nostalgia seeing that jazz bar. Thought I was it every time I went there.*

God, me too. Even in my lace leotard + trainers phase.

Babe, you could definitely still pull that off.

I was looking at an old pic the other day. You can see my entire nipple through my top. Not the outline, I'm talking full-scale areola. It's astounding.

Sounds it.

Remember those pink trousers you had a penchant for, K?

Ha! And that yellow top? I looked like a rhubarb-and-custard sweet.

My fave was Liv's pleather trousers. The way they squeaked!

God, I remember peeling *myself out of those after a night out. They were like wearing a giant condom.*

Good times.

Agreed xxx

Her heart skittered and her breath fluttered. These girls – these women. They were both; they would always be both. They held her past and her future, her youth and her yearning, her wildness and her wisdom. These loves of her life – how lucky she was.

She reached the park, the spot where Chris's friend had bumped into her, that hint of Chris's maybe-new relationship. She touched her hair reflexively. It had grown into a bob, now, feathered around her ears. She had learned to spray it with saltwater and ruffle it carefully-carelessly, and it felt something like her long waves, but older.

The park was filled with the shrieks and buzz of countless lives: dogs galloping joyfully; children learning to ride bikes and skateboards; fragile hungover coffee-sipping and bacon-roll-nibbling; motivational sit-ups and sparring. How strange it was that the same multi-layered activity could make you feel alone and adrift, or cocooned and safe. She remembered walking here just a few months ago and the exquisite sting of all those faces, all those voices – not one of them understanding or appreciating the pain that shivered through her body. Now, the same multiplicity was comforting. Life went on.

On the other side of the park was a pub, doors already flung open and people scattered across its outdoor tables. Only one was empty. With a snap of decision, the most natural thing in the world, Katie walked inside and ordered a glass of dry white wine. She sat at the empty table, and pulled the heartbreak handbook from her bag. She watched, and sipped, and read. Alone but not lonely; alive and anticipatory.

Leaves and layers of words from her friends; the acknowledgement of pain; the advice on how to manage it. The first pages were blotchy with spillages and tears, the corners crumpled by her own agonized hands. It was so recent, and it was a lifetime ago.

The rages and the reckonings; the tears and smudges from throwing the book, screaming at the book. Liv's furious words echoed in her skull; the anger that had made their years of intimacy seem so fragile. Dee's anguished face flickered across her vision, gripping her mother's hand. Mel looked wise, but wan.

Katie swallowed. How innocent she had been, to believe that only a lover could break her heart.

She held her phone above the book and took another photo. This time she captioned it *More than memories*. The past and the future entangled together; a relic of their lives, and a looking forward. *That needs to take pride of place in our house*, one of the girls – the women – replied.

Laughter was ringing from the tables around her, as dozens of strangers exchanged stories and jokes, stretched languorously, listened. A couple were sitting at the next table – next to each other rather than opposite, for the ease of gently kicking each other, running hands up and down each other's forearms and – yes – leaning in for kiss after kiss. A man not dissimilar from Chris – muscles that suggested attention, nondescript but well-fitting white T-shirt, jeans and brown boots – who was straddling the bench seat in a slightly ostentatious way. A woman with a striped sundress and an Afro tied under a red-and-orange scarf, sitting tall and fiddling with her dangling earrings. They were drunk on each other and still slightly self-conscious; they were pouring themselves out to each other and still sitting on the edge of something. First few months, Katie decided.

And she waited, wondering, for a stab of pain, but its shape had changed. Something mournful, something grateful. *Our relationship was nine years long.*

She took out her phone and scrolled to Chris's name. He was last online thirty-two minutes ago. His photo was one she didn't recognize. Their messages – their story – sat like an insect in amber. Her thumb hovered and her heart quivered. *Our relationship was nine years long.*

She tucked the phone back into her bag, and sipped her wine. The world moved on, fantastic and full.

Closure?

It is impossible to tell in advance when it will happen. You will wish you could. You will stretch and search for it. You will ask people, ask books, ask the internet: when will I feel better?

And there will come a time when you wake with a lightness you had forgotten, and a sense of anticipation, of looking forward more than you are looking back. You will pour your coffee and butter your toast and savour everything: bitter sharpness; silky richness; thousands of luxuries in every day.

You will think of them and you will feel something softer than you ever imagined. It might be simple – it might not – but its sharp edges will have been rubbed away. Their colours will be muted, their voice muffled. Their imprint will be left on you for ever – but so too will the imprints of the books you read, the music you dance to, the views you swoon over, the interviews you flunk – and triumph – the windows you roll down, the air you breathe.

You will look at the sky and see birds. You will think of swimming in the sea, and climbing hills, and sitting in bars with the world buzzing thrillingly close to you and the best people in the world hugging even closer to you.

You will look back and know that to be heartbroken is to be human. It is a reaction to the loss of that which we love. To love is to risk a broken heart, but to refuse to love is no protection. You were made to love. You were made to be loved.

You will look ahead, and see the string pooling out into the places you are going to live, and the people you are going to meet, and the love you are going to feel. Great, bountiful, overflowing love, rivers of love, oceans of love.

Acknowledgements

First thanks must go to Lucy Morris – still the sender of the most exciting emails, maker of the most exciting phone calls, and the best agent I could have ever hoped for. Thank you to Alice Gray for offering *Instructions* such a wonderful home at Pan Macmillan, and to Lucy Brem for stepping into her editorial shoes so perfectly when, early on, life turned out to imitate art a little more than we expected. Thank you to Rosie Pierce for holding my hand through the past crazy year.

Thank you to the wider teams at Curtis Brown and Pan Macmillan for guiding me through this childhood dream journey so expertly, particularly Liz Dennis, Rosa Watmough, Becky Lushey, Chloe Davies and Caoimhe White. Thank you to my international publishers. A younger version of me is still pinching herself.

Instructions for Heartbreak is a work of fiction, but its message – that friendship will scaffold your broken heart – is one I am lucky enough to have a wonderful blueprint for. Thank you to Mat Moss and Luke Winter for the appropriately grey and gloomy beach walks, to Emma Dodd and

Lauren Bond for the beds in Leamington and Manchester – and to Lauren, also, for introducing me to the inane joys of *The Other Woman* at the perfect time. Thank you to Hannah Whitfield for the wine-fuelled heart-to-hearts in the Warwick students' union bar, to Joey Connolly for the beer-fuelled heart-to-hearts in the Lord John Russell, and to Joe von Malachowski for the anything-fuelled heart-to-hearts all over the place. Thank you to Duncan McCaig and Jon Sanders for the short but very sweet stint at Holly Street, and to my Derby Road housemates – Rachael Davison, Sian Hughes-Kroon, Rachel Mannering, Alice Ridgway and Zoë Tweed – for making Manchester magical. Thank you to Columba Achilleos-Sarll, Bella Davies-Heard, Rowena Fay, Lewis Gray, Robynne Hodgson, Lucy Morton, Annabel Robertson and Claire Robinson for your companionship at significant times. Thank you to Eve Smith for Edinburgh tables, Manchester graveyards, always understanding and never being a nightie brigader. And thank you, always, to DASH – Ruth Davidson, Alice Langley, Clare Skelton-Morris and Hannah Walker – my wild hikers, swimmers, drinkers, dancers, agenda-makers, note-takers, left-over-right girls – women.

To my parents and siblings – Rob, Helen, Charlotte and James – thank you for my foundations.

To Oscar and Georgie, thank you for napping enough to enable me to edit, and for allowing the years of your respective births to be (nearly) upstaged by *I've got an agent!* and *I've got a publisher!* How lucky I am to be your mum.

Finally, to Ed, thank you for everything else and, indeed, for everything.